CW01513338

THE CONFERENCE OF THE BIRDS IN TEHRAN

THE
CONFERENCE OF
THE BIRDS IN
TEHRAN

Anahita Tishtar

MENMA BOOKS

ISBN: 978-1-9192986-1-0

Copyright © Anahita Tishtar

No part of this book may be reproduced or transmitted in any form or by any means electronic or mechanical including photocopying, reprinting, or on any information storage or retrieval system, without permission in writing from Menma Books.

MENMA BOOKS

www.menmabooks.eu

West Cork, Ireland

Main cover image copyright © 2011 by Peter Sís, used with permission of the artist.

To My Sisters

"To tell the truth: that is the first Persian virtue.
Have I made myself clear?"

FRIEDRICH NIETZSCHE, *ECCE HOMO*

WORLD ONE

IN PURSUIT OF MITHRA

YALDA NIGHT

METAMORPHOSIS

THE SEVEN VALLEYS

ARRIVING

WORLD TWO

CHARACTERS IN ORDER OF APPEARANCE

Parto – Iranian woman returning home after sixteen years abroad (*Goose*).

Hooman – Poet and writer (*Owl*).

Atossa – Courageous, independent woman (*Woodpecker*).

Sam – Early forties, facing personal and professional collapse (*Ostrich*).

Ava – Sam's partner (*Crane*).

Babak – Gay man and veterinary surgeon (*Nightingale*).

Dara – Tailor, Babak's partner (*Turtle Dove*).

Shirin – Babak and Dara's close friend (*Hummingbird*).

Farhad – Shirin's husband (*Nightingale*).

Rambod – Friend of Hooman, struggling with addiction and illness.

Neda – Young student hunted by the IRGC (*Swallow*).

Zhina – Courageous Kurdish student, Neda's friend.

Roxy – Glamorous, vulnerable woman (*Canary*).

Kamran – Cosmetic surgeon and Roxy's partner (*Pheasant*).

Bijan – Host of the Yalda party (*Blue Jay*).

Persis – Bijan's enormous, fluffy white cat, calm and affectionate.

Banoo – Wise and warm, a motherly figure for Bijan.

Giv – Banoo's husband, long-time friend and caretaker in Bijan's household.

Mr Kayvon – Old family friend, retired lawyer, and self-made historian.

Gitti – Mr Kayvon's wife.

Jav – A family acquaintance of Bijan's (*Turkey*).

Surena (Suri) – Young, sharp, and witty, twin brother to Pouria (*Kestrel*).

Pouria (Pori) – Thoughtful, analytical twin who balances his brother with calmness (*Kestrel*).

Twins' Mother

Akbar – Orthodontist and neighbour of Bijan's.

Mohsen – Akbar's cousin.

Gohar – Courageous and resilient mother (*Wood Pigeon*).

Ayda – Young, observant daughter of Gohar (*Sparrow*).

Leyla – *Tar* player.

Fereydoun – Late arrival at the party with two small dogs.

Huma – Flamboyant, striking features, and last to arrive at the party.

WORLD ONE

IN PURSUIT
OF MITHRA

He who overcomes himself is divine. Most see
their own ruin before their eyes; yet they still go
into it.

LEOPOLD VON RANKE

A long time ago, on a cold winter day, the Simorgh took a sharp turn and began to soar. He swung around in a full circle in the sky. The last of the pale sunlight shone on his broad chest; he shimmered and flashed in the sky like a winged sun disc from a distance. He drifted west, then veered east, and wailed out his sorrow.

Leaving Damavand, the highest peak of the Alborz, the Simorgh turned his head and looked down for the very last time. He let slip a teardrop, then a feather.

As fast as a shooting star, he reached the final ascent and disappeared into the clouds. The sky went dark.

The warm teardrop rolled down and grew as cold air rose from the ground. Like a diamond, the crystal tear cracked the frozen surface of the crater. The mountain woke with a flare and an eruption of sulphur—but the feather still circled, making its fall, seeking those who search for a way.

A *KINTSUGI* BOWL

PARTO

'AT PRESENT, if you are Iranian, this is likely to be always slightly emotional. Whether inside or outside the country, it is always there, even faintly, but pulsing, oscillating, like a current flowing somewhere deep inside you. Isn't it?"

Parto overheard the snatch of conversation between two other travellers in the check-in queue and nodded. She dropped off her luggage and walked straight through the departure gate.

Meeting the baggage allowance felt like an achievement; typical passengers from Iran often carry overweight bags, ambitiously trying to pack their entire lives within the 23kg limit.

But this time was different. She wasn't leaving Iran. She was returning.

Walking down the aisle, she spotted her window seat. It was occupied by a middle-aged man with a scraggly beard.

"Excuse me, I think this is my seat," Parto said, showing her boarding pass.

"Are you sure?"

"Yes, I am. I booked the window."

The man grumbled and moved, reluctantly.

She continued politely, "I haven't been in the country for many years and wanted to see Tehran from the window."

The man rolled his eyes, unconvinced.

Parto had left Iran sixteen years earlier, on her own, in search of a new life.

She had moved between a few countries, eventually completing a degree, finding a job, and becoming a European citizen. Surprisingly, she hadn't missed home much in those early years. There were enough grim memories to escape—and so much to learn about her new world. She had no family left in Iran. They had all adopted new countries; they were everywhere but home. She no longer knew where was where. Only in the last few years had she begun to feel the urge to return.

She was in her mid-forties, robust and slightly masculine; she had to be. But her face told a different story. Her eyes were a deep Persian black, and when she smiled—which she often did—it gave her the warm, reassuring look of an eager listener. Yet there was something strange and hard to define about her; something between uncertainty and confidence, wit and seriousness, calm and wild.

Her head was glued to the window; she could feel her rapid breath touch the glass and rush back to her face.

Breathe in. Breathe out. The clock was ticking.

Her eyes were fixed like a hawk on the view outside. Her heart was pounding. This was the second leg of her journey. With only a few direct flights to Iran these days, she had to stop in Istanbul and take this flight to Tehran. There wasn't long left now. She kept checking the screen monitor, waiting for the first glimpse of Iran. When it finally showed East Azerbaijan, she shivered.

She was in.

Crossing over the landscape, she felt like a bird flying back across the countless mountains and lands she had once left behind. She wondered how she'd managed to navigate it all. Was it luck—or perhaps a gut feeling, knowing where to go and where not to? She remembered reading a story in which a grandfather told his granddaughter how messenger pigeons were released at the front during the war. They had to fly over battlefields to get home, without ever looking down. *"You must look forward, or you'll never reach your destination."* It had become her mantra.

"Was that brave?"

The voice of Hooman rang in her ears. This was his response when she told him the story a couple of years before she left. One autumn day, when the air was still mild, they had laid down under a cedar tree in the garden of their mutual friend, Bijan. They were looking at the fast-moving clouds.

It was a bit early in the season for the sky of Iran to host migratory birds, which mostly arrived towards the end of December, heading from the north to the southern, warmer countries; but there were masses of them that autumn, roosting talkatively on the tree and travelling overhead on their tracks.

Hooman was listening to her, but he was taken aback when he said, "You really think that was a brave thing to do...not to look down?"

Parto said no more and just looked up at the sky, at the migrant birds, that day.

The sun had swept over the mountains. Their white tops were paved with snow, sloping downward to the gentler ridges and valleys, then rising again.

"Mountains! I hadn't realised how much I'd missed them."

Parto thought about the paradox of the land's tranquil beauty and the horror of its narratives—grief, brutality, and terror. She looked away for a moment, weighing her tangled feelings about her motherland. It wasn't just her. She knew many Iranians struggled to define themselves.

It was true, as one writer commented, that "Iran is less a country than a continent."—a land where things were not necessarily what they seemed on the surface. We Persians, she thought, had been hanging around since as far back as the Bronze Age—with all those empires, invasions, cultures, conquerors, poets, architects, charismatic thinkers, and dark villains. And, after all, we have been speaking Persian for as long as the other Indo-European languages—which is why mother was *madar* and father was *pedar*. How could Farsi have survived so long?

She recalled how surprised her English teacher was when she told her that Farsi didn't have feminine or masculine nouns or pronouns, where everything was referred to as "it"—woman, man, dog, tree, sun, bird, mountain, everything! It was as if, when the language was crafted, it was too early on in civilization for people to divide the genders, or perhaps they were too civilized to designate them, and everything equally had one label. Even if someone was non-binary 5,000 years ago, they could be "it" or, not too weirdly, "they."

Parto then thought about Iran's ancient faith, Zoroastrianism, which had an elegantly simple philosophy: "Good Thoughts, Good Words, Good Deeds." Unlike some other religions that commonly consider human life on earth as hard and preordained, it had always given positive value to the human struggle.

Following his free choice, man had come to earth to stand by the Sire of Truth, Ahura Mazda ("the Lord of Wisdom"), in his millennial fight against darkness and falsehood. Choice, thinking, and free will.

Then we had been given Islam. After the Arab invasion in 650 CE, we may have gradually switched our religion to Islam, but not to its language. People generally read the Quran in Arabic without understanding it—but they believed in it. Perhaps this, she thought, was the miracle of the Quran.

And yet, some ancient Zoroastrian learning had been kept intact. We still celebrated the seasonal festivals, and the spring equinox—Nowruz—was still Iran's official New Year and the most important holiday in the calendar, just as Yalda Night, at the winter equinox, remains a significant event.

Parto pushed her head back in the seat and pondered: *Who are we really?* On one side, a culturally confident nation; on the other, a deep nostalgia for a lost generation, disappointed at what we had become.

She thought about England's defeat of the Spanish Armada and how it changed the course of history—inducing a rush of patriotism and giving England the confidence and power to command the seas and build a global empire. Was that luck or competence? If the Armada had succeeded, it would have brought England a Spanish Inquisition and a very different history.

There are many more moments like this. What would the world be without the French or Russian revolutions? What if Hitler had won the war? And what about Iran?

What would the world be if we had prevailed over the Greeks, the Moguls, the Arabs? Or more importantly, what if we hadn't been torn apart by the Islamic Revolution—still an enigma, with no clear sense of why it happened or what it truly signified?

What would Afghanistan, Iraq, Gaza, Lebanon, or even Russia be, if the Shah had stayed in power?

Was it all a series of unfortunate coincidences that led us here—or was this what we deserved? Did the clerics really mastermind the overthrow of the monarchy, or was it a foreign force? Was it fear of communism? Or a conspiracy? None of it made sense to her, which was frustrating. Yet she believed history mattered—not just because she had studied it, but because she believed it shaped people, much like memory, and could not be ignored.

What is the true Iran? Could she ever find out?

She sighed, exasperated by her confusion over how to perceive her own country today. But deep inside, she still believed there was something good about Iran—something it had yet to share with the world.

She had been thinking for a while of Iran as a *kintsugi* bowl. Zen teaches that a damaged bowl, cup, or pot should not be neglected or thrown away, but must continue to attract respect—and that we should attend to its repair with great care. The whole process symbolizes a reconciliation with flaws and the accidents of time. Rather than hide or suppress the cracks, it is better to admit them, learn from them, and find a way to mend them. Throughout history, Iran had broken and shattered into pieces many times—but had always been put back together.

The metaphor of a bowl had come to her in a dream, a couple of months before she decided to take this trip.

In the dream, there was a bowl in her hands, full of paint in many different colours, swirling and mixing together. It was as if the bowl were a well, springing with colour. Suddenly, she felt dizzy and dropped it. The bowl broke into pieces, and the colours vanished into an abyss of darkness beneath her feet. She was terrified, especially as she herself began to fall into the void. *This is the end*, she thought. But then, she flapped her arms and rose above her fear, hearing a clear voice say: *The only way out is to find Mithra.*

When she woke up, she knew she had to return to Iran.

She came to herself and looked over her shoulder to check on her neighbour. His face looked grim, and his eyes were still closed. He kept them shut, even when she informed him that the stewardess was there with refreshments—her attempt to be friendly.

It was mid-afternoon and still sunny when Parto finally spotted the magnificent peak of Damavand. She gasped. The silver crown of Tehran was covered with snow; it stood there, timeless—just as proud and splendid as when she had left.

So, this is it. Here it is. Tehran.

She removed her neck scarf and wrapped it around her head, glancing around to see that all the other female passengers were busy doing the same to cover their hair. The transformation was sad and submissive—and, at the same time, faintly funny. They raised eyebrows and exchanged sympathetic smiles.

She got into position, her head glued to the window, her eyes glowing and dilated, ready to welcome the first glimpse. But the closer they got, the less she could see. A thick, dark-brown smoke blurred her view. Damavand was buried under it too; only its peak stuck out.

A few minutes ago, it had been sunny and bright. Now she could hardly see. Was something burning?

The captain announced they would be landing shortly. As the aircraft descended, the smoke gave way to a yellowish smog. A deserted land slowly came into view.

Over the years, away from Iran, unexpected aromas would awaken her memories—a waft of mint, the sweet breath of honeysuckle, or the soft fragrance of roses—carrying her back home in an instant. Her memories of Iran's scents were rich and vivid, woven with taste, texture, and colour. After years of living with these memories, now, within minutes, they would rise up to enfold her once again.

The man was fidgeting in his seat. His eyes were open now, and he glanced at Parto from the corner of his eye—now wearing a headscarf. He leered, his head half-averted. *Oh, that was it,* she realised. That was why he had seemed so tense: he was one of those men who couldn't look directly at a woman's face without the hijab.

She made her way down the aisle to the exit and turned to someone in the line. "Sorry, sir. Do you know where this thick smog is coming from?"

"It's the non-standard petrol—after the sanctions," the man replied, adjusting the mask over his face. "How long have you been away?"

Parto stepped out of the plane. The chilled air drifted in and touched her face. She took a deep breath, filling her lungs. Her heart skipped a beat.

It wasn't the smell of Tehran.

It smelled of burnt diesel—and pain.

She sobbed.

OUR OLD COURTYARD IS LONELY

HOOMAN

IT WAS EARLY afternoon on December 21, and the sky over Tehran hung low, heavy with a dark, suffocating haze, shrouded in a dense veil of pollution. In cold weather, the air was always worse—smoke and carbon dioxide lingered, trapped, until wind, rain, or snow swept them away.

Hooman sat alone on a bench in Tulip park. He wasn't bothered by the dim light; these days, he wore sunglasses outdoors regardless of the weather. The park was empty and bleak. He didn't mind that either. He sat quietly, sunk deep in thought, reworking the lines of his new poem in his mind—*Midnight Angel*.

He was in his mid-forties, long-limbed with broad shoulders, carrying himself with a kind of dismissive nonchalance. His eyebrows were as thick as an Owl's—sometimes needing a quick comb—and his wavy hair was greying at the temples. He flicked away his cigarette, then stood up, stretching his arms and yawning. "Ahh...been sitting too long."

Pushing back his hair, he looked up at a passing flock of birds, blackening the sky, and murmured, "Where are they going now? Anywhere but here."

He strolled toward the gate. When he was a very young boy—maybe six or seven—he used to come to this park with his father, and sometimes with friends. There was one spot that always brought back a particular memory.

He and a friend had shared a Walkman and a single set of headphones. That was the mystery of music—it acted like a time machine, preserving moments just as they were. The song was *Ma Baker* by Boney M, probably the last piece of Western music he'd heard before the Islamic Revolution.

He often thought of his mother there too—and that pained him. They used to dance together to that song when he was small. Hooman always sang the first part: *"Freeze! I'm Ma Baker—put your hands in the air!"* And his mother would raise her hands, pretending to be scared. They'd laugh, jump, and dance all the way to the end.

It was the happy sound of his boyhood. But now, both his mother and the song were gone.

He passed through the little lanes that led back to the main road, now bustling with traffic and thick with the smoke of roaring exhausts. A bit further up, he stopped at a grocery shop, torn between what to buy for Yalda. *Watermelon or pomegranate?* He liked them both.

An array of pre-cut watermelon wedges was displayed out front—covered in cellophane, tied with ribbons, and decorated specially for Yalda—but they looked rather unappealing. Hooman turned to the pile of whole watermelons stacked in the corner. He picked a medium-sized round one with dark green stripes and tapped on it, pressing his ear gently to its belly, as if waiting for a reply. His face beamed as it rang hollow.

"This one, please."

"That? Why that one? You didn't like the cut ones?" the shop owner asked, his voice tinged with disappointment.

"You took all the fun away man! This one should be good. We say life is an uncut watermelon, don't we—until you cut it."

"At least you see what you're buying," the shop owner insisted. "You're not leaving it to fate."

"Fate?" Hooman shrugged. "No, I just prefer to choose and cut it myself."

Slapping a clump of notes on the counter, he added, "I always choose. Don't you? Do you believe in fate yourself?"

"Some do… Not for me. But I believe in my faith. If I don't know the answer, I always do Istikhara." He slid the watermelon into a bag and pointed to the ceiling. "Allah knows best."

"You consult God even on buying watermelons?" Hooman grumbled, taking off his sunglasses and frowning sarcastically at the shopkeeper—almost as if he wanted to *show* him that his left eye was scarred, having once been shot. "I believe we all have a choice," he repeated.

The man looked back at him without sympathy, smirked oddly, and muttered something under his breath.

Hooman grabbed the bag, raised his thick eyebrows, and gave him a dry, pointed look before dashing out.

On the wall opposite the grocery shop was an enormous image of the sullen face of an older man, with a hefty grey beard and a large black turban. Many walls across the city were covered with similar portraits—of him and his allies. Their eyes seemed to follow people everywhere, always watching. He paused and whispered, *"Big Brother is watching you."*

Hooman often wondered why everything they produced was purposely unpleasant. The unspoken brief seemed to be: *"Do it as ugly as possible."* In their bid to make their mark, there was a wilful attempt to demonise—to cut the trees, dry the rivers, kill the dogs, and cloak the women.

He could hardly recall a single refined piece of art created by the government in the past forty-odd years. Even the few mosques and shrines they built lacked any true sense of beauty.

At the word "beauty," he paused—and for the first time, it struck him why. Beauty itself was the problem. *"Beauty awakens the soul to act."* The voice of his friend Rambod echoed in his mind, reading from Dante. *That's why they fear it,* he thought.

Beauty has a profound, awakening effect on the human spirit; it stirs something deep within. It is powerful, it makes the world better, and they cannot afford that.

He shrugged and wandered off, the carefully chosen watermelon swinging gently back and forth in its bag.

I AM KAVEH, A BLACKSMITH

"I am Kaveh, a blacksmith," he said,
striking his head with clenched fists,
his voice shaking with rage and grief.
"What have I done wrong?
Why have my sons been taken?
You've destroyed all I built.
My back is bent beneath years of despair.
Speak! —are you a king, or a monster?
And why must my son's brains feed
the hunger of your vile serpents?"

—from the *Shahnameh*, the Persian Book of Kings.[1]

ATOSSA

IN THE HALLWAY, Atossa leaned forward in front of the mirror, ran her fingers vigorously through her hair, encouraged some curls down on both sides, and dabbed on a quick touch of lipstick and a spritz of perfume before dropping her makeup bag into her purse. The lipstick suited her red mahogany hair, and her stature seemed to gain more vigour from the scarlet colour.

She was usually spoken of as incredibly forthright, without being offensive, so that when she chose a word, she knew exactly where to land it. She was not yet fifty, but her forthrightness perhaps gave the impression of someone older, as did the fact that she lived independently and ran her own successful catering business.

Feminine fashion, for her, was not just a matter of personal taste but a way to show courage and a love of liberty—something that could always entail risk. Atossa was well aware of that but didn't care.

Stepping back, she allowed more of herself into the mirror, looked at her reflection, adjusted her large silver Faravahar necklace[2] on her polo neck, and patted it gently over her heart.

The phone rang in the other room. She rushed to answer it.

"Taxi is waiting for you, Madam."

She grabbed her shawl and wore it loosely, smoothed back from head to shoulders, then heeled down the stairs. The car chugged, and a thick gauze of exhaust filled Atossa's nostrils as she opened the door and plopped herself down in the back seat with an apology:

"Sorry you've been waiting so long."

The driver turned his head. "Don't worry, Madam. That's part of my job."

He briefly pulled down his pollution mask while speaking; an exhausted, bony face with short black stubble appeared beneath his grizzled eyes. He was too young to be patient.

Atossa studied him with her sharp, narrowed eyes, shook her head slightly, and grumbled, "Another Master's or PhD graduate? Am I right?" The driver cast a quick glance at the rear-view mirror and, with an apologetic smirk, said, "Well spotted! Master of Electronic Engineering—unemployed for two years."

"Ridiculous!"

"That's okay, Madam. Like any job, you get used to it. To be honest, it was good at the beginning—you know, paying the bills—but even this"—he tapped the steering wheel—"isn't easy now… rationing petrol, lack of spare parts… So, I do some electrical work too. Any problem at home—washing machine, fridge-freezer, lighting, you name it. I also install satellite dishes. As many channels as you want: CNN, Al Jazeera…"

He bowed slightly, rummaged through the glovebox with one hand, and flipped a shabby business card into Atossa's hand. "Sorry, this is the only one left. My number's there, if you need any job done at home."

Atossa took the card and asked, "How's the driving?"

The young man rubbed his forehead and replied, "Snapp is good—they copied the same model as Uber. There's a map, which really helps drivers like me. As you can tell from my accent, I'm not from Tehran. Without this system, it'd be impossible…I'd get lost ten times a day. Tehran is gigantic, isn't it?"

Atossa nodded.

"And growing like a mushroom, hourly. No one can tell where its head is, the tail, or even the centre anymore! The city pushing up against the Alborz Mountains… no harmony, no breathing space, no greens, no birds, no air to breathe!"

She sighed deeply. "Tell me…all those old dead trees on Valiasr Street[3]."

[15]

The driver nodded. "Exactly! They're even selling the right to the sky now. What do poor children see from their windows in this city? Just wall to wall—dark and grey. I think this city desperately needs a healer. But even if someone wanted to change it... how? Imagine if an earthquake..."

Atossa suddenly began to worry. Someone had once told her that a taxi driver with a Samand car might be a government spy. Damn! She had forgotten to check what kind of car this was. She glanced nervously at the dashboard, searching for a logo or make—but there was no clue.

The taxi slowed down; the traffic had almost doubled since the beginning of the journey.

"This is because of today's demonstration," the driver said, pointing to the stream of heavy traffic ahead. "They closed the main highways, and the drifted traffic is building up. Well, it's Yalda too. By the way—Happy Yalda!"

Atossa's heart ached—her jailed cousin was one of the reasons behind the demonstration. She felt frustrated; her family had banned her from getting involved today. That decision came after her last appearance at a gathering in front of Evin Prison, when her outspokenness could easily have landed her in jail. Her family didn't want to lose another member.

She pulled herself together and put on a blank face, replying politely, "Ah yes, of course. To you too. Do you have anything planned?"

The driver shrugged. "We can't plan much these days, can we? If I get home in one piece, I'll meet up with some friends later."

"I know, but hopefully you'll get to them. Don't forget—it's the longest night of the year!" she said jokingly, then added, "Any family here? You said you're not from Tehran?"

"Correct. I'm originally from Nishapur. I came here for university and stayed on to work and support my family—my parents and brother. Do you know where Nishapur is?"

"Of course! The city of Attar and Omar Khayyam. How old is your brother?"

"He's fifty-four."

"Fifty-four?" Atossa said, surprised. "Why are you supporting him? Normally the eldest—"

The driver cut in. "I know. But he's unwell. He was a soldier on the front during the war with Iraq. He narrowly escaped a major explosion, but the blast wave hit him hard. He never recovered—he's mentally ill now, very dependent on my parents."

"Ah, I see. I'm sorry. It must have been so difficult for your family. How old was he when he got injured?"

The driver rose slightly in his seat to see Atossa better in the mirror. His eyes spoke volumes. In that moment, he suddenly looked older—mature and tense.

"Not sure you really want to hear this, Madam... He had just turned fifteen. Spring of 1983. He was one of those many child soldiers on the ground, made to walk through minefields. They used them as fodder—as live mine sweepers to clear the road. And now they're all forgotten... either dead or disabled. His mother died three years later, and my father married my mother after a while. Ali is my half-brother."

"Did they really force them to walk on mines? We heard so many different stories."

"Yes. Brutally—but very cleverly, through their sophisticated propaganda machine. They stole those boys' minds with all kinds of tactics. They were only teenagers. Do you remember that poor boy, Hossein Fahmideh?"

"Of course."

Atossa's mind travelled back to those days—the way the regime had made a war hero out of Fahmideh, a boy who left home without telling his parents to join the front-line forces in the defence of Khorramshahr. He had wrapped himself in a grenade belt, pulled the pins, and thrown himself beneath an advancing Iraqi tank.

She recalled that famous statement by Ruhollah Khomeini, once scrawled across the walls of so many schools: "Our leader is not me, but that thirteen-year-old child who threw himself with his little heart against the enemy. He is worth more than a hundred pens or a hundred tongues."

She remembered "Student Day" in the official calendar—the day that marked Fahmideh's death. Atossa had been a schoolgirl herself back then. On Student Days, there were no lessons; instead, the agenda was filled with slogans, ceremonies, and war-related visits and events.

She recalled one particular Student Day, when the plan was to take the students to visit the family of a schoolboy who had recently been killed. She had been very young, and instead of listening to the poignant war stories told by the boy's sister, all she could focus on were the mouth-watering, cream-filled puff pastries the family had arranged to serve afterward.

Following Fahmideh's example, many boys—probably bored with school—went off to war, eager to prove their heroism and strength to the Imam. They were too young to understand the danger, too small to even hold a gun properly, but the regime had found a use for them—on the minefields.

The driver turned his head slightly and said, "I think that was the dumbest way anyone could die. The truth is, grenades don't destroy tanks. And above all, it wasn't even necessary to throw himself under it—he could have just thrown the grenades without sacrificing his life."

The topic of Hossein Fahmideh led the driver to speak about the night his brother was injured.

"My brother was brainwashed," he said. "I heard an unbelievable story from one of his comrades—someone who used to joke about seeing the Twelfth Imam during the war. He and my brother were in the same regiment. Before they sent them to the front, they were told stories about surprise visits from the Imam, who only appeared to brave soldiers.

"When the night of the operation arrived, they were very close to the front lines but under heavy Iraqi artillery fire. Many around them were killed. This guy remembers feeling something hot burning on his back. He looked at his hand and realized his arm was injured. As he and many others—including my brother—began retreating through the carnage of limbless and headless bodies, they suddenly saw a white horse and a glowing figure that looked like the Imam, shouting verses from the Quran and commanding them to return to the front."

"Filled with new energy from the vision, and despite their injuries, he and my brother joined the others in an attempt to go back and regain lost ground. But then an explosion hurled them into a trench.

"When he regained consciousness, he dragged himself out in agony and saw a light in the distance. He began crawling toward it. And when he got there, he saw the white horse—wounded—with motorbike headlights powered by a car battery strapped tightly to its saddle. Next to it lay the body of one of their commanders, dressed up as the Imam—dead."

Atossa gave a small groan. Neither of them knew what to say, and they sat in silence for a while.

The volume of traffic was growing heavier, and cars had nearly come to a standstill. The driver decided to take a shortcut and turned down a side street. It was a mistake. They were now stuck, and a U-turn was impossible.

Atossa felt a bit dizzy. A headache was coming on, and she opened the window. The driver looked at her in the mirror.

"Sorry," Atossa said. "I needed some fresh air."

"Of course. But outside is even worse—denser and more polluted. Far from fresh. This domestic petrol is worse than poison. It'll kill us slowly. It doesn't even work in brand-new cars like Mercedes-Benz or BMWs. Can you believe it? A friend of mine tried it..."

Atossa jumped at the opportunity. As she shut the window, she asked casually, "So... what's your car?"

"This piece of metal? It's a Paykan."

"Oh... phew!"

He caught her expression and chuckled. "What? Did you think it was a Samand? Thank you very much, Madam. Do I look like one of *them*?"

Atossa shrugged. "Well... sorry, but in that case, maybe you shouldn't *look* like them, I guess."

They both laughed.

Then, suddenly, Atossa stopped laughing and asked, "Have you read the *Shahnameh*?"

"The *Shahnameh*? Sort of... I've heard some of the stories."

"What happened to your brother reminds me of the story of Zahhak—the demon king who brought an end to Jamshid's throne and glory."

Atossa told the driver the story of Zahhak, who had transformed from a supernatural monster into an evil human. "He was a cruel ruler, with two black snakes growing from his shoulders. Every time he cut them off, they rose again—until Ahriman, Satan, appeared disguised as a skilled doctor."

"He told Zahhak, 'Leave the snakes. Don't cut them anymore. You must feed them to keep them calm. Give them human brains—especially young ones.' So every day, Zahhak's spies would seize two youths and execute them, just to feed the snakes. And that's how Zahhak ruled for thousands of years."

Suddenly, the car in front stopped. Doors opened, people spilled out onto the road, voices rising in alarm. The driver looked ahead, tense.

"Something's happened," he muttered. The car behind blared its horn. A man approached their window and knocked.

"Did you hear that? The gunshots."

"Gunshots?" the driver said, startled. "No, we didn't... only one?"

"No. Many."

The woman behind them finally took her hand off the horn and got out too. People began gathering, speculating aloud:

"...It was close..."

"...Tear gas..."

"...Security forces chasing them..."

"...Better to stay inside..."

"...Protesters..."

"What do we do now?" the driver asked. "Seems like we're stuck."

"Don't worry, I can walk," Atossa said.

"No—it's more dangerous. Better to stay in the car and wait. It'll calm down."

"You can see it on your map—look, there! It's not far from here, where I'm going. Sitting here is more stressful."

The driver looked at her, concerned.

Atossa opened the door. "Thank you. Go home as soon as possible. It's not safe to work outside today."

He nodded. As she was stepping out, he called, "Wait!"

Atossa turned. "What is it?"

"What happened to Persia after thousands of years of Zahhak?"

Atossa stared at him, slightly baffled, then smiled. "The end of the *Shahnameh* is a good one! Haven't you heard it? Something *did* happen. Fereydoun, along with Kaveh the blacksmith, rose up against Zahhak and defeated him—two young men from our country who had kept their brains safe."

The driver's face lit up with quiet satisfaction.

Atossa winked as she stepped away. "You should read the *Shahnameh* more."

HAFT TAPPEH

"Susa, the great holy city—abode of their gods, seat of their mysteries—I conquered. I entered its palaces and opened their treasuries, where silver and gold, goods and wealth were amassed. I destroyed the ziggurat of Susa. I shattered its shining copper horns. I reduced the temples of Elam to nothing; their gods and goddesses I scattered to the winds. The tombs of their ancient and recent kings I devastated, exposed them to the sun, and carried away their bones to the land of Ashur. I laid waste to the provinces of Elam and on their lands, I sowed salt."

—attributed to Ashurbanipal (669-631 BCE), king of the Neo-Assyrian Empire, after the Battle of Susa.

SAM AND AVA

IN HIS FLAT on Vanak Street, Sam lay in bed. Barely lifting his head from the pillow, he glanced at the clock from the corner of his eye. It was around midday. He grumbled something under his breath, then slid his head beneath the pillow and clamped it tightly with both hands.

The past few weeks had been tough. Yesterday made it worse—Ava had said she was thinking of leaving him.

They had been together for over ten years, and he still loved her. It was impossible to imagine life without her. And yet... he felt little physical desire for her anymore.

The more he loved Ava, the less he craved her body—which felt strange. Someone he barely knew, or didn't care for at all, could still drive him mad with longing. But his desire for Ava lived only in his mind now, not in his body. *Does she know how awful I am?*

A sharp globule of acid reflux rose in his throat, forcing Sam to sit up suddenly. He threw the pillow to the floor and sat motionless on the bed.

The issue with Ava wasn't the whole problem.

For the second year in a row, the Ministry of Agriculture had failed to pay the incentive owed to the syndicate of sugar-cane farmers. The bank had once again declined to advance funds for factory workers' wages. Ownership of the privatised sugar-cane industry had changed hands multiple times, each shift offering fresh opportunities for corruption. The authorities had plundered the country—poor farmers and workers not excluded.

Sam had fought to keep the Tehran office running—for the sake of his team and their families—but now that, too, had failed.

It was painful to witness the slow deterioration of an industry. He remembered travelling around the factories, listening to stories of the sector's glorious past. One memory stood out: a farewell party for a retired colleague at the main factory.

"This is the end... the very bitter end, son. Very bitter."

They had been sitting on a bench opposite the factory canteen, the air felt heavy with the familiar whiff of brown molasses.

"The end? Come on... retirement is the beginning of—"

"The end of the sugar-cane industry, I meant. The end of me was years ago... you know... I wish I hadn't seen..."

The old man paused, suddenly turning distant. His eyes lost focus as he continued: "But I *saw* those days," he said, shaking his head. "When the factory was in its early years."

He pointed toward the main building. "It was the sixties, around the time of the 'White Revolution,' when the government went crazy for agriculture and had just changed the whole land ownership system. It was a big, brave move—a fantastic time for farmers.

"Imagine! For the first time in our history, Iranian farmers were getting support through agricultural cooperative banks—no more moneylenders or landlords. It was a game-changer. But it wasn't just about loans and money.

"They thought about everything. Thousands and thousands of kilometres of feeder roads were built. And again, for the first time in history, most Iranian villages became connected to the main markets."

"You know, it was mostly the Italians who built those roads—in some of the most challenging areas of Iran. They're good at building roads, going all the way back to the time of the Roman Empire." He chuckled. "And we were looking after them—with cold beer. Yes! Cold Iranian beer! I can still taste it... You were too young to remember—or maybe not even born. How old are you... remind me?"

"Forty-three."

"Bless you, son. You were born too late!"

"I know."

"We saw those good, happy, glorious days! We had the *White Revolu-*

tion—and sadly, your generation only saw its opposite, the *Black Revolution*."

Sam knew he was referring to the White Revolution of 1963, a reform era known for its rapid economic growth and redistribution of wealth to the working class.

The Shah's vision had been for every Iranian to enjoy an educated, healthy, and prosperous life, with the long-term goal of transforming Iran into a global economic power. Land reform was the cornerstone of that vision. The government bought land from traditional feudal lords at a fair price and sold it below market value, with long-term repayment terms, to the peasants, who had lived like slaves under the landlords.

Next came the privatization of government-owned enterprises, allowing both the old feudal families and the public to buy shares in manufacturing plants and contribute to industrializing the country.

These economic reforms came alongside significant social change: granting women the right to vote, and investing heavily in education, health, and environmental resources.

The old man sighed deeply—his breath was heavy with the weight of history. His head shook in a mix of despair and resignation. Then, his gaze drifted from Sam back to the factory—a silent, hollow shell that now mocked its past.

"Listen to this final point. Technically speaking, that building was state-of-the-art across the board. Absolutely first class. You see these water shortages now? The muddy brown water we drink? Back then, they built twelve major dams in a decade—more than one a year. They knew agriculture mattered. Not like these fools today, obsessed with nuclear bombs, drones, and weapons."

He turned his eyes away from Sam and looked off into the distance.

"And now what? Most of the people who saw those days died in the war. I envy them. I really do. They were lucky. They didn't live long enough to see this suffering, this disgrace.

"I haven't been paid in years. I live with my son and his family. He hasn't been paid in six months either. And *that*—"he pointed at the factory"—is a wreck."

The old man was right. The factory at Haft Tappeh had once had a magnificent beginning. It was part of a dream to bring prosperity to Khuzestan—something beyond oil. In 1978, the factory had produced a record-breaking 100,000 tons of sugar. After the Islamic Revolution, however, it declined rapidly. During the eight-year war with Iraq, Haft Tappeh was bombed multiple times. Years of poor management followed.

Then came the so-called sugar mafia. In 2007, the import tariff on sugar, which had been 150 percent, was suddenly slashed to just 10 percent. That year alone, the Syndicate of Iran imported five million tons of sugar—when national consumption was only around two million. The beneficiaries were religious conservatives and certain traditional bazaar merchants.

The workers' trade union staged periodic strikes, protesting broken promises by officials. One of their placards read: "Leave SYRIA, think about us!", referring to the regime's policy of supporting proxies but neglecting its own people.

There had been many arrests. Seven activists were imprisoned in Susa, sentenced to a combined total of 110 years—plus 74 lashes each.

Sam recalled one young man—a human rights activist and freelance journalist—who had been tortured and was still serving a long sentence.

But what happened yesterday was beyond imagination.

He'd heard an incredible story: security forces had raided the factory and beaten several employees who were on a hunger strike. Some were arrested, and others were threatened—told they would be replaced by Chinese workers if they didn't end the strike.

The protests had intensified after an inflammatory radio interview with the managing director, who declared, "The donkey belongs to whoever is riding it. And now, as you can see, we are riding it—and we won't get off. We won't leave this firm."

Haft Tappeh lay near the ruins of the Elamite civilization, close to the ancient city of Susa—where they had taken that young woman, and many other protesters, to prison.

To Sam, it all felt like a violent collision between a new barbarism and the glorious, ancient past. He covered his face with his hands; his skin felt cold and stubby.

He'd spent hours awake last night, unable to sleep—just lay there, watching Ava. She had rolled to the far edge of the bed. By morning, she was barely on it—then got up and left for work without looking back. He could sense her movements from familiar signs: the sound of the shower running, the scent of her body lotion, the click of the fridge opening, and the sound of the apartment's main door closing.

He pulled aside the curtain and watched her walk until she disappeared around the corner. It was still too dark. Looking at her frail figure had pained him.

A sudden breath of cold air brushed against his face, and he stood there, disoriented, until something shiny caught his eye in the misty twilight.

A bird.

He pulled the curtain fully aside to get a better look. It circled once, then stooped, landing on the neighbour's balcony. He squinted, leaning closer. It was unusual—maybe a winter migrant. White, ghostlike.

It looked exactly like an albino crow.

By the time he reached for his phone to take a picture, the bird had flown.

Back on the bed, Sam thought the real tragedy of living under a regime of terror didn't always unfold in dramatic events—it revealed itself in the quiet erosion of domestic life. It crept into every house, every room. Everything soured slowly, until it rotted completely.

He thought again about the corruption at work, the many years of despotism. He couldn't shake the face of the bank manager he had spoken to. That sleazy piece of work! The man was one of the *Aghazadeh*[4]—the privileged children of Ayatollahs and regime elites, corrupt to the bone.

They were like weeds in a garden, multiplying fast and choking everything. They had the power to do whatever they pleased—even sending their families abroad. For them, the "evil West" was suddenly acceptable when it came to their children's comfort.

Maybe that was the true rot: it spread like a spider's web—silent and unseen at first—until one day you woke up, caught fast in its sticky threads... rotten, too.

After an hour, Sam dragged himself to the bathroom. He tried not to look in the mirror—he didn't want to see himself. He wanted to be someone else. But his eyes caught a glimpse, and he was trapped by the sight of a hunched, hapless older man, much older than he thought he was. A stranger and a failure looked back.

He sat there for a long while, head resting on his knees, numb.

Then, a text. Ava.

"What do you want to do about tonight?"

"Tonight?"

"Yalda at Bijan's."

He had completely forgotten. They were invited to Bijan's for Yalda. *Damn*. Bijan held on to traditions, no matter what, hosting a party even when no one felt like celebrating. Sam thought of texting to cancel.

Another beep. "So?"

"I don't know. Maybe we should cancel... it's the middle of the week anyway. We'll think of something to say."

"Cancel then?"

"No, I mean... it's up to you, Ava."

"So, as always. I should decide?"

She was right. Ava always decided. She had decided they would marry, and now she had decided they would separate. Sam simply followed.

"Yes, please. My mind doesn't work right now." He imagined her reading that and thinking, *If it ever had worked properly.*

A few minutes passed.

"Better we go. It's a distraction."

"Sure."

"Ask Yars if we can get a lift."

"Ok, will do."

Nothing felt the same anymore.

He tossed the phone onto the bed and walked to the hallway. From his coat pocket, he pulled out a crumpled cigarette pack and fished for a lighter.

Then he stopped—his eyes caught on the shoe rack. One pair of Ava's shoes sat next to his. Crouching in front of it, he slowly moved his head closer. Lighting the cigarette, he blew out a long, silent stream of smoke. A shiver ran through him as his eyes lingered wistfully on the rack.

THE PIGEON'S BLOOD IS RUBY

BABAK AND DARA

BABAK AND DARA, known collectively to their friends as Yars, lived as a gay couple but kept it a secret from everyone except their closest friends. To anyone who asked, Dara was Babak's cousin who had come from his village to work and live with him as a lodger.

Dara was in his late thirties—slightly chubby and bald—with dark eyes that seemed to hold a gentle warmth. Though he wasn't considered handsome by most, there was something undeniably winning about him. His features came from his mother, as he liked to joke: "Everything from Maman except my hair; she definitely wasn't bald."

A skilled tailor, Dara was known for transforming the *manteau*—the long over-garment mandatory for women—into bold fashion statements. These days, everything was a platform for the fight, and the style of his garments had become almost a political statement.

Babak, who worked as a veterinary surgeon, was a bit younger—slender and tall, with soft brown hair usually slicked back neatly. His family came from somewhere in the north, which explained his unusual green eyes that could shift from amber to hazel depending on the colour of the shirt he wore.

In his early years, Dara had experienced violence and rape—memories he was never able to expunge. One story told of how he was discovered in a hotel room with another man when he was young. Facing the possibility of the death penalty if arrested, he begged the hotel manager—who was working with the Revolutionary Guard—not to hand him in.

The manager agreed but in return demanded sexual favours from him and also made him available to be abused by a gang of his friends. It was only when the manager died that he escaped to Tehran, where he found a job at the surgery where Babak worked, thanks to Sam, a mutual friend. The trauma he had suffered was still an open wound, and the surgery—where he received the unconditional love of the animals, and eventually that of Babak—proved a saviour. After a while, he and Babak decided it would be better for him to return to tailoring and work from their apartment.

It was the last day of autumn, and at the usual time, Babak left home to walk the few minutes to the station, where he would catch a train to the surgery. Diesel fumes thickened the cold morning air, and he adjusted his neck scarf to cover his nose. At the metro entrance, he stopped at the newspaper kiosk to pick up a copy of The Citizen; even though he never read it, it made him happy to see the newspaper boy's smile.

The boy shouted, "Happy Yalda!"

Babak replied the same while crossing the barrier and slowly made his way down the stairs toward the platforms. He checked the time on his mobile and saw that he still had a few minutes. While waiting, he noticed feathers blowing in the wind. A bit further up, the body of a Wood Pigeon lay on the ground, a mess of soft white feathers; one wing was sprung sharply back and moved tortuously. He crouched down and carefully turned the bird over with both hands. Its breast was tattered with blood. It seemed to have been hit by a train. He decided to take it to the surgery and spread the newspaper open to use as a carrier.

The newspaper was instantly stained with blood. The bird didn't struggle much and slowly relaxed its wing. As soon as he got on the train, one of the other passengers gave him his seat. He placed one hand over the paper, and the other naturally wrapped beneath it; he could feel the warmth of the panting body.

The other passengers grew curious, looking at the bird with sympathy and asking questions. The one most entertained was the kid selling goods in the carriage—he tried to pour drops of water from a bottle onto the bird's mandible. It was only three stops to the surgery, so it seemed likely they could make it.

"But just before the last stop, everything went black, and the train came to a sudden stop in darkness."

"Damn!"

"There must be a power failure!"

Babak stroked the bird and, using the light from his mobile, saw the Pigeon's eyes flicker—still alive. The atmosphere grew tense after a few minutes without any announcement, and a cacophony of noise filled the tiny space. The temperature started rising, children were scared and sobbing; some passengers panicked, banging on the doors, while others tried to open the windows.

One passenger began to scream, "We are dying here!"

[28]

"It's only a power outage," a man said.

"Power in this country went forty years ago, not just now!" another man retorted, which was followed by muffled applause and a stream of similar comments.

After about fifty minutes, someone shouted, "Shush... I said shush!" and pressed his ear to the side of the carriage. They could hear movements—running, calling, banging—in the distance... something was happening and frighteningly close. Suddenly, the train jolted and began to move. People cheered and hugged each other, but as soon as they arrived at the station, they were met with a scene of chaos.

A group of women not wearing hijabs were being confronted by the morality police, who suddenly opened fire. The crowd scattered in panic toward the exits, leaving the bodies of two young girls on the ground. Inside the carriage, everyone began screaming and piling on top of each other on the floor. Babak was too shocked to move. He didn't know how long he sat there, but the train had begun moving toward the next station as if nothing had happened, and finally, the carriage doors opened.

As he joined the heaving crowd trying to leave the station quickly, a damp feeling in his hands made him look down: the Pigeon's body was flexed to one side, dead, already giving off a slightly rancid smell. A small patch of blood oozed from the cover of *The Citizen* newspaper onto the palm of his hand. He shrieked hysterically, "Blood... blood," but in the chaos, no one noticed—except a younger man pressed between others in the rush of the crowd, who looked over at him intently and said,

"The Pigeon's blood is ruby."

Babak didn't understand what he meant and yelled, "What?"

"You can't wipe it... It stays... drips to gemstones... look!"

But the man was pulled into the crowd and disappeared before Babak could ask him more.

About thirty minutes later, after being almost carried along by the crowd, Babak found himself outside the station. It was less chaotic; most people had dispersed, and the sirens of the security guards' vehicles were fading into the heavy traffic. His mobile rang as he stepped outside. He pulled himself together, placed the dead Pigeon next to a tree on the street with care and respect, and answered the call.

Dara had heard about the shooting inside the metro, and his voice was anxious. Their conversation was short, but the few words exchanged calmed Babak. Words like "Come home" and "died thousands of times" were filled with genuine love and carried an energy that quickly dispelled the last feelings of terror.

He decided it would be safer to walk home. He felt a need for support and wondered how difficult and empty it would be without Dara.

He recalled the time they met, a couple of days after Dara had joined the surgery. Everyone seemed to like the new fellow already. Dara was wearing the surgery's dark blue uniform and was busy cleaning the crates of discharged animals when Babak went to say hello. They exchanged a few words about Sam, their mutual friend. Dara said he would change and come to the office when he finished. That day, they talked for hours, Dara sitting there with his childlike eyes and insatiable curiosity.

"The animals—don't they feel pain like us?"

"Of course they do!"

Dara had asked about the halal and kosher methods of killing animals. He was almost in tears when Babak confirmed that the animals were conscious when their veins are cut, dying slowly as the blood flowed from their severed throats, finally leading to brain death. It was very different from stunning, where the brain shuts down first.

"Why? Why do we do this? Can this improve something? The meat?" Dara asked.

When Babak said it made it worse, he was shocked. "Really? It degrades meat quality, too?"

"Yes. It makes it tougher, and it goes off quicker. It's all about the pH—the balance of alkaline and acidity. Stress makes it more alkaline."

"And then we eat that!"

Dara had a hypothesis, that this might be one of the reasons the region was violent. "If that stress changes the meat, and we eat that meat, it will change us too!"

That made Babak think. "Maybe."

As all the abattoirs in Iran were halal, Dara stopped eating meat from that day.

Although they shared a similar outlook on the world, they were very different people. Dara had a rougher edge, while Babak was educated and from a good family.

Their gods, too, were different. Dara's God was beyond time and not in need of a house, temple, or shrine. He called it *It*. In contrast, Babak's God—shaped by family tradition—was tangible and familiar, had a thousand different names, was kept in purposely made buildings, and required offerings.

Yet their different gods had brought them closer. Differences kept them who they were; if they were one, it wasn't just because they thought alike. Also, if one God didn't bother much one day, the other would.

Just as today, Dara's God had worked remarkably to save Babak.

COCKROACHES

SHIRIN AND FARHAD

WHEN SHIRIN arrived at the Yars' home, it was early afternoon, and Babak had returned already. Dara opened the door to her and gave her a big smile.

"How is he?" Shirin asked.

Dara nodded. "Okay. Come in, darling, he will be better to see you."

Babak hurried out into the hall. The three hugged each other with closed eyes for a few moments before they sat down on a long sofa covered with cushions near the heater. Shirin removed her neck scarf and flung it to the far corner of the floor with contempt. That used to be her headscarf, but not anymore. She usually had a dazzling smile, which never failed to put strangers at ease, but today her mouth was rigid except for a twitch on one side of her lip. She brought her hands to her face and sighed deeply into her palms.

"So, you saw those girls in the metro?" she asked.

"Only briefly... the train went by quickly," Babak replied in a low voice, looking at the floor.

"Briefly? That must have been long enough. A scene as horrifying as that can never be brief. It stays long somewhere—maybe forever!"

She shook her head, then took Babak's hand in hers, squeezed it, released it, and leant back on the sofa.

"It was terrible out there," she continued. "I was coming from the Pardisan area. First, I saw the crowd, and I thought it was one of those daily protests about the cost of living, or maybe about the hijab and a confrontation with the stupid morality police. But when I got closer, I found out that a large number of people had gathered at the Environment Department building, demanding that the environmentalists who had been arrested on spying charges be released."

Dara and Babak were well aware of how eight conservation scientists and researchers from the Persian Wildlife Heritage Foundation had been accused of using their project to track critically endangered wild Asiatic cheetahs as a front for espionage. They had the government's permission and worked closely with the Department of Environment, but they somehow drew the suspicion of the IRGC[5], as they seemed to have got close to a nuclear plant while tracking a cheetah. They were convicted at a secret trial. One of the accused died in suspicious circumstances while under interrogation shortly after his arrest. The rest were sentenced to between six and ten years in prison.

Shirin continued. "Myriads of IRGC forces, like insects, were scattered among people, and they looked scary—like lice. Frightening. I noticed a few suspicious-looking ones without uniforms too... lurking among the crowd. But their chilling eyes were revealing. I tried not to stare at their dirty faces, but I was sure they were undercover morality police, in case the gathering triggered a bigger protest."

Dara said, "I know that... chilling faces. There were many of them at last month's gathering in remembrance of Bloody November. Monsters. I hate them—hate them!"

Shirin went quiet for a while, as if there were no more words that could describe the terror and suffering of the people of their own country. But suddenly she shook, as if she had found something new, and muttered, "Unless..."

"Unless what?"

"Unless they're not even Iranian! The Islamic government... I know it sounds like a conspiracy theory, but where else in the world do they open fire on their own innocent children like this? All these killings, all the beautiful young girls... the deliberate poisoning of schoolgirls... where else? There must be something powerful in women that scares them. Why are they so scared of women—mothers, daughters? Why don't they want us to be seen? Now men too—fathers, brothers, sons... how many of us do they want to shoot?"

"At least everyone can see now—we don't want them," Babak said quietly. "It's clear we're fighting back. But, you know, so many people... their names just get forgotten. Like Homa Darabi. She was a doctor, a paediatrician, who... set herself on fire because they wouldn't let her work after she refused to wear the chador. That was ages ago—1994. Most of the protesters now weren't even born then."

He paused, looking away for a moment. "And then there's the 'Blue Girl'—that innocent girl who just wanted to see a football match—she did the same. Set herself on fire because she was dressed like a man to watch the game. And they charged her... just for not wearing a hijab."

Dara sighed, shaking her head. "It's just too much. Too dark. Too cruel. Like I keep saying, we don't have a leader. If we did... maybe they wouldn't have got away with all this—forty years of killing, violence, and executions."

At the word "executions," Shirin shifted, gripping her handbag tight. Dara said he'd put the kettle on, but as he got up, she interrupted, "Wait... did you see this? It's gone viral today."

Her hand trembled as she pulled out her phone and showed them a picture from Instagram. Dara sat back down. It was a photo of a hand-written note, stamped by the Isfahan Central Prison Library. Babak leaned in, squinting to read.

"We ask you, fellow citizens and compatriots: Do not let them kill us! We need your help. We need your help —" Saeed, Saleh, Majid, Sons of Iran 6. None of them said a word. Babak looked down at the floor and saw a cockroach skitter across the room, climbing up the edge of the wall. Being a vet didn't help his phobia of cockroaches, but instead of rushing to kill it, he followed it with his eyes as it crawled toward the ceiling.

"They've invaded our homes and made those intimate spaces their own.... those greasy... smelly...slimy things... a physical embodiment of filth and germs... their black skin stained with faeces and vomit.... They're everywhere to show us we've failed to keep clean... they're everywhere to paralyze us. How can we carry on? Live... go to work...take our children to school...go to bed... go to the kitchen to eat? They creep up on us. This is what we get... this is what we get when we fail to keep clean."

His voice was breaking.

"We can't function because we're always on the lookout... we're pro-grammed to fear! Do you... do you know why they reek of the toilet? Because they wallow in filth and store urine and shit..." He took a long, despairing breath, then, more like a vet this time, continued, "They're incredibly prolific and hard to get rid of... very, very hard."

He was still looking at the ceiling, his head leaning back on the sofa; tears rolled down from the corners of his eyes. Shirin squirmed in her seat and took her eyes off the ceiling to exchange an anxious look with Dara.

Babak covered his eyes with both hands and wept as he spoke more words. "And we all breathe in the stink of these creatures... their whiskers waggle... I can hear them on us... I can feel it in my hair, on my arms, in the beat of my heart and the shortness of my breath—that piercing noise… scratch, scratch, the scratch of their spiky feet. We thought we could stop them. They're eating us… they're eating us..!"

At that, Dara stood up and shouted, "ENOUGH! STOP IT!" Grabbing a cloth from the kitchen, he jumped over the table and tried—unsuccessfully—to reach the ceiling and kill the cockroach. Shirin shrieked and jumped. Then Dara knelt down beside Babak and looked at him intently.

"We will get them out of here. We will get our country back, you hear me?"

Babak just nodded.

Shirin and Dara encouraged Babak to shower and rest while they prepared some lunch, and things gradually became calmer. They talked about Yalda and the gathering at Bijan.

"I can get ready here," Shirin said. "I have everything I need in my bag."

"Good," Dara said, looking at Babak. "Sam called me and asked if they could come with us."

"Of course," Babak said.

"He said he saw a white crow today!"

"A white crow?"

Shirin's eyes widened in surprise.

Shirin was married to Yars' best friend, Farhad. Since Farhad's departure seven years ago, she had also grown very close to them. She had a typical Persian look—black eyes and long, silky black hair, with a prominent nose. Unlike many others, she ignored the taboo and stigma around it and refused to succumb to the popular trend of rhinoplasty surgery.

She often joked with her friends, "My nose reveals my ancient Persian-Assyrian genes. It's like the Hoopoe's crown—that's what defines the Hoopoe as Hoopoe. Plus, my nose is very sustainable."

She had heard somewhere that besides genetics, local climate contributed to nose size: the higher the temperature, the bigger the nose, so it can inhale more air to cool off the body. But most of her friends had theirs reduced. She believed they became new people, changing not only their noses but their voices, their upper lips, their smiles, and even the way they laughed.

With her deep longing for Farhad, she had immersed herself in her large group of friends, keeping close contact with them and often inviting them to her flat, but she still felt lonely.

Was it loneliness that drew her to the mountains? For years now, she had been organizing expeditions to the mountains north of Tehran for various university groups and, on rare occasions, tourists. Mount Damavand had become her refuge. She enjoyed the peace and tranquillity the mountain bestowed and the fresh air—just what she needed to compensate for living in a swarming, polluted capital. She always returned from there energized and happy.

Although nature didn't discriminate, not many women were involved in climbing—perhaps because of the mistaken belief that outdoor sports were only for men or the difficulties in dressing appropriately. This was a topic Shirin often discussed with Dara; they even had ideas to start a business together creating sports brands for women. In this way, she grew closer to Dara, while Farhad was more Babak's friend—not only because they went to the same school, but also because they shared a love of music. Farhad was a rapper who ran an underground band in which Babak sometimes played guitar.

The IRGC were informed about the anti-regime elements of Farhad's songs and were on his track. This was one of the reasons he and Shirin decided to emigrate to Canada under the "Skilled Worker Scheme." Farhad's degree in Metallurgical Engineering could achieve a considerably higher score than Shirin's career, so he became the principal applicant. They filed their documents, but in 2004 the relationship between Canada and Iran drastically deteriorated when Zahra Kazmi, an Iranian Canadian freelance photographer, was arrested and later killed in custody in Tehran. Consequently, they had to send their documents to the Canadian embassy in Damascus.

The processing time for immigration could range from a few years to more than a decade, depending on factors such as the applicant's country of residence and the type of application. For them, it took only two years before they were called for their first interview in Damascus. The interview went very well, and they were pleasantly surprised by how much they loved the city. It felt good to unwind after the stress of the process, even if just for a couple of days. They returned home cheerful, carrying a large bag of Syrian souvenirs—handmade Aleppo soaps and boxes of Ghraoui chocolates.

They had to wait again. There were a few possible scenarios: in some cases, a second interview was required before the application could be finalized; in a few lucky instances, the file was approved without any further steps. But they had also heard of unfortunate cases that ended in formal rejection. They waited anxiously for an answer.

Finally, a letter arrived from the embassy—Farhad, as the principal applicant, was asked to attend a second interview in Damascus. It was the final days of winter, just before Nowruz. Shirin told everyone they had received the best early New Year present imaginable. She joked that they wouldn't need to do any spring cleaning this year—they were leaving soon.

The interview was scheduled for 10:30 a.m. on Tuesday, March 15, 2011, at the Canadian Embassy in Damascus. From early that morning, Shirin was on the phone with Farhad almost every hour. "Don't forget to make eye contact... a proper handshake—not too firm or too loose, and short... don't talk too much... and keep smiling. You'll be fine."

She stayed on the phone while he ironed his shirt and dressed in his carefully chosen suit, finishing with the tie Dara had given him. "It's French silk," Dara had said. "It works."

When it was time to go to the embassy, Shirin said, "Remember to put the lucky charm in your pocket—it'll help. And... breathe! Before you go in, be confident. Breathe... just imagine us there. Love you, and good luck."

About two hours later, he called home to give Shirin the news: they had been approved for immigration to Canada. They both screamed with joy and cried tears of relief. Seven years of uncertainty were finally over.

Farhad could hardly contain himself—speaking faster than usual, his sentences scattered as he told Shirin every detail about the Canadian immigration office, and about the desperate people still waiting in the queue.

He said he couldn't stay in the hotel until checkout—he was too excited—so he decided to walk into town. He texted Shirin later that afternoon. The streets, he said, were full of military—very different from their last visit together. Some shops were closed, including the famous chocolatier they had gone to before, but many things still seemed to be functioning normally.

They were aware of unrest in Damascus following the Arab Spring of 2011, but at that point, travel to Syria still wasn't considered dangerous. The last message Shirin received from him came when he was waiting for a taxi to go to the airport:

"Get packing, my beautiful Canadian goose! See you tonight 😊 💚 💚
💚 *P.S. Wait to tell Granny—I should prepare her myself when I'm home
tomorrow. Love you "*

That was the last Shirin ever heard from Farhad. He had checked out
of the hotel, but he never made it to the airport. And then—nothing.

Since that day, Shirin had returned to Syria again and again. She enlisted
every organization she could find, followed every lead, searched hospitals
and morgues—sometimes during airstrikes. For months, then years, she
clung to the hope that he was alive somewhere, that he might be held in
a prison, unable to contact her, still waiting to come home.

But over time, his name became one of more than 100,000—men,
women, and children swallowed by the chaos of war—missing since the
start of the Syrian civil conflict.

CANTO

RAMBOD

HOOMAN had kept adding to the poem he'd begun years ago—
Midnight Angel—wanting to read each new verse to his friend
Rambod and ask for his verdict.

The new verses were inquiries into the night: how the sun extinguished
itself; the crushing weight of darkness; the chill settling deep into the earth;
the faded habitations; the consumed towns with their trees and birds; the
muted noises; and the colours fading slowly into black.

On his way home, Hooman decided to stop by Rambod's place to share
the latest verses. Since Yalda was always entwined with poetry, he planned
to persuade him to join Bijan's party. It was unlikely Rambod would
agree—these days he hardly left home—but there was no harm in trying.

Rambod let him in through the macramé curtain hanging in the doorway of his studio flat, then carefully locked the door with double chains.

The room was airless and dim, the blinds drawn low. A carpet patterned
with large red flowers on a black background made the space feel even
smaller. In one corner, worn cushions were scattered around a musty divan,
while piles of books and papers cluttered the floor.

The heavy air in the flat made Hooman take off his bulky fur coat. "This
was my old man's trademark, remember?" he said, leaning over Rambod
to hang the coat on the hook. "Looks like I'm turning into him!"

He took off his sunglasses, revealing his injured eye—but that witty glint
was still there, untouched. "It's as if you're locking the door of a jail, man!"

"Well, it is indeed a jail," Rambod said resentfully. He checked the
door chain again, looping it around the little nub and pressing it until
the master lock clicked. "My very private prison, Boof—where I'm both
prisoner and prison warden."

Boof was a nickname that Rambod had given Hooman years ago because of his thick, bushy eyebrows—like an Owl's. Hooman liked it. To
him, nicknames were funny and personal; they made people feel closer.

"Did you see the girls?"

"What girls? No, I didn't."

"If you'd come a minute earlier, you would have seen them—two young—I mean, very young—girls from Karaj, heroin addicts. Honestly, Boof, as if I'm a dealer. I wanted to bang my head against the wall when they asked if they could stay the night… honestly! Then they made up a story that so-and-so sent them to get some opium because they were on meth and the runner was late and now wanted to re-up! But I could tell from their wary eyes, their skinny, desperate faces, that it was pure heroin—totally wrecked. I'm in this shit, I know what it is."

"Mate, you're not a heroin ad…"

"No difference… let's leave it." He shuffled out to the kitchen, grunting some swear words.

Hooman sighed deeply. Iran had the highest rate of drug addiction in the world. While opium remained culturally more acceptable, heroin and methamphetamine were rapidly overtaking it as treatments for depression. This surge was driven by high youth unemployment, inflation, and the influx of cheap heroin from Afghanistan. Some believed it was a government strategy to keep young people off the streets. This was also behind the rising cases of HIV—Rambod included.

But their friendship—and their shared love for literature—remained untouched. They spent hours discussing writers and poets from Iran, along with whatever international works they could get their hands on. Rambod would usually lean back, rub the back of his neck, and listen generously.

He had his own way of offering criticism: "inky" if a piece didn't impress him much, or "clanking… clanking" when he sensed something was starting to take shape. And on rare occasions, when something truly moved him, he'd raise his hand in the air and declare, "Glorious!"

Until recently, they could talk for hours. But now, it was hard for Hooman to watch as Rambod's mental and physical health declined day by day.

Rambod adjusted his heavy-framed glasses, which looked too large for his gaunt face. He took the notebook from Hooman's hand, flipped through the pages, and scanned the final verses of the poem. Then, gazing thoughtfully into the distance, he handed it back.

"Let's hear it," he said. "Can you read it aloud, Boof?"

Hooman sat upright and read in his low, husky voice—sometimes with a tinge of sadness.

As he read , Rambod prepared the charcoal. He carefully cut a lump from the sticky, dark brown paste of opium, which he kept wrapped in a crumpled piece of foil. He shaped it into a small ball and pressed it to the end of the ceramic bowl of a long pipe.

When the coal heated up and turned red hot, he picked up a piece with a pair of tongs, held it over the little ball, and blew on it hard. A distinctive, pungent, bitter smell filled the room.

Hooman stopped reading. The process was familiar to him, although he never took part in it.

In the beginning, they had rows, and Hooman made many attempts to stop him. Now, with Rambod being ill, there was no point in hassling him—but it didn't lessen the sheer sadness Hooman felt for his friend.

Rambod exhaled and leaned back against the wall, mumbling about the poem. Hooman wasn't listening anymore; his eyes were fixed on his friend's ravaged face and his rotten, crumbling, worn-out body. *Would he ever rise again?* A deafening blow struck his heart.

He noticed Rambod was falling asleep and recalled how they had talked about Frank Baum's *The Wonderful Wizard of Oz*—how Dorothy falls asleep in a poppy field after the Wicked Witch casts a spell on her. In his mind, he repeated the lines as best he could remember.

"Poppies, poppies, poppies will put them to sleep!" Dorothy did not know this, nor could she get away from, the bright red flowers that were everywhere around her. Her eyes grew heavy, and she felt she must sit down—to rest, and to sleep... "If we leave her here, she will die," said the Lion. "The smell of the flowers is killing us all."

They had once compared the Ministry of Guidance to that witch who cast a spell to make people sleep. They laughed that day—but today, nothing was funny.

Then he thought about the irony: it was a flower that was to blame for making his friend sick. "Can one put a petal back after it has fallen?... Can one put a petal back after it has fallen?" he murmured several times.

Staring at his friend for a long moment, he felt utterly inept, as if his hands were made of cement.

In that instant, he had a strange vision: overlapping circles, geometric patterns of repeating spaces—of dark and light. They gradually resolved into six-petal rosettes shaped like a lotus flower. It was a peaceful, comforting vision of a complete flower, a glimpse of another reality.

He bent forward and shifted slightly, reaching out to touch the flower—but then everything snapped back to what it was before.

He found himself still staring at Rambod. Running his fingers through his hair, puzzled, he thought, *Oh well... what a weird experience.* He assumed it must have been the narcotic effect of passive smoking.

Rambod had drifted into a doze and didn't respond when Hooman called him. He let him be and looked around—the place was a mess.

The room was heavy with smoke, so he picked up the brazier tray with the half-burned coal and placed it in a safe corner of the kitchen. Then he leaned forward, gently pushed a cushion behind Rambod, and whispered, "I'm leaving, okay? It's Yalda tonight..."

Rambod nodded and smiled with closed eyes, lightly lifted his hand, then rolled onto his back. His eyes opened—unfocused—staring at the ceiling as if he were seeing something there.

With a crack in his voice, he said, "You mentioned your old man. It reminded me—I had a dream last night... about my father

It was strange. We were in a ditch, and I saw a large, dark moving cloud. And when I warned him that a storm was coming, he clenched my hand and dragged me up to the edge and said, 'Look, son, that is not a storm. They are birds... a murmuration!' I felt good, Boof, really good. I think I wept with joy."

Then he closed his eyes again.

"What a nice dream, Rambod, that is a good sign!" Hooman smiled softly, leaned forward, kissed his forehead, and noticed the flurry of ash from coal deposited on his friend's eyelashes, making them look grey-white.

Before he left, Hooman quietly removed a small wad of notes from his pocket and looked around for somewhere to leave it for Rambod. On the bench was a book under a half-eaten banana and a chain of keys and locks; he tried to slide the money onto the open page and noticed it was a poem:

> *"Can you enter the great acorn of light?*
> *But the beauty is not the madness.*
> *Tho' my errors and wrecks lie about me,*
> *And I am not a demigod—*
> *I cannot make it cohere."*

—Ezra Pound, Canto XCV

1384

NEDA

AT THE FRONT DOOR of his house, Hooman paused, set down the watermelon, and said playfully, "Don't move!" Then he dug deep into his pocket for his keys.

His flat was in a ten-floor apartment building, centrally located just a few minutes' walk from one of the main Valiasr junctions. The building's walls were plastered with ads and flyers, stuck randomly around the array of apartment doorbells:

Fast internet... Kidney B+ for sale... Plumbing service... Tehran's cheapest mini pizza... Invest in Belarus... Visa and immigration (FAST)... Bone marrow and kidney without the middleman (all blood types) ... IELTS, ISI, TOEFL only in thirty days...INFESTATION?? Don't worry! We are here! The instant killing of cockroaches!

He got the key and turned it in the lock a few times, but it was stuck. He tried again, pulling the door slightly with his other hand, and this time it gave way. The door hissed open, and just before he stepped inside, a warm, heavy breath brushed the back of his neck. Suddenly, someone shrieked and shoved him forcefully through the doorway.

Hooman froze. Images of thieves and violent gangs flashed through his mind. Terrified, he thought he was about to die.

He turned around and, to his astonishment, saw a very young woman recoiling in fear, pleading in a low, shaky voice, "Help... please!"

Her body trembled with small convulsions, her face deathly pale, and a pair of swollen, red eyes stared at him. Hooman was still in shock. He noticed she had wet herself, a puddle of pee around her skinny legs.

He pulled himself together.

"For heaven's sake! Who are you... damn ... what happened to you?"

The girl was panting like a hunted bird. She wasn't wearing a hijab; her dark brown curls were flattened to her forehead with sweat. She looked down at the floor and whispered, "Sorry... I'm sorry," then sank to her knees, covered her eyes with both hands, and shuddered with sobs.

Hooman was beginning to recover his presence of mind and reached out his hand toward her.

"That's okay." He almost stepped into the puddle around her. "Let's help you out... come on... easy... tell me what happened to you."

The girl held her limbs as if trying to stop them from shaking and slurred, "I was chased... by them..."

"By them?"

"The IRGC."

Hooman held his breath for a moment, then said, "Fuck!"

"I will leave soon... if you'll just let me wait here... please... until they're gone... please... I will leave."

"You can't stay. I mean, here in the hallway like this!" He glanced at her wet trousers. "Come on! You need to get changed. There are others in this building, too. Hurry up! Give me your hand—let me take you to my flat. Can you walk okay?"

"Are you sure? Sorry... let me clean this first."

Suddenly, both of them lifted their heads toward the ceiling. They could distinctly hear footsteps coming from the upper floors.

"Leave it, leave it... move, please, will you?" Hooman pulled her hand, which felt as cold as ice. He plopped himself and her into the lift.

As he went to open the apartment door, he realized he had left the key at the building's main entrance. He smacked his head. "Oh shit, I left the keys at the door! Bugger! Wait here!"

He ran downstairs, leaned very close to the door, and slowly opened it. The watermelon hadn't moved. He took a deep breath, grabbed the keys and the watermelon, and ran back upstairs.

He showed the girl to the bathroom and gave her a towel; she was still shivering.

"Sorry, I'm sorry." She convulsed in tears.

"Listen! Stop saying sorry, will you? Wash up first, then we'll decide what to do next. Okay? You're safe here! Calm down. And wait..."

He grabbed his pyjamas from the bedroom and tossed them toward her. "You can use these for now." He shut the bathroom door behind her and stood outside, frozen stiff. His heart hammered loudly in his ears. He closed his eyes, trying to make sense of everything, then opened them wide as if he'd just found a solution. He grabbed his mobile and called the only person he knew who could help.

Atossa and he were old friends. She ran her own business and had a natural ability to take control of any situation. Years of managing a full kitchen staff had taught her how to work under pressure—and how to handle things when they went wrong.

"There's a girl in my bathroom!"

Atossa chuckled on the other end of the line. "What? Good for you, Hooman! Is she a ghost? Or did one of your ex-girlfriends come for revenge?"

But when Hooman told her the story, the laughter died.

"Okay, Hooman, listen—take a few deep breaths and stay calm. I'm at Nana Khanoum's now. I'll get a Snapp and be there in half an hour. Okay mate?"

Nana Khanoum, Atossa's grandma, had come out of the kitchen, all ears, and listened to the whole conversation. Every Yalda, Atossa would go to her house to pick up the 'Problem-Solving Nuts.' Grandma always prepared them with care, genuinely believing that eating them and making a wish on Yalda night would resolve all problems.

Nana Khanoum looked at Atossa with a penetrating gaze. Her face was thin, her wavy hair pulled away from her bony, brown-coloured face and braided into two knots resting on her shoulders; it made her look like the head of an Apache.

"What is the matter, darling? Hooman making trouble again?"

"Don't worry, Nana, nothing important. I don't know yet, but I'll find out more when I go there!"

"You just arrived!" Nana groaned. "In this chaos, I'm not sure if the taxis are still running... It's going to snow... the weather is bad." She moved back to the kitchen irritably, crying quietly and muttering, "In this chaos... chaos..."

Atossa knew Nana Khanoum's concern wasn't really about the weather, but about her other grandchild, Nilofar, who had been taken to jail.

As Atossa waved outside for the Snapp, a flock of migratory birds made their way across the sky above. She looked up. Nana was right—it was going to snow, the first of the year. No surprise: winter was officially arriving in just a few hours.

Nana Khanoum stood behind the window, watching her leave. Finally, she smiled and waved; Nana and the old balcony hung there as if they were permanent fixtures in Atossa's sky.

As Atossa sat in the car, she returned the wave—then noticed a re-fined-looking man standing at the entrance of the building she had just left. *How did I miss him?* she wondered.

He had a distinctive black moustache and wore a long black raincoat with a matching tie. With two small dogs by his side and a travel bag in hand, he appeared to have just returned from somewhere. He stood there in the cold, feeding the birds.

As the taxi drove away, Atossa looked again through the back window. The man smiled at her.

When Atossa arrived, Hooman ushered her into his room, closed the door, and quietly—but impulsively—asked,

"Outside? Did you notice anything suspicious? Anyone at the door?"

"No… it looked very normal to me. Where is she? Did you get her to talk?"

"In the kitchen. No, I was waiting for you."

"Okay, let's go! Leave it with me. What's her name?"

"I don't know," Hooman shrugged.

"For goodness' sake, Hooman! This is ridiculous! You could have asked her name, at least!" She opened the door and strutted confidently toward the kitchen.

The girl stood up and said hello, her head averted nervously, as if she couldn't make eye contact with Atossa. Hooman's giant pyjamas covered her body up to the chest, with her spindly hands dangling at her sides. The look made Atossa smile.

Atossa put her hands on the girl's shoulders, looked keenly at her, and with her low, gravelly voice, said, "Don't be frightened. I'm Atossa, Hooman's friend… by the way, he is Hooman!" She looked sarcastically at Hooman and continued, "…who most probably has forgotten to introduce himself yet. What's your name?"

"Neda."

"Nice name! Okay, Neda, why don't you sit down and relax, please."

They all sat around the kitchen table. A bit uneasy, Neda glanced surreptitiously from one to the other. Atossa narrowed her eyes, pulled one of her managerial faces, and leaned forward. "Look, if you want us to help, tell us the story. What happened to you?"

Neda stayed silent for a few moments, then said, "You've already helped a lot. Honestly, I can leave…"

Before she could finish, Atossa pounded her hand on the table. "Listen, young lady! We can't just let you go, not knowing what the hell happened to you or why you're here!"

"Okay, okay… right! I was on the run. The IRGC is looking for us."

"For *us*?"

"My friends and me… the IRGC—they were undercover agents."

"Fat rats."

Atossa sucked in a breath and shook her head. "I know they're everywhere. You've been protesting, right? Let me guess… one of those anti-hijab clashes? Or the one this morning about prisoners' freedom?" She felt a sharp twist in her gut, thinking of her cousin Nilofar.

"No, they broke into the university at lunchtime." Neda paused, then said irritably, "I think we had leaks. Someone ratted us out. These days, it's easy—they snare people with food or money."

That was the longest sentence Neda had uttered, and she instantly realized she had said too much. She looked around with her big, dilated eyes and went paler.

Hooman asked her to explain more about the reason for the raid. Neda hesitated, biting her lip like she was telling herself it was okay to speak. "All right… I'll tell you—They might have found out we're 1384s—I mean, members of…"

Leaning back against the chair, Hooman suddenly jumped up and exclaimed, "1384?? No way!" He looked at Atossa and said, "Do you know about this, Atoss? It's the latest anti-government student movement. Ha! Fantastic!"

"I'm leaving now. Please let me," Neda said, standing up.

Atossa half rose from her seat, leaned forward with a hand on her hip, and in a big-sister tone said, "Sit down, please! You're not going anywhere! And you too, Hooman—can you shut up and let me think for a minute? We're anti-government too, aren't we? In case you can't see that, Neda!"

Hooman removed his glasses slowly and set them on the table.

Neda gasped at the sight of his scarred eye, then dropped her eyes to the floor. With her voice barely above a whisper, she said, "Sorry."

Atossa kept her gaze locked on Neda. "Where's your home? Any family or relatives?"

"Not in Tehran. I'm a student on my own. I live on campus—Tehran University. I'm from the south."

"And how old are you?"

"Twenty-one. Soon to be twenty-two."

"Where are your friends now?"

"I don't know. We separated. We can't call each other for a couple of hours—that's the rule."

"That makes sense." Atossa nodded thoughtfully. "Tell me, Neda... what's 1384? What's the ideology? The name's strange. Is it a code or something?"

Hooman coughed and cleared his throat. "I think we have bigger issues to resolve here than learning about resistance groups, Atoss!"

"Come on, Hooman! Step by step—surely we must educate ourselves!" She lowered her head and tapped it lightly. "What do you think this is, Hooman?"

He braced himself and grimaced. "Don't make that face at me—answer the question!"

With some effort, Hooman replied, "Your big head!"

"Correct. Thank you! And that's exactly what you're missing!"

Neda chuckled but quickly said, "Sorry," dropping her head briskly to hide her smile.

Atossa looked at her. "There's no crime in laughing. Now, tell me about 1384—I'm curious."

Hooman shrank back slightly and said languidly, "Okay, I'll make tea then."

He got himself busy at the counter—brewing the tea, setting out three glass cups, and finally placing the tray in the middle of the table when it was ready. The comforting scent of black bergamot tea filled the room, making everything feel just a little more normal.

He dropped two spoonfuls of sugar into his cup and stirred it noisily

Neda sat, head bowed in thought, her fingers wrapped tightly around the cup as she drank in slow, quiet sips.

She wore a thin white polo-neck jumper tucked into Hooman's pyjamas, which hung loosely on her—several sizes too big, nearly as long as her black manteau. She had already hung that, along with her trousers, to dry in the bathroom. She was thin, with dark olive skin, large eyes, and dark brown curls. Meanwhile, Atossa had started chatting with Hooman about

Nana Khanoum, giving Neda space to settle

After a minute or two, Neda unclenched her hands and placed her palms on either side of the cup. She slowly slid her fingers forward, took a deep breath, and finally decided to speak.

Something sparked across her face—excitement, or maybe defiance. For a moment, she seemed older, sharper, as if a different version of herself had emerged. She swept her curls behind her ears and rolled up her sleeves.

"If you want to hear it, of course. Have you read the novel *1984*? Or maybe seen the film?"

Hooman straightened in his seat. "George Orwell's?"

"Exactly. That grim vision of a dystopian society."

"Big Brother is watching you!" Hooman smirked.

Atossa nodded. "Yes, I've seen the movie. It's funny how people always call it 'George Orwell's *1984*,' like there are a dozen versions floating around. I mean, as if there's another *1984* out there. Okay, yes—go on."

Neda looked at them and nodded. "We believe that kind of frightening world isn't just something out of Orwell's imagination—it's the reality we've lived under this government for more than forty years."

Atossa said, "I read that book ages ago. I barely remember—just a few bits." She squinted, resting her chin in her hands as she tried to recall.

Neda began to explain, "The world in *1984* is a dystopian society in the future, totally controlled by a political party led by Big Brother—who might be a real person, or maybe just a symbol. The Party's only goal is to hold onto power.

"They use telescreens to watch everyone all the time—even in their homes. There's this new language called Newspeak that's designed to limit how people think. And doublethink—that's when you're forced to accept two contradictory things as true at the same time."

She paused briefly, then added, "There's a Thought Police that arrests people just for thinking the wrong thing. And the Party keeps rewriting history, constantly changing the past to match whatever they say now.

"There are four ministries. The Ministry of Truth handles lies and propaganda. The Ministry of Love deals with torture and brainwashing. The Ministry of Plenty keeps everyone poor, and the Ministry of Peace is in charge of never-ending war."

"Society's split into three groups: the Inner Party—just a tiny elite; the

Outer Party—a bit larger; and then the working class, which is like 80% of the population. Most of them are kept distracted and uneducated."

She looked down briefly, then said, "Love and real relationships are banned. Sex is only permitted for reproduction!"

Neda paused and looked at them. "Does that ring any bells?"

Hooman and Atossa exchanged a glance, then both nodded.

"I think it was banned here? Not totally sure... and in some other country—oh right, Belarus too!" Hooman said.

Neda leaned forward slightly and, in a quieter voice, said, "The similarities go deeper than most people think."

"First, there's the totalitarian control—one party with absolute power, using a sophisticated propaganda machine to shape a false reality. In the book, that was the job of the Ministry of Truth. Our version? It's called the Ministry of Guidance.

"Then there's the idea of perpetual war. In *1984*, Oceania is always at war—with either Eurasia or Eastasia—it doesn't even matter which. What matters is that the country always has an enemy. People are expected to remember who they've defeated and always feel grateful for being 'safe.' The Islamic Republic did the same. They created the idea of a never-ending war to justify their power. It gave people a false sense of unity and purpose—and a reason to be thankful for freedoms that don't really exist.

"None of the wars were accidents. Take the eight-year war with Iraq—there's a reason Khomeini rejected the ceasefire in '82. And there's a reason he branded the U.S. as 'The Great Satan' and the U.K. as 'The Little Satan'—they needed constant enemies. Look at how they've used Syria, Iraq, Lebanon, and Yemen—just battlegrounds for their dream of becoming a Shia superpower. Add in Quds Day, the chants about conquering Jerusalem... it's all part of the same script."

She gave a dry smile. "War is Peace, right? Sometimes I seriously wonder if the regime copied its entire playbook from Ingsoc and Big Brother."

She looked at them. "And we all remember the 'Two Minutes Hate,' don't we? Lining up at school every morning, clenching our fists and yelling 'Death to this' or 'Death to that.'"

Atossa and Hooman both nodded, silent.

"The next parallel is newspeak, Oceania's official language," Neda continued. "They replaced English with a stripped-down, redefined vocabulary to deny facts and control thoughts. That's exactly what's happened here—except ours came wrapped in Quranic language with its Arabic roots. A calculated policy of deculturisation and de-Iranisation. "Language is the artery of culture. Damage it, and the culture dries up. That's why so many writers, singers, and artists were executed—or forced to flee. The regime's greatest enemy was never a foreign power. It was thinking."

Then she added quietly, quoting Orwell: *"If thought corrupts language, language can also corrupt thought."*

Atossa closed her eyes, pressing a hand to the Faravahar necklace around her neck. "Yes. Good thoughts, good words, good deeds."

They sat in silence for a moment, then began trading more eerie parallels.

"The Party dress code," Hooman said, "and our mandatory hijab laws... same obsession with controlling bodies."

"And the Thought Police," Neda added, "basically our morality police. Different name, same purpose."

"Sex allowed only for reproduction," Atossa murmured. "Passion is dangerous. Desire is rebellion."

Hooman raised an eyebrow. "Music, dancing, singing—banned, because they 'encourage individuality.' Can't have people expressing joy freely, right?"

"And above all," Neda said, "the only pure love allowed is for Big Brother... or in our case, the Supreme Leader."

Atossa gave a dry chuckle. "Slavery is Freedom." Then, suddenly, she smiled. "Do you know what I remember the most? The chocolate ration. Sorry—I'm a foodie."

She rolled her eyes and said it like it was breaking news: *"'Chocolate ration increased to twenty grams a week!'* You remember that part? It was already thirty grams—but they cut it and called it a gift, and everyone cheered like it was a treat."

She shook her head. "Just like us, really. They reduce meat, bread, everything—but then during Ramadan, they run a discount and people queue like it's a luxury. And no one remembers that last year we had more."

She turned to Neda. "We had food coupons starting in '79. You weren't born then."

Hooman leaned forward, hands tucked under his chin. He looked amused, but thoughtful. "And Room 101? You know what it is here?"

Neda raised her eyebrows but stayed silent.

Hooman turned to Atossa with a sly grin. "Come on, Atoss—you've got the big brain. Tell us. What's Iran's Room 101?"

Atossa hesitated. She knew the answer, but saying it made something tighten in her chest. She shrugged, keeping her expression cool. "I don't know...go on. Enlighten us, oh genius."

"Room 101," Hooman said, smiling, "is Evin."

Atossa felt a familiar twist in her stomach but just muttered, "Damn it. Yes. Clever—for once." Her voice dropped as she quietly added, "Ward 209."[7]

Hooman smiled, then grew quiet. "Orwell was a damn genius. I wonder what he'd make of our time. What side he'd take. What war he'd fight. He died too young—only forty-six. Tuberculosis."

Atossa said, "You know, maybe it's better he didn't live long enough to see this dystopia for real."

They smiled, and Neda, imagining his character, said, "Agree. I bet he'd be some kind of activist—maybe a climate activist or something..."

Atossa jumped in, smiling, "Totally. Probably a vegan too, right?"

Neda chuckled, "Maybe. But absolutely political. And I don't think he'd ever get on social media—Instagram or X or whatever. He'd definitely stay away from all that stuff... the platforms and data monitoring that now shapes public opinion. But he predicted it all, though."

Hooman nodded. "For sure. The guy was a total genius."

"There are some passages in *1984* about the twenty-first century that stunned me," Neda said, then continued, "like when he wrote: *'Human equality had become technically possible, and long-abandoned practices—imprisonment without trial, the use of war prisoners as slaves, public executions, torture to extract confessions, the use of hostages, and the deportation of whole populations—had not only become common again but were tolerated by people who considered themselves enlightened.'*"

The three of them fell into silence.

ZORRO

'INCREDIBLE!" HOOMAN SAID, breaking the silence. Atossa looked at Neda and asked, "But wait—how does all this connect to your group, 1384? Are you trying to build some kind of utopia?"

Neda shook her head. "Good question, but no. There's no utopia. No perfect society. What we want is to stop this ongoing dehumanization. This regime—the root of all evil in Iran and the region—wants total control over people. Orwell nailed it when he said, *'You don't create a dictatorship to protect a revolution; you make a revolution to create a dictatorship.'*"

Neda sighed deeply, her voice heavy with sadness. "But there's a bigger problem. We suspect this goes far beyond Iran. They're all connected—an international network of Big Brothers creating dystopian states wherever they go... Iran, Afghanistan, Syria, Yemen, Iraq, Lebanon. And that endless fire fuels the ongoing war between Palestine and Israel."

She paused, then added, "Like Orwell said, the Party believes a permanent state of war must exist—for two reasons. First, to keep the wheels of industry turning without actually increasing the world's real wealth. So it's not just about destroying human lives, but also the products of human labour. Second, it's about controlling the thoughts of the masses. Since no decisive victory is possible, it doesn't matter if the war goes well or badly—as long as it continues and consumes the surplus.

"Ironically, 1984 turned out to be a year of massive destruction. In March of that year, Iraq launched its first large-scale chemical attack, unleashing tons of sulphur mustard and nerve agents on Iranian soldiers at the Majnoon Islands battlefield[8]. This horrific campaign went on for several years.

"Even though the Geneva Protocol clearly banned the use of chemical weapons, no Western country openly condemned Saddam for using them. In fact, they supported his regime in other ways—supplying precursor chemicals, technology, and the know-how to help develop the weapons. The thing is, while the 1925 Protocol banned their use, it didn't actually ban making or owning them.

"But it wasn't just about chemical weapons. The list of countries involved in selling arms is long— the USSR, the US, European nations, and even China, which saw its first major opportunity to become a key arms supplier in the Middle East.

"Crazy—I never noticed that. never connected it to that year," Hooman said. "Did you, Atoss? Maybe it's because we use a different calendar… or maybe we've just blocked that whole time out. It was so damn dark."

Atossa nodded slowly. "Me neither, Hooman. But honestly, it's a tragic kind of dark comedy. We all know that a few years later, those same countries turned on Saddam Hussein—pretending to chase the very weapons they helped him build."

"Exactly," Neda said, then continued: "And then came the Gulf War, and the flames are still burning across the Middle East. If you look at all these conflicts, religion keeps getting twisted into the excuse—Shia, Sunni, Jewish… all just the chariots of gods carrying fire, dragged by human ignorance."

She leaned forward slightly, her voice quieter but more intense, "But seriously, what's the point of religion if all it does is divide us? To draw borders? Separate people? Aren't we all the same? Aren't we all connected in the eyes of the God who made us?"

Hooman got up as if to make another round of tea but just stood there, arms folded, staring at the kettle.

Neda glanced at Atossa. "Sorry, I got sidetracked. You asked about the name of our group. Aside from the Orwell reference, the year 1384 (2005) in the current Iranian calendar marked a turning point. Ahmadinejad came to power, and the regime's propaganda machine kicked into full gear. That was the year the nuclear program escalated—uranium enrichment, global tensions, the whole package. So, 1384 made more sense than 1984."

"That explains it!" Hooman said with a nod.

Neda smiled, glancing from Atossa to Hooman, and said with quiet confidence, "There is a way out. A hopeful message is hidden in that dystopian book."

Atossa and Hooman stared at her, intrigued. She let the moment stretch before finally saying: "Love."

They both looked startled.

Hooman chuckled, rubbing his forehead, "Oh my God."

"Love?" Atossa said. "Are you serious? You want to fight this monstrous regime with *that*? The love between Julia and Winston? You mean that kind of love…?"

Neda, calm and steady, spoke like she had practiced this moment a hundred times. "Our manifesto comes down to three things: choosing love over hate, fighting for liberty, and refusing to stay silent. Love is our first act of resistance. And it's not soft—it's the hardest thing to hold onto when everything around you is falling apart. But it keeps us human.

"Oppressive regimes know that. That's why they try to make the world ugly—because beauty sparks love, and love gives people courage. So we fight back with art, with music, with connection..."

Hooman nodded. "Hard to argue with that."

Neda went on.

"But hate is seductive. It's primal. It spreads fast. That's why so many followed Khomeini. Why so many admired Hitler. We have to be careful—because a society built on revenge will rot from the inside. You can't fix a broken system with the same poison that broke it."

Atossa leaned in. "So what's next?"

"Liberty," Neda said. "The regime survives by erasing people. It doesn't want citizens—it wants obedience.

"Ever notice how small countries rarely become totalitarian? It's not a coincidence. Without the masses, the machine falls apart.

"They want us to forget that every person matters. But when you start seeing people as individuals again—really seeing them—everything shifts. One voice can break the spell."

She glanced at them both, making sure they were still with her.

"And last, refusing to stay silent—we speak, even when we're tired. Because if we don't—who will? Oppression doesn't just live on violence. It lives on indifference. On people saying, 'It's not my problem.' On people looking away."

Neda looked up at both of them, signalling that she had finished. After a moment, Hooman turned to Atossa and said softly,

"Remember, Atoss... at her age, we were kind of a mess. Naïve, confused, insecure... I mean, seriously—nothing like her. Neda's generation is something else. Maybe they really *can* fix what we couldn't. Maybe they're the ones who'll actually save us."

Atossa looked at Neda with admiration. "The phenomenal Generation Z."

Hooman smiled. "Generation Z! Indeed—Z! You know, it reminded me of an old television series called *Zorro*. I loved it when I was a little boy. You might remember it, Atoss—but you won't, Neda.

"Zorro was a hero, a defender of civilians against tyrannical authorities. He had a horse, a cloak and a cape, a long sword, and a mask. I was so excited about all of it—I even got his costume as a birthday gift.

"In the movies, Zorro always left a distinctive mark: a Z, cut with three quick strokes of his sword to sign his work. When Atoss said 'Generation Z,' I unconsciously pictured a massive Z slashed across the map of the Ayatollahs' Iran by this new generation—as a sign of victory."

Atossa smiled at Hooman's boyhood memory, then looked at Neda with motherly concern.

"You must be very careful, Neda. Very careful, please... We need you. Aren't you scared of them?"

"Every single minute. But there are more important things than my fear."

Hooman's mobile rang. They looked at each other anxiously.

"Shhh, be quiet," Hooman said as he rushed to answer it. He listened for a moment, then turned to them with a smile.

"Don't worry. It's only Bijan."

He turned back to the phone. "Hi, Bijan... yes... good... I'm coming, of course. Atossa is here too—she's got Nana's nuts, and I have the watermelon."

He paused, glanced at the kitchen table, and added, "Bijan, listen... we might have a guest with us too. A young lady... do you mind?"

BIRDS ON THE TIGHTROPE

AVA

AVA WAS a primary school teacher. She had arrived an hour early for her class and spent most of that time motionless, holding a pen tightly in her hand and staring at the blackboard, rewinding the pictures from the memory of the night before. The conversation with Sam had been painful. Recalling some of the argument cast a gloom over her face, as if everything in her features was drooping, from her eyebrow to her pinched lips, as if she was in agony. But as the children began pacing in, she quickly recovered her smile. Work helped her momentarily forget the troubles waiting for her outside the school walls.

Once the children were settled, coloured pencils sharpened, and sketch paper handed out, Ava walked between the desks, admiring the children's work. She loved seeing them so engaged in drawing. Painting—and occasionally crafts—were the only subjects in the arts curriculum. Music, dance, and performing arts had been excluded.

Art wasn't a desirable subject from the government's point of view. Parents raised their children from an early age to focus solely on becoming doctors or engineers. But Ava knew many children still possessed a natural artistic drive and curiosity that refused to be extinguished.

Ava hated that in Iran, every sphere of artistic expression was curtailed and closely monitored. Freedom of expression was a fundamental human right—but the Ministry of Culture and Guidance, overseen by the 'Guardian Council,' saw art as a barrier to bringing those who had strayed back onto the path of 'righteousness.'

They claimed music stirred only unclean feelings; it was like a drug. Dance was deemed immoral and sinful in any form—including the mystical dances of the Sufis. Theatre, they said, "raped the country's youth and stifled their spirit of virtue and bravery."

Children were encouraged only to perform *Ta'zieh*, where they dressed as little imams re-enacting the battle of Karbala.

It was enough for Ava to glance around the school walls to see the message: banners bearing famous quotes that reflected the regime's emphasis on martyrdom and control:

"Every land is Karbala; every month is Muharram; every day is Ashura."

"Hijab is chastity for a girl."

But the worst form of suppression and control, she thought, was the enforcement of the hijab—the patrolling of the streets by the Morality Police. Under Article 638 of the Islamic Penal Code of Iran, women and girls as young as nine must cover their hair and conceal the shape of their bodies beneath long, loose robes. Violating this law could result in up to sixty days of imprisonment, seventy-four lashes, or fines adjusted for inflation. It was outrageous and inhuman.

It was sad—no, more than that, it felt *wrong*—that some Iranian women, like Zahra Rahnavard, supported this law. She had been one of the early revolutionaries against the Shah. Alongside her husband, former Prime Minister Mir-Hossein Mousavi, and future President Hassan Rouhani, she helped push for the mandatory hijab right after the revolution, even published a book, titled *Beauty of Concealment and Concealment of Beauty*. The title itself spoke volumes. A woman with an art degree yet standing behind something so limiting and oppressive.

Ava looked away from the students and walked toward the windows, their glass opaque with layers of pollution. The grime dimmed the entire classroom. She scratched a tiny circle with her index finger and winced at the sticky dirt clinging to her skin. The air felt suffocating.

She had a sudden urge to open the window but struggled with the hinge, stuck tight from years of neglect. The windows needed washing. The whole school did.

She stepped back and sighed. Cleaning the building felt like too much to ask—when there were far more urgent problems, like the inhuman conditions teachers were forced to endure.

Payment for most outsourced teachers—including Ava—had been de-layed for the second year in a row. All her colleagues had second or even third jobs. Without Sam's income and a bit of support from her family, she wouldn't have been able to survive.

Official contracts were reserved for teachers employed directly by the Ministry of Education, which most were not. Instead, they were hired through private contractors on temporary agreements the government exploited. They earned much less than a dollar a day, with no benefits, no medical insurance, no overtime, no holiday pay—despite the fact that the public school system couldn't function without them.

Ava thought back to her own school days nearly forty years ago. She had been a tiny, shy girl, and to help her build confidence, her teacher had put her in charge of distributing the free school meals. At 10 a.m., students up to the eighth grade were given fruit, milk, and calorie-rich biscuits. She remembered carrying the baskets and placing a portion on each desk—triangle pouches of Pak milk, Nan-e-Razavi biscuits with their buttery taste, which she could almost still savour.

She glanced back at the children now. Hijab was mandatory for girls from the age of seven—the start of elementary school—even though all the schools were single-sex. They had to keep their veils on in the classroom, as if rehearsing for a lifetime of wearing them.

At the back of the room, one girl bent her head closely to her desk. Her hijab slipped forward, hanging over her paper, nearly covering her work. Ava walked over and gently tapped her on the shoulder. As the girl lifted her head, Ava helped her push the veil—and her messy hair—back behind her ears.

"Now it's better, isn't it?" Ava said.

The other girls giggled, and the student quickly returned to her sketching.

"Let me see... oh, this is a huge fluffy cat, sitting in the sunshine. And what's this? A boat?"

"No, miss—that's not a cat. That's the map. It's Iran."

Ava felt a bit embarrassed and smiled. "Oh! Yes, of course—I see it now."

The map of Iran *did* resemble a cat, but somehow, she had missed that.

"Great work! But what's the boat for? ...This wasn't exactly what I asked for."

She looked up, then gently reminded the class, "Remember, the topic was *Yalda*."

The girl said confidently, "That's not a boat, Miss! It's a watermelon wedge—see? Green on the bottom and red on top. It's for Yalda. Everyone in Iran eats watermelon, and the sun is coming to shine!"

The class burst into peals of laughter.

But Ava stood still, silent. It reminded her of the first page of her favourite book, *The Little Prince*—and how the grown-ups had mistaken a drawing of a boa constrictor digesting an elephant for a hat. Now she had made the same mistake. She smiled to herself. *The grown-ups never understand...*

She looked at the girl keenly and said, "Well done. Well done!"

From the front of the room, another girl called out, "Finished, Miss!" and held up her paper.

The painting showed two tall trees connected by what looked like a tightrope. A group of birds—some big, some small, like a little family— were tiptoeing across it from one tree to the other. On the ground below were small, red fruits.

Ava adjusted her glasses and smiled so deeply that it crinkled her whole face.

"Okay... let me see. Very interesting." Then, curiously: "Tell us more. How does this relate to Yalda?"

The girl pointed to the red fruits. "Those are pomegranates."

"Aha! Nice... and the birds? Walking the rope instead of flying—why's that?"

The girl replied, "Well... they needed it to keep their balance. They don't know how to fly yet."

Ava went quiet, her eyes fixed on the drawing.

The girl, growing impatient, wiped her runny nose with the edge of her hijab and added softly, "They're scared to fly, Miss."

Ava slowly lifted her gaze from the paper and looked at her with full attention. "Ah... of course they are," she whispered.

DRUNKEN HORSES ON THE ZAGROS MOUNTAINS

ATOSSA AND HOOMAN were in the living room, chatting and getting ready for the party. Hooman pulled back the curtain and shouted, "Snow!" They both leaned closer to the window.

Neda looked at them and smiled. She was still in the kitchen, drinking her second glass of tea, sitting on the far side of the table next to the heater, waiting for her trousers to dry and occasionally turning them.

She glanced around the room surreptitiously; the place seemed tidy and normal. On the kitchen table, a newspaper was spread open: a half-full glass of water, a bowl of sugar loaves, an ashtray, a red notebook, and a bottle of eye drops. It felt surreal to be among people she'd only learned existed a few hours earlier. Though self-conscious at first, she no longer felt like a complete stranger.

She thought about Hooman's injured eye, likely the result of a shooting by the security forces. Birdshot—a type of shotgun pellet—had been deliberately aimed at the eyes of many protesters. The bullets had blinded many of them but not dimmed their vision.

As kind as Hooman and Atossa had been, Neda began to feel anxious about being there; she feared she might be putting them at risk and worried for her friends too—it had been a few hours since they had separated. Holding her mobile tightly between her hands, she felt a wave of apprehension as her breathing quickened.

She shook her head a few times, as if trying to shrug off the negativity. Neda was most worried about her friend Zhina, because she was a Kurd. Although the totalitarian regime cast its shadow over everyone, it was worse for women in general—and for Kurdish women in particular. Many female Kurdish political prisoners had recently been prosecuted and given exceptionally long prison terms.

In 1979, during the referendum to establish the Islamic Republic, despite the overwhelming 'Yes' vote, the situation in the northwest of Iran was more complicated. Iranian Sunni Kurds boycotted the vote. As a result, the regime launched a war against Kurdistan. The bombardment began shortly after the revolution's victory, hitting many cities across Iranian

Kurdistan. The Kurds suddenly found themselves under threat in their own homeland. It was widely seen as an act of revenge—a brutal response by the regime, which continued until the present day and included mass executions as a punitive measure against the Kurds for their resistance and refusal to align with the regime.

Neda recalled the stories Zhina had told her about the courage of Kurdish women who had become soldiers and joined resistance groups to fight oppression. While many Iranian women—especially in the big cities—complied with the regime's rules on headscarves, Kurdish women resisted compulsory veiling and were among the last to surrender. Due to their distinct cultural identity and ongoing struggle against the central government, Kurdish women often viewed the imposition of the hijab as another form of state control and an attack on their cultural freedom. It took the regime significantly longer to enforce Hijab in Kurdish areas compared to many other parts of the country.

The air from the heater was blowing the pages of the calendar on the wall above Neda's head. She noticed that *Yalda* was marked with a red circle, and the name *Bijan* was lightly scribbled in pencil. She raised her hand, pressed it against the calendar to stop the page, and traced her index finger around that little red circle a few times.

The circle reminded her of their last night on campus, when she and her friends had talked about *Yalda* too. A discussion about the different regional traditions for the occasion had led them to try a Kurdish hand-holding circle dance in secret. They had fun standing together in a circle for a few minutes, trying to learn it from Zhina. But now, all Neda could see was the word *Yalda* and a big, round, empty circle. It felt like a hole, a void—a huge gap.

Zhina told them that even something as simple as teaching that dance could lead to prosecution. There were horrifying stories of how the regime sentenced several Kurdish women to long prison terms just for teaching the language.

To be Kurdish was to be fragmented. What fascinated Neda was that if someone was Kurdish, there was a good chance that person came from Turkey, Iran, Iraq, Syria, or even Armenia. But no matter how many borders divided them, they still identified with a distinct culture. From the northern Zagros[9] to the eastern Taurus[10], they all knew how to dance hand in hand in a circle. It was no wonder the regime feared dancing and singing—it was the bond that reminded the Kurds who they were. That was their code, a sacred secret.

"All right?" Atossa came back into the kitchen with a broad smile and a glint in her eyes. She stood by the heater and dropped a small floral-patterned bag on the table.

"Hey! Come on, we're going to the party. Let's put the lippy on... see what we've got here." She rummaged through the make-up bag and, with a persuasive voice, continued, "Look—here's a little mirror, lipstick, powder, face cream... all you might need to freshen up!"

She began applying red lipstick herself, then looked at Neda. "Too much?"

"No, that's perfect for Yalda," Neda answered politely.

"Your hair is so pretty—curly black," Atossa said, "and looks so healthy compared to mine!" She pointed at her straight, mahogany-highlighted hair, which looked damaged from too much dyeing. "Look! How boring mine is! I've always wanted curls!"

Neda blushed and said, "Thanks, but believe me, sometimes I have to do a lot of work to straighten it!"

She tried to be polite by keeping her smile and engaging in conversation, but her face had gone pale again, revealing some nervousness.

"Feeling anxious still? Can't blame you, really. Let me see if Hooman has Borage tea—it will soothe you. You don't have to come with us, dear... we just thought it might help. They might still be there. It would be safer if you went back later."

"It wouldn't be inappropriate, would it? I don't want to be a nuisance... I already am..."

"Aw, of course you're not," Atossa said, taking Neda's hand. "Come on, let me show you something." She pointed to one of the pictures among the fridge magnets; it was a photo of a group of friends. Neda recognized Hooman and Atossa among them.

"That's our friend Bijan! Look—we're going to his place. He knows you're with us. Hooman mentioned it on the phone, didn't he? They're a cool bunch, maybe a bit old and boring for your age... but they're easy-going and funny. Don't worry. Look at this lady—she's like his mother, called Banoo. This was years ago. They love guests; you'll see for yourself."

"Come on, girly, help yourself." She unzipped the bag fully. "If you like, put your lippy on and we'll be ready to go!"

Neda smiled in consent. Dusk was falling, and the continuous beeping and smell of fuel from the traffic outside filled the air. It was late in the day. Neda was restless. She glanced hesitantly at her mobile and said quietly, "Just don't know what happened to my friends yet..."

Having returned from the front room, Hooman dropped into a kitchen chair, grabbed the eye-drop bottle from the table, tilted his head back, and positioned himself for a drop.

Atossa ran over and said, "Give it to me." She held his head steady, pulled his eyelid, and squeezed in a drop. It made Hooman jolt. With his face still tilted up, he said, "Why don't you turn your phone on? It's been a good couple of hours now—it should be okay."

Neda felt a crust of cold sweat on her forehead, and with shaky fingers, she switched on her mobile. The three of them stood still, holding their breath for a lingering minute. Atossa put one hand on Neda's shoulder and the other on her Faravahar necklace.

A text came through.

Neda read it, then held the phone in the air for everyone to see and smiled. "'Spaghetti for dinner?' This means it's safe to call!"

Atossa screamed, "YES!" Hooman ran his fingers through his thick hair and muttered, "Phew."

But the joy didn't last. Neda's face contorted as she spoke on the phone. When the call ended, she placed her mobile on the kitchen table. The story was that her friends had shaken off the IRGC and returned safely to the hostel. But an hour later, the IRGC raided the residence hall again and took Zhina for questioning on university grounds. She was returned after a while—but something had changed. She seemed different, as if they had injected her with something, a drug to extract information.

Neda looked like a bird that had been shot. She sank to the floor. In her mind, she heard Zhina's voice: "They make horses drunk to cross the Zagros." [11]

She remembered the story of the Kolbars that Zhina had told her, about the people who transported smuggled goods across the Iran-Iraq border. For many Iranian Kurds, it had become the only source of income. Among the Kolbars were children, elderly men and women, and educated young people who were jobless due to high unemployment and deep-rooted discrimination in Kurdistan. They carried merchandise as small as medicine or cosmetics, and sometimes as heavy as 120 kilograms, strapped to their backs for ten to twelve hours through treacherous mountain passes and mined border terrain.

In winter, the path could be buried under a metre of snow. Death or life-altering injury was common. And that was in addition to the constant risk of being shot or captured by border guards. Those with horses or mules sometimes spiked their animals' water with alcohol to help the long-suffering, overburdened creatures push through the harsh, snow-covered mountains, a testament to the sheer physical demands of the routes.

Neda suddenly exclaimed, "No!" Then, with her hands on the edge of the table, she rose abruptly—as if she had just retrieved her defiant superpower. *There must be another reality*, she thought. *This has to end. They had to survive, to make it through this difficult path.*

Her eyes, red and unfocused, turned toward Hooman's and Atossa's anxious faces. She was visibly shaking but took a long, deep breath to calm her nerves. Then, as if searching for something on the table, she picked up the little floral bag, removed a mirror, and gazed at herself for a moment, frowning intently—like seeing something beyond her own face. After a moment, she grabbed a lipstick, uncapped it, and circled it a few times across her lips.

"I'm ready now."

"But what about your friend?"

"Zhina will carry on. My friend is strong. She is one of the children of the Medes and Cyaxares.[12]"

CONTAGIOUS

ROXY AND KAMRAN

PROPPED UP with cushions, Roxy lay on the bed before a big flat screen. Her face was masked in thick makeup, and her long, dyed blond hair was blow-dried into a bouffant. Her eyeliner and mascara heightened her black eyes but still came second to her plumped-out lips. This was thanks to Kamran's skilled injection; he made it seem natural and not too obvious, although his skills as a cosmetic surgeon were now less in demand since lip fillers promoted by Kylie Jenner, the youngest of the Kardashian family, had hit the market and were now being smuggled into Iran.

Kamran was her boyfriend; they began dating shortly after first meeting at his clinic. He turned out to be a warm, sensual man, far from his image as a serious doctor only interested in his work. Kamran was married but had been separated from his wife for a few years. Not long after they started dating, Roxy moved in with him.

The Fashion Channel was showing on the television screen, which was almost as large as the wall behind it. This was something Roxy usually loved watching, but tonight she was barely paying attention. She browsed through her mobile as if searching for something that could lift her spirits. Her natural cheerfulness had begun to fade recently, and she often found herself slipping into acute, momentary bouts of depression; it was like someone pulling a cord and switching off the light inside her head. These episodes had become more frequent and lasted longer, and she worried that she might finally sink deeply into a pit of depression.

Roxy had to get ready for Bijan's party, but she kept delaying, scrolling through the photos from the last party on her phone; they were enough to put her off tonight's event. "Oh hell... look... silly idiots..." she murmured to herself.

Meeting Kamran had allowed her to join a small minority of wealthy people whose affluence did not depend on direct connections to the regime and who lived in a bubble, as if nothing else existed outside. She had begun to realize, however, that none of them were happy; their lives were ruled by drama, confusion, unpleasant stories, obsessions, and pathetic affairs.

She came from a family that had little and had understood from the beginning that the poor and the rich lived in two very different worlds. When she was poor, despair made sense and often pushed her to build a better future. But now that everything she needed was provided, what reason was there for her depression?

We are all becoming sick, she thought.

Something was very wrong, though she couldn't yet name it—a vague, intangible weight. It was like being trapped in a room lined with mirrors, unable to see beyond, forced to face only their own reflections.

She had been finding it increasingly difficult to shrug off her doubts and convince herself that things were fine. A trip to the best holiday resorts in Thailand, shopping in Dubai, buying a branded watch, or importing a fancy car couldn't cure it. They had become involuntary actors in a dark fantasy comedy, which was growing emptier over time.

Lies are like plastic, she thought. *They don't decompose and always come back to haunt you. Was this reality also part of the lies?*

She wondered how long they could keep pretending, clinging to this hollow comfort. Maybe there was another reality—just out of reach. One they had lost or chosen to forget.

She put her mobile down on the bed and stared at the ceiling, as if looking into a dark, heavy cloud.

Kamran, lying next to her, shifted slightly and placed his hand on Roxy's lap, as he often did. But this time, the warmth of his touch burned through her laced chemise. It landed exactly where Kamran's best friend had placed his hand the night before at the party. He had smirked, nodding toward the corner of the room where Kamran was deep in conversation with another woman.

She moved her leg the same way she had the night before and said exactly what she'd said then: "We should go, it's late."

She sat on the edge of the bed.

Kamran jolted, switched on the light, and grabbed his mobile. "Let me call her again, and then I'll get ready," he said, walking into the hallway.

Roxy removed her chemise and looked at her long, skinny legs, her belly with its slight bump, and her round, plump breasts—another masterpiece of Kamran. She didn't like her body much. Not even her height. She was tall for an Iranian woman, and Kamran was short.

She took the same dark purple Versace dress she had worn the night before out of the cupboard, held it in the air, then brought it closer and slipped it on, extending the neckline wide and moving her head carefully so as not to disturb her makeup.

She sat on the edge of the bed to put on her stockings and shoes. Rocking herself back and forth, she was still thinking about Kamran. He was kind. She knew there was something between them that was still, to a degree, intact. But she was never quite sure about the rules of the world in which he lived. She could only see half of Kamran's face; the other half was turned toward the wall. His visible cheek was flushed—his skin always turned red when he was agitated. He was talking to his daughter in the U.S. about the exchange rate. The dollar had risen another 30% that week, a historic high—even someone as wealthy as Kamran was feeling the strain.

His daughter, following in the footsteps of her older brother, had left for college only a few months ago and was now at university. Roxy thought she was a spoiled and clumsy girl—but she also knew it wasn't fair to judge. She didn't have children, and she never interfered.

Still, in this situation, she felt for the girl. Kamran was behind on the tuition fees, and it had become difficult to send money from Iran. His daughter was now at risk of dropping out and returning home.

Kamran noticed Roxy watching him and walked into the bedroom with his nimble steps. A small, well-proportioned man with short, neatly cut silver hair, he came to the head of the bed, gently kissed her forehead, then pointed at his mobile and shrugged as if to justify the long conversation that was making them late for the party.

Roxy smiled, lifted her hand in approval for him to carry on, then left the edge of the bed to stand by the window. She pushed the curtain slightly apart and held it open. The cold from the glass breathed back onto her face.

It was snowing. She thought about changing her shoes and putting on boots—but didn't bother. The party was inside Bijan's house, only a few steps from where they usually parked in his garden, so it would be fine.

She kept looking out. The night, she thought, had an extraordinary variety of forms. When it was cold, the darkness was blacker—more secretive and scarier. But when it was warm, the night felt sultry and seductive. This one felt strange and heavy, the kind of night that made you want to see the stars.

In her head, a song called *Love Night* played. It was one of Hayedeh's songs that had stuck with her after she'd watched an old clip on her mobile earlier. Recalling it helped as if someone had switched the light on again. The clip was a black-and-white video of a picnic area in the old days of Tehran, maybe fifty years ago or more. People were scattered around: some preparing a barbecue, smoking shisha, drinking tea, playing backgammon, children making a swing on a tree. Their faces looked so pure and genuine.

She thought that something must have gone very wrong to have metamorphosed those beautiful people into the beastly society she was now a part of.

Her mind lingered on one part of the clip—where a young couple danced, trying something more modern for that time, hilariously so. The crowd had huddled around them, cheering.

Whispering the same song to herself would transport her into that crowd, and it felt more real than the present. Roxy thought she was that girl in the clip—the young woman dancing, fearless and light, as the crowd huddled around her, cheering.

"Sorry, honey. Finished."

Kamran returned to the bedroom, threw his mobile on the bed, and said he'd go change. The smell of his aftershave still lingered in the air from the bathroom.

Roxy leaned on the doorframe and asked about his daughter.

"Fine," he said. "Just a bit anxious. The short-term solution is for her to stay with a friend for now."

"She must be very stressed at that age," Roxy said. "By the way, the guy finally showed up. He only had your auntie's medicine—I left it on the console. But he couldn't get the eyedrops for Hooman or any dermal fillers this time."

Kamran raised his eyebrows and faintly smiled. They'd been waiting over a month for the guy to turn up. "At last, something." He paused. "Did you check the expiry date?"

Roxy nodded. "Yes, I did... You remember how he was? A very big man? But you wouldn't have recognized him. He's grown a beard, lost weight, and looked very nervous. He couldn't answer our calls—his Kolbars were stranded on the route, you know, by the border forces. He sounded rough. There had been shooting, and some..." She paused, unable to finish her sentence, and just said quietly, "Poor man."

Kamran made a strange bellowing sound, muttered a few words, and came out wearing dark trousers with a white shirt, collar up and fully buttoned. He changed his tie twice and looked frustrated. He draped both ties loosely around his neck and turned.

"Which one, Rox? Quick—we must dash. Gosh, it's already 8 p.m.!"

"Hmm... none. Why don't you try your green-purple striped one?"

"Ralph Lauren?"

Roxy nodded. She put on her winter jacket, looked in the mirror, rounded her lips, and carefully adjusted the corner of her mascara with the tip of her little finger. Then she stepped back and asked,

"Do you believe in déjà vu?"

DISORIENTED

A broken skull is
Not a broken brain, monsieur!
The war that you have waged
Is one of thought, and it
Cannot be fought with
Knives, or guns, or even fire extinguishers.
Napoleon was right when he observed that
Only true imagination gives the masses might

—Anno Birkin [13]

IN THE DARK, Babak sat in the front seat of the car next to Dara. They were discussing the quickest way to pick up Sam and Ava on their way to Bijan's house in the old part of Tehran near the French Embassy, at the Neauphle-le-Château junction. That area had turned into a commercial district, but Bijan's house was one of the rare buildings that had miraculously escaped the property developers' eyes and hadn't been demolished yet.

Shirin sat quietly in the back of their big, old van, which rattled like a tank. She seemed to have turned in on herself again.

Dara checked on her in the mirror. "You okay?"

Shirin nodded, looked at the snow falling through the beams of the headlights, and thought the air would be fresh tomorrow. She always checked the weather in Damascus, too, it had become a habit. She knew temperatures shifted drastically in Damascus during autumn, but snow was rare.

It was a shame; Farhad loved snow. They used to go to the Dizin ski resort in Tehran together. Now, she had mixed feelings whenever it snowed.

But was Farhad even there? No one could say for sure.

Dara banged hard on the steering wheel as the car passed along Khaled Islambuli [14] Street.

"Oh no! Mistake again—I took the wrong turn!"

"No... what mistake? We're good," Babak said.

"I know, but honestly, I can't bear driving down this street with this absurd name again! It's beyond irritating. Can you name a single country that has a street named after an assassin? It's preposterous!"

"Agh, come on! You're making a big deal out of this," Babak said, "It's just a name. Call it by its old name if you prefer. Remember the stamp they issued in his honour?". He took a deep breath, cleared his throat, and continued, "We just need to ignore it, Dara. That's all."

Dara grew serious. "That was one reason, but also, at the top of the same bloody street, Hooman got birdshot in his eye!"

Babak looked at him quizzically. "I thought it was further down?"

"No, it was here. I'll show you the exact spot. We keep ignoring everything! No wonder we're in this deep mess!" Dara turned around to get confirmation from Shirin. "Don't you think?"

Shirin looked out the window with vague, unheeding eyes and said, "I think it might snow in Damascus tonight, too."

Dara and Babak exchanged glances. Babak raised his eyebrows.

They stopped just before Ava and Sam's flat, which was in a four-floor building. The couple were waiting outside in the cold. Babak jumped out of the car and offered his seat. Ava preferred the back, so Sam went to the front.

From the back seat, Shirin and Babak, on either side of Ava, said, "Happy Yalda, guys!" The two new arrivals were quiet. Sam only nodded, and after a pause, Ava said in a low voice, "To you too."

Meeting them, Shirin returned to her usual self. She leaned closer, took Ava's hand, pulled her gently, and whispered, "What's happened? Had a row again?"

"Same old... but we're done this time." Her voice trembled as if she wanted to cry, but then she breathed deeply, turned her face aside, and quietly said, "More later."

Shirin pressed Ava's hand more firmly. Babak half-heard them but pretended he hadn't, then suddenly said, "You look amazing tonight!"

"Oh, really, me? Thanks, Babak-jan [15]. I haven't changed even... straight from school."

The mood lightened and relaxed as they chatted.

Traffic swelled, and a heavy flow built up, heading toward the junction where they would join Tehran's central artery, Valiasr Street. But encountering a lurching SUV and a dented Peykan taxi coming the wrong way sparked concern. They were stuck far from the intersection and couldn't tell what the issue was. A squeal of tyres came as more cars ahead made sudden U-turns. Something was happening.

"Might be an accident?" Dara pulled the window down, stuck his head out, and waved at the turning car.

"What's the matter?"

"Bloody stop and search... for Yalda!" The driver cursed and sped up.

"We should have stayed home," Sam grunted.

Babak muttered, "Shit!" and shoved the CD selection he had under his shirt; the touch of cold discs on his bare belly made him shiver.

It was gridlock now. Taking advantage of the standstill, children dodged among the cars to sell flowers, chewing gum, tissues, and cigarettes. Some offered to wash the windows or were selling Fal-e-Hafez—pamphlets containing poems by Hafez that claimed to tell one's future.

Ava said sadly, "There are no statistics for these poor kids, no plan, no past or future, as if they don't exist!"

Shirin asked, "Where do they usually come from, do we know?"

Ava said, "Well, it's a mixed bag. Some are maybe children of Afghan refugees, but the majority are from very poor Iranian families. My heart aches for them, especially the girls, and how they're forced to grow up and mature quickly. Imagine the awful things they have to go through—you name it: exploitation, rape, harassment..."

"Best not to imagine!" Shirin said.

Three children—two boys and one girl, about six to ten years old—were hovering near them. The girl looked older than the boys and had a backpack with a faded Disney character printed on it. Like a clown, she had painted her nose red but hardly smiled. She was trying to coordinate selling stuff from her bag with the two boys.

One boy walked briskly, zigzagging his way around the cars. He banged on the van's window. "Tissue? Gum? How about flowers for the ladies?" He looked playful.

Sam pulled the window down; a fog of cold air came inside. He took a bouquet in exchange for a few notes. The boy giggled and looked cheekily toward the back of the car when Sam held the flowers in the air without looking at Ava.

Ava didn't move. Shirin took the flowers and placed them on Ava's lap.

Suddenly, Ava jolted and asked the boy to wait. "What is she selling?"

she asked, pointing at the girl standing nearby.

"Fal-e-Hafez."

"Give me one."

The boy waved at the girl; she approached with a stack of pamphlets and stood by the window. Normally, a little trained bird would hop out and pull a pamphlet randomly with its beak, but in this case, it was only the girl.

Shirin jokingly said, "Where is the bird, then?"

The little boy replied, "The bird, Madame? We had one. Died—it didn't survive."

Ava handed the girl a note, closed her eyes, and took one. Then she asked the girl why she had painted her nose.

The boy laughed. "For Yalda, to make people happy."

Then, with a more serious face, he added, "She is deaf, Madame."

The girl stood there, visibly shaking; her teeth were clattering from the cold. Ava leaned forward and gently held the girl's chin, which was ice cold, then removed a pair of gloves from her bag and handed them to her.

"You don't need to make anyone happy, darling. Put the gloves on. They're a bit large, but they'll help keep you warm."

The girl took them and smiled.

Shirin said, "Poor thing, she needs a gauntlet to survive out here in these streets."

Cars began to move slowly. Drivers fought for each inch, bumper to bumper, until they finally reached the Revolutionary Guard patrol.

Two armed, bearded guards wearing Basij uniforms waved and stopped their van.

Dara pulled down the window and, with a grin on his face, said, "Salam Alaikum, brother."

His attempt to appear friendly and use their vocabulary was ignored. The guard gazed suspiciously inside the car and said, "Pull over!"

Dara obeyed and stopped further up the road.

Shirin glanced over her shoulder. Other bearded men stood beside the guard in plain clothes—legs wide apart, puffed up and confident. A minibus marked "Guidance and Morality Police" was parked nearby. A female officer in a black chador was dragging a girl toward the bus. The girl struggled, bent forward, and was pushed inside. Her forehead hit the top of the door, and she floundered on the floor of the vehicle.

Ava and Shirin gasped.

The woman in the black cloak slammed the bus door shut. Shirin leaned forward, squinting, and spotted two other women inside. A chill ran through her. "There are more girls in the bus."

"Don't stare!" Babak said.

One of the chunkier bearded men approached, leaned into the open front window, and gruffly fired off questions: Who were they? How were they related? Were they married? Where did they live?

His bad breath filled the car. He looked like someone hunting for prey, gazing at Ava and Shirin with dark, vacant eyes, as if calculating whether any wisp of hair had been left uncovered.

Ava and Shirin didn't move; they simply straightened slightly in their seats and stared back at him.

For a moment, it felt as though they were watching an animal ready to devour its victim; one mistake could be their last.

Finally, he gave up and growled at Dara to open the boot.

Sam had tucked his head into his chest; eyes closed under a frown of disapproval.

Ava glanced in the mirror and saw the guard opening a soft drink bottle and sniffing it. Her hands were cold; she pushed them into her manteau's pockets and touched the crumpled Fal-e-Hafez. She had already caught a glimpse of it from the corner of her eye: *Arrive the glad tiding that grief's time shall not remain, Like that remained not. Like this shall not remain.*

Ava raised her eyebrows and pushed the Fal-e-Hafez back into her pocket.

Babak's pulse raced, thumping in his ears. When he was very young, he had been arrested for drinking and packed into a minibus with the rest of the partygoers. At the detention centre, they strapped him to a metal bed, pulled off his shoes, and tied his ankles to it. The guard's voice banged in his head and echoed through his memory: "What's your shoe size? Forty-four? After I'm done with you, it'll be fifty-four." Babak couldn't walk properly for months after receiving seventy lashes on his back and soles. He shifted in his seat and nervously pushed his feet deeper into his shoes.

When the search was finally over, the guard grunted to Dara, "Move!"

Dara heaved a deep sigh of relief.

After a few moments of silence as they drove on, he said, "Okay, guys.

I think we've had enough of their ugly faces. Don't worry—I know what to do now. We don't want to risk another patrol, do we? So I'm taking a different route and avoiding the main roads."

The atmosphere in the car lifted slightly, and they all began talking again. No one really cared which way Dara went.

After a while, as they drove up a side road, he suddenly pulled over and said, "I think we're lost."

"What?"

"What do you mean we're lost?" Babak asked, looking around.

The area seemed strange, like a wasteland or an abandoned industrial zone. Ice covered the bare earth, and the only structure in sight was a derelict warehouse in the near distance.

Babak shouted, "Bloody hell—how did we end up here?"

"I have no idea," Dara said. "Let's go to the end of this road, and then I'll figure it out."

They began to travel down a long slope. On one side was a half-bulldozed ditch; uprooted trees jutted from the earth, covered in frost and icicles.

Shirin said, "Oh my God! What is this?"

"Looks like... an uprooted forest."

"It's like a scene from a ghost movie, guys."

"Can we reverse, please? It doesn't look right!" Ava said, holding Shirin's hand.

The road was getting narrower and bumpier. The car jolted over a deep pothole, and there was no room to turn around.

Suddenly, a huge, rusty wreck of an electricity pylon emerged in the headlights. It blocked the road completely.

Shirin screeched and held her head.

Dara slammed the brakes and looked at Sam, his eyes wide with panic.

Large dead birds lay crushed beneath the wrecked pylon, their bristled feathers frozen stiff. Only Dara and Sam could see them. They were too shocked to speak.

"Reverse! Reverse... I said reverse!" Shirin kept screaming from the back.

Visibility worsened; it was pitch black now. Dara slammed his foot on the pedal and reversed as fast as he could. They heard scraping sounds, as though the car was disentangling itself from the frozen wreckage around them.

Finally, they arrived back at the junction where they had turned off the main road.

Dara stopped the car. It was cold, but he was panting and sweat ran down his face.

"I'll find someone to ask, okay?"

He pointed at a warehouse on the corner with its lights on.

As he opened the door, the reek of a broiler chicken farm wafted through. Ava felt sick.

He checked the tyres briefly and walked toward the building. They watched him in silence through the rear window. Babak got out too and followed him. They disappeared into the security room.

When they came out, they were with someone wearing a long, peculiar dress and sporting a Mohawk hairstyle. The person gestured animatedly, waving their hands in the air to show directions.

Shirin leaned forward and asked Sam, "Is that guy a woman?"

Sam moved closer to the window. "Hard to tell."

They watched as the person held both hands outstretched like wings, pointing in opposite directions.

Back in the car, Dara started the engine. "We missed the turn," he said.

"I didn't notice a turn, did you?" Shirin asked. "Maybe we were too busy talking."

"We must be blind, then," Sam shrugged.

"We missed the turn for sure," Babak added. "Did you hear what that guy said? 'There's always a turn'—didn't quite get that... weird man."

Dara said, "Listen, we are where we are now. Let's focus. There are two options—either we head back to the city, or we take the turn he mentioned."

They agreed to take the turn.

NOTES

1 Based on the translation of the *Shanameh* by Arthur George and Edmond Warner, (London: Kegan Paul, Trench, Trübner & Co., 1905–1925), vol.1

2 A necklace that features the Faravahar symbol, one of the most recognizable icons of Zoroastrianism. The Faravahar is widely worn as a symbol of Persian cultural identity and heritage

3 Valiasr Street, formerly Pahlavi Street, is a major boulevard in Tehran, Iran, stretching about 18 kilometres from Railway Square in the south to the Alborz foothills in the north. It is the longest street in the Middle East, known for its tree-lined sidewalks, shops, and cultural landmarks.

4 Aghazadeh refers to children of the elite in the Islamic Republic, often seen as beneficiaries of nepotism and privilege.

5 The Islamic Revolutionary Guard Corps, an elite military, political, and economic force established after the 1979 Islamic Revolution

6 In November 2022, Majid Kazemi, Saleh Mirhashemi, and Saeed Yaghoubi were arrested following their participation in protests in Isfahan amid nationwide demonstrations triggered by the death in custody of Mahsa Amini. On May 19, 2023, they were executed in the early hours of the morning.

7 Ward 209 in Evin Prison is a notorious security ward controlled by Iran's Ministry of Intelligence. It is primarily used for political prisoners, journalists, academics, human rights activists, and dual nationals, often held in harsh conditions including prolonged solitary confinement, constant surveillance, and psychological pressure. Prisoners in Ward 209 frequently endure blindfolded interrogations, limited contact with the outside world, and torture.

8 The Battle of the Marshes (1984) was a major offensive during the Iran–Iraq War targeting the oil-rich Majnoon Islands via the Hawizeh Marshes.

9 The Zagros Mountain range stretches across Iran and Iraq, forming a significant part of the historical and current Kurdish homeland in those countries.

10 The Taurus Mountains are located in southern Turkey and are also a crucial part of the Kurdish homeland in Turkey.

11 This quote is inspired by the 2000 film, *A Time for Drunken Horses,* directed by Bahman Ghobadi .

12 It is a common cultural and historical assertion in Kurdish tradition that modern Kurds are descended from the ancient Medes and their king, Cyaxares (known as Keykhosrow in the epic tradition), a lineage proudly referenced in the Kurdish national anthem, "Ey Reqîb."

13 Anno Birkin, *Who Said the Race Is Over?* (Laurentic Wave Machine, 2003), p. 52.

14 Khaled Islambouli was an Egyptian military officer who led the assassination of President Anwar Sadat on October 6, 1981. He was executed for his role in the assassination on April 15, 1982.

15 Jan is a term of endearment commonly added to a person's name or a title.

YALDA NIGHT

Even the darkest night will end, and the
sun will rise.

VICTOR HUGO, LES MISÉRABLES

PANDEMONIUM

Pandemonium: (a) the capital of Hell in Paradise Lost by John Milton; (b) a wild uproar or chaotic situation. Derived from Greek Pan, meaning "all," and Daemonium (daimon), meaning "evil spirit." [1]

THE BRUTE squatted on a cliff edge, staring into the pit of the gorge. As dusk fell, it turned its eyes upward to search through the dying light until it finally heard the vultures' calls echo through the valley' it began to whimper with excitement.

The vultures circled a few times before descending into the darkness of the gorge where the writhing body of a youth lay tied to stakes. The brute began to dance in a frenzy to the sound of the youth's screams, as the body was pulled apart piece by piece. When silence came, the brute knew he had to act quickly. He bounded down the side of the gorge with loud cries, scattering the protesting vultures. He crouched over the eviscerated body and tore its head away, breaking it like an egg on a rock to extract the brain. The brain must always be saved; it was for something else.

He began to walk heavily toward a large metal gate on the side of the gorge. One by one, he unfastened seven chains. Cockroaches scattered at his feet, crushed under his heavy stump. The steel rollers screeched loudly as he pulled the gate back.

A lone rusted cage creaked as it dangled in the darkness. The brute placed his offering over it.

The beast known as Zahhak came to life, his elongated neck uncoiling into two snakes. He twisted his head and shrouded himself in black cloth. The serpents hissed and slithered out from under the shroud to feed on the young brain.

PARADISE

Paradise: (a) a garden where, according to the Bible, Adam and Eve first lived: Eden; (b) a wonderful place where people go after they die if they have led good lives: Heaven. Also, a place or state of bliss, felicity, or delight —a form of complete happiness. This word entered English from Old Persian, where it meant "walled garden."

SCARLET pomegranates and ripe apples hung over clusters of vines. Birds glided upward, nightingales serenaded, peacocks unfurled their majestic tails, and pink roses bordered a small fountain. At the heart of it all, a cedar tree stood tall against a golden background.

Bijan stood there, staring in admiration at the Qashqai carpet, which showed a stunning depiction of the Tree of Life[2]. Portraying a single, intricate tree at its centre, this one was exceptionally elaborate woven by a tribe of carpet weavers and left to him by his father. He leaned down, his fingertips gently brushing the surface of the carpet, and closed his eyes. As he traced the weft with his touch, each knot seemed to speak to him, like Braille, bringing forth the echo of his father's words.

"The first thing we all perceive in a carpet is the central design, and the last are the margins. But sometimes—like in this carpet—the margins are just as important. They represent the enclosing walls of the garden. Zoroastrians believed the garden should be protected by rings of walls, or seven valleys, so that Ahriman—or evil—could not enter it. Remember, authentic Persian carpets have seven margins: one main border, separated by two small margins from two medium ones, each bordered again by smaller ones—making seven in total."

When Bijan asked him about the beautiful red paisley patterns on the margin, he told him: "There are different interpretations. One is the bent cedar—it refers to the strength of the cedar, which bends in the wind but never breaks. Others say it is a teardrop, or a flame of fire, even an almond. But I favour Professor Dakoda's explanation[3], which says the paisley represents the wings of a bird—maybe the mythical Simorgh, or the royal Shahbaz in the Standard of Cyrus."

BIJAN'S HOUSE

BIJAN, who was well past fifty but whose smooth skin made him appear younger, was standing in an oblong room on the ground floor, overlooking the garden. It was his childhood home—a distinctive building called *Khooneh Bāghi* ("House within Fruit Orchards"). In the past, many of Tehran's homes had similar orchards, but most were destroyed by developers. According to the law, an orchard could not be built upon, but developers found a way around this: they would dry the trees using cement and lime, then apply for building permits.

Those that still had orchards were usually owned by elderly couples whose children lived abroad. Once the couple passed away and the heirs sold the house, the tree-drying would begin—paving the way for apartment blocks.

Bijan could never let that happen to this house. A place without memory, he believed, was a lost place.

The house maintained the soul of the old days. Three tall windows with their original ornate carvings stood on each side of the door to the garden. The stained-glass panes, darkened by Tehran's air, allowed only a dim blue light to beam faintly across the hall.

Bijan pulled the heavy curtains to the end of their runners and frowned, wishing the windows had been cleaned before tonight's party.

At one end of the room near the hallway stood a grandfather clock. Bijan dusted it; it no longer worked, but he cared deeply for it. Persis the cat curled on the floor nearby, her favourite spot. She was an enormous, fluffy cat, resembling a white pillow. She didn't bother to move while Bijan cleaned the clock, but just purred at the peacock feather duster.

Bijan liked antiques. He didn't collect them just for their value, but for the stories behind them. They reminded him that, even in these ever-darkening days of Iran, the power of tangible, beautiful objects could still endure. There had been a good time, even if he hadn't lived it. He was the fourth generation of a merchant family dealing in carpets. His great-grandfather had been among the first to exhibit Persian carpets in Hamburg. The business was now small, having nearly ended after Bijan's father died, but he had managed to keep it alive by focusing on Gabbeh rugs.

Bijan's true passion, however, lay in music, and his tastes were as diverse as they were deep—ranging from traditional Persian melodies to grand opera. He lifted the lid of the vintage Grundig turntable, a treasured gift from his father before the revolution, and began sifting through a stack of records. Babak had promised to curate a CD playlist of old Persian songs for the party, so that was settled. But Bijan was searching for something else, a particular tune, the one he often played during Yalda nights.

Mozart, "Die Zauberflöte", conducted by Herbert von Karajan

He blew on the turntable's surface before placing the disc on it. Lifting the arm slowly, he squinted to check the stylus. "Be careful, don't break the needle!" his father always warned each time they turned it on.

Humming *pa... pa... pa*, Bijan wandered through the house, moving from room to room. This was the place he had called home for nearly all his life, a house full of countless corners, each one holding a memory. It was one of the main reasons he had never wanted to leave Tehran.

Yet tonight, the house felt strange and unfamiliar, as if it had quietly grown distant from him. A subtle unease crept in, and he couldn't shake the feeling that this might be his last Yalda here. A wave of unexpected nostalgia swept over him—though he immediately questioned it.

He sank into the sofa, crossed his arms, and muttered to himself, "But nostalgia for what? Really, for what?" It was the voice of self-mockery that always pulled him back when he teetered on the edge of depression. After a long pause, he looked around, sighed, and said with a shrug, "Oh well." Rising abruptly, he adjusted the sofa cushions and rearranged the family pictures on the console table.

Was this his solitude? he wondered. *It shouldn't be,* he answered, knowing he was not a lonely man. His house was always full of friends who genuinely cared for him. And he also had Giv and Banoo.

Giv and Banoo were among the family's earliest additions. Giv was born in a small village in northeastern Iran, where Bijan's father met him—and later Banoo—while serving in the Literacy Corps, a program that sent young men to teach in remote areas as part of their national service.

This was before Bijan was born, but he had heard the story from his parents many times.

Even though compulsory state education had been in the statute books since the early days of the Shah's father—who aimed to centralize and secularize public education by decreeing compulsory schooling for all

Iranians and building many schools—literacy rates, especially in rural areas, remained very low. Nearly two-thirds of the rural population in 1963 remained illiterate. Before the Pahlavis, education was largely informal, decentralized, and religiously oriented, primarily managed by the clergy and traditional guilds. Teachers were often reluctant to work in villages due to poor facilities and resistance from the Mullahs, whose view of education was limited to Quranic studies and reserved solely for boys.

In response, the Literacy Corps was launched as part of the White Revolution of 1963, sending teachers to remote villages—often as married couples, as Bijan's parents had been. The presence of a female teacher was crucial in gaining the trust of village women and encouraging them to send their daughters to school.

Bijan's parents always considered that time as one of the most rewarding experiences of their lives.

After his parents returned to Tehran, Giv and Banoo found work at Kanoon, an organization dedicated to providing a wide range of cultural and artistic activities for children. They loved their jobs, relishing the opportunity to introduce children in their own village to an extensive collection of books and resources that were otherwise out of reach.

In the summer of 1968, Bijan's parents received heartbreaking news: Banoo and Giv had lost their infant son and nearly all their relatives in the devastating Dasht-e-Bayaz earthquake. Concerned for the grieving couple, they insisted that the couple come to Tehran and stay with them, hoping the distance from the tragedy would help them heal. They agreed.

Banoo was the only girl in a family of seven children; her father held the title of Khan, the head of the tribe in the area—the Khan of Lower Hill. Although Banoo was her father's darling, being the only girl in the family, her education was confined to sewing, cooking, carpet weaving, milking cows, horse riding, and falconry. School wasn't for girls.

Banoo and Giv first met at the *Chovgan*⁴. Disguised as a man, she played on the team opposing Giv's. As she raced after the ball, Giv followed closely.Banoo's mount, a skittish young pony, suddenly raised its front feet in the air and threw her off. Before she managed to jump back on, her thick black hair fell from underneath her hairband, and Giv was shocked to see that his rival was a girl. They looked into each other's eyes for a brief but penetrating moment.

Shortly after the match was over, a messenger arrived with Banoo's hairband and a note: "Let's spend the rest of the game together." Banoo was proposing to him. Giv always said that his destiny was to be at a rebel's service. She would look over at him with a smile and say, "Yes. A devoted rebel!"

Banoo's voice called from downstairs. "Bijan, Bijan-jan... aren't you going to get changed?"

Bijan didn't answer. He simply smiled, turned off the music, and walked briskly toward the basement, where the kitchen was. Warm air drifted up, filling the staircase with redolent smells as he descended.

The kitchen was the most used space in the house. It was cozy and old-fashioned. The walls were lined with original wooden shelves, over-loaded with cups, plates, copper trays and pots, large jars of pickles, and bundles of garlic and peppers hanging from hooks. There was even a tandoor, though it hadn't been used in many years.

On the counter sat a massive electric samovar, gurgling noisily. Its steam fogged the glass door at the far end of the kitchen, which opened onto the garden. Through the misted glass, part of a tree and a small pond could be seen, dimmed behind the haze.

Bijan paused on the stairway, quietly watching Banoo and Giv at work below. Banoo stood at the big wooden kitchen table, dressed in her red pais-ley-patterned gown—the one she wore only for Yalda and Nowruz. Her long silver hair, parted carefully down the middle, was tied back with a matching paisley ribbon. The scene felt suspended in time, as if nothing had changed.

Banoo moved with quiet confidence, her body at ease, as if every part of her were perfectly attuned to each gesture. Her neck was long and up-right, her face warmed and weathered by sun and time, lines deeply etched around her eyes and lips like stories written on skin. Her arms stretched steadily over the table as she added the final touches to a dish she had likely prepared a hundred times before.

Giv stood at the sink, slowly washing pomegranates. He was tall and all bone, as if the muscle beneath his skin had quietly vanished over the years. His gait had always been lumbering, and over time, he came to resemble the Pink Panther—a comparison that eventually became a nickname.

"Need a hand?" Bijan called, tying up his sleeves.

The large kitchen table was covered with small dishes of mezze: *Sangak* bread, big pieces of carefully wrapped dolmas, *Lighvan* cheese, walnuts, heaps of mint and basil, dishes of smoked aubergines, olives, and much more.

Bijan leaned against the sink, helping to dry, and announced jubilantly, "There you go! Another Yalda!"

Giv uttered in his craggy voice, "Indeed!" He shook the water from his large hands, then asked, "I hope they're coming... in this situation, people might not bother."

"Of course!" Bijan protested. "They're all coming—we have a full house and maybe a couple extra, too."

"The more the merrier," Banoo smiled.

Giv leaned forward, his round, serious eyes locking onto Bijan's face. "Be careful then, son! Keep the music down. No singing! They're around today—I saw two of their cars."

Bijan looked disappointed and grumbled, "Oh no! Leila is coming with her *tar* [5], and we're going to practice with Banoo. It's Yalda, come on..." He glanced at Banoo, silently begging for support.

"Good God, a full band then!" Giv said. "You know them—they don't care if it's Yalda or not. If you and Banoo want to spend Yalda night at Evin, go for it!" Giv was always very cautious.

"We shall see, darling, okay?" Banoo replied, offering a playful wink to Bijan to end the conversation.

Giv was referring to the government building next door, known as the *Nofel Loshato* Innovation Centre—a place with a few offices, conference rooms, and a private meeting room. It was often empty, but sometimes at night, the lights were on and a couple of luxury cars were parked outside.

Bijan continued to grumble as he dropped the tea towel on the bench and took a piece of bread from the mezze table. Before putting it in his mouth, he pointed to the top of the fridge and exclaimed, "What's that up there?"

Banoo beamed. "Persimmon! How did we forget to tell you? Giv spotted it and picked it this afternoon. Isn't it amazing?"

Giv looked pleased with himself. "We had to bring out the big ladder to reach it. It was right at the very top!"

Bijan's face lit up as he stared at the fruit. He whispered, "The Yalda Sun."

[87]

Banoo nodded. "Yes, indeed. We have the Yalda Sun this year..." She didn't finish her sentence, only sighed deeply before adding, "It was like yesterday... your mother..."

Bijan recalled how his mother and Banoo would pick the fruit when it matured in autumn. In Tehran, persimmons rarely stayed on the tree until early winter, after which they were brought inside to ripen in the kitchen. They were a deep, fiery orange—like rays of sunshine. If one or two remained on the tree by Yalda, his mother would take it as a good omen—the "Yalda Sun," as she called it. But in recent years, the tree had become unpredictable, yielding only a few fruits, just enough to feed the crows. No "Yalda Sun" had appeared, when the story had almost been forgotten.

Looking at them now, he remembered a dream he'd had a few weeks earlier, in which he was a young boy again, running to tell his mother about the single persimmon left on the tree.

"Go and pick that for me," his mother said.

The tree was very tall—taller than it was now—and he was frightened.

"I can't reach that," he replied. She looked at him and said, "Why don't you fly?"—as if it were the most natural thing in the world.

Strangely, he knew he could. He flapped his hands a few times but hesitated when he saw a giant crow perched nearby and decided to wait until it left the garden. But as he waited, the fruit slowly dissolved into nothing. When he looked back, his mother was gone.

For the next half hour, the three of them worked in silence, focused on preparing the food. Bijan made several trips between the kitchen and upstairs, carrying plates, cutlery, dishes, the large samovar, and a tray filled with glass cups. Afterwards, he shovelled the snow from the driveway and cleared the porch, getting everything ready for the guests.

He stamped his boots heavily on the mat, then stepped back inside. The corridor was thick with the sharp scent of Giv's 4711 Eau de Cologne—one Bijan had brought him from Germany many years ago.

"Phew, Giv!" Bijan called out. "That stuff is getting worse. When are you going to let it go?"

Giv, now dressed in the dark brown suit and wide tie he'd bought a decade ago, stood calmly in front of the mirror. "But why?" he replied. "What's wrong with it?"

Bijan rushed upstairs to change. He reappeared clean-shaven, wearing a white shirt, brown cardigan, and dark blue trousers. In one hand, he carried his guitar, which he leaned against the wall next to the turntable, ready for later. Giv raised an eyebrow but said nothing.

Back in the lounge, the three finally sat on the sofa to relax before the guests arrived. In front of them, a tray held three glass cups of tea steaming with the scent of bergamot and cardamom. Persis sauntered over and leapt onto the sofa, stretching herself out across Banoo's lap.

Bijan pulled up a stool and rested his legs on it. Gazing around at the walls, he said, "The house feels different tonight."

Giv shrugged. "Of course. It's been cleaned—maybe we should do it more often."

Bijan smiled faintly. "No, it's not that... there's something else."

***

The doorbell rang frantically several times. As soon as Bijan opened the door, Atossa darted into the hallway. He smiled and kissed her cheeks.

"Hooman's right behind me—with our guest, a young lady," Atossa said, glancing nervously around. "Has anyone else arrived?"

"You're the first, of course. Hooman said you were bringing a guest. Is something the matter, Atoss?"

"It's been a day... I'll tell you—it's a long story." Bijan raised an eyebrow but said nothing.

Later, after Hooman explained, Bijan quietly passed the story to Banoo and Giv in the kitchen. Moments later, Banoo came upstairs and walked straight to Neda, arms open.

"There you are," she said softly. "Our very special Yalda guest—my brave girl. Welcome, darling. You've brought light back into this house tonight."

She sat beside Neda, stroking her back as if she had known her for many years. Atossa smiled, placing her granny's old tin of problem-solving nuts on the table and nudging her gently. "See? I told you—they already love you."

Bijan stood nearby, watching with a quiet smile.

***

To reach Bijan's house, Parto took a taxi from her hotel. The city she was born in—and once loved—now felt strange, almost unrecognisable. It had grown larger and louder. The streets had shifted, the buildings altered. But what struck her most was the ocean of faces she passed—their eyes scanning desperately, searching for something: rain, thunder, fresh air... a change.

The taxi crept through the chaotic tangle of cars and motorbikes, but Parto barely registered the noise. A ghostly ring of tinnitus had taken over, growing louder in her ears with every turn. As the driver weaved through the streets, she could almost hear the shatter of windows, the pneumatic thud of bullets, the hiss of tear gas sinking into the city's very bones. This city had been abused—layer upon layer—physically and mentally.

"I'll get out here," Parto said, pointing to the white door on Nofel Loshato Street. The house seemed smaller now, sunk into the shadows of taller buildings. But the old shoe shop still stood at the top of the road—a small detail that lifted her spirits.

Parto stood at the door, her hand hovering over the bell. She paused before pressing it, drawing in a slow, steady breath. Her heart was pounding. She was about to see them all again... and above all, him. Was he there too?

She wouldn't let her heart give in. No... no, she couldn't let that happen again. She had to be careful.

The pain of their separation had once devoured her. Those first few years had immersed her in a fog she couldn't quite escape. But time had softened the edges. She had learned to live with it. *Yes... she must be very careful now.*

Beyond that door lay a chapter of her past—one she had left behind long ago. How would they look now? Had they changed, like she had? Older, perhaps a little flabbier, a little rounder... a touch greyer.

The door opened, and there stood Bijan.

"Oh my God! Oh, my dear, my dear... Parto-jan, here you are at last!" he exclaimed, tears welling in his eyes.

They embraced, holding each other tightly. When they finally pulled back, their faces lit up with pure joy.

"Like the old days, when everyone was still here..." Bijan said, his voice cracking with emotion.

Behind him, Banoo and Giv stood waiting, their arms wide open.

"Look at you, beautiful Parto! Oh, don't just stand there—come in, it's freezing tonight!" Banoo said warmly.

Parto smiled, noticing the change in them both. They had shrunk just a little in the years that had passed. Bijan caught her eye and gave a small, knowing wink—as if to say, *Yes, I see it too.*

Parto nodded and followed him inside, but paused when her eyes landed on the grandfather clock. "Oh! This... it's still here!"

"Yes, of course," Bijan said proudly. "And still doesn't work—lazy beast—but I don't mind. It still gets polished."

Before they entered the main room, Parto paused, her heart pounding. She looked at Bijan and quietly asked, "They're all here... aren't they?"

Bijan held her gaze for a moment, then gave a slow nod. "Yes... almost," he said softly. "They're waiting for you."

When they entered the room, Bijan shouted, "Look who's here!" The others' eyes lit up as they rushed forward to greet her with kisses, embraces, handshakes, and countless questions.

"Oh my dear... I've just... when did you arrive? Happy Yalda... welcome... snow... jet lag?... can you breathe here?... headscarf... monsters... did they stop you?... airport... you haven't changed a bit... IRGC... passport..."

Everyone was so nice and friendly, but Parto felt they were different from what she remembered—their interactions, the new words or slang they had adopted. *Had she changed too, in their eyes?*

And then... there he was, standing silently in the corner of the room, looking at her. Parto's eyes caught his. Her first impression was of how much he had changed. He seemed leaner now, with a more prominent nose. His once thick, wavy black hair had thinned and turned grey, and his brows were fuller, more unruly. He wore a pair of spectacles that made him seem even more distant.

They stood there, staring at each other in silence for a few moments. Finally, Hooman began to move toward her, and the eyes of everyone else in the room followed, sensing the unspoken tension between them. Bijan, aware of the weight of the moment, turned the music up, giving them a brief bubble of privacy.

"Look at what you made of me," Hooman said softly. He paused, and then—after a long moment—pointed at himself with a trembling hand. "At last, a man."

He felt tears roll down his face but let them flow.

[91]

They didn't hug. Perhaps neither of them could bear it. Parto leaned forward slightly, then stiffened, frozen in place, her heart pounding in her chest. In an instant, a flood of scattered memories surged through her—visions of their former life flashing like scenes from a film. She finally managed to pull herself together.

"We have changed."

Hooman nodded, and his voice cracked with a lump in his throat. "Welcome home."

Parto looked down at the floor; her eyes welled with tears, and she wished he hadn't used that word. *Home* had become a sensitive and challenging term for her. Having left her motherland behind, she now found herself with more life, friends, and family outside Iran than within it. She felt a deep sense of confusion.

Once, a colleague had asked her where home was, and she had surprised herself by answering, *"The space conjured up by the scent of honeysuckles or verses of Hafez."*

Giv interrupted, holding out a glass of hazy pink liquid. "Home brew. Try!" he said, eyebrows raised with a playful grin, as if they needed to celebrate the occasion.

Bijan, standing behind him, added excitedly, "Vintage 2000. I had to dig all over the garden to find where we buried this one..." Giv cut him off, "You had to dig? Actually, I did the digging, and he was only watching. You remember how lazy he was? Hasn't changed a bit!"

Parto looked at the homemade wine and sniffed it before tasting. It smelled like vinegar and had a strange, sharp after-taste.

"So?" Giv and Bijan fixed their eyes on her, waiting for the verdict.

"Hmm... nice!"

"Really? You're not just saying that?"

"Oh no... it is marvellous!" Parto said, realizing that her standards had now been set much higher.

Some new guests arrived, and Bijan left to greet them. Dara made his way to the kitchen to help. Atossa was there at the counter, pouring drinks.

"Dara, come here, dear... did you meet Neda, the young lady who came with us?"

"Yes, briefly. Poor thing. Hooman told me the story."

"Okay then. Hooman was looking after her, but after meeting Parto, his head is all over the place. Can I ask you to look after Neda and make her feel at ease? She's sitting alone, and I don't want to be sticking to her like glue all the time... you know what I mean?"

In the lounge, Neda stood with her arms folded, eyes fixed on the grandfather clock.

"Tick, tock, tick, tock," Dara said, trying to catch her attention. "Ancient and beautiful, isn't it?"

"Yes," Neda replied softly, "but it doesn't seem to work!"

"As far as I remember, it never has," Dara said, waving at Giv. "Hey, Giv, has this clock ever worked? It always seemed like more of an ornament... a giant one, of course!"

Giv scratched his head. "Well, good question. You see, Bijan's father inherited this—I'd guess it's over 100 years old and used to work perfectly."

He paused, as if hearing something. "I remember its chimes. It never failed us until maybe over forty years ago, when suddenly one day it stopped and hasn't worked again. Bijan's father was still with us then. We brought lots of people to repair it, but no luck. Bijan even contacted a couple of Swiss and Dutch clockmakers when he was in Europe—you know how good they are with clocks..."

Bijan, who had returned from greeting the new guests, was listening. "Ninety-eight years, to be precise. If you look closely, you'll see 1925 written there."

Dara and Neda leaned forward to see a small faded golden plaque.

"Oh yes! I wonder how the chimes sounded," Neda said.

"Very musical. Ding... dong, ding... ding..." Bijan smiled and wandered off.

Dara said, "Well, that's the clock! Now meet the most handsome man here—my partner Babak." He pointed him out. "Tall and fine in his red polo neck. I'm not exaggerating, am I?"

Neda nodded, and they laughed.

Bijan was worried the party seemed a bit sombre and slow to start, but as mezze dishes were passed around and the bootleg drink flowed, the mood relaxed, and the guests began to mingle more.

Each time Parto faced Hooman, he looked away. She wondered if she did the same unknowingly. She was relieved he was alone—selfish, yes, but it would have been harder otherwise.

Catching up with friends was delightful after all those years, but there was still something strange about seeing them. It was as if she had walked onto a movie set where the actors wore make-up to make them seem older.

Suddenly, Parto spotted Shirin. After embracing, they left the main room to find a quiet corner.

Sitting on a bench, Shirin folded her legs against her chest and held them tightly with her arms.

Parto had heard about Farhad but wasn't sure Shirin would be willing to talk about him at the party. But she did—telling her the whole dreadful story and her ongoing quest to find him.

She lowered her gaze, fighting back tears. Parto noticed a corner of her lips twitching. When Shirin finished, she leaned back against the wall and closed her eyes.

Parto held her hands tightly, looking helplessly for a soothing word.

"It's the time we live in," Shirin said. "I wish it were only me and my story... but look—everywhere, everyone lives in horror, as if they've taken the whole country hostage. Everyone has something to grieve for..."

As Parto listened, she felt guilty for the peace she enjoyed outside and often took for granted—and for the fact that they had once planned to emigrate together, though Shirin's attempt had ended so dreadfully.

Sensing Parto's unease, Shirin changed the subject.

"Why didn't you stay with me, silly girl? You know I'm on my own... acting like a stranger, after all these years. The hotel must be so unwelcoming. How about your uncle—the one in Tehran, the brainy lecturer?"

Parto answered, "Oh, he finally left too. It's been a couple of years now."

"To where? Through the university, I guess?"

"No, no... they tried, but that didn't happen. Then a window opened, a scheme in... in Canada..."

At the mention of Canada, there was a pause.

"To... to look after old people in remote areas. Mind you, he's not young himself, but they went for their son's future. They had one son—my cousin."

Shirin said, "Oh well, at least one future saved!" She moved closer with a cheeky smile and quietly asked, "Did you talk?"

Parto asked sheepishly, "To who?"

"Hooman, obviously!"

She blushed. "Only a few words. It was hard."

"I bet."

A cold breeze came through the two large windows in front of them. Parto turned her head toward the glass and saw the silhouette of the cedar tree in the garden. Snow was falling from every direction, turning the branches white. It reminded her of the giant Christmas trees that were everywhere back home.

"How similar Yalda and Christmas are," she said—but inside, she was burning to learn more about Hooman.

She finally asked, "But what happened with that girl—the actress? I'd heard they were living together. I was surprised he's alone... maybe expecting someone to join him later?"

"No, that didn't last. As far as I know, he's never had a long relationship. Many girls came and went... but you know."

Shirin wanted to tell Parto that perhaps he had never truly recovered from their separation—but instead said, "He keeps himself busy with his writing—poems, plays... but the poor thing couldn't for a couple of months after his operation. But now..."

"What operation?"

"Oh, sorry—you didn't know? His right eye was badly injured in a demo last autumn."

Parto's face crumpled in shock.

"It was birdshot. Three pellets hit him. One crushed his ear's top—fortunately not his head—and one struck his left eye. He's lucky to keep partial sight; many lost theirs in the protests. Didn't you hear?"

Parto placed her hands on her head, her voice trembling. "Oh my God, yes, but not about Hooman!"

"He keeps his glasses on, even indoors. Maybe that's why."

Parto shuddered, as if a cold wave had washed over her.

Shirin gently urged, "Let's go back inside. It's freezing out here."

Parto followed her, feeling like a sleepwalker—dizzy from the news.

THE *KORSI* ROOM

Off the main room, beside the stairs leading to the kitchen, was a long, spacious study—once the reception area of the original house, now transformed into a TV room. For tonight, Banoo had redecorated it—removing the sofa and television to make space for a *korsi*: a low table covered by a thick blanket with a heater underneath. Divans and cushions were placed around the *korsi*, where guests could relax and stretch their legs beneath the warmth.

On the blanket lay a rustic red quilt, a few books, a small bowl of problem-solving nuts, and a silver dish heaped with seeded pomegranates.

When Shirin and Parto entered the room, they found six or seven people sitting close together, giggling like children. In the corner, Banoo stood by a small side table with a samovar and glass cups, pouring tea with a radiant smile.

Bijan peeked his head through the door, smiled at Banoo and the guests, and said, "Cozy, isn't it?" Then he slipped away.

"Where did you two disappear to? Come here, warm yourselves," Banoo said.

They joined the others; their legs comfortably tucked under the *korsi*.

"Wow! This is so homely... it's like a nest," Parto said. "Well done, Banoo, for keeping this tradition going."

That turned the conversation into the origins of Yalda and its rituals.

"Growing up," Ava said wistfully, "I always thought Yalda was just about staying up through the longest night and finishing all the fruits and nuts at home. My mother always prepared a special feast for it, though."

Sam, sitting directly across from Ava, stayed silent, occasionally glancing at her from the corner of his eye.

"Listen! Our village—honestly, it was the best!" Dara said, excitement thick in his voice. "Everyone would huddle around the little communal fire. We'd stay up till dawn, telling stories and reading poetry... They'd put piles of pomegranates—seriously, like a mountain of pomegranates." He brought his hands together, forming a triangle to mimic a mountain, and continued, "The lovers would disappear into the night... some people sang, some danced... it was amazing!"

Banoo placed the tea tray in the centre of the *korsi*, and everyone shifted to make room for her.

Shirin turned to her. "How was it for you, Banoo-jan? Was it the same in your village?"

"My father always said that evil forces, or Ahriman, were at their peak on Yalda, the longest and darkest night," Banoo said. "So, he'd stay awake most of the night and wouldn't let us sleep until midnight. The whole village stayed up. The idea was to stay awake, just in case misfortune was lurking. It was good fun, though. People would gather with friends and family, share the last fruits they'd preserved from the summer, and spend the long night in good company. And everyone tried to wear red, like I did tonight!" She smiled, her wrinkles deepening around her eyes.

Her tone shifted to something more serious. "I think there's a message hidden in this tradition. We must stay awake, stay together in winter, in the darkness, in the cold and difficult times."

She paused, looking around the table as if letting the message settle. "Our house was always full of people on Yalda. And sometimes, for the newlyweds or newborns, there'd be gifts wrapped in beautiful white tulle, tied with red ribbon. It was a big thing in Khorasan villages."

Shirin said, "Oh, the gifts! We did that too. My parents would always send small bags of nuts and candy to the orphanages, I remember we used to make them."

"The Celebration of Light—that's what Yalda was originally called," a craggy voice said. It was that of Mr Kayvon, sitting among the others at the *korsi*. He was an old family friend, a retired lawyer, and an amateur historian. To those who knew him, he never seemed to change, as if he had reached his full evolution years ago and decided to stay that way for-ever—small, skinny, and brittle, always in his dinner jacket and cravat. His thick spectacles more like magnifying glasses, inspecting everything before him to build a corpus of knowledge he liked to share at every opportunity.

His wife, Gitti, was a plump, easy-going woman with a good sense of humour. An excellent baker, she had brought a massive tray of baklava to the party, and others were already asking for her recipe.

"The Celebration of Light?" Dara raised his eyebrows.

Mr Kayvon nodded and continued, "Our ancestors knew—or more accurately, discovered—that after this night, the nights would gradually grow shorter. So they called what we now call Yalda 'the eve of the birth of Mithra.' Mithra, or Mehr, was the ancient Persian deity of the rising sun."

At the name *Mithra*, Parto sat upright with a jolt; she felt again the same sequence of feelings she had experienced in her dream. First came the fear she had when dropping the bowl into the abyss, followed by the hope sparked by a voice telling her the only way out was to find Mithra.

A flicker stirred at the edge of her memory—something from the dream.

Not just a voice this time, but wings cutting through air, feathers like metal. A figure—part human, part bird—soared above a scorched horizon. She couldn't remember its face, but the feeling was unmistakable. She shivered.

Mr Kayvon continued explaining, "Mithra is also a judicial figure, a protector of truth; you see, the connection between light and truth makes perfect sense."

Gitti took a piece of sugar loaf and, before dropping it into her tea, held it in the air between her fingers, as if trying to stop her husband from talking. "Kayvon! Not more history, don't bore them... this is a party!" She always referred to her husband of fifty years by his surname.

Parto quickly interjected, "No! Please, let Mr Kayvon tell us more."

Gitti stirred her tea faster and shrugged.

Mr Kayvon continued, undeterred. "So, to be precise, we don't celebrate the longest night; we celebrate the victory of light over darkness and the birth of Mithra, the deity of the Sun." He paused, peering around the *korsi*, then asked, "Tomorrow is the first day of winter, but can anyone tell me the beginning of which month it is?"

"The month of Day,"[6] everyone replied, looking at one another, intrigued by where he was going with this. Gitti shrugged and asked, "So?"

His eyes lit up like a child's. "I was curious, so I checked the etymology of the word 'day' in an English dictionary. It turns out it comes from a Proto-Indo-European word meaning 'bright' or 'to shine.' There you go!"

Neda raised an eyebrow. "Does that mean the English word 'day' is somehow connected to the birth of Mithra?"

"Well done!" Mr Kayvon nodded. "That's my assumption!"

Sam smiled disparagingly, his expression silently saying, *"What the hell?"* Tomorrow might be the first of the month, but to him, it was just another failed payday.

For Parto, this was genuinely fascinating. She acknowledged that much about Iran invited debate or critique, but its ancient calendar born from the centuries of wisdom remained beyond reproach. Unlike so many others shaped by religion or politics, Iran's calendar was firmly grounded in the logic of the cosmos. She remembered the effort it had taken to explain this to friends abroad, until she finally found a simple way to put it:

"Our year is divided into four seasons. Each season has three months, and the calendar is anchored by four celestial events: two equinoxes—

when day and night are equal—and two solstices, marking the longest and shortest days.

"Nowruz, our new year, begins with the spring equinox, usually between March 19 and 22. It's all about the light—measuring the light. The true beauty lies in the fact that these dates are not arbitrary; they are fixed, set by the Earth's steady orbit around the Sun."

Gitti stopped stirring her tea and said, "Well, we learn something every day, don't we? Let's say everything came from Iran, then! Wouldn't that be easier?"

Everyone laughed.

Her husband leaned forward across the table. "Zoroaster's teachings say that life in this world reflects the cosmic struggle between light and dark, good and evil. Mithra is closely tied to the Sun and the protection of divine glory—or *farr*, as it's called."

One of the guests at the table, a youngish man with glossy oiled hair pushed back into a tight ponytail, threw a walnut in the air and caught it in his mouth. Still chewing, he said drily, "God of Sun, darkness, evil, and all that! Aren't they just fairy tales, Mr Google?"

Gitti gasped audibly, but her husband ignored him.

Atossa had returned to the room and was standing by the door, listening. Before anyone could speak, she leaned forward and lifted the medallion around her neck to show everyone. "Look! I always carry this with me. I know it's connected to *farr* and is a Zoroastrian symbol, but I'd love to learn more about its history."

Mr Kayvon squinted at Atossa's necklace. "The 'winged sun disc,' or as it's also called, the 'Faravahar,' indeed represents *farr*."

The sight of the medallion reminded Parto of the last time she had seen Hooman before leaving Iran. At the airport, as they said goodbye, he had given her a Faravahar bracelet—but she had refused to take it. She sighed and lightly rubbed her wrist with the tips of her fingers.

"But what exactly is this *farr*?" Atossa asked, smiling shyly. "Okay, I know I should know, but I guess I'm not the only one." Several heads around the *korsi* nodded in agreement, and Shirin raised her hand. "Me too!"

"The most obvious is sometimes the most neglected," Mr Kayvon said. "What if someone asked how many teeth you have in your mouth? We think we know, but we need to think for a moment before answering it, so don't worry!"

He cleared his throat and continued. "*Farr* represents divine glory. In ancient Persia, it was tied to legitimate kingship and rulers, embodying moral and spiritual excellence. In the Avesta, Jamshid, blessed with *farr*, ascended to the throne and ushered in a golden age. Under his rule, prosperity and happiness flourished thanks to his wisdom and innovations. But over time, his arrogance caused him to lose it. His *farr* was taken by a falcon, who hid it for safekeeping in the waters of a lake..."

The pony-tailed man chuckled. "Keep it safe in the water of a lake... are you serious? Come on!"

The others laughed, and Gitti scowled, shushing them.

Mr Kayvon's expression flickered with surprise for just a moment, but he quickly regained his composure and smiled as he continued with energy. "This myth reveals three powerful lessons about *farr*. First, it's not a gift that sits still—it's ever-changing and can slip away if someone doesn't live up to its high standards. Second, when dormant, it lies hidden beneath the surface, like something waiting to be discovered, representing its fluid, unpredictable nature. And third, to truly possess *farr*, it must rise from the depths, emerging from the water, denoting its awakening and potential."

He referred to a brick wall at Persepolis, where a striking relief showed these three stages: a seed resting beneath the water, a cluster of lotus flowers emerging gracefully on the surface, and, at the final stage, a vibrant sunflower fully in bloom—symbolizing the complete unfolding of *farr*. Each image and stage told a story of transformation, growth, and the journey from potential to perfection.

"Is this for kings only?" Neda asked.

"For kings and queens, the weight of responsibility is immense—they can't afford the same mistakes that others might. However, *farr* is so much more than just a symbol of political power. It's a gift granted to those who stand firmly by the principle of truth. And here's the astonishing part," he said, pausing to scan the faces around the room, his voice low and intense, "Every single person has the potential for *farr*. No exceptions! As I mentioned, it's like a seed hidden beneath the water's surface—waiting to be discovered and, when nurtured, capable of blossoming into something extraordinary."

Ava was only half listening, her mind consumed by the previous night's argument with Sam. Why didn't he want to talk about it? They both knew what had happened. Shirin had advised Ava to let it go for a while, but she couldn't. Something had shifted. Among the images flickering through her mind from the night before, she recalled a strange bird—like a white crow—hopping and swaggering behind their window in the middle of the night. Was that real, or just a dream? Like the falcon in Jamshid's story, it felt as if that bird had taken Sam's *farr* from him. From that point, Sam was finished for her.

Dara scooped a generous portion of seeded pomegranate into his bowl and jokingly asked, "Wait a minute—how did we end up here?" He chuckled. "We were talking about Yalda!"

Mr Kayvon picked up a glass from the second round of tea, taking a long sip noisily. Setting the glass down, he continued in his usual calm and measured tone:

"Well, it was all about light. Light is the most profound force in human life. But it becomes even more fascinating when we look at it beyond its physical form—into the realm of metaphysical or inner light, which is at the core of Zoroastrianism. Consider the grand model of the cosmos, the rhythm of days, nights, and seasons. Now, think of the human being as a microcosm, a world in miniature. We often forget that we're part of this vast universe, but the same cosmic principles also apply to us."

The pony-tailed man suddenly broke into a passionate speech about East and West: "Sorry, but honestly? Really, in this age of AI, we are still banging on about the ruins of Persepolis! No wonder we are in this deep shit. No wonder the Middle East is in such a state—because we are so naïve and superstitious. We don't live in reality, do we? Wake up, man, wake up! The intellectuals from the West are right to laugh at us!"

"Darling, please!" Banoo said, widening her eyes and looking embarrassed. Gitti suddenly stood up to leave but then hesitated and sat back after her husband shook his head at her. Parto, who had become more and more absorbed in the words of Mr Kayvon, gave a start and quietly asked Shirin, "Who is he?"

Shirin, who was sitting beside the offender, muttered, "Later."

Mr Kayvon let out a heavy sigh, removing his glasses with deliberate care as he studied the young man. "My dear son, what a pity you are so bored by history. But history matters. Intellect takes many forms. Eastern intellect is fluid and more relaxed, drawn from the warmth of the Sun, compared to Western intellect, which is more rigid, shaped by logic. But the differences are not the problem; we ignored the similarities, and that is the real tragedy."

Parto nodded. "Totally."

The pony-tailed man turned towards Parto. "I guess you're just visiting, aren't you? If there are enough similarities, why don't you come back and live in Iran?"

Parto let out an awkward laugh, caught off guard by his sudden shift in tone and the cold intensity in his eyes. She remembered he had been sitting quietly in the corner when she arrived, observing as the others welcomed her, so he clearly knew she was a visitor.

"Yes, laugh! Laugh!" he sneered. "Just as I expected! Just as I said. Living in the West, you should laugh at us! But tell me this—when someone asks you where you originally come from, do you squirm? And I'm sure you hide when they ask if you're a Muslim, don't you? Be honest. Just be honest with me!"

Parto's face flushed deep red. "I've never been ashamed of being Iranian. This country left enough for us to be proud of, even in these darkest days." She was breathing fast. "In the West, those 'intellectuals' you speak of don't often ask about someone's religion. That is a private matter! But if they did, or if I had to fill out a form, I'd always answer: I am a pagan!"

"What? Pagan? What the hell?"

"Yes, when Mr Kayvon highlighted the similarities, do you know what similarity came to my mind before anything else?" She paused for a moment, still breathing fast; her gaze fixed directly on his eyes as she said, "It was religion! Damn, boringly similar... yes, always the same story: a man hears the voice of a god and tells us what to do, what not to do. It doesn't matter if it's East or West, Judaism, Christianity, or Islam. But you know what our ancestors worshipped—whether in the East or the West? Nature. That was it! Simple, clear—no lies, no manipulation, no class division, no dogmatism or ethnicity! No holy wars, no crusades, no jihad.

So, of course, all the religions condemned pagans, despite stealing their celebrations! Yes, there was a Christmas before Christ—called Yule in the West—and Yalda right here. No one, not even the pagans, knows where we came from or where we're going, but at least they respected what was beneficial while we were alive on this planet." She paused, her eyes sweeping across the room to ensure everyone was hanging onto her every word.

"Think about it. Imagine if, instead of churches, synagogues, or mosques, we could simply look at the Sun, the Moon, and the stars. They're there equally for all of us—and are free! Isn't the Sun rising every morning enough of a miracle? And why not have many gods, to honour the diversity of nature? If God is good, let's have many! I see no harm in that... and let's not forget Goddesses, too. With the pagans, men and women were equal. Feminine divinity and nature were the most important. And now, look at us! After centuries of ignoring these truths, we find ourselves trapped in the belly of the giant whale of religion, fighting for both women and nature.

"So yes, of course..." she said, her voice steady and full of conviction, "I'd prefer to be a pagan!"

There was stillness in the room. Ponytail had found a whole walnut among the nuts and pressed the sharp edge of his key into the shell until he finally cracked it. Then he shrugged and said, "Whatever!"

As she looked at him, Parto's mind drifted back to a dream she had a few nights before her flight to Iran.

In the dream, it was dusk, and she stood by a pond she knew well—a quiet spot in a park near her home. Out of nowhere, a boy tossed a stone into the water, and to her shock, a giant fish emerged from the depths.

"Don't throw stones," Parto called out, her voice urgent. "You'll wake the fish."

The boy glanced at her with a mischievous grin and shrugged. "Don't worry, it was just a walnut. They eat it."

The dream hung in her mind as she stared at the pony-tailed man.

Mr Kayvon broke the silence and asked, "But isn't Paganism a religion, too?"

Parto hesitated for a moment, then replied, "Well, it is, and it isn't. This was a label that early Christians slapped on others, and if we want to consider it a religion, at least it's non-Abrahamic and not part of the systematic, organized kind! For me, it's what we naturally acquire... as natural as nature itself. It doesn't need to be defined as a cult or religion!"

"Zoroastrianism? What do you think about that?" Mr Kayvon asked.

"Well, these days, no one really knows who they are, and, sadly, I have little knowledge, too. I know they share some values with pagans."

Mr Kayvon stayed silent.

Parto then leaned forward, extending her hand across the *korsi* to shake hands with the pony-tailed man. "I don't think we've introduced ourselves yet. My name is Parto!"

"Jav," he replied curtly, shaking her hand without much enthusiasm.

Banoo, who had been quietly listening to the exchange, felt a little sorry for him. She knew Jawad—or Jav, as he preferred to be called—well. He was about fifty, the son of a friend of Bijan's father. Like so many, he had tried—and failed—to emigrate. The story was that had an altercation at one of the embassies, and that had been held against him. He had been married once, but the relationship had been a series of volatile arguments, even in public. Divorce followed, though he claimed his wife had left him for someone else. In the end, she too had left Iran, taking their daughter with her.

Just then, Persis, leapt onto the *korsi* table, tipping over a cup and splashing some tea.

"There you go!" Gitti said. "Now it's her turn!" Everyone laughed. Banoo began to clear the cups, and Sam got up to take the tray from her. Then she pointed to the books on top of the *korsi* and said, "Let's recite from these wonderful poetry books. May the spark of light illuminate us from within and bring joy to all our hearts."

Mr Kayvon reached for the Hafez book, his fingers touching the cover with reverence. Then he respectfully kissed it before opening it.

CULTURAL REVOLUTION

Ten to twelve people were in the living room, talking in small groups.

Bijan sat on a stool beside the vintage turntable, casually strumming his guitar as he chatted with Hooman and Babak. They had talked about politics, the crackdowns on the streets—but something more personal lingered just beneath the surface.

Finally, Bijan glanced at Hooman and, in a soft but probing voice, said, "All right? How was it? It must be hard, seeing each other again after all this time."

Hooman didn't reply. Babak gave him a gentle pat on the back.

Bijan broke the silence.

"Sorry, mate. I just wanted to make sure you're okay... you know..."

Hooman nodded. "'Course. I know... I know. Okay, this is it. Strangely... I still love her!"

Bijan and Babak exchanged a brief, knowing look.

Hooman paused and took a deep breath before speaking again. "And my love for her... it's completely free of the past or the future. It's... it's a kind of annoyingly pure love," he added with a bitter laugh, his voice cracking at the end.

Bijan sighed, handing the guitar over to Babak. "It's a pity."

Babak took the guitar, cradling it without playing.

Hooman stood up abruptly. "I'm going for a cigarette," he muttered before walking off toward the garden.

"Poor man, totally fucked up," Bijan muttered.

Babak sighed. "Yeah, I thought he was over it... I really feel for him. Honestly, Bijan, today I realized just how powerful love is. I know it sounds like a cliché, but after that terrible shooting in the metro and then hearing Dara's voice on the phone—it was like magic. It pulled me back from the edge. It gave me something to hold on to, something to believe in. Love is powerful, man. Really powerful. Poor Hooman... I can't even imagine what he's been through if he's still this deep in love."

He set the guitar down carefully, leaning it gently against the wall. Bijan watched him for a moment, a sense of shared understanding passing between them.

"Won't you play?"

"Not in the mood, really," he replied. He glanced around the room, which struck him as rather sombre.

Bijan said, "Doesn't help, does it? If we all give up? Let's change this, even if only for a few hours."

Babak nodded and then put on a song from the seventies called *Vay Vay*, turning up the volume and shouting, "Time for a dance, guys!"

Bijan stood up, syncing his lips to the song, moving his head slightly with the rhythm, and opening his hands wide as a gesture of invitation.

No one bothered.

Kamran and Roxy had just arrived and were already deep in conversation with two twin brothers in their early twenties, who had attended the same school as Bijan's son in Tehran.

Kamran heard Babak's invitation to dance and grimaced. "Dance!? Really? What planet are you on, man? I can hardly stand on my feet. May I ask—what should we dance for?"

His face grew tense as he continued. "Yes, maybe we should shake our legs because each day we wake up to the news of one of us being hanged. Or perhaps we can gloss over the fact that Iran's currency is the worst in the world? I'd rather sit and cry!"

"Ah, come on, darling," Roxy said. "This is a party. Save your tears for later... for me!" She made a face at him and winked at Bijan, who looked disappointed and was heading toward the turntable to stop the music.

Roxy then pulled Kamran's jacket sleeve. "Did you hear that, Kami?" she said, bringing him back to the conversation in which one of the twins mentioned that the Ministry of Education had removed all the girls' illustrations from the third-grade textbooks.

Surena and Pouria—known as Suri and Pori—were identical twins. Both had bright black eyes and uniquely kind smiles brimming with vigour. Their differences were subtle, noticeable only to those who knew them well.

Suri, the more flamboyant of the two, was slightly broader in build. His hair was gelled into a deliberately messy spike, and he wore a dark green checked flannel shirt, unbuttoned over a white T-shirt and jeans. In contrast, Pori was tidier and more reserved, wearing a sleek black jumper and sharp grey trousers.

Surena chuckled. "The funniest part... the most stupid point... is that the illustrations were cartoons. Just imagine their sick minds."

Roxy frowned. "Disgusting! Think how sad it is that they want to diminish women, given that the first woman to win that big mathematics prize was Iranian."

"That's it, I know. Maryam Mirzakhani?" Pouria said. "That was the Fields Medal, the Nobel Prize in math."

Surena took over. "And listen to this! Recently, there have been talks about replacing English lessons with Chinese, so now the first language kids will learn is Arabic, and then the second option is Chinese!"

Kamran chuckled.

The twins' mother, a slender woman wearing a striped polo neck, stood a little behind, listening eagerly. She stepped forward and, in a low, respectful tone, said, "There's nothing wrong with learning Arabic or

Chinese—in my opinion, those are great languages too. But the fact that they're dismissing our rich Farsi language and English, the international language of communication—that's exasperating!"

"Actually, to be very fair here," Kamran scoffed, "that fits perfectly! Millions of people—from newlyweds to the elderly—save money every day to make a pilgrimage to the Shrine of Imam Reza, don't they? They recite in Arabic there, but to reach that place, they'll bypass Ferdowsi's tomb, which is only half an hour away. I think we can agree that Iranians owe the survival of Farsi to Ferdowsi, yet visiting his tomb isn't a priority for many. So with that mindset, what do people really need most—Arabic or Farsi?"

The twins' mother shook her head. "You're right, but I wonder if it's simply a lack of knowledge. I'm not sure how many people read the *Shahnameh* these days. We tried at home when they were young— I used to read the stories aloud, remember, boys?" The boys nodded, and Surena recited a verse: "Mighty is the one who has knowledge."

She smiled and asked, "Does anyone remember how this used to be printed on the cover of our old school textbooks?"

"Ah... yes! I do! I do!" Roxy said, crossing her arms over her chest and giggling. "I'm showing my age here, aren't I? I had my primary school before the revolution!" But her giggles faded quickly, her voice flattening as she continued, "Burning books... you remember?"

The images from that time flickered vividly in her mind. It was one of those cold winter nights in 1979 or 1980. The Revolutionary Guards had piled a mountain of books in the middle of the road, preparing to set them on fire. She was a little girl, one of many children who had gathered to watch. The smell of burning paper, the crackling of the flames devouring the books, were etched deeply in her memory.

She could still recall the faces of those around her, smeared with the sticky black residue of smoke. When she got home, her face was as black as a coal miner's. Her mother scolded her sharply, saying, "Paper ashes are the worst ashes!"

Roxy unconsciously touched her own face as she told the story. "They wanted to leave us in the dark—the Ayatollahs. They knew very well that knowledge is power, and they were terrified of books. It all started like that—with burning books. It was even before compulsory hijab, right, Kami? Was it before that?"

"It was the Cultural Revolution!" Kamran said, looking intently at Roxy. "Darling, it was all part of the same package and happened around the same time. They copied the idea from Mao's Cultural Revolution—which the Chinese possibly borrowed from the Soviet Union. Like the Chinese, the regime here also targeted the Four Olds!"

"Four Olds?" the twins asked in unison.

"Yes. The Four Olds! Though the regime didn't use that exact term—it was actually coined by the Red Guards during China's Cultural Revolution in 1966, referring to the pre-communist elements of Chinese culture they sought to destroy: Old Ideas, Old Culture, Old Customs, and Old Habits. In Iran, the goal was to change these Four Olds as well. Of course, this happened years before you were born—and far different from the version they fed you in school."

The boys looked at Kamran with curious eyes, eager to know more.

"It was the early days of the Islamic Revolution," Kamran said. "Khomeini's remarks during a Friday prayer in the early '80s—'We are not afraid of economic sanctions or military interventions; what we fear are the universities training our youth under Western influence'—was enough of a green light for his supporters, who called themselves Hezbollah, a name you'll find very familiar now."

He paused, giving them a sarcastic look before continuing, "Anyhow, that very night they attacked the Tehran Teachers' Training College, leaving the place looking like a war zone. This spread to other cities and became systematic. The Cultural Revolution Headquarters was established within weeks. In the first phase, the academic community was purged of Western and non-Islamic influences to align it with Shia Islam. Then they targeted cultural institutions—cinemas, theatres, galleries—and, most importantly, all universities were closed for three years, from 1980 to 1983. When they finally reopened, many books were banned, and thousands of students and lecturers were expelled.

"It was then transformed into the Supreme Cultural Revolution Council, and the chairman of the Council has always been the President of Iran. This body remains a powerful force in the government, ensuring that education and culture in Iran remain one hundred percent Islamic—rather than Iranian. So basically, a reformist Iranian president is a myth. The worst and most fake presidents were those who called themselves reformists!"

Babak interjected, "It was their way of purging the ranks. Just like Hitler's obsession with race, the Ayatollahs fixated on our culture. In fact, they even called it 'cleansing'! My father was expelled as a lecturer during the Cultural Revolution. We still have his dismissal letter—stamped boldly with the word 'Cleansing' at the top. But after nearly five decades, they still haven't succeeded..."

The twins' mother began to look uncomfortable. Her father had joined the cultural revolutionaries before going off to fight in the war, where he became a martyr. She was proud of his sacrifice during the war with Iraq but never spoke of his involvement in the Cultural Revolution, except to her mother. She offered Babak a polite smile. "Thank you. I think the boys got the idea."

"Hang on, Mum!" Surena interrupted, eager for more. "I've obviously heard about this, but I've never really understood it. Why did people let the books burn? Had they lost their minds? It seems so primitive. I mean, if people were educated, why did the revolution happen at all?"

Surena's question hung in the air, until a man who'd been quietly listening spoke up for the first time.

"Let me take a step back," he said, rising to address the group.

Roxy looked at the man, then at Kamran, and said with a polite smile, "We actually spoke earlier, didn't we? I apologize; I seem to have forgotten your name!" She looked a bit embarrassed, then grinned and added, "But you're the dentist from next door, correct?"

"Yes, no problem. I'm Akbar, an orthodontist... or, well, a dentist," the man replied with a broad smile. He then launched into an impromptu lecture about the political climate before the revolution, recalling how he had been sent abroad on a scholarship. He explained how he mingled with various opposition groups from outside Iran—Communists, MEK, and others—discussing their views and ideas that helped shape the events leading up to the revolution.

"Well, we were young and a bit full of ourselves. At the time, everyone thought the revolution was a good idea. We believed life could be better, you know?"

"Better life? Are you serious?" Kamran interrupted. "I was a student then too! I remember when the rial was one of the top seven currencies in the world. People had an amazing lifestyle. Students could even buy cars from abroad and drive them back to Iran. I did it myself. I remember passing through Turkey—a miserable place with a terrible economy. And now look at them! What were you thinking—'a better life'? Just a bunch of students…"

"We were not 'just a bunch,'" Akbar snapped back angrily. "It was the majority of the population. It was legal—we had a referendum!"

Kamran waved his hands dismissively. "Oh, a referendum! Thanks for reminding us how 'legitimate' our government was!"

Bijan began to feel uneasy. His neighbour Akbar had invited himself to the party in a passing conversation with Giv in which he said that his family was away and he'd be alone for Yalda. Bijan didn't know him well and had no idea about his political leanings. Now, he realized he needed to defuse the tension before things escalated. With a friendly gesture, he spoke up.

"Hmm, referendums… always a tricky subject, aren't they?"

"What trick?" Akbar snapped, his tone defensive. "It's democracy!"

Babak felt his stomach tighten at how casually the word *democracy* was being linked to the regime, but he bit his tongue, aware that Bijan was trying to keep the peace.

Bijan gave Akbar a calm, measured smile. "Democracy, yes—the term invented by the Greeks. But even Socrates wasn't a fan of the idea."

"Really?" Surena asked, his curiosity piqued.

"There's a beautiful story about it," Bijan continued. "One day, Socrates asked another philosopher, 'If you were heading out on a sea voyage, who would you choose to be in charge of the ship—some random passengers, or a well-trained captain?' The other person replied, 'Of course, the captain.' And Socrates responded, 'So why would we let just anyone manage the ship—or the state?'"

Babak nodded emphatically,

"I guess, Socrates' point was that voting in an election or a referendum is a skill, and like any skill, it needs to be taught. Without that knowledge, it becomes an irresponsible act—like putting random people in charge of a ship during a storm. They'll never reach land. They'll sink… just like Iran is sinking now."

Akbar turned his face away, staring blankly into the distance, as if he hadn't been listening at all. Kamran couldn't help but flash a shrewd smile.

Pouria, always thoughtful, asked, "But what would Socrates suggest instead? Did he believe only a small number of people should vote?"

Bijan shook his head. "No, not at all. His point was that only people who think clearly and deeply—not emotionally—should vote. Think about it: if you ask a kid who's better for them—a doctor or a candy seller—they'll pick the candy seller every time."

He paused. "That's the tragedy. Socrates lived it. In his seventies, he was a household name in Athens," Bijan went on. "He spent his life asking hard questions, poking holes in lazy thinking. Then three powerful men accused him of corrupting the youth and dishonouring the gods—and the city turned on him."

He exhaled. "Five hundred citizens sat on that jury. The vote? 280 to 220. Barely tipped."

Roxy leaned in. "And then?"

"They sentenced him to death," Bijan said softly. "Made him drink the poison himself—hemlock."

He paused, his tone softening. "Socrates' death shows the difference between intellectual democracy and democracy by birthright."

The twins' mother asked, "So, do you mean that age shouldn't be the only factor when it comes to voting?"

"Precisely! Voters must earn the right to vote—they must own it. Democracy is not a given entity, but something that must be constantly nourished, like a delicate flower."

Akbar let out a snort of laughter. "A delicate flower? That's hilarious." Still chuckling, he turned to the twins, saying, "You see... Anyway, it's hard to explain now. We wanted change, and you would've done the same back then."

The brothers exchanged doubtful glances, and Surena exclaimed angrily, "Don't laugh like that! We're not that stupid, and I doubt we would have."

Pouria chimed in, "You older guys say this now. You had a great life—getting sent abroad by the last government for education—but you betrayed it."

"Guys, that's enough!" their mother intervened.

Akbar looked taken aback but continued to talk. "I know where you're coming from, boys, but this is naïve. That regime also had its faults—like SAVAK, the brutal secret police—or the extravagance of all those celebrations for the 2,500th anniversary of the Persian Empire, and..."

Babak cut him off. "Wait! Take responsibility for what you did! Yes, yes, there was SAVAK. Like any other country in the world, Iran needed security and intelligence services. But if they were, as you claim, *brutal*, the revolution wouldn't have succeeded. Look what the government does *now* with protesters and students."

Roxy made a quick warning movement, glancing sideways at Kamran nervously. She ran her fingers through her hair, growing impatient with the escalating argument.

"Guys, please. Kami, leave it—we've said enough. Let's get some mezze. I'm hungry."

But Kamran was fully engrossed, his eyes narrowing, oblivious to her.

Babak turned to the man and raised his voice. "Let me tell you something—I believe it's pretty good going for any government if their worst fault is spending too much on one ceremony. A celebration of 2,500 years of Persepolis was the best legacy he could have left us. He understood his people well. He took the criticism of extravagance but lit a candle that is still burning—to show us the way."

"Ex–cell–ent," Bijan said, emphasizing each syllable. "Well said!"

Babak pressed on, his voice growing more passionate. "That ceremony wasn't just for the world—it was for us, for dark days like now, to remind us of who we were. He knew how forgetful and naïve we can be. It took that level of extravagance for us to truly appreciate our heritage. People watch those clips now and are reminded of our glorious past."

Babak wasn't done. He leaned forward, glaring at Akbar, his voice laced with rancour and bitterness.

"But time hasn't softened those hard edges! There's no going back for the thousands buried in long pits, or for the millions who died in the war, or for the uncertain future of these guys." He pointed at the twins.

Their mother immediately raised her hands in protest. "I said enough, please!"

Unfazed, Akbar settled back into his chair, propping a cushion behind him—staking a claim to his space. A grudging smile tugged at his lips, as if to say, *This is it. If you don't like it, you can leave.*

Kamran cleared his throat and turned to Bijan. "Babak-jan, did you want to put on the music? This might be a good time."

GODZILLA VS KING

With the heat of argument still hanging in the air, the brothers left for the calm of the *korsi* room, where others continued to read and recite poetry. Their mother immediately followed, intending to say something but stopped at the door before entering.

Babak was right, she thought—they were in uncharted territories, and the future of her sons, like so many others, wasn't promising in this cursed country. She felt that familiar feeling of regret well up in her body again. Why hadn't she let her ex-husband take the twins abroad with him? They could now be studying at a university, just like Kamran's son.

Her husband had called her "selfish" and "irresponsible"; it hurt to know he was probably right. She countered this unpleasant thought by telling herself there was no point in standing here miserably all night—this was a party, after all. Then she asked herself, *Was it?* It didn't feel like a celebration, but rather a gathering of angry, frustrated, and hopeless people—together for what? To share their miseries on the longest night of the year?

It felt like a desperate attempt by the dwindling middle class—if they could still claim that title in this economic disaster—to hold onto civility and celebrate tradition, no matter the circumstances.

Yet, she realized, as strange as it seemed, this party was still a dream for the lower classes—most Iranians—who couldn't even afford basic necessities, let alone the fruits and nuts of the occasion. The middle class was quickly fading, swallowed by the widening gap between the poor and the super-rich. She couldn't help but feel a deep regret for what people had done in the past, actions that now seemed to resurrect this suffering. Would there be a saviour, or would they only sink deeper into the swamp with each passing day?

She closed her eyes, sighed deeply, and pressed her palms against the doorframe.

Roxy noticed her and came over. "Are you okay, lovely?"

"Ah, yes. I'm fine, all good. I just had an awkward moment."

"We all have those, especially after that friendly exchange we had!" Roxy said, walking her back to the main room.

In the hallway, not far from the *korsi* room, Neda spotted a *daf* resting quietly against the wall. She picked it up, settled onto the sofa, and began gently playing with its rhythms. Though the twins couldn't see her, they followed the sound weaving through the room. Surena, with his easygoing manner and confidence, approached and spoke as if he had known her forever, "Good thing you weren't in that room; we had quite a storm!"

Neda put the *daf* aside and looked up in surprise. "Sorry?"

Pouria stepped in, pointing at his brother. "I'm Pouria, and that's my brother Surena. Suri and Pori, if it's easier."

"Neda," she replied.

Surena, still curious, asked, "You play the *daf*?"

"I wish," Neda smiled. "My friend plays it, and I was just trying to copy her."

"What do you study, if you do?" Surena asked.

"Medicine," Neda replied.

"Cool! Me, physics!" Surena said.

"Philosophy," Pouria chimed in, winking at his brother.

Neda quickly relaxed around them; their easygoing conversation made her feel comfortable. When they asked how she ended up at the party, she nearly shared the story of 1384, but something held her back; it felt too risky to reveal too much too soon.

"Tell me more about that conversation," Neda asked, curious. "What did you say you were debating in the next room?"

"Godzilla vs King!" Surena answered and chuckled.

"What?" Neda looked confused.

Pouria came to the rescue. "Godzilla—you know, that monster from those old Japanese movies? Suri called the regime's top brass 'Godzilla'."

"Oh my God! Haven't you seen it?" Surena asked.

"Well, I've heard of it. It's pretty famous, but it's not my kind of movie." Surena's brow furrowed.

Pouria let out a light chuckle. "You've really disappointed him! Ever since Suri was a kid, he's been obsessed with movies. One whole wall of our room was plastered with Godzilla posters. You can imagine what we had to put up with."

Surena sighed, shaking his head. "You have to watch them! They're massive, destructive creatures powered by nuclear radiation—nearly impossible to kill, and they regenerate quickly!"

"Are they like dinosaurs?" Neda asked.

"Kind of," Surena replied. "But even bigger and more complicated! They can hide deep under the ocean and stay undisturbed for ages. They're awakened—or mutated—by human activities like nuclear testing. Their very existence is tied to what people do."

Neda caught the mention of 'under the water' and 'undisturbed'—a strikingly similar concept to what Mr Kayvon had said about *farr*. That made her pause. "Under the water?" she asked. "Did you say under the water? Really?"

"Yes, deep under the ocean," Surena answered, raising an eyebrow. "Why?"

Neda shrugged. "Nothing," she said, though she was clearly intrigued. "Go on"

Surena continued, "Godzilla was originally created as a metaphor for the United States and the atomic bomb. That's why its skin is scaly and heavily furrowed—it's meant to resemble the scars of those who survived Hiroshima and Nagasaki. But the creature also represents the wider human impact on the environment."

Neda tilted her head. "And what about the connection to the regime that Pouria mentioned?"

Surena's expression tightened, a grimace crossing his face. "Well, take Sadegh Khalkhali, for instance. He was a mullah who became Chief Justice of the Revolutionary Guard in '79. He's known for executing thousands— laughing all the while. What he did to Azar, the Shah's horse, was something even Godzilla might baulk at. First, he broke the poor animal's legs, then blinded her, cut out her tongue, and finally shot her."

Neda shuddered, her face twisting in disgust. "Oh no! Please... no, that's... it's sickening."

Surena raised his hands, a cloud of regret crossing his face. "Sorry, I'll stop there."

"No, please carry on," Neda urged, though her voice was laced with disbelief. "But surely you're not suggesting the leaders of the regime aren't human... are you?"

Surena looked at her with steady, resolute eyes. "This is exactly what I'm trying to say, Neda."

"Come on! How could that even be possible?" Neda asked, confusion mixing with disbelief.

Surena's eyes darkened, his voice turning sterner. "I'm serious. It's not as far from reality as you think."

After recounting the earlier argument over the cultural revolution, he added, "Listening to that arrogant slob in the other room, I'm convinced the Ayatollahs are real monsters. And the sick minds of people have manifested them. In a way, it's our own people's cruelty and twisted thinking that have fed these demons—imbued them with dark energy and power."

Neda stared at him, disbelief written across her face, and asked, "As simple as that? Can it really be like this?"

Surena jumped to his feet, disappointment flooding his face as he exclaimed, "You call this simple? Seriously? You call this simple?!"

Pouria grew conscious and said, "Suri! Bring your voice down!"

Neda squinted, pouting slightly as if trying to make sense of it all. She turned to Pouria. "What do you think? Do you agree with your brother?"

Pouria raised an eyebrow and glanced at Surena, who looked at him expectantly, waiting for support. After a pause, he spoke. "Well... yes. 'Our own people.' I think he means we have this horrifying ability to create our own monsters and fuel our own destruction. The monsters are always lurking beneath the surface, like creatures sleeping deep under the ocean—but it's people who awaken them."

Surena's lips curled into a slight smile as he glanced at Neda.

Pouria went on, "Of course we weren't born then. Our parents were still young in '79. I'm talking about our grandparents—most of whom we never even met. Except for one grandmother, who always refused to acknowledge the revolution."

He leaned forward slightly. "But we can't just excuse it—or pretend it didn't happen. Ninety-nine percent voted yes. How? How could they accept Khomeini as their leader? What did they see in him?"

"We've had our fair share of conspiracy theories," Surena added bitterly. "Some say it was MI6. Or the Marxists. Others blame Jimmy Carter. I'm not saying they played no role—but the root cause?"

He paused, placing a hand on his chest.

"This was us—the people of Iran. It wasn't a coup, for God's sake. It was a revolution. A proper one. No foreign interference could've pulled this off in a place like Denmark. Or Japan. Their people wouldn't have fallen for it. But here? No one realized how tightly religion held this country in its fist."

Neda, listening intently, asked, "So... you think it was religion?"

Pouria nodded, backing his brother. "Religious dogmatism."

He paused, then added, "There's this concept—people say one thing in public but believe another in private. Like under communism. There's a term for it: *preference falsification*. I came across it in a book by an economist. Back in '79, most Iranians probably had more in common with the mullahs than with the Shah's officials—but no one admitted it. They hid behind intellectual masks. The pressure kept building... and eventually, it erupted."

Surena's eyes lit with defiance. "But it's the same now, isn't it? The people and the regime—once again, they've got nothing in common. Maybe we're cursed by the ignorance and choices of our revolutionary grandparents. But it's time to fix it."

TUS FESTIVAL[7]

Jav, who had been scathingly dismissive of Mr Kayvon's explanation of *farr* just moments earlier, was now pacing the *korsi* room with his phone held high, desperately trying to catch a signal. He wandered across the room until he reached Neda and the twins, who were huddled together on the floor.

"Hey, you guys!" he called out. "Got any signal?"

Surena hesitated before checking his phone and gave a shrug. "Nope."

"Damn it," Jav muttered, staring at his screen in frustration. "I just got a WhatsApp a second ago, and now it's gone again."

He glanced down at the three of them sitting dismally on the floor. "Look at the state of you! Why don't you join us over there? We just had free history lessons!" He caught Neda's eye and added with a smirk, "Didn't we?"

Neda recoiled slightly at the memory of his earlier behaviour at the *korsi* table but managed a stiff smile.

Jav grinned sarcastically. "And now, even better—they're reciting poetry!", he scoffed, laughing as he started toward the door. But then he stopped in his tracks. "Ah, that's it! It's working here!" he exclaimed, his fingers flying over the screen of his phone.

Surena, still watching him, tilted his head toward the door where Jav stood and murmured to Neda, "Who is that guy? Do you know him?"

Neda sighed, shaking her head. "No idea. He was arguing with the others earlier. He's... a strange character."

Before Surena could respond, the distinctive, earthy scent of espand [8] drifted into the room. Just then, Atossa appeared in the doorway, carrying a tray of food in one hand and a small copper espand burner in the other. The burner's smoke spiralled gently, weaving through the air around her. Her eyes immediately landed on Neda, and she broke into a warm smile.

"There you are! I was looking for you," she said, then glanced at the twins. "Looks like you have made some friends!"

She stepped forward and held out the tray with a cheerful expression. "Try these, guys—they're so good."

Jav's eyes locked onto the tray like a hawk: warm Sangak bread and vibrant mezze—green olives, ruby pomegranate seeds, and crumbled cheese with crushed walnuts. He couldn't resist. Before anyone could react, he darted over, snatched a couple of olives, and popped them into his mouth—still talking on the phone.

"Oh—hallo, hallo... shit, I shouldn't have moved... damn it... lost it!"

He spun on his heel and bolted back toward the door, his ponytail whipping behind him.

That was enough to send the others into a fit of giggles.

Atossa peeked over at the *korsi* and raised her eyebrows in surprise. "Wow—they're reading the *Shahnameh*! Look over there!" She smiled. "Come on, let's join them, shall we?"

Sharing a look of curiosity and excitement, they followed Atossa across the room to see what the fuss was about.

Mr Kayvon was reciting beautifully, his voice smooth and rhythmic, but he paused as Atossa placed the tray at the centre of the *korsi* table. She gave the copper espand burner a gentle swing, releasing fragrant clouds into the air—like a priest swinging a thurible during a church vigil.

Sam coughed a few times. Atossa glanced over and grinned. "Sorry, mate—better than cigarette smoke! Disinfects the place! Actually good for your lungs!"

Sam kept a straight face and doubled down with exaggerated coughing.

Atossa smiled and threw up her hands dramatically. "Okay, okay—enough. I'll take it back to the kitchen!"

"Go on, Kayvon!" Gitti said firmly.

He nodded and resumed reading.

...Now Khosrow wept and asked : "What is your name?"
The angel said. "I am Sorush. I came
In answer to your faith, and soon you'll be
The world's king, glorious in your sovereignty:
You'll reign for thirty-eight long years if you
Act righteously in everything you do."
He vanished, and the world has never known
A vision like the one Khosrow was shown. [9]

Well, there's so much more to explore in this book," Mr Kayvon said, then paused. "But maybe the big issue is this: we don't read the *Shahnameh*—or connect with our history—nearly enough."

Neda leaned toward Surena and whispered, "Do you read the *Shahnameh?*"

Surena leaned in closer and muttered, "We did a bit when we were little."

As he spoke, his face hovered so close to hers that his nose brushed lightly against her ear. Neda felt the warmth of his breath, the nearness of him. She turned to meet his gaze—and instinctively recoiled, catching a gleam in his eyes that seemed meant only for her. Heat flushed her cheeks as she pulled back, startled by the wild, new feeling stirring inside her. Was she even ready to admit it to herself? The surge of emotion was overwhelming. *Silly girl,* Neda chided inwardly. After all, wasn't love what they were fighting for in the 1384 manifesto? And so, she let it bloom— bold, raw, unfiltered.

Mr Kayvon closed the *Shahnameh* and tapped his index finger several times on the cover. His gaze drifted into the distance, a quiet sadness settling over his face.

Gitti leaned forward, trying to catch her husband's eye. "Kayvon?" she said softly.

"We have a big problem," he replied, with a serious tone. "We have a national book—and we don't bother to read it."

Gitti let out a sigh of relief. "Oh, good God, man! You really had me worried with that look." She filled a plate with mezze and gently placed it between them, nudging him to eat. He ignored her, wrapped in his self-imposed silence. After a long pause, he spoke again.

"What does it take for a nation to read its own epic? Ferdowsi under-stood the power of stories—he knew. Throughout history, we've seen how stories shape people... entire civilizations. Just look at religion. It's the greatest story ever told—insanely powerful. It split one world into two and made the afterlife feel inevitable, as if what happens after death was always certain."

He paused, letting the weight of his thoughts settle before turning to more recent examples.

"Or take *The Epic of America*—the term "American Dream" was first coined by its author, James Truslow Adams, during the early, most devastating years of the Great Depression, when the United States was in a state of severe economic crisis. He described it as the dream of a land in which life should be better, richer, and fuller for everyone. Since then, it has become a defining narrative for the United States—shaping the country's self-image as a land of opportunity and fueling national pride."

His voice grew more intense. "And then, of course, there's *The Communist Manifesto* by Marx and Engels. The impact of that book is immeasurable. And don't even get me started on how literature has shaped national identities—*Les Misérables* by Victor Hugo, *Macbeth* by Shakespeare, or *Ulysses* by James Joyce!"

He took a breath, looking at them intensely.

"It's always a book!" He paused again. "Now—do you see the super-power of books? The magic of storytelling? There's something almost otherworldly about them—the way storytellers can transport us to different worlds, evoke emotions we didn't know we had, and make us see life through new lenses."

"Do you see this? Stories hold a power to connect us in ways nothing else can. And yet, we don't read them enough in Iran. We could talk about this until our tongues bleed."

"Our *Shahnameh* is timeless, echoing the drumbeats of the past and telling Persia's epic story while inspiring our future. It's a powerful tale of heroism, destiny, loss, and the struggles that shape a civilization. So my question remains: how do we get a nation to actually read its national epic?"

Gitti raised her eyebrows, stopped eating, and set down her fork. She pursed her lips and reluctantly pushed the small plate aside. The room fell silent.

Mr Kayvon suddenly turned to Banoo and Giv, as if struck by an idea. "Tell them about the Tus Festival," he suggested. Giv glanced at Banoo, who nodded. She was more talkative and better at storytelling.

"Well, you've asked me to go back a long time, maybe fifty years!" Banoo said. "There was a festival in Tus, the birthplace of Ferdowsi, aimed at promoting the influence of the *Shahnameh* in Iranian culture from many perspectives—literature, painting, music, plays, you name it. Even international scholars were invited to discuss his work.

"This idea came from Queen Farah Pahlavi and was first suggested at the Shiraz Arts Festival, another annual international festival we had back then. She genuinely believed in Iran as the land of myth and legend, and her love for art, our rich heritage, and cultural identity was ingrained in her..."

As Banoo spoke, Giv closed his eyes. The scent of espand still lingered in the air, unlocking a rush of memories from the Tus Festival that flooding his mind. It pulled him back to the woody tang of frankincense and espand smoke filling his lungs that day. The rhythmic beat of drums echoed in his ears, and the chants of performers and storytellers rose around him once more. He saw the re-enactments, the gleam of sweat on the wrestlers and pahlavans, the pulse of tradition alive in every gesture.

At the centre of it all stood their hostess—the Queen—radiant in her full majesty, as they gathered beneath the dome of Ferdowsi's marble mausoleum.

It was July 1975—a scorching day, especially gruelling for anyone in costume. Giv was there as a dancer, part of a Khorasani Choob Bazi troupe. Banoo had a role too, playing the *daf* for the storytellers. Both had been noticed by representatives from the Ministry of Culture during a visit from Kanoon and had arrived a few days early to rehearse for the event.

Giv snapped out of his nostalgic reminiscence at the echo of Banoo's voice.

"Do you remember, Giv? ...Darling?"

"Sorry, what?"

"The epic storytellers... the *Naqali* performers. I said they were the best! Weren't they?"

"Oh yes, yes," Giv replied with a nod. "They were incredible!"

Atossa suddenly exclaimed, "Why don't you perform something for us, Giv? Please—it's Yalda!"

Giv sighed. "Good heavens."

Banoo laughed. "He's shy."

Giv groaned. "I'm not shy—just stuck. It's my back pain..."

Banoo smiled knowingly.

Neda went to fetch the *daf* from the corridor, and Banoo took it with steady hands—her left hand supporting the bottom, her right thumb pressed firmly against the rim. She struck it hard.

The deep, resonant sound of the *daf* filled the room, drawing the attention of twenty or so guests gathered around the *korsi*. Banoo rose to her feet, lifting the *daf* higher, her hands moving faster as the metallic jingles echoed through the air.

Parto was captivated—the *daf* was beautiful, bold, and full of life. She marveled at its simplicity; it might have changed very little over the centuries. A *daf* player was even carved into the ancient Bisotun inscription, a testament to how long the instrument had accompanied stories and songs. The frame remained wooden, the drumhead still usually made from goat skin, and while the jingles may have evolved, the sound itself had likely remained almost unchanged.

After a few minutes, Banoo lowered the *daf* and began to recite a passage from the *Shahnameh*.

When Banoo finished, the room erupted in applause. Bijan looked at her with admiration.

"Which part of the *Shahnameh* was that from?" Ava asked.

"Rostam's Seven Labours," Banoo replied.

"I've used the expression before— 'Rostam's Seven Labours'—but I never really knew what the seven tasks actually were," Ava said.

Banoo smiled. "Well, they were seven nearly impossible tasks that Rostam had to complete—always with the help of his loyal stallion, Rakhsh."

She began counting them off on her fingers. "First, *The Lion*—Rakhsh fights a lion. Second, *Crossing the Desert without Water or Grass*. Third, *Killing the Dragon*. Fourth is *Defeating the Temptress*."

She paused. "And the fifth... oh, what was it, Giv?"

"*Killing the Demon*," Giv answered. "Then *Rescuing the King*, and finally, *Killing the White Demon*."

"The White Demon?" Neda echoed, surprised.

"Yes," Banoo said. "The most dangerous of all. In the myth, the White Demon captures the king and his commanders, blinds the Iranian soldiers, and throws them into dungeons. Rostam's battle with him is the climax of the story. His victory is the triumph of good over evil."

Giv added, "But some say the White Demon also represents something deeper—a hidden enemy."

"Like what?" Jav asked.

"Like ignorance," Giv said.

MONARCHY OR REPUBLIC

Neda quietly said to Surena and Pouria, "Godzilla, White Demon—what's next?" They giggled.

Surena approached the *korsi* table, pointed to the large book and asked Mr Kayvon, "May I?" He nodded. "Wow, this is bigger than our copy at home," Surena said, bending slightly to lift the heavy book. He called out to Neda and Pouria, "Look!"

Together, they flipped through the pages filled with vibrant miniature paintings of kings, princesses, horses, orchards, mountains, birds, and demons. Banoo pointed out where the most famous stories originated.

Surena paused for a moment, deep in thought, then asked, "Are these stories real? Based on history?"

"A mix of myth and history," Mr Kayvon said. "Ferdowsi was really grieved by the fall of the Sassanid Empire after the Arab invasions. So, his whole effort was about preserving the memory of Persia's golden age and passing it on to the next generation. His main goal was to save the language and the pre-Islamic legacy—both myth and history. But the book also teaches important values like love of country, family and helping the poor. He called it the *Shahnameh*, or the Book of Kings, but it's so much more than just a list of kings in order. It tells their stories—an epic mix of myth, legend, culture, history, and the timeless fight between good and evil."

"Did we always have kings and queens?" Surena asked.

"Yes, as far back as history goes, right up until the Islamic Republic was established in 1979," Mr Kayvon answered.

"Just our bloody luck—born at this time!" Surena muttered, glancing at his brother and Neda.

Jav shouted, "So, you're a royalist then?"

"We're not sure yet what we are!" Pouria replied.

But then Surena added quickly, "Is there any government you know of that offered more freedom than a monarchy?"

Neda paused, startled. She considered herself politically aware but had never really thought about that question before.

Jav grinned. "Aha! I knew it—you're a royalist!"

Irritated, Pouria retorted, "He just asked a question!"

Jav shot back, "Can't he speak for himself?" Then he smirked and added, "Oh wait, maybe you twins share the same tongue?"

Surena half rose from the floor and looked at Jav vehemently, but before he could say anything, a loud voice stopped him: "Well, I... I am a royalist. And a proud one!"

It was Bijan, who strode into the middle of the room, holding up his hand to signal that he expected silence for what he was about to say. Jav slowly let his jaw drop and sank back into his seat with a begrudging smile, while Surena continued to stare at him contemptuously.

Bijan began to make his case. He argued that the end of monarchies in Europe after World War One created a power vacuum, fuelling instability and helping totalitarian regimes rise. While he acknowledged that other factors, like economic hardship, played a key role, he believed the collapse of monarchies contributed to the chaos that led to World War Two.

"Auschwitz and the Gulags—those were the by-products of what came after the monarchies! The horrors of the concentration camps didn't come from the palace, but from the Nazi regime. You know, I studied a bit in Germany. Do you know what 'Nazi' stands for?" He paused, scanning the room. "*National Socialist German Workers' Party*!" He grinned wryly and added, "In his vision of the Third Reich, the very 'national socialist' Hitler had no place for monarchs. And if you didn't know, 'Reich' means 'empire.'

"In Russia, the Bolsheviks, despite their claims of democracy, gave birth to the oppressive Soviet Union, which quickly became a totalitarian state. Today, under the guise of a Federal Republic, the Russians have an elected president—and, not by accident, an ex-KGB officer, no less! In my view, for a country as vast as Russia, bringing back the monarchy is the only way to get rid of Putin. Instead of sending troops and weapons to Ukraine, they should knock on the door of the House of Romanov!"

Some clapped, and Pouria let out a sharp two-fingered whistle. Bijan chuckled, but from across the room, Giv shouted, "Too late, son!"

Bijan pressed on. "Look at the region after the Shah left—conflict, carnage, destruction. The Iran-Iraq War, Afghanistan's ruin, the Gulf War, Syria, Lebanon, Yemen... and now Israel and Palestine. We're on the edge of another global war..."

Akbar, the orthodontist, stood at the door with a smug grin. "Throwing the crown back on us, huh? So you think the world's problems would vanish if monarchies returned everywhere? I wish it were that simple, my friend."

Bijan studied Akbar intently. To him, his face was intimidating, with piercing eyes and smiley but bloodless lips framed by a neatly trimmed goatee.

Babak exchanged uneasy glances with the twins; it was clear they were uncomfortable with Akbar's presence in the room. Bijan shrugged and said politely, "Oh, my apologies, Akbar! I didn't quite catch that—could you say it again?"

Akbar moved to the center of the room, taking a moment to scan the faces around him. Parto offered a polite smile, as did Mr Kayvon. Gitti stared, Jav continued munching on nuts, Shirin leaned against Ava, Atossa listened intently with her arms crossed, Sam appeared bored, almost dozing, and Babak kept his head down. Akbar's gaze locked with the twins and Neda. Lowering his head with a deeper, more triumphant smile, he said,

"Well, nothing—except your take on Russia really caught my attention. After all, communism found its place in the grand scheme of things. Look at China... and you were suggesting bringing back the monarchy." He paused briefly and said, "Anyway, I came to find—ah, there he is!" He waved toward Giv at the back of the room. "Do you mind more guests? I just got a call from my cousin Moshen, he's nearby. I told him I was here. Hope you don't mind if he joins us? Oh, and by the way, your clock is slow..." He checked his watch. "Anyway, he'll be here soon, if that's okay. It's Yalda, after all..."

Giv and Bijan exchanged surprised looks, both blurting out, "Of course... of course!" Giv grimaced slightly, as if to shield Bijan from the conversation, and said, "Son, you mentioned Auschwitz and the Gulags—I want to add one more to the list: the suicide bombers. This new, mad, terrifying phenomenon.... You know, I had a long chat with a man at the bakery the other day while waiting in line. He made an interesting point. He said if countries like Iran, Afghanistan, or even Syria and Iraq had kept their kings, this horrific trend might never have emerged. He believed monarchy insulates against extremism—and pointed out that, even now, the safest places in the Middle East are the Arab monarchies. Thinking about it, the dynamics of the region are far more complex, and maybe the guy over-simplified things a bit—but he might've been right in some ways, like—"

Akbar interrupted. "Which bakery do you go to?"

"That Sangak naan place, next to the bank... right up the main street. Do you go there too?"

"Oh no," Akbar replied. "I don't have time for bakery queues. I prefer baguettes—I shop at the supermarket next door. I know the age group of the retired guys who go to the bakery. Anyway, it's no surprise what that man told you, since the countries you highlighted as the safest in the Middle East also happen to have the richest oil resources. After the mess with Iran and Iraq, no one wants to mess with them."

Bijan listened carefully, then said to Akbar, "No, no... I disagree! Look at Jordan. It doesn't have significant oil—in fact, it imports oil. On top of that, it lacks natural resources compared to its neighbours. The country is landlocked, has barely any access to the sea, and very little else. But it's still one of the most stable nations in the region, all under the rule of their kings! Did you know the population is mostly West Bank Palestinians who fled war in 1948? And their currency is one of the strongest—stronger even than the British pound!"

"Incredible!" Akbar exclaimed. "But how?"

"Petra!" Bijan said with a smile.

"Petra? You mean the ruins?" Akbar asked, puzzled.

Bijan laughed. "Ha! What you call 'ruins' is actually one of the main reasons their GDP has grown! Tourism is huge for Jordan's economy, and it also brings in a lot of foreign investment. For example, they're one of the world's largest exporters of pharmaceuticals and medicines. So no, it's not always about oil."

Akbar grinned. "Doesn't make sense, does it? You mean the republics are undemocratic?"

Suddenly, the room erupted into a cacophony of voices—some defending republics, others tearing them down.

Jav, joining in with a grudging and pompous tone, said, "Guys, this is the Middle East's case for monarchy... mind you! People aren't educated enough to understand the kind of democracy a republic would bring! Otherwise, what's wrong with republics? Like... like—oh yes! France! Tell me what's wrong with France's republic?"

Bijan turned toward him, leaning in so he could stare directly into Jav's eyes.

"Oh, come off it, Jav!" Bijan shot back. "We can't generalize like that and say all Middle Easterners are uneducated! What's wrong with you? About the French Revolution, I could talk about that until morning! Was it really perfect? I'm not so sure! They paid a hefty price to become a republic, but tell me, is France stronger now compared to what it was before? Is it still leading the world? Look at how divided the country is! And okay, let's forget Europe and look at countries that are more similar to the Middle East. Let's go to Africa..." He turned to Akbar and asked, "Morocco or Algeria? Which one would you choose to live in?"

Akbar replied bluntly, "Well, before I answer that, I'm still waiting for a reply to my earlier question. Are you suggesting republics are undemocratic—yes, or no?"

"Well, I just answered that," Bijan said with a shrug.

"So you mean they aren't, then? Okay, at least that's clear."

"It depends on your definition of democracy," Bijan replied.

"A government elected by the people," Akbar said firmly.

Bijan raised an eyebrow. "Is that all? In my definition of democracy, other factors matter more—individual freedom, prosperity, human rights, the rule of law."

He began counting on his fingers, listing countries in the air. "Norway, Denmark, Sweden, Finland, the Netherlands, Belgium... Look, I've done my research. More than half of the world's top ten democracies are monarchies!"

Parto, who had been mostly quiet—half-focused on finding Hooman and half-listening—nodded at Bijan's comment and said, "And those countries are far more prosperous and happier, aren't they?"

Jav looked at her gravely. There was a palpable cynicism in the air.

Parto had felt it ever since returning to Iran—a strange, almost sour tension beneath every conversation. It was the third major shift she had noticed since coming back. First, the growing poverty. Then, the booming beauty industry. And now, this: a heavy mood of suspicion and disgust that clung to people like a second skin.

But maybe it wasn't just the country. Maybe she had changed too.

Had she always been this cynical before she left? Living abroad had softened something in her. One of her first shocks had been the trust—the casual openness of strangers, the kindness in their eyes. It stood in jarring contrast to the closed-off, guarded faces she saw now.

And then, yes... there was something else she had forgotten—the Labubu dolls. These grinning idols were scattered everywhere, lavish symbols of joy that most people could hardly afford. Perhaps that, more than anything, was the quietest kind of tragedy.

The countries Bijan had listed clearly seemed happier. Iran felt like the opposite. Everyone here appeared either deeply insecure or brashly overconfident—as if the weight of totalitarian rule had etched a particular madness into their smiles. It was the same haunted energy she associated with the Russians, Parto thought: a shade of cynicism inherited like a scar that would never heal.

Mr Kayvon, sitting nearby, noticed Parto had withdrawn into herself. Her earlier mention of pagans had piqued his interest. He leaned toward her and spoke softly. "So, you're just visiting?"

"I am."

"When was the last time you were in Iran?"

"Oh, a long time ago... nearly sixteen years."

"Oh dear!"

They chatted for a bit before he asked, "Did you say you study history?"

"European history," Parto nodded.

"Fascinating! What era?"

"Modern—though I'd love to study the Age of Antiquity... maybe for my PhD one day."

"Ah, so you've got a Master's. Impressive. What stood out most to you?"

"That's a good question. Hmm... it's hard to say. The World Wars in Europe really shocked me—especially how little we learned about them in Iran. But what about you? You clearly know a lot about Iranian history. Where did you learn all that?"

Mr Kayvon smiled humbly. "Curiosity! I just love to read. Tell me, what was your paper about? Was it on the World Wars?"

"Oh no, something quite different—historical paradoxes. I'm fascinated by them."

"Paradoxes?"

"Yeah, like 'What ifs'—counter-factual history and the alternative outcomes historians explore."

"And what was your 'what if' for Europe? If Hitler had won, the war?"

"No, that one's been done to death. You might laugh, but mine was: *what if Liechtenstein had bought Alaska?* It was actually offered to the Prince of Liechtenstein by the Russian Empire in 1867, but he declined. The U.S. ended up buying it for $7 million. There are still Orthodox churches there today! I looked at what might've happened if Alaska had ended up in European hands—or stayed with Russia. Imagine Russia and North America sharing a land border...especially in winter."

"Wow, that's fascinating! So what did you find—just the short version?" Mr Kayvon asked, clearly impressed.

"Okay, super short?" Parto smiled. "If Alaska had gone to Europe, it could've completely reshaped 20th-century geopolitics—new alliances, different wars, even different borders. And if it had stayed with Russia, there'd be a direct land link between the two superpowers—right at the Bering Strait. It's technically maritime, but in winter, it often freezes solid. That creates a kind of seasonal ice bridge. So yes, during those months, you could actually *walk* from one superpower to the other."

Their conversation was cut short by a sudden shift in the room—Bijan and Akbar's argument had escalated into open hostility.

Akbar's eyes burned with anger as he glared at Bijan, who maintained a sarcastic smile, nodding occasionally—just enough to add fuel to the fire.

"Seems you've done your reading, my friend," Akbar said sharply. "But let's not forget Saudi Arabia. Isn't that a kingdom too? Any sign of democracy there? Women's rights? LGBT rights?"

Bijan shot him a dry, ironic look and replied firmly, "We have to compare apples to apples. Saudi Arabia is an absolute monarchy, not a constitutional one. There are no political parties, no judicial precedent—though technically, the king must follow Sharia law."

Akbar fired back, "But it's still a monarchy. And we have Islamic Sharia laws too. We're a republic—and functioning better."

Bijan grimaced and interrupted, dragging out his words. "Oh yes... yes, Doctor, thank you for the reminder. But we have the most *special* republic in the world—the Islamic Republic!"

A ripple of laughter ran through the room.

"We get to elect our president and parliament democratically... and then we get something extra. Something cute—*the Guardian Council!*"

The laughter grew louder.

"Yes, they care for us so much. Not just one or two, no! We get *twelve* super-duper guardians—mostly Mullahs. Their specialty? Overseeing our elections. First they vet the candidates, then they bless the results. So generous!"

"They also watch over the parliament," Bijan continued, "just to make sure everything complies with Islamic law. And who appoints the Guardian Council? Surprise, surprise... the man of God—the Supreme Leader!" He chuckled gruffly. "It's the biggest joke for a republic."

The argument kept spiralling, both sides digging in deeper.

Bijan's voice grew louder, more forceful. "The reason people cling to failed political ideologies—like communism—is because they're too proud to admit they can't fix the world. Sure, the ideas look good on paper—but they don't work. Just look at seventy-eight years of the Soviet Union!"

Akbar let out a spiteful laugh and jabbed a finger toward him. "Ha! Did you say seventy-eight years? So it *did* work!"

As much as Giv tried to mediate, neither of them showed any sign of backing down.

Surena, Neda, and Pouria sat in silence, wide-eyed, watching the exchange unfold—innocently—even though it was Surena's question that had sparked the entire debate. Gitti glanced at them, then at her husband, who had quietly resumed talking with Parto, the two of them seemingly choosing to stay detached from the storm brewing nearby. Suddenly, she shrieked, "Kayvon! Say something!"

Mr Kayvon excused himself from Parto and looked around at the room, now a blur of raised voices and clashing opinions. "Guys! Listen!" he called out—but no one heard him.

Gitti quickly grabbed the *daf* from the floor and struck it hard. The sharp beat cut through the noise, silencing the room. Mr Kayvon raised an eyebrow, surprised, then smiled gratefully at his wife.

"Look," he said, projecting calm, "I appreciate the passion. We humans always seem to crave something grand, complete, and extraordinary—and when we don't have it, we invent it. But here's my take: both systems—monarchy and republic—*can* work. The key is knowing what fits where. Not every country is suited for a monarchy. It depends on historical context and cultural values. For example, you wouldn't expect a monarchy in the

U.S.—it just wouldn't make sense. But in nations lucky enough to have the right cultural and historical foundations, a constitutional monarchy might actually offer the best chance at a fairer, more unified society."

Akbar raised an eyebrow. "How would that even work?"

Mr Kayvon opened his hand and looked around,

"People are like the fingers of a hand—different in faith, ethnicity, and belief, especially in a place like Iran. But each has a function. And here—" he pointed to his palm, "—this is the place of the monarch, in our case 'Padeshah'."

He slowly closed his fingers into a fist.

"See? The monarchy is what binds them. All those traditions—the pageantry, the parades, the cavalry with swords drawn and trumpets, the jewel-studded crowns, silk robes... our emblems like the Lion and Sun or the Peacock Throne—they aren't only theatre. They serve a deeper, almost sacred purpose: to root a nation in something beyond politics. They speak of identity, and continuity. They remind people not just of who they are, but of who they have been—of the unbroken thread of meaning that stretches across generations.

He paused for a moment, letting the words sink in.

"And most importantly, in a constitutional monarchy, the monarch helps *sustain* democracy—by rising above political factions and offering neutral space for debate. Political parties still govern, but the crown binds them to something older and greater than themselves."

Mr Kayvon looked around the now quiet room.

"In the UK, the monarchy helped prevent fascism in the early 20th century. Orwell once said the monarch acts as an escape valve for dangerous emotions. Today, as Britain grows more multicultural, only the monarchy can hold it together. Without it, the whole thing might fracture."

Neda, surprised, leaned forward. "Did Orwell really say that?"

"Yes, he did."

"Where? Which book?"

Mr Kayvon nodded. "It was in one of his essays."

"I've never come across that."

Mr Kayvon smiled, "I'm pretty sure. Orwell said something even more remarkable. He wrote: *'In England, the real power belongs to unprepossessing men in bowler hats. The creature who rides in a gilded coach behind soldiers in steel breastplates is really a waxwork. It is at any rate possible that while this division of function exists, Hitler or Stalin cannot come to power.'*

Half an hour later, when everyone had finally exchanged their views and the arguments began to cool, Bijan leaned back and took a deep breath.

"Well, guys, we should do what Spain did—re-establish the monarchy after Franco's dictatorship. Honestly!"

Akbar's face turned red with fury. "Don't wrap it up just yet! What about the *hereditary* part? How do you explain that?"

Jav groaned under his breath. "For heaven's sake... not again!"

At that moment, Banoo re-entered the room carrying a tray of clean glasses. She checked the samovar, quietly listening, her eyes flickering toward Bijan. Then, in a voice filled with distant memory, she said: "We kept bees when Bijan was little." A soft smile tugged at her lips. "His mother was a master beekeeper. This house was surrounded by orchards—just a few buildings here and there. The rest was green, bountiful... alive."

Her gaze shifted to Akbar, her tone softening into something almost wistful. "Right where your dental clinic stands now... that used to be a cherry garden. Full of trees. Especially beautiful in bloom—Springtime."

Akbar stood motionless, his expression unreadable.

Bijan's face lit up at the memory. "I can still hear it," he said. "The buzzing, when Mother opened the hives." Banoo nodded gently. "She always used to say, 'Every single bee has the potential to be the queen.' And when we asked her how, she'd smile and say, 'The magic of metamorphosis.'"

Akbar's jaw tightened. His eyes narrowed. With a sharp, unsettling jolt, he turned to Bijan, a cold sneer spreading across his face. "Well, my friend," he spat, "I'll leave the beehive to your Queen." With that, he stormed out, Giv following close behind.

Babak, watching Akbar's exit, couldn't help but grin. With a twinkle in his eye, he chimed in, drawing on his veterinary background.

"Yes, exactly," he said, with a lively tone. "Worker bees pick a few ordinary eggs and place them in special cells, feeding them only royal jelly. And from that, one eventually transforms—becoming the queen. She's the most capable, the strongest... humble, tireless, a warrior, and a goddess all in one."

Neda's eyes sparkled. "So all we need is some royal jelly, then!"

Mr Kayvon smiled. "Yes, we do. Ours, however, is kept under the water."

ASIAN GAMES 2584

No one really noticed when Shirin left the *korsi* room. She had managed, for a while, to suppress the anxiety that had crept up on her, but it returned like a small, hostile animal, gnawing even more at her stomach. At home, she would lie on the floor and breathe but didn't want to draw attention at the party. So, quietly, she poured herself a glass of water and headed upstairs.

Tucked between the bedrooms, a small lounge offered a quiet retreat, its walls lined with bookshelves. A woody, herbal scent filled the space. Shirin noticed a still-warm oil burner on the coffee table. She bent over it, took a deep breath, and exhaled a few times; it was soothing, helping to push back her tension a little. She sank into a rocking chair in the corner and closed her eyes. The noise of the crowd downstairs felt louder. Of course, they were her friends—nice, lovely people—but like almost everyone living in this cursed country, they were immersed in their own problems.

We're becoming so weak, Shirin thought. *We should've stayed on the streets, shouting for freedom—not at each other. None of us have the guts anymore...*

It felt petty. But she couldn't resent them. They were family now, especially after Farhad disappeared.

What would it be like if he were here, at this party? She pictured him: What would he wear? Which side would he take?

The garden lamp glowed outside, snow drifting through the light slipping in between the curtain slats. *Farhad liked snow,* she thought. *Or likes it....* What tense should she use when thinking of him?

She tried to make sense of her anxiety. It was raw and sharp, unmistakable —like a creature living inside her: sometimes quiet and curled into sleep, other times stirring, restless.

Shirin placed her hands gently on her belly. For the first time, she felt not fear, but only pity for the small, inner presence. It was her anxiety, now reframed as a sick, jaundiced child needing care. That unfamiliar tenderness brought with it a strange sense of calm, dissolving the panic into a simple act of mothering.

Her eyes roamed over the books. Even just looking at them, she thought, added to the warmth of the place—like the comforting smell of coffee or baking bread. She spotted a few old volumes of children's books and rose from the rocking chair; they were first editions from Kanoon. Banoo and

Giv must have kept them from when they were working there.

The Kanoon logo—a bird perched on an open book, singing—made her smile, as it always did, bringing back memories of her childhood. She placed the books back on the shelf and glanced at the other titles, a mix of subjects from *The Art of Cooking* to *My Uncle Napoleon*.

But then her eyes fell to the bottom shelf, and she gasped at the sight of a few rare titles—*A Brief History of the Lion and Sun* by Kasravi, and a series of Sa'idi Sirjani books: *The Fables*, *The Short Sleeves*, and *Zahhak the Snake Shoulder*. Shirin picked up the last one and noticed it had been personally dedicated by Sa'idi himself.

To the defiant descendants of Iran—the Faranaks, the Fereydouns, and the Kavehs.

On another shelf, a series of poetry rested in quiet elegance—works spanning Ferdowsi, Hafez, Rumi, Forugh, and Sohrab Sepehri. Her eyes lingered on a volume by Attar: *The Conference of the Birds*. She lifted the heavy book and settled onto the floor, fingers lightly turning the pages. It was richly adorned with exquisite miniature paintings—birds in flight, towering mountains, delicate flowers, and ancient trees.

Shirin recited some verses, her whisper floating through the quiet room. Her fingertips traced the colourful illustrations: golds that shimmered like sunlight, turquoise as deep as the sky, and reds and greens so pure they seemed drawn from the earth's own pigments. It felt natural and timeless.

Suddenly, a tide of sensations swept over her—first apprehension, a dizzying rush; then, gradually, as if she had been swallowed by the paintings themselves, she was soaring like the birds atop a mountain. For a fleeting heartbeat, an unfamiliar tranquillity rose within her—a delicate mixture of stillness and motion, where reality and dream entwined. Shirin quivered and turned her hand to look at it, but the vision had already vanished. Bewildered, she shuffled through the pages and noticed a postcard tucked inside the book. The postcard was printed with six small drawings of athletes in various poses. In the centre was an inscription: *The Shiraz Asian Games 2584.*

What was that? she wondered. Perhaps it was from the old calendar. She remembered that the last year of the Imperial calendar was 2537—the year of the revolution, or 1979—meaning 2584 would be now.

After the Islamic regime came to power, the Imperial calendar was abolished and replaced by the Hijri Shamsi [10] calendar. It had been decades since anyone in Iran used the old system. The current year was 1404, according to the calendar introduced after the Islamic government's arrival. From then on, all dates followed the Hijri Shamsi calendar.

Someone's being very funny, *she thought*. Maybe it was Bijan who made the card a joke—yes, that was very him. She flipped it over and saw familiar handwriting on the back:

See you there, Farhad X

Shirin sat frozen, the card in one hand and the book in the other. She didn't hear Dara's heavy footsteps as he entered the lounge.

"There you are! You disappeared! Are you okay? ...What is it, Shirin-jan? What's wrong?"

Shirin placed the card and book gently beside her. She stood up slowly, her body trembling. Before she could steady herself, Dara was at her side, wrapping her in a comforting hug.

For a moment, she rested in his arms. Then, taking a deep breath, she stepped back and whispered, "Just look at this!"

But there was nothing inside.

"I think I put it inside the book!" she said, holding it out to him.

Dara took the book cautiously. "Oh, this beautiful book of Attar—magnificent miniatures..."

"No!" Shirin gasped. "Look at the card. There was a postcard inside."

Dara flipped through the pages but found nothing. Shirin snatched the book back, her hands trembling as she searched frantically. The card was gone.

She scanned the floor desperately, but it wasn't there either.

"I swear, Dara," she said, with a shaky voice, "I saw that card. I'm not lying."

"Of course, Shirin-jan," Dara said, pulling her into a tight hug. "Maybe it was just similar handwriting."

"No!" Shirin shook her head emphatically a few times. "It was signed, too. His signature is very distinctive."

Dara exhaled slowly. "Okay, Shirin-Jan, that's alright... maybe it's just one of those episodes again. Come on, let's go back to the room. Let me make you a cup of tea."

Shirin placed both hands on her stomach, pressing down. "You go...

I'm going to rest here. My stomach is churning... Please, Dara, go. I'm better off here. I can't stand the fighting we had tonight. Why do we keep insisting on seeing each other?"

Dara chuckled softly. "You know them well, don't you? Honestly, if they behaved, I'd be worried!"

Shirin smiled faintly. Dara insisted on staying with her until she felt more relaxed, then they'd go downstairs together. She moved from the floor to the rocking chair, while Dara settled on the sofa across from her.

To distract her, he suggested a little game: they would each pick a random book from the shelf, then choose a random page number and read a few lines from the top.

They went through a few books.

"Okay, that was a good one," Dara said, grinning. "Your turn now!"

Shirin thought for a moment. "Upper shelf—fourth book from the right."

Dara grabbed the book and pulled it from the shelf. "Good choice. This one's a big one. What page?"

"Hm... let's say 544," Shirin replied.

"Okay, got it. Ready?" Dara smiled, flipping to the page.

He began reading aloud as Shirin listened intently.

> *There is a great black mountain. It's human stupidity. There is a group of people who push a boulder up the mountain. When they've got a few feet up, there's a war or the wrong sort of revolution, and the boulder rolls down—not to the bottom; it always manages to end a few inches higher than when it started.*
>
> *So, the group of people put their shoulders to the boulder and start pushing again. Meanwhile, on the top of the mountain stand a few great men. Sometimes they look down and nod and say, 'Good, the boulder-pushers are still on duty, but meanwhile we are meditating about the nature of space or what it will be when the world is full of people who don't hate and fear and murder...'*

Shirin looked at Dara with curiosity and snapped, "Who's that by?"

Dara shut the book and smiled. "Doris Lessing—The Golden Notebook."

"Goodness me! That was so spot on—the story of us, the boulder pushers... as if she copied it from us," Shirin said, her voice a mix of amusement and intrigue.

Dara laughed. "No, I guess the world's full of boulder pushers everywhere." He raised his eyebrows with a smirk. "Mind you, she was born in Iran!"

[136]

MOTHERS OF TULIP PARK

The doorbell rang, and Giv opened the door, letting two women step into the hall. Banoo hurried to greet them, throwing her arms around the older woman and kissing the younger one's forehead. "I'm so glad you made it!"

Atossa peeked out from the kitchen and gave them a warm smile.

Banoo called out, "Bijan-jan, Bijan... come here! Gohar and Ayda have just arrived." Then, turning to Gohar, she added, "Make yourself comfortable over there. Look, I've set up a *korsi* in that room. It's warmer there."

In the kitchen, Parto placed a tray of glasses by the sink and asked Atossa, "Do you know them?"

"Yes, sort of... That older lady is one of the Mothers of Tulip Park. Their official name is the 'Mourning Mothers of Iran,' but we see them every Saturday evening at the solidarity vigils in Tulip Park, so everyone calls them that."

Atossa paused for a moment before continuing, "Her son was arrested at home, right in front of his family, just a few days after the student protests were crushed in 1999. Three months later, he was allowed a brief phone call from Evin Prison. He told his family to follow up on his case, but they never heard from him again. Evin officials have refused to release any information about him. No one knows what happened. He was 23 then—so if he's still alive, he could be nearly 50 by now. Gohar still holds on to hope. The other mothers... they've had similar stories, or lost a son or a daughter."

"The Mothers of Tulip Park became a larger movement over the years, as the regime's pattern of killing protesters continued. Their name evolved, and other similar groups emerged—like the 'Mothers of Khavaran,' 'Mothers of Aban,' and 'Mothers of Justice.' As the groups grew, the regime began to feel threatened and tried to silence them through the IRGC and undercover agents. They raided homes, had members dismissed from their jobs, and many were taken to Evin."

Parto asked, "On what grounds?"

"Being involved in an illegal organization that threatened state security. They received lengthy sentences and were often even beaten and tortured while in prison."

Parto found it unimaginable. Things had only become worse during the years she had been away. While social media revealed a lot, it still couldn't capture all the stories.

"We insisted Gohar and Ayda join us for Yalda," Atossa said. "The family is under pressure from the government not to talk about their son. They don't go out much to reduce the risk, but we didn't want them to feel isolated. And honestly, we just wanted to be with them on this special night."

Parto asked about the younger girl.

"She's Gohar's daughter, Ayda. We should go and say hello to them," Atossa replied. As she was heading out of the kitchen, she paused and added briskly, "Lovely, would you go get Hooman for me quickly? Tell him they're here... he knows them from the park."

Before Parto could respond, Atossa gave her a playful wink and a cheeky smile, fully aware of the awkwardness her request might cause.

"I know, Parto-jan, don't make that face—this is really urgent!" she said, before breezing off to greet the two women.

Parto blinked, fighting back the grin tugging at her lips. Classic Atossa—still pulling people into her whirlwind, whether they liked it or not. A familiar twinge stirred in her stomach. She knew exactly what was behind Atossa's request. She paused. Part of her wanted to go find Hooman; the other part wasn't so sure.

At that moment, Persis rolled on the floor, purring contentedly, her eyes fixed on the counter as if something invisible were lingering there. Parto followed her gaze but saw nothing—at least, nothing she could identify. She frowned, watching the way the cat's pupils dilated, as though tracking something in the air only she could sense. What if there were other worlds, just out of human sight, visible only to creatures like Persis?

The thought was unsettling, and it pushed her out of the kitchen to search the house for Hooman.

She checked every room, walking through the house with growing impatience, but there was no sign of him. She returned to the kitchen in case he'd gone there unnoticed. Again, nothing. The cat had disappeared too.

Parto stood still for a moment, her pulse quickening. "Okay, that's enough," she muttered to herself, trying to shake off her anxiety. "It's not meant to be!"

But still, a restless energy gnawed at her—the same unease she had worked so hard to bury over the past sixteen years: the hurt, the yearning, the uncomfortable possibility that her love for him might resurface.

"Desperate... desperate... desperate...," she whispered to herself as she touched up her lipstick and poured herself a shot of arak, swallowing it in one go, the bitter liquid burning her throat.

As guests began trickling into the kitchen, their chatter filling the space, Parto slipped quietly toward the hallway. She felt pathetic—a woman trying desperately to hold herself together while everything inside threatened to unravel.

A cold draft swept down the hallway from the garden, slipping through a crack in the door. Parto shivered as it brushed against her back. She moved to close the door, but as she reached the threshold, she spotted him in the garden—a tall shadow against the white snow, the glow of his cigarette faintly illuminating his face.

She was uncertain what to do. She could shut the door quickly and pretend hadn't seen him, but finally gave in to the leap of her heart, which pushed her forward almost involuntarily.

Hooman heard her footsteps pressing heavily on the snow and turned around, squinting. The night was too dark for him to see clearly, but he knew who it was.

"Ah... you came," his voice rich and warm. "It's cold here...but it is a beautiful night!"

There was something about the way he spoke—gentle and inviting—wrapped around her like a soft woolen blanket, a subtle touch she felt more than heard.

They stood side by side for a few minutes without saying anything. The house loomed behind them as they gazed at the cedar tree. Unease hung between them, like a cord pulled too tight.

Finally, Parto spoke, a slight tremble in her voice. "You... still writing?"

"Yes," he answered, his tone quieter now. "A little. Mostly poems and plays these days... it's been hard with... everything else..."

"Your eye? Shirin just told me. I didn't know. I'm very sorry... I could have..."

"Oh... no! Don't worry, I can still write."

"Which eye is it?"

Hooman turned his face slightly, removing his glasses, and their eyes met briefly. She leaned forward to see better; they were so close now that the mist rising from his face mingled with hers.

Just as Parto opened her mouth to speak, a sudden rustle came from the dark depths of the cedar tree, followed by a low creaking. It made her jump.

Hooman looked away. "It's just the wind... I guess!"

The sound changed to footsteps. Parto's gaze turned toward the end of the garden path, where a figure emerged from the shadows, clumsy and unsteady.

"Hi, guys!" he called out. "Good to see you! I'm the neighbour—well, the cousin of the neighbour, to be exact. Here for Yalda, just jumped over the back of the garden...was shorter than going all the way to the front door... the snow's pretty deep, huh?"

He laughed awkwardly, his words tumbling out in a rush. "Look at this beautiful garden—it's huge! Sorry to interrupt, looks like you were, uh, cozying up under this tree... romantically?" He giggled. "You... guests too?"

Parto's face flushed with embarrassment, and they both nodded, caught off guard by the man's odd, almost intrusive energy.

"I'm going in," the man said. "That door's open, right? Don't you want to come inside before you freeze?"

The suggestion felt abrupt, but it was cold, and Parto's hands trembled as she instinctively reached for her pockets. She felt exposed, like something delicate had just been ripped away. With her voice barely more than a whisper, she said to Hooman, "Maybe we should go inside."

BONYAD

Sam shivered as he walked from the front door to where the van was parked to get his packet of cigarettes. The street was quiet and dark. He lit one, the small flame flaring like a protest against the biting cold. He wasn't enjoying the party, but the thought of it ending felt worse. It meant facing the days ahead. A future without Ava. What a long, lonely road that would be.

His eyes were fixed on Bijan's house, standing dark against the snow, its windows faintly glowing with an indigo light among the bare trees. The blackness of the house seeming to intensify the dark thoughts swirling in his mind. He thought of his own home, how dark it had become. A tightness seized his heart. He turned his head away and looked toward the sky, closing his eyes to let the snow land on his burning eyelids.

He sought solace in the good memories of his life with Ava. She was the daughter of his football coach, and they met at the pitch when she had come to pick up her father. Ava's father was a man of integrity; the family wasn't wealthy, but they were educated, grounded—good people. Sam had promised Ava's father that he would look after her, that he wasn't interested in politics or getting into trouble, but in keeping a low profile and building a comfortable life.

They couldn't have children, but that at least allowed them to travel more often. They were happy once. But look now—how things had crept up around them like weeds. How did they end up here? Really—how?

He flicked away his second cigarette, half-finished, and decided he'd had enough of the freezing cold.

Inside, Sam stood with his back to the room, warming his hands by the heater, when he felt a tap on his shoulder. He turned around and found Mohsen—someone he knew through work but hadn't seen in years.

He noted how Mohsen had settled into middle age, with thinner hair and more weight around the midriff. When Sam first knew him, he was a builder working on a construction project in Hafftapeh, but he had since transitioned to property development and made a fortune for himself.

"Hello, stranger!" Mohsen said, laughing. "Look at you!"

"Goodness, man, what are you doing here?"

"Accident," he chuckled. "I just came to see my cousin Akbar, who's got a dental clinic next door. He was invited to the party, so I tagged along. You know his family's away in Canada. He's half here, half there."

He laughed again. "Do you know how many times I've tried to buy this house? But Bijan won't bloody sell it. The guy loves the place, but to me, it's like a ghost house. Someone even said it's haunted. Maybe Bijan's possessed by this pile of bricks...but the land—just think—I could make two commercial centres out of this and the garden. Easy!"

He then asked, "You? You know them well?"

"Yes, Bijan is an old friend. He's my wife Ava's distant cousin. Did you come with your wife?"

"Which one?" Mohsen chuckled. "The Quran promises us more than one in heaven, right? So I thought I'd start practicing now!" He laughed again.

"You're sure your wife—the main one—doesn't know?" Sam asked.

"My wife? She knew from day one. But as long as she's shopping in a mall in Dubai, she's happy. I'm happy. God is happy. Everyone is happy. Civilized!"

Another laugh—but this time, Sam noticed his teeth were unnaturally white.

"Good," Sam said, unsure if Mohsen would catch the sarcasm in his tone.

Mohsen then launched into a tale of his business acumen during the crisis—his collection of high-rise apartments in north Tehran, which he called his *"safety net"*—before bragging about his latest pharmaceutical investment.

"Pharmaceuticals?" Sam raised an eyebrow. "How did you get into that without any background?"

"It wasn't a problem," Mohsen replied with a grin. "Thanks to the sanctions! It's a brilliant opportunity, Sam. We're operating like a network—clean and easy. You're welcome to join us."

He paused, raising his hand, and Sam noticed the same brown *Aqeeq* ring tightly pressed on his finger.

"Here's an example. We buy a bottle of simple Feroglobin—an iron supplement—for a maximum of $8 per bottle, delivered in pallets at the Turkish border. Guess how much we sell it for?"

Sam shrugged indifferently. "I don't know."

"Give me your best guess!"

"Really, I have no idea... let's say, for argument's sake, $10 per bottle?"

Mohsen laughed. "Ha! No wonder you're broke! Aim higher, man—open your eyes! It's going for $20. Easy!"

Sam frowned. Mohsen leaned forward, his face inches from Sam's.

"The secret is," he said conspiratorially, "when people are sick or dying, they pay—especially for things you can flag as cancer treatments, stuff like that. And look, I'm so proud that we create jobs, we provide medicine to terminally ill people, and they're happy to pay! I'm happy. God is happy. Everyone is happy. Civilized!"

A wave of shame and anger washed over Sam—shame at his own failures, and anger at the blatant greed and corruption Mohsen was flaunting.

Just then, a new guest entered, carrying a large *tar*. She looked like a musician. Mohsen's eyes locked on her, and he nudged Sam, whispering, "Almighty God! Look at that penthouse."

Sam raised an eyebrow, surprised by the expression. "What?"

But Mohsen was too distracted to explain and resumed bragging about his success, his voice growing louder.

"You see, I run everything myself. Don't trust anyone, Sam—not even your brother! That's the key!"

Sam's mind flashed back to Mohsen's older brother, who had been involved with Bonyad at the start of the revolution.

"By the way, how's your brother?"

"Which one?"

"The one who was in Bonyad?"

Mohsen hadn't been expecting this. "Naser? You've got a good memory. He moved to Boston with his family."

"Boston, America?"

Mohsen nodded, quickly realising he'd said too much.

"Oh, has he? I thought he was anti-US! How did he end up in the Great Satan?"

Mohsen shrugged emphatically. "His wife is doing her PhD there."

"I see."

Sam went quiet. He was thinking about the *Bonyad*[11]—a charitable trust and one of the richest government-linked organizations in Iran. It was originally set up by Ayatollah Khomeini after the 1979 Islamic Revolution, supposedly to help the poor and disadvantaged.

Its initial wealth came from real estate and the confiscated assets of people who had either fled the country, been executed, or imprisoned. Since then, it had grown massively and was often described as the second-largest commercial force in the country after the state oil company.

Its operations stretched across a huge number of sectors, and its wealth was often estimated in billions of dollars. The board of directors operated under the direct supervision of the Supreme Leader. They reported only to him and not the government. *Bonyad* also enjoyed a high degree of autonomy, avoided public scrutiny, and was exempt from taxes.

There were many similar religious and charitable organizations, such as Astan-e Quds Razavi (AQR), which gained its wealth from managing the Imam Reza shrine in Mashhad and other religious institutions. All were corrupt to the bone—funding terrorism, illicit activities, and, of course, the *Aghazadeh* (the "Good Genes"), like Mohsen's brother, whose wife was related to one of the Ayatollahs.

Sam knew a lot about the AQR. It controlled massive assets across a range of sectors—agriculture, energy, construction, and finance. It also had major investments in sugar production and related industries. Some said it was responsible for at least ten percent of the country's total sugar output and held shares in three sugar companies.

AQR was considered one of the most powerful religious charitable foundations in Iran. It didn't pay taxes like most others, and its head was chosen directly by the Supreme Leader as well.

The profits were huge. Meanwhile, companies like Sam's Haft Tappeh were struggling—but the money kept flowing, not to them, but into the military and Iran's proxy forces, including those in Lebanon.

He couldn't help but wonder: *How do we, the people of Iran, tolerate this?* Maybe we've forgotten who we were—lost our sense of self.

That was the regime's plan from the beginning: to erase our past, dismantle our culture, rewrite our history, silence our language, even change the way we looked and dressed. It was essential for their survival. If we wake up each day with no memory and no identity, then we're nothing. And if we're nothing, they can do anything they want to us. They've abused our minds—and we've let them. For far too long.

Mohsen was still talking, but Sam was lost in thought, unable to hear him as the words drifted past. He only saw Mohsen's mouth moving, opening and closing repeatedly. At some point, Mohsen leaned in, jabbing his finger at him. Sam felt the tap of Mohsen's *Aqeeq* ring against his shirt.

Lowering his voice, Mohsen whispered, "Let me know if you're stuck. You need some friends!"

Sam felt Mohsen's breath on his skin, and hate rose in his throat. His anger erupted like a volcano, and he pushed Mohsen back violently. "You bastard!" he shouted. "You told me not to trust anyone a minute ago. I don't need a friend like you! With your bloody mushrooming high-rises and that disgusting, filthy medicine smuggling you call business—your breath is infected. Get away from me! Get away!" The room froze into silence.

When Ava heard her husband shouting, she ran from the *korsi* room to see Sam gesticulating wildly at Mohsen. Ava tried to grab his hands, holding them tight, and exclaimed, "Stop it, Sam. Stop... What happened? What's going on here?"

Sam kept his eyes fixed on Mohsen. "Cannibal! You are a cannibal!"

Ava was shocked and embarrassed by the intensity of Sam's anger. "We should have stayed home… What a mess. Sorry, Banoo. It's my fault… What a mess!" Banoo rushed over and held her tight as she wept in her arms.

Sam looked at Ava as if he had just noticed her presence. His face softened, the anger melting away to reveal the vulnerability of a frightened child. He knelt beside her, tears flooding as he cried.

THE WEEPING *TAR*

After the quarrel, the mood inside the house was sombre. Banoo cradled Ava, who was still trembling like a baby on the sofa. Shirin found a blanket and spread it over her. Banoo gently adjusted her arm so that Ava's head rested more comfortably on the cushion but remained seated by her side.

At the far end of the room, Mohsen and Akbar spoke with their heads bent conspiratorially close to each other. They turned to look pleadingly at Giv, as if expecting him to do something—or at least sympathise with Mohsen. He shook his head from side to side in response. He watched, powerless to stop them, as they made the decision to leave

As they turned to go, the mood in the room seemed to lift.

Bijan led Sam to the kitchen and closed the door behind them. He tried to calm him down, but Sam, unheeding, lowered his aching head onto his folded arms on the table. A tight pain was spreading across his chest, creeping into his left arm.

In the *korsi* room, no one spoke until Hooman came in after Gohar and her daughter and said, "Did you hear that? Typical married couple! Makes me glad I'm still a single man."

They smiled but didn't look convinced. Atossa scowled—this was a bit too off-kilter.

As the silence stretched, Banoo suddenly stood up from the sofa and looked around the room. "There she is!" she said, visibly relieved. "Leila, darling, would you play something for us?"

Leila, a petite woman in a peacock-blue vest and red skirt, looked like a Qajar-era beauty with her long black hair and joined eyebrows. She smiled and nodded as she carried a *tar* into the room.

Banoo called out, "Let's all sit by the *korsi*. It might be too cramped for all of us, but it's cosier, isn't it? I'll make some borage tea. It's the best calming tonic—good for the heart, good for the mood."

She bent over Ava, kissed her forehead, and whispered in her ear, "Come over, darling—only when you feel like it, okay?"

Ava sat up and nodded. "Sure. Thanks. I'm better now."

Banoo returned with the tea and, with Atossa, lit the candles in a round copper tray and placed it on the *korsi* table. The little flames whirled Sufi-like, while the scent of frankincense and espand from the incense burner in the centre filled the room.

Leila sat crossed legged on the floor, the bowl of the instrument resting on her lap, one hand on the long wooden neck as she tuned it.

Kamran was excited to see her—Leila had once been one of his patients.

"I knew you couldn't forget me... that aquiline nose," Leila said as he greeted her.

Kamran laughed and introduced Roxy, who, in a playful nod to her husband's skills, asked, "So, where is that nose now?"

Just then, Ava entered the *korsi* room with Parto, casting a rueful smile around the space before settling into a corner. There was little room left, and a few guests had begun to gather at the doorway.

Atossa exclaimed, "Oh! Look at us. Let me count—one, two, three... oh goodness me, we're over thirty!"

Once everyone had settled, Leila's fingertips gently strummed the *tar's* strings. Her music slipped into the room like breath. Some smiled softly; others closed their eyes and swayed gently.

As the night carried the music along, a mournful solitude settled over the room, as if the melody of the *tar* had slipped into their souls, expressing the words they couldn't speak.

Leila paused to rest her fingers, which now felt oddly wet and clammy. She looked around and noticed a few tear-streaked faces. The room had fallen into heavy silence.

Bijan, remembering his duty as host, lifted his eyes from the floor and said softly, "Thank you, Leila-jan. That was beautiful."

Leila raised her glass of tea and took a sip. "Well, it seems I've made everyone more depressed. Should we blame the *tar*? They say it's like water—its tune always takes the shape of the audience's mood."

Shirin tried to hide her tear-streaked cheeks with a tissue, but her trembling voice gave her away. "No, don't blame the poor *tar*. It's us. I guess everyone's just... vulnerable. On edge."

Jav shouted from the other side of the room, "To be precise—we're all fucked up!"

The twins' mother, who was waiting for the right moment to take her boys and leave, raised her eyebrows and coughed politely.

"Well... that's not the word I would use," Shirin said dryly.

"Tonight is Yalda, for God's sake!" Roxy exclaimed. "We've had enough, guys. Leila, darling, play something fun, and I'll sing along. How about that?"

Kamran looked at Roxy admiringly. "Oh, sweetheart—will you?"

Roxy nodded, tilting her head with a coquettish smile. "Yes... well, I've had one of Haydeh's songs in my head all day—*The Love Night*."

"Good choice," Leila said. "But a bit tricky with the *tar*. Sing a bit, and I'll catch the rhythm and join in."

Roxy began to sing.

> *Tonight is a night for love.*
> *We have just this night—for love.*
> *Why don't we leave the story of pain for tomorrow?*

Leila whispered the lyrics, then reached for the *tar* to play—but shrieked the moment her fingers touched the strings and dropped the instrument.

"What is this? Look!" she cried.

Everyone leaned in toward her. The *tar* was wet. The strings were weeping.

Leila stared, struggling for words. "I... I thought my hands were sweaty, but... look!"

"Good God! I thought you'd seen a cockroach!" Babak said, visibly relieved.

Jav leaned forward and grabbed the instrument. "Let me see, young lady." He pointed toward the ceiling. "It might be condensation—hot air from the old *korsi* and the cold weather outside." He gave the *tar* a gentle shake. Drops rolled onto his palms. He shuddered. "Weirdo piece of crap! Can someone turn on the lights? I can't see anything in this bloody candlelight!"

The lights were switched on. He examined the instrument more closely. Surena gave it a try—it was definitely wet.

"Let me see from the other side," Jav said, asking Surena to hold the *tar* by the neck. He bent in, squinting. "Hmm... Let's put it outside in the open air to dry."

Leila quickly grabbed the instrument's case and ran after him. "Not in the ice and snow, though! Be careful, that's a precious instrument—all mulberry wood!"

Banoo sat upright, motionless, as if holding her breath. Her eyes met Giv's, and she gave him a subtle nod.

Understanding the cue, Giv moved to the top shelf, retrieved a box, and handed it to her. It was an old, traditional Isfahani *khatam* box, adorned with intricate geometric patterns.

Banoo gently dusted off the lid and opened it. Inside were slips of paper, small stones, and dried leaves, which she carefully removed—revealing a cloth-wrapped object beneath. She unwrapped it slowly: a small, pale flute.

"I thought it might be interesting for Yalda," Banoo said softly.

Leila leaned in with curiosity. "Is this a flute?"

"Maybe a *ney*?" Babak suggested.

Leila shook her head. "No, it's much shorter than that. A *ney* is at least four times as long."

Banoo held the flute aloft, her voice quiet but certain. "Yes, it's a type of flute. A bone flute—made from bird bone."

"What?" Neda and Pouria asked in unison.

The bird bone passed from hand to hand, each person murmuring something about its delicate craftsmanship.

Jav guffawed. "That odd weeping *tar* wasn't enough—now we've got this antique!"

Mr Kayvon leaned in, his eyes alight with intrigue. "How fascinating. I've read about these. They must be very old. How did you come by it?"

Banoo smiled, shaking her head gently. "It's not as old as you might think. It was made for me when I was in the mountains—maybe fifty years ago, or a little less."

Giv, standing nearby, nodded. "It was right after the big earthquake."

Bijan looked up, surprised. He hadn't heard this story before. His gaze flicked between Banoo and Giv. Banoo met his eyes.

"Your mother knew about it, darling," she said.

Giv nodded again in agreement.

Bijan looked slightly disappointed. With his love of music, he was surprised they'd never shown him the instrument.

Across the room, Parto didn't notice Hooman watching her. Her eyes lingered on the bird bone, lost in thought. Her mind drifted back to a lecture she had once heard in which the professor had shown images of some of the oldest known wind instruments made from perforated bird bones. He spoke of the uncanny parallels between human arms and bird wings—so different in purpose, yet so similar beneath the surface. Both shared the same bone structures in their forelimbs, evolved for different functions.

Bird bones, she remembered, were remarkably light. Their inner cavities hollowed out to make flight possible—perfect for transforming into flutes. Primitive, yes, but powerful. In some ancient cultures, they were believed to hold mystical properties. Blowing air through the hollow bones, people believed, could summon the spirits of the dead, awaken ancestral memories, and connect the living with a long-forgotten past.

As the flute came back to Banoo, she carefully extended it toward Leila and said, "Leila-jan, would you like to give it a try?"

Leila took the flute in her hands—and began to play.

FEREYDOUN

The doorbell rang. Bijan said, "I'll get it." Banoo's face beamed as she hurried after Bijan to the door.

A refined-looking man with two small dogs appeared out of the mist at the entrance. Carrying a small travelling bag, he seemed to have arrived from a distant place. The dogs darted inside, leaving a trail of snow behind them in the hallway. He called to them and laughed apologetically at the mess.

His deep-set eyes gave him an air of intensity. He had dark hair, a neatly styled moustache, and wore an elegant black raincoat with a matching tie.

He held Banoo's hands and kissed them respectfully. Giv arrived to greet him, and they embraced for a long moment. Bijan watched with a polite smile, recognizing the man's face but unable to place where they had met.

The dogs barked at Persis. The cat bristled but then settled by the clock. When Persis hissed, the dogs quickly retreated to their owner.

Bijan crouched to pet the dogs and asked their breed.

"That little devil, the white one, is a German Spitz, and the grey one's a Poodle," their owner explained.

The noise of the dogs and the late arrival of the surprise guest piqued everyone's curiosity. Atossa snuck a peek at the hallway and reported in a low voice to the rest of the curious faces. "It's a guy and two puppies; he looks like someone..." She craned her neck for another look. "He has an Omar Sharif kind of face! Oh no! Wait... maybe Queen."

"The Queen? I heard a male voice!" Hooman said.

"Duh, Hooman! I meant the singer. Freddie Mercury!"

Banoo and the guest entered the *korsi* room, hand in hand. "We have a very special guest who's travelled a long way to see us," she announced, pausing with a broad smile before adding, "No need for further introduction: Fereydoun Farrokhzad!"[12]

The room fell into a rigid silence, too flabbergasted to speak.

Fereydoun strode confidently to the centre of the room, radiating the poise of a showman. "Thank you, Banoo-jan, and happy Yalda to all of you. Tonight, I'm here as a storyteller to help make this long, frosty night a little shorter." Everyone stared at him in stunned silence. Finally, Atossa plucked up her courage and said politely, "Well, excuse me, but we thought... we thought... how do I put this...?" She paused and glanced at Banoo quizzically. "This is a joke, isn't it?" Banoo's face was motionless.

Atossa looked back at Fereydoun and said, "But... we thought that you were dead!"

Fereydoun guffawed. "Don't worry, that's fine. What's your name, darling?"

"Atossa."

"Atossa. Beautiful. I love your *Faravahar* necklace."

Atossa smiled and put her hands on her pendant.

Fereydoun continued, "I knew this question might come up tonight! So yes, everyone thought I died—but, in fact, I didn't!"

The questions came pouring in. Guests, now emboldened, asked about the story of his "murder" in Bonn and where he had been since.

Fereydoun remained remarkably calm as he replied, "Alright, alright. I can't deny it—I thought I was dying too when those criminals stabbed me. It was brutal, excruciating; there was blood everywhere. I honestly believed that was it—that *this* is how someone dies.

"But here's the thing: there's no such thing as 'dying.' You just adjust to a different level of being."

Kamran raised an eyebrow. "As simple as that?"

Fereydoun nodded. "Yes, exactly. As simple as that!"

Kamran frowned more deeply and then, with a wry smile, turned his head slightly away. "Well, that's funny. It reminds me of the ghost stories I used to tell my son when he was little."

Jav chimed in, "Try harder man!" Then, grinning, he added, "It's Yalda, not Halloween—but what could be better than a ghost story on a night like this, complete with a proper chill?"

With that, he walked to the wall and switched off the light.

The room plunged into darkness, and some of the guests let out startled screams. Neda felt the warmth of Surena's arms wrapping protectively around her.

"Please, switch it back on," Banoo requested softly.

Jav flipped the lights back on and chuckled. "Oh, I didn't mean to scare anyone!"

Fereydoun remained unfazed. "Don't worry," he said with a quiet smile. "Whether the light's on or off, it's still dark in here. Can't you see?"

He turned away from the guests and walked toward the small window at the far end of the room. Gently wiping the mist from the old glass, he leaned forward to peer through the tiny circle of clarity. His posture sagged, his head lowered onto his shoulders, and he hummed a solemn tune.

> *Even such made me that beast without peace,*
> *Which, coming on against me by degrees,*
> *Thrust me back thither*
> *Where the sun is silent...*
> *Where the sun is silent...*
> *Where the sun is silent...* [13]

As if shaking off the weight of the moment, he glanced back at the guests. His eyes flickered over the faces in the room—confused, suspicious, yet intrigued. Then, offering a knowing smile, he spoke.

"After it happened to me, I couldn't help but wonder: why do we make such a big fuss about death, really? Everything is complicated *and* simple—both, at once.

"If we think of death as a mystery, then isn't birth just as mysterious? Maybe even more so."

He paused, then placed a hand over his stomach, eyes widening with a playful expression. His strong jawline caught the candlelight, made sharper by his smile.

"Imagine something growing inside you—completely unknown. We have no idea where that soul comes from. But do we question it? Do we fear it? No.

"We don't—because we *think* we have control. We can see it, hear it, feel it. And, honestly, babies *are* adorable, aren't they?

"But that's the thing: we rely too much on what we can sense. And anything beyond that... unsettles us."

His tone shifted, growing more serious. "Death is tragic—not because it's more mysterious than birth, but because we can no longer perceive the person. And let's face it: people aren't cute when they die. "He paused, then added with a wry smile, "Trust me, I know from experience."

A few nervous chuckles flickered around the room.

"But here's the thing: if we could somehow take our *senses* out of the equation, we'd see that birth and death are two sides of the same coin. The end meets the beginning—seamlessly, in their own time."

A wave of murmurs rippled through the room.

Pouria turned toward his brother and mouthed a word. Surena, seated beside Neda, caught it from across the room. He frowned, puzzled, and whispered, "Ghost?"

Their mother, noticing the exchange, gave them a knowing wink—then silently mouthed back: *"No. Game."*

Suddenly, Hooman—who had been listening intently—raised his hand and asked, "Hang on a minute. If that's true, then how do *we* see you? As far as I know, we haven't changed our level of being... have we?"

"Good question!" Fereydoun said, his eyes lighting up. "Well, the best way I can explain it is by telling you a story."

A hush fell over the room.

"The story I want to tell is *Sir Orfeo*—a beautiful medieval poem, inspired by the Greek myth of Orpheus and the Underworld... or, in this case, the Land of the Fairies."

He paused, then laughed softly and continued,

"In the poem, the princess Heurodis falls asleep in a garden beneath a tree and dreams that she'll be stolen away by the King of the Fairies the next day. Terrified, she tells her husband, King Orfeo. He surrounds her with armed knights, determined to protect her. But they can't stop what's coming. Despite every effort, she slips away—crossing into a land beyond mortal reach—and vanishes.

"Grief-stricken, Orfeo abandons his crown and riches, retreating to the wilderness. There, he plays his harp, pouring his heart into his music, and it becomes his key to unlocking the supernatural. His music is so powerful that it can move mountains.

"For many years, Orfeo lives in solitude, his beard growing long and tangled. Then, one day, he watches a hunting party pass through the forest, led by the King of the Fairies. Sixty ladies, falcons perched on their wrists, ride by. As he watches the falcons, Orfeo smiles, remembering his past life and love of falconry. Drawn by the sight, he walks toward the women. And there, among them, he sees his wife.

"In that moment, Orfeo realizes that he has finally crossed into the Otherworld. He plays his harp for the Fairy King, who, moved by the music, agrees to release Heurodis. After a poignant reunion, Orfeo is granted permission to bring her back to the mortal realm. But there's a catch: he must not look at her for the entire journey home.

"He follows the rule and returns to his kingdom, where he is restored to his throne. He regains his power and wealth, and his people rejoice in his return. Heurodis also returns to the mortal realm with him, and they live out their days in peace and happiness."

He smiled. "Nice ending, isn't it?"

His expression then turned serious.

"So, the reason I share this myth with you is this: the Otherworld isn't some distant, hidden place deep underground or up in the sky. It's a parallel realm, right beside you. Things can slip between the boundaries, crossing from one world to the other. Just as Orfeo entered the Otherworld with nothing but the music of his harp, tonight, the *tar* wept with sorrow for your souls, and the melody of the flute pulled me into this place."

He paused, his voice softening. "I love music—always have, deeply. There's a power in it that transcends the boundaries of our worlds. Believe me, it touches the unseen and reaches beyond the ordinary. Through music, I have reached you. And now, through music, you can see me!"

Hooman still didn't look convinced. He wanted to say something to Fereydoun, but his lips wouldn't move. Instead, he kept his eyes fixed on the floor.

Parto sat just behind him, as puzzled as everyone else, but her thoughts lingered on Hooman. She watched him run his fingers along the back of his neck—that familiar gesture spoke volumes. His hair had turned grey, and lines now marked his face. Yet despite all these changes, that small habit had remained unchanged. It was the same gesture he used when searching for the perfect word in a poem, or when startled or deep in thought.

That simple, unchanged detail brought a warmth to Parto's heart. As she listened to the tale of *Sir Orfeo*, a fleeting thought crossed her mind. For a moment, she longed for an Otherworld of their own, where playing a song could transport them to something beyond what they had—something more than the life they had created and the reality they now faced.

Roxy giggled, as if to reassure herself, and gave a playful glance at Banoo and Bijan in turn. Tilting her head to one side, she flashed a cheeky smile and asked, "Come on, guys, what's going on? This feels a bit mischievous, doesn't it? Is this some kind of murder mystery game? If it's not, then I'm afraid it's all far too complicated for me."

Bijan shrugged innocently, as if he were just as puzzled, and Banoo simply smiled.

Mr Kayvon reached over and gently held Gitti's hand, offering her a sense of reassurance; she seemed anxious and clearly wasn't enjoying the encounter.

Sitting cross-legged on the floor, Dara straightened his back, clasped his hands in his lap, and spoke up. "No offence, but I have to agree with Roxy. This is either some kind of entertainment for the night—sorry, again, no offence—or it's just way too complicated. The story you're telling..." He trailed off, then looked at Babak, gauging his reaction. Babak nodded slightly, confirming Dara's words.

Fereydoun's voice remained steady and confident as he explained further, "Your logic relies on the idea of change—and I understand that. But change is the only certain thing in the world: the fundamental nature of the universe, the framework for everything else. It's a law."

"Our universe is sustained by it. Everything—down to the atoms—is in a constant state of transformation. Every second. That's the principle the universe follows. It's not optional. It's non-negotiable.

"So, even though I have died, the law of constant change allows for this: for me to be both dead *and* not dead at the same time. Does that make sense?"

Kamran couldn't stay still. He walked from one corner of the room to the other, his hands clasped tightly behind his back. "So, suppose it does. But what's the point then? Are we doomed to just repeat and repeat?"

Fereydoun smiled gently,

"No, it's not as boring as it sounds, my friend! Change is only the backdrop for the scene, the stage upon which everything unfolds. But the real work—the true challenge—is yours! You must weave the story. You must conjure up a world for yourself to live inside, with all its senses, sounds, smells, tastes, movements, and objects. Just as a writer brings characters to life through imagination, you are the creator; you shape it all."

"You are the storytellers, the architects of your own existence. You hold the power to craft whatever world you wish. You can travel to anywhere, anytime—past, present, future—it is all within your reach."

"You mean...time travel then?" Pouria asked.

"You've watched too many movies!" Fereydoun chuckled. "No, I mean that you have the power to choose and shape the road you want to travel right now, in the present."

He leaned forward slightly, and lowered his voice. "The past and future exist simultaneously, but only the present gives them meaning. And the present, my friend, is shaped by your feelings."

"But how come I remember the past but not the future?" Pouria asked.

"Ah, that too falls under the same law—the law of change," Fereydoun replied. "To form a memory, you must have passed through change. That's what makes the past visible to you."

He paused, letting the room settle into silence before continuing.

"But just because you don't remember something, doesn't mean it hasn't happened—or won't happen. You meet your future constantly, moment by moment. It's already there... just remains unknown to you until you live it."

Ayda looked at her mother. They'd sat in silence since arriving, but now she leaned forward and directing a question at Fereydoun , "So... did you choose to be murdered?"

Fereydoun nodded, a hint of a smile on his lips. "Yes, I did. I've always loved a mantra from Zoroaster: 'Happiness comes to those who bring happiness to others.' I kept it pinned to my work desk. And yes, I wanted to be a source of happiness, no matter the cost. I wanted to sing, play music, speak the truth. It seemed like a wise decision. As you can see, I'm still living in your happiness—whenever you listen to my songs." He winked, his voice edged with humour. "And I always knew—in our society, the living hero never lasts. So, to be remembered, I had to be... well, dead."

Ayda caught a flicker of relief in her mother's face—as if the thought that her brother might still exist, even after death, offered a strange kind of comfort.

A ripple passed through the room. The mood shifted—from horror to something quieter. Something like wonder.

Persis strolled into the *korsi* room with calm indifference, made a bee-line for Banoo's lap, where she settled comfortably. The two dogs, having busied themselves sniffing around the house, stood patiently by the door, tails wagging eagerly. Fereydoun rose and opened the door, releasing them into the garden. The dogs shot out like arrows into the snow, weaving wild circles around the cedar tree, their joyful barks ringing clear in the crisp air.

When Fereydoun returned, he crouched down and gave the cat an affectionate rub. "Happy now that I let them out?" he asked with a grin.

Parto asked, "Have you always had dogs?"

Fereydoun smiled warmly. "Yes, I've always loved them. They're loyal in a way most people aren't—and they bring so much joy."

Mr Kayvon nodded slowly.

"Back in ancient Iran—in Zoroastrian times—dogs were seen as noble, even sacred. They were part of the family. Hurting a dog? That was serious. Like, almost the same as hurting a person. You could be severely punished, even damned for it. It's sad how far we've strayed. We've really forgotten our good manners..."

Dara let out a sigh. "Now it's just barbaric. People have to sneak their dogs into Babak's clinic."

Babak nodded.

"It's senseless. I don't get where all that hate for the poor animal comes from."

Mr Kayvon's face darkened. "Awful," he murmured, then looked at

Fereydoun. "But here we are, son... Sometimes I wish I'd died years ago..."

Gitti, looking concerned, gently touched her husband's hand and said softly, "Don't, Kayvon. Please... don't say that."

But his eyes stayed locked on Fereydoun as he said, "When you were with us—in the '90s—Iran was already in trouble. A land of shadows. But you wouldn't believe what's happened since... Could you have seen this coming? The corruption, the abuse, the killings, the wars... If, like you said, we're the storytellers, then look at the story we've told. A dark one. A tragedy we, the people of Iran, have woven with our own hands."

A long silence followed.

Fereydoun looked down for a moment, then back up. "Let me ask you something: why don't elephants in India break free? As babies, they're tired and struggle until they give up. When they're grown, the same weak rope holds them—but they never try to escape. They're trapped by belief, not by strength. That rope? It's like dogmatic religion—strong enough to hold us long after we've grown strong enough to be free."

Kamran spoke up. "I think we *do* want to break free. The problem is—like in chess zugzwang—there's no good move. Any move we make leads to checkmate."

Sam leaned on the door, hands on his head. "We're numb—like frogs slowly boiled alive."

Ava sighed, rolling her eyes. She wished he'd shut up for the night.

Shirin jumped to Ava's defense. "Numb, frog? Not me, Sam. I'd rather feel the heat than go numb—no matter how hard they try to boil us."

Atossa, who usually had something to say, sat in silence, lost in thought. Something clicked—Fereydoun wasn't just a lookalike of Omar Sharif or Freddie Mercury. He was the same man she'd seen earlier, feeding birds near Nana Khanoom's house, in the same raincoat, with the same dogs. She kept this to herself, unsure what it meant. Her thoughts shattered when Fereydoun's voice cut through the quiet.

"Let's pause the politics," Fereydoun said warmly. "I'm here to listen, share stories, and above all, to sing. To bring hope—hope for today, for tomorrow, and for a better future for our children and theirs."

Parto felt a rare kindness in his voice, a fading warmth from a forgotten Iran.

Turning to the crowd, Fereydoun asked, "What's your favourite song?" Without hesitation, they called out, "Sad Easterner!"

Leila leaned over to Jav. "Hey, could you bring the *tar*, please?" He handed it to her with a faint look of reluctance. She plucked a string, studied it for a moment, then quickly tuned it. Across the room, Banoo tapped the *daf*'s skin in rhythm, while Bijan lifted the bone flute and tested a note. Then Fereydoun's voice rose above the chatter—and suddenly, the room bloomed with music.

You, Sad Easterner!
You're like a mountain of light,
Don't let our sun fade away.
You're as pure as the morning,
And as proud as the sea.
Don't let the silence grow stronger.

As the music faded, his final line—"Don't let the silence grow stronger"—hung in the air, stirring a deep, unspoken bond between them all.

Gohar was the first to speak, her voice trembling with emotion. Tears streamed down her cheeks, untouched. "Thank you, Fereydoun, for reminding us we can no longer stay silent." Banoo gently took Gohar's hand, sensing her thoughts drifting, as always, to her missing son. "You didn't stay silent. My son didn't. Both live on within us."

Ayda's voice cracked, heavy with longing. She clutched her fist to her chest. "So many want to fight... if only we had a leader."

Surena shook his head, with a sharp bitterness in his voice: "A leader? I wish. But who would dare captain this wreck? This sinking ship?"

ARMAGEDDON

Armageddon: (a) the last battle between good and evil before the Day of Judgment (as described in the Bible); (b) Any dramatic, final, or catastrophic conflict—especially one likely to destroy the world or the human race, such as a nuclear war; in short, the end of the world. The word originates from the Hebrew term Har Megiddo, *meaning "Mountain of Megiddo." Megiddo refers to an ancient city, located about thirty kilometres southeast of Haifa. It was strategically situated on a key route between Egypt and Syria and had been the site of numerous historical battles.*

'SINKING SHIP…" BIJAN murmured, resting his chin in his hand as he stared at Surena. The term had a percussive effect—it struck him like a physical blow.

Iran—once a land of promise and beauty—had fallen apart. Paradise lost, swallowed by the pandemonium that had devoured everything. The madness had dragged on for years, but to Bijan, *'sinking ship'* felt like the most fitting description. It wasn't just chaos anymore— it was something even worse: a crushing finality.

The metaphor marked the end of an era—an era beyond salvation. There had been no turning back for a long time—not just for Iran, but for the entire region. Everything now felt beyond rescue.

It was the end.

He let out a heavy sigh. "What I don't get," Bijan said, almost to himself, "is how we let this happen. How did it sneak up on us like this? When did everything go so wrong—and become irreversible?"

"Metamorphosis!" Shirin burst out, leaning forward suddenly. She pressed her fingertips to her forehead. "Metamorphosis, that's what it was! Little by little, year after year—they turned us into *this*!"

Jav nodded vigorously. "Yes, exactly! We've been turned from human to…" He crouched down suddenly, crawling on all fours and braying like a donkey: "Hee-haw! Hee-haw!"

"Stop!" Shirin cried, her voice trembling with frustration. "This isn't funny at all. Don't you realise…?"

Jav got back on his feet and said, "What's the matter? I just showed what you said. Everyone's being super-sensitive tonight!"

Fereydoun listened , head bowed, stroking Persis in his lap.

Neda's voice shook as she spoke. "We're desperate for change. We're fighting for it—really fighting. But it feels like we're just wasting our time... like screaming into a void." She curled her hands into fists, slowly tightening them, as if trying to squeeze her frustration and fear into something solid. Then she continued, "And that dream... I've been having this recurring nightmare. It haunts me. Every time it comes back, it leaves me anxious. But last night... last night was different. God, it felt so vivid. So real." She paused, catching her breath, struggling to steady herself.

"I dreamt I was running through a barren wasteland. The ground was frozen, coated in frost. It was bitterly cold. And I felt this overwhelming urgency to run—like something was chasing me."

Then I saw a black mare gallop past. She was heavily pregnant—and somehow, I could see inside her, like her womb was transparent. She was carrying twins.

The mare stopped and lay down in front of me, ready to give birth—but she was struggling. I wanted to help her, but I didn't know how. I felt helpless.

Then, without thinking, I put my fingers in my mouth, like I was trying to make myself throw up. Somehow, I believed that if I made my own body contract, it would help her.

And it did.

She gave birth—first to a perfect filly, who stood up right away. She was strong. Alive.

Then came the second foal. It didn't move.

When I looked closer, I saw the umbilical cord had twisted into a noose around its neck. It was choking. I panicked and started running again.

And that's when I woke up."

Neda paused, her chest rising and falling with heavy breaths. Atossa quickly crossed the room, gently placing a hand on Neda's shoulder.

"Sorry," Neda said, her voice steadying, though her eyes remained distant. "I'm fine. It's just... the whole dream unsettles me. And today, when I was running from the IRGC forces, it felt like I was right back in that nightmare. Like no matter how fast I ran, I couldn't escape."

At the mention of the IRGC, a silence fell over the room. Surena and Pouria exchanged glances —surprised by her words.

Atossa leaned in and hugged her. "Ah, darling Neda... but you made it, didn't you? You're safe now. With friends, Neda-jan. You're with friends."

Hooman shifted slightly and gave her a quiet, reassuring thumbs-up.

Ayda stepped forward, "Neda is right, I have been having nightmares too. Mine are always about drowning..." She paused, swallowed hard "It is suffocating. We scream, but our voices are scattered, fading into the dark."

Fereydoun set Persis down and stood.

"Listen, brave daughters of Iran," he said firmly.

"The two worlds—the divine and the dreadful—may seem apart, like the radiant filly and the lifeless foal in Neda's dream. But they aren't. They're bound together, held in the same womb.

Our motherland is in labour, gasping with pain and contractions before you. It's up to you to help her deliver. The reins are in your hands. You have a choice."

Pouria's frustration broke through his calm. "I wish this was our choice." His eyes flicked toward his mother. "What our parents did..." He paused. "I'm not blaming them, exactly. But their generation—that wasn't our decision." Surena spoke up quickly. "If it were, we'd have fixed it by now." Their mother's gaze lingered on them and said, "There's little hope for young people today. Not much they can do. Otherwise, it's the same tragic story and nothing ever changes." She glanced at Gohar and Ayda sheepishly, then fell silent.

"You mean the danger of protesting?" Neda asked. The twins' mother nodded slowly.

"It's worse when you're afraid," Ayda said. "The snakes look deadlier if you try to run."

Neda nodded. "You have to face the fear... but it's hard. I know. If only I could stop running and stand still."

"But darling, you don't have to," Roxy said gently. "You shouldn't have to pay for the mistakes our generation made... it's not fair."

"Rox, that's true," Kami replied. "But who else? Us? Fine, us... At this stage, we don't have much left to lose—generally speaking. But the future belongs to the young—"

His words were cut off by Jav's sharp voice. "Alright, enough! Let's sort this out. Two groups: the 'honourable old farts'—you lot get a spot on one side. We'll hand you industrial-grade mops to clean up four decades of shit from the Islamic Republic. The rest of you? Stand on the other side and enjoy the show. I'll be the referee. Fair?"

Some chuckled, but Sam, still at the door with his head in his hands, groaned, "You don't get it. We're dead already. Walking corpses. We can't change a thing."

"Come on, guys, we can't think like that!" Shirin said firmly. "No matter our age or ethnicity—Kurd, Gilak, Arab, Turk—we all live in this country. Even if we're outside its borders, if we're Iranian, we're responsible. Right? Or should we wait for some foreign power to rescue us? And then... you know what would happen."

Shirin's words struck Parto deeply, stirring guilt. She'd done so little—just a few scattered protests, liking posts on Instagram. It all felt distant, disconnected from the real fight. Then the dream came—vivid and urgent—pushing her to return to Iran, to find Mithra. But who—or what—was Mithra? A person? An ideal? A philosophy? A leader? The questions echoed unanswered.

Parto took a deep breath, turned to Fereydoun, and asked, "Is there any hope—any path we haven't tried? Do you know anyone who could bring us together? Someone to lead us?"

Her question hung in the air. Hooman stared, wide-eyed, caught off guard.

Fereydoun's face lit up with a smile. "Yes," he said confidently. "I believe I do."

"Why didn't you tell us before?"

"Because you never asked. If you want something, you have to ask."

The room fell silent, thick with anticipation. Every eye was on Fereydoun. Breath held. Waiting.

"Only if you're truly ready," Fereydoun said.

A chorus of voices rose in agreement.

Bijan, flushed with excitement, called out, "Of course—we couldn't be more ready."

Fereydoun's smile deepened, but his tone grew serious. "Good. I ask this because there's something you must consider. You must understand—there's a journey ahead. A journey to find your leader. This is non-negotiable."

Questions flooded in. Where would they go? How long would it take? Was the leader inside the country, or outside? Was it a man or a woman?

Fereydoun raised a hand, silencing them. "Listen—there's no time to answer everything now. Like every great journey, this one has a guide."

His eyes flicked toward Banoo, a brief, knowing glance passing between them as if they shared a secret only they understood.

"Now, it's time to meet your guide. Trust me, all your questions will be answered soon." Fereydoun's eyes gleamed. "In the over thirty years I was away; I met many remarkable people—one of them is Huma. An extraordinary one."

Surena's voice cut in, sharp and wary. "Is he dead too?"

Fereydoun chuckled. "Huma is neither he, nor dead!"

Atossa interrupted happily, "So Huma is a woman? I love the idea of a female guide!"

Fereydoun laughed again. "Sorry to disappoint, but Huma is neither man nor woman. In our Persian tradition, beings like Huma don't fit into gender categories. Huma isn't bound by 'he' or 'she.' It's like our language—Persian doesn't distinguish gender; everything is simply 'it.'"

Mr Kayvon, who had been listening closely, finally spoke. "Language reflects the mind. In a true Persian mindset, everything is equal—we don't make those divisions. I've read about Huma in several texts. Huma has never been seen as a gendered figure, but rather as a protector and guide—an embodiment of something greater than individual identity."

Fereydoun nodded firmly. "Exactly."

Surena's eyes narrowed with curiosity. "Did you say it's not dead?"

"No—not the kind of death you imagine," Fereydoun said. "Huma is part of the cycle. It burns in flames at the end of each era, only to rise again reborn from the ashes." His strange words hung in the air, leaving everyone reaching for meaning. Was he joking? Or revealing a truth too heavy to accept?

The silence broke into uneasy whispers—still raw from meeting him. Nervous chuckles followed, half incredulous, half uncertain. The moment felt suspended in a Yalda legend—part ceremony, part warning, with the chill of a deeper truth lurking just out of reach. For Bijan, the phrase "end of the era" landed like a cold slap. So that was it. *The end.*

Breaking the tension, Fereydoun lifted the bone flute and turned to Leila. "Will you play something for us?" His voice was soft, carrying a quiet weight—like a secret waiting to be unlocked.

[163]

NOTES

1   There is a Persian root parallel to "demon" in the word div, which descends from daēva. In both Greek and Persian, the words daimon and daēva originally referred to divine powers or gods but gradually came to mean fiends or demons over time.

2   A "Tree of Life" carpet is a type of rug or textile design that typically features a central motif of a tree, symbolizing the interconnectedness of life, growth, and nature. In Persian and other Middle Eastern carpet traditions, the Tree of Life motif is deeply symbolic, representing the cycle of life, the universe, and the harmony between the spiritual and physical worlds.

3   Allameh Ali-Akbar Dehkhodâ was a prominent Iranian literary writer, philologist, and lexicographer. He was the author of the Dehkhoda Dictionary, the most extensive dictionary of the Persian language published to date.

4   Chovgan: An ancient Persian equestrian sport, considered the precursor to modern polo.

5   A long-necked string instrument

6   دی in Farsi, pronounced day.

7   Tus (also spelled Tous or Toos) is an ancient city located in the northeast of Iran, in the Khorasan province, near the modern city of Mashhad. It is renowned as the birthplace of the epic Persian poet Ferdowsi, author of the *Shahnameh*. It played a crucial role along the Silk Road before suffering extensive damage during the Mongol invasions in the 13th century.

8   *Peganum harmala*, or Syrian rue, is a perennial herb from the Nitrariaceae family, traditionally used in medicine and rituals throughout the Middle East, North Africa, and Central Asia.

9   By Forugh Farrokhzad, taken from *The Fall of Heaven: The Pahlavis and the Final Days of Imperial Iran* by Andrew Scott Cooper (New York: Henry Holt and Co., 2016).

10   The Hijrah ("the migration") refers to the Prophet Muhammad's pivotal emigration from Mecca to Medina in 622 CE. This event marks the starting point for all Islamic calendars, including the Hijri Shamsi (Solar Hijri) calendar used officially in Iran and Afghanistan.

11   The name Bonyad is an abbreviation of Bonyad-e Mostazafan va Janbazan, which translates to the Foundation of the Oppressed and Disabled (or Wounded Veteran).

12   Fereydoun Farrokhzad (October 7, 1936 – August 7, 1992) was an Iranian showman, poet, actor, singer, and political activist. Following the 1979 Islamic Revolution, he was forced into exile in Germany. In 1992, he was brutally murdered in what is widely believed to have been a politically motivated assassination, likely orchestrated by the Islamic Republic.

13   Dante Alighieri, *The Divine Comedy*: Inferno, Canto I, translated by Henry Wadsworth Longfellow (1867).

METAMORPHOSIS

Just when the caterpillar thought the world
was over, it became a butterfly

CHUANG TZU

HUMA

Assembly of birds, the Hoopoe spoke,
I am the Messenger Bird
For the Visible and the Invisible.
— Attar, *The Conference of the Birds* [1]

THE DOORBELl rang, and Fereydoun went to answer it, Banoo and Giv trailing close behind as everyone stared in apprehension toward the hallway.

Like a bolt of lightning, a lithe figure burst into the *korsi* room, wearing a flamboyant hat and a robe of orange, brown, and black, darting across the floor like autumn leaves swirling in the wind. A face of undeniable allure emerged from the shadow—high cheekbones, a sharp nose, and large, expressive eyes.

Fereydoun was struggling to keep pace behind. "Ah! You're still too fast for me, Huma!" he chuckled.

"Happy Yalda, dazzling revellers of the solstice!" the new arrival cried out in a high, operatic voice that could fill the heavens, and then turned to Fereydoun.

"Indeed, I am fast—always on the move, ever traveling. Don't forget it! These endless cycles of resurrection and rebirth demand immense energy, but each journey only strengthens me. This time, I was in Shiraz when your call reached me—clear and profound, echoing through the longest night, drawing me back to fulfil my duty once more."

Hooman leaned toward Atossa and whispered, "So this one... who comes to mind?"

Atossa's eyes flicked to the stranger, taking in the sharp cheekbones, the striking eyes, the aura that seemed both alien and magnetic. *"David Bowie?"* she murmured. "That kind of face..."

Hooman raised his eyebrows. "Come on, Atoss! This is a woman—one hundred percent!"

Atossa, amused, pressed a finger to her lips, signalling for silence.

On the other side of the room, Kamran squeezed Roxy's hand and whispered in her ear, "Sent by the US?"

"A spy... you serious?" Roxy replied, half-laughing.

"Shhh... perhaps! Let's see," Kamran said. "But this may be a good sign, Rox. Perhaps someone is finally doing something!"

Roxy shrugged.

Huma studied the audience, sweeping over their uncertain faces. "Don't look at me with those shocked eyes!" she said. "You encounter far stranger things every day and simply look away, pretending it's nothing—don't you?"

She turned back to Fereydoun. "This lot doesn't seem too enthusiastic for the journey ahead."

Then, sensing they needed more than just a rebuke, she spoke in a tone that was softer, calmer, yet carried the weight of time and experience. "Listen! I have travelled through history, across many lands—always serving as the unwavering messenger, a role I have carried since the time of King Solomon and the Queen of Sheba.

"I journeyed from Yemen to the Levant—it was I who brought Solomon the news of the Queen and her people, revealing that they worshipped the sun, and that this was the secret behind their prosperity in that distant land.

"I was loyal then, and I remain so. The message stays with me—always safe, always carried."

Fereydoun, observing the scene with a quiet intensity, said, "I believe the group is simply lost... just a little confused?".

"Ah, is that the reason?" Huma said. "Allow me to see... there may be just the thing to guide this company from the shadows of forgetfulness, to remind each one of who they once were."

With a fluid, elegant motion, Huma reached beneath the thick robe, rummaging for a moment before emerging with a large, ornate pitcher whose intricate design caught the faint light, glimmering with an otherworldly allure, raising it high and declaring, "This is it—the elixir that will awaken the heart, soothe the soul, and induce love: the wine of Shiraz!"

After Giv poured wine for everyone, Huma's eyes sparkled as the glass was raised. "Shiraz gave birth to this wine, but it's you who give it soul. Here's to our journey! *Salamati, Saḥtik, Sağ ol, Ser çavan!*"

Fereydoun smiled, a familiar glint in his eye. "Some things never change," he said.

He glanced around the room with a nod toward Huma. "Still speaks every language she's ever touched."

A ripple of warm laughter passed through the group.

"Well, just a few from the map of Iran—Farsi, Arabic, Azari, Kurdish. All cousins to *sante, saluti*... even Armenian—*urakhut'yun*. Different words, same wish: to your health."

Kamran leaned close to Roxy and whispered, "What did I tell you? The guy is probably ex-intelligence. No one just picks up that many languages."

Roxy stifled a grin.

Huma began to speak again. "In Iran, with all our many dialects, the wine of Shiraz is our shared language—a timeless voice that rises from the soil we all call home."

Glasses were raised, and a quiet warmth spread through the room as each guest lingered over the Shiraz wine.

Leila lifted her glass, closed her eyes, and took a long inhale. "Wow... that's something else."

Hooman leaned in, swirling his wine as if it were a puzzle. "Huh... interesting. Peculiar, even... Wait—I know this. I've smelled it before... I'm having a Proustian moment!" He rubbed the back of his neck, eyes narrowing as he hunted the memory.

Leila took a slow sip, tilting her head. "It's carnal, isn't it? Full-bodied, velvety... like a spoonful of pomegranate molasses." Her mischievous smile hung in the air, while Hooman sank into the memory the wine had stirred in him, as if the flavour itself were alive and just out of reach.

Across the room, Parto watched them from the corner of her eye. There was something in the ease between Leila and Hooman that unsettled her. She turned back to her wine glass, drawing in a slow breath, but for Parto the experience was different—certain words always unlocked distinct flavours or fragrances in her mind.

Shiraz was one of them. It brought the scent of narcissus to her senses—sweet, heady, almost overwhelming. She couldn't tell whether the aroma came from the wine... or from her own thoughts.

Bijan, still admiring the ornate pitcher, took a slow, deliberate sip. "Crisp at first..." His eyes closed. "Then it lingers. Plum, dark fruit... something deeper, Complex—layers unfolding like a story in my mouth."

Kamran took a sip and grinned. "What an opulent taste! Try it, Rox!" Then he turned to Huma with sudden certainty. "Californian Shiraz?"

"No," came the firm reply. "This is different. It's made in Shiraz—the last case from Khollar."

"Khollar?" several voices echoed, intrigued.

Huma nodded. "Yes. A small village near Shiraz, where the roots of this wine's legacy still run deep."

Apart from Banoo and Giv, who shared a knowing look, the others looked puzzled. A few exchanged sceptical glances.

Roxy spoke up. "Never heard of it."

Huma sighed. "Not surprising. Khollar today is unrecognisable. When I picked up this bottle, it looked like a war zone—just rubble. The life that thrived there for a thousand years, going back to the time of Jamshid, is gone. All of it. Just within the last generation of the Islamic Revolution. What used to be a vibrant town is now cut off, swept away by waves of political and social upheaval. The vineyards that once flourished? All dried up. Turned to dust. Desert. This... this is the only bottle that survived. And I brought it for you."

Mr. Kayvon nodded thoughtfully. "I've read about the origins of wine—fascinating stuff. Some say it began in the Caucasus—Georgia, Armenia, even parts of Iran. And Shiraz is often mentioned in the early traditions. But you mentioned Jamshid—now I'm curious. What's that story?"

Huma smiled. "According to legend, the roots of wine trace back to Khollar. The story credits Jamshid, one of Iran's ancient kings, with its discovery. It's said his wife fell seriously ill—and then made a miraculous recovery after drinking a fermented liquid. Grapes that had fallen into ditches during a storm had fermented on their own. She drank the liquid, and it healed her. "Astonished, Jamshid brought settlers to that very place, and it's believed they founded Khollar. He even built a dam to support agriculture and winemaking—some believe that site is the famous Dasht-e-Murghab[2]."

While Mr Kayvon kept chatting with Huma about history, the rest of the group gathered in clusters, sipping the wine and engaging in animated conversation. Roxy made here way over to Babak, Atossa, Dara and a few others and whispered conspiratorially: "We think this whole thing's a setup—and that Huma's been sent by foreign forces. Kami's convinced Huma is a US agent!"

"Hallelujah!" Atossa grinned, rubbing her hands together.

Dara's eyes sparkled. "Oh, you can totally tell by the accent. It's like a foreign accent, you know? 'Happy Yalda' sounds kind of like the hip-hip-hooray that English speakers say."

The Twins' mother, grinning knowingly, jumped in. "I thought the same! Maybe Israeli, right? That face... I mean, the nose..."

"No matter where Huma's from," Ava said with a dramatic flourish, "even if it's another planet at this point, as long as she gets us out of this mess, I'm all in!"

Roxy dropped her voice to a mock-serious tone. "And let's not forget—who in Iran wears a mohawk? That's just... weird."

"Oh my God, yes!" Atossa gasped. "I thought it was a hat at first!"

"Me too!" Ava said.

"Not male or female, like Fereydoun said earlier—that was pretty odd, huh?" Dara added, raising an eyebrow.

Babak nodded. "But it's clever—a disguise tactic. Well done, Kami, you're a genius!"

Roxy puffed up with pride. "Yep! He's brilliant at this kind of stuff—reads tons of spy novels," she giggled.

Kami's face grew serious as he spoke. "But," he paused and looked at their faces with conviction, "we must not tell Bijan about this. As the host, he should have been involved! He pretends and keeps insisting that he's never met Fereydoun and Huma. Nonsense! Especially when Banoo and Giv seem to know them so well." They all nodded.

Meanwhile, Jav stood quietly beside the twins and Neda, trying not to get too caught up in the conversation. Inside, though, he was nervous—his thoughts tangled in a mix of unease. He drank his first glass quickly and felt a bit tipsy. Fereydoun waved at him and winked, which made Jav even more uncomfortable.

Shirin stood among the others, but a sharp pressure built on her forehead—her migraine was returning. Frantically, she searched her bag for painkillers but came up empty. "Damn it," she muttered in frustration and hurried to the bathroom, splashing cold water on her face. It offered momentary relief. Her hands gripped the sink, the water still running, but her mind raced with unsettling thoughts: that mysterious card, the Asian Games 2584, the eerie return of Fereydoun, and now Huma's arrival.

What is going on? Who are they? They seemed so real, so fascinating... but at the same time, unsettling, suspicious, and supernatural.

Shirin turned off the tap and shook her head, trying to clear her mind. She pressed her forehead against her arm, attempting to push away the migraine and the uncertainty that clung to this strange story. Then an ant caught her eye, climbing her wrist with relentless determination. How very similar! Does this ant know it's my hand it's trying to conquer? Does it know how far it should go?

A quiet sympathy washed over her, a silent kinship with anyone who moves forward in uncertainty. Perhaps trust isn't in seeing the whole road, she realized, but in walking it anyway.

Just outside the *korsi* room, in the corridor, Parto still hesitated before drinking the wine, her attention focused instead on her reflection in the dark red surface. She swirled the glass gently and watched as her image rippled with the movement. For a moment, the ripples settled—and then, with an almost imperceptible shift, her reflection transformed. It was no longer just her face, but something else—something delicate, like the soft petals of a narcissus flower blooming within the liquid.

Entranced, Parto leaned in closer, her gaze fixed, unable to tear herself away from the shifting image. The reflection seemed to beckon her, pulling her deeper into its quiet mystery, as if it held the answer to something she couldn't yet understand.

At that moment, Parto felt a soft tap on her shoulder. She turned to find Shirin, heading toward the *korsi* room with an empty glass in her hand. "Try it," Shirin said. "I just did, and it made my migraine vanish with just half a glass."

Parto glanced at the wine—the fleeting image now gone—and for a moment, hesitated. But then, with a deep breath, she took a cautious sip, unsure of what to expect.

THE LEADER

There is a leader for us, I tell you,
Who lives over there, in Mount Qaf.
Simorgh is that Beloved's name, the leader of all birds,
Who is closer to us than our own blood veins;
Yet we stay far from that Great One, so very far!
—Attar, *The Conference of the Birds*[3]

NOT LONG after drinking the wine, everyone began to feel a bit different—not drunk, but as if the world, even the smallest details, had taken on a startling clarity. Atossa stared in wonder at the blue and red arteries standing out in relief beneath her skin. The room seemed to hum with electric energy; glances were exchanged, as if everyone were silently asking: *What is this?*

Pouria felt the sounds in the room briefly shift into tangible forms—an array of disorienting shapes that flickered, then vanished. He gave Surena's shirt a quick tug. Surena blinked, his eyes unfocused, lost in something unseen, as if caught in another experience. The tug broke the moment, and they returned to themselves.

Across the room, Sam sat frozen on the edge of a chair, struck by a vision. Inside the heart of a pomegranate seed resting on the table, he saw himself—his entire existence suspended within its core. He sank back into his seat, spellbound, unable to look away.

Parto turned to Hooman, her breath catching in her throat as their eyes met. What she saw went beyond the surface—into something deeper, something raw, a wound carrying an untold story. It was as if she could feel the weight of it, an invisible ache that resonated with her own.

Each person caught a fleeting glimpse into hidden depths—a brief vision of what lay beneath the surface, intensely personal and unique.

All of a sudden, Huma leaned forward theatrically, "And that's it—the final sip! The bottle's tale comes to an end. So then—shall we get to work? I hear you're after a sovereign, a leader—well, here I am!"

"You mean... you're the leader?" Surena asked.

Huma smiled. "I'm not the leader, but I know who is. I'm here to guide you to find your leader!"

"Yes! That's exactly what we needed!" Ayda exclaimed, her excitement mirrored by Neda and the twins. They exchanged looks, a silent understanding passing between them. It was as if an impossible dream was about to be realized.

Kamran cleared his throat and asked Huma, "Can you elaborate? Is this leader perhaps outside the country?"

"Outside? No, don't worry—the leader is inside. No visas or passports required."

"So, is the leader Iranian?" Hooman asked.

Huma looked momentarily bored. "Could you ask less obvious questions, please? Yes, of course. Where else would the sovereign of Iran come from? What a question!"

Hooman lowered his head but murmured defensively, "I just asked because the current leaders don't seem very Iranian... they even struggle with Farsi."

Huma snickered. "Ah, I see where you're coming from, my boy. But here's the thing: the current regime isn't leading—it's looting, plundering, and abusing the country. They don't deserve a foothold here."

"So, who is this leader?"

Huma paused for a moment, then replied, "The leader is known as the Simorgh."

A ripple of surprise spread through the room.

"Simorgh? Peculiar!"

"Is that a nickname?"

"What a funny name!"

"Maybe it's a password?"

"Simorgh? Wasn't that the name of a bird?"

Ignoring the flood of questions, Huma firmly insisted, "Yes, indeed. Simorgh is the name of our leader!"

Shirin squinted. "Wait —wasn't that a fictional bird? Was it in the *Shahnameh*?"

Atossa chimed in, "Yeah, I was about to ask that too..."

Mr. Kayvon jumped in, "Yes, it's mentioned in the *Shahnameh* and a few other books. It's the one that always rises from the ashes, representing power, wisdom, and change." He paused, then added, "Oh, and yes, like its name suggests, it's a bird. 'Si,' as we know, means 'thirty,' and 'morgh' means 'bird.' The Simorgh is usually seen as a massive, powerful, benevolent bird, but sometimes it's a mix—a creature that's part bird, part lion..."

Jav rolled his eyes at Mr. Kayvon and slurred, "Yeah... yeah, fine! Whatever!"

Then he turned back to Huma. "And where exactly is this grand Simorgh now? Do you know?"

Huma replied confidently, "Yes, I do. Highness Simorgh resides on Mount Alborz."

"Alborz?" The room trembled with disbelief.

"Yes, that's right," Huma replied. "Did you expect to find your leader on the Moon again?"

Babak, wide-eyed, turned to Dara. "We can see Alborz... I mean, the peak of Damavand from our kitchen window, can't we?"

Dara nodded, then moved closer to Huma. "You mentioned a journey ahead. Alborz is practically at Tehran's doorstep, isn't it?"

"Exactly, but don't be fooled—the journey to the Simorgh is far from simple. It's not about proximity; it's about what lies ahead. We'll focus on seven peaks along the range, as the Simorgh moves between them and their valleys."

Mr. Kayvon objected, "Did you say the range? But the mountain range runs from the border with Azerbaijan in the west, along the south of the Caspian Sea, and ends in Khorasan in the east! This is a huge area!"

Huma nodded thoughtfully, acknowledging the insight. "Precisely. We are exactly in the middle of the mountain range. Tehran—the city at the base, at the very foothills of Alborz. 'Tah' and 'Ran'—'the end' and 'the slope'—symbolize the beginning of a journey, the start of something larger. Just like the name of the city, our journey to the Simorgh begins at the bottom, but where it will take us, no one can say."

Huma paused, letting the significance of the words hang in the air before continuing, "My friends, those peaks guard secrets, ancient and untold. As I said, the path to them is not a simple one; it will test every ounce of your courage, every fragment of resolve you have. What you seek is not handed out easily! It is a trial, a challenge that will push you to your limits. But if you can face what lies ahead, if you can unlock what the mountains are hiding, you may find what you have been searching for."

Huma's voice softened, but the words still hung powerfully in the air.

"The journey won't be easy. But remember, nothing worth finding ever is!"

Roxy, still processing the weight of the revelation, asked, "So, are we supposed to just drive up there? Or maybe take the Tochal Telecabin⁴? Could you tell us what the means of transport are? Would you provide the sat nav, maps, guides...?"

"Each valley we cross has its own guardian—a native expert climber to help guide you toward the peak," Huma explained. "I too will be your humble guide, but it is you who must take each step with courage. The path to what you seek is before you. Will you take it?"

Kamran took another sip of his wine, frustration creeping into his voice. "But you're keeping us in the dark. We have no idea who this person is, how to find this so-called Simorgh, or what he or she stands for!"

Huma's eyes flashed with intensity. "I've told you everything you need to know! First, the leader is called the Simorgh. Second, there is a journey—an important one—that will take you to the top of Mount Alborz to find your leader. And as for their identity—well, it could be female, or it could be male. I can't confirm that just yet!"

Neda gave a subtle nod. "That's all we need, really."

Kamran turned to her in disbelief. "Wait... wait a minute, young lady! Don't be so naïve! This sounds way too good to be true! We know nothing about this person! How can we trust him—or her—to lead us? All we've been told is that the person is Iranian, has a mysterious name, and might be hiding in a cave on a mountain! How is that enough to put our faith in this so-called leader?"

"Ah, now that's a great question!" Huma responded. "I love this discussion, and I'm glad you're questioning the leader's credibility. But here's the thing—the whole point is for you to go on this expedition and judge for yourselves. That's what this journey is all about."

"Last time, when Iranians blindly chose a so-called leader—brought back from exile without question—no one bothered to ask if he was even qualified. As Hooman pointed out, the man couldn't even speak Farsi properly! He emerged like a poisonous mushroom, feeding off the backs of all the major opposition groups of that time—Communists, the MEK—and just like that, people bought into the idea that he was some Imam sent by God, dropped from the sky.

"No one asked why he'd been preserved in France or protected by the

Shia fundamentalist group, Fad'iyan-e-Islam. He understood something the people didn't: at that time in Iran, the path to power ran straight through the gutter of ignorance. And he was right—his shadow soon eclipsed the light, and people started seeing his face in the Moon. A very dangerous game, that one."

Huma's voice sharpened. "Was he a fake? A fabricated puppet meant to undermine the glory of Iran? Or was it a calculated scheme to wipe out Communism in the region? Whatever the reason, the Islamic Revolution happened for one major reason: the people's ignorance.

"Khomeini wrote books—supposedly for religious guidance, for Marja'[5] status. But did his followers ever read them? Did they even understand who they were following?"

Huma paused, then said, "Let me share a few gems from Khomeini's *Resaleh.*"[6]

"It is Halal to eat a grasshopper caught by hand, but not if it comes from the hand of a non-Muslim."

A few chuckles rippled around the room. Atossa winced and muttered sarcastically, "Seriously? *Grasshopper*? We should definitely follow that one."

"If a man has intercourse with his brother-in-law or father-in-law, his marriage remains valid."

Jaws tightened. Eyebrows rose. No one spoke for a moment—until Jav broke the silence with a grin. "Oh no! I wish I'd known that before!"

Some laughed at his joke, though the laughter sounded more nervous than amused.

"If a man sleeps with his aunt, he should not marry her daughter—his cousin."

The smiles faded. The silence grew heavier.

"A father should be proud if his daughter gets her first period at her husband's house."

No one dared make a sound.

Huma said, "And the last one for now—

"Intercourse with a woman is not allowed unless she attains the age of nine years regardless of whether the marriage is permanent or temporary. There is, however, no objection in other enjoyments like touching lasciviously, hugging and rubbing the thighs, even with a suckling infant."

Neda shouted, "Please stop!" A stunned stillness followed and then Ayda blurted, "You're making that up! Please tell us this isn't true!"

Huma shook their head slowly. "If only I were—and yet the people of Iran chose this man as their leader in 1979."

Huma's gaze swept the room, lingering on each face.

Heads hung low, No one met anyone's eyes.

Roxy wiped away a tear with the corner of her finger. Shirin muttered under her breath, "Criminals..."

Dara shook his head, dazed.

"What kind of drug were people on?" Hooman snapped. "What could've made them so high that they believed in him?"

Surena leaned forward. "I'd rather imagine Iranians never read those books... than think they read them and accepted it all blindly."

The room fell silent again, the weight of it all hanging in the air.

Finally, Fereydoun broke the stillness. "Let's say you're right—and honestly, you probably are. *The Resaleh* was originally published in Arabic in the '60s... so maybe people didn't read it then, but the Farsi translation has been available since 1989." He paused. "That's unforgivable."

He then looked up and said in a more sharpened tone, "But here we are. And now, you've been given a chance. So, what's the hold-up? The choice is yours—but nothing happens without action."

Just then, the conversation stopped. Everyone turned toward the deep, echoing chimes of the clock.

Bijan rushed into the hallway, the others right behind him.

He dropped to his knees beside the clock. "Good gracious... what's going on? It's—it's chiming again," he said, staring at it like it might explain itself.

He turned to Giv and Banoo with wide eyes; they stood motionless.

As the last chime faded, a stillness settled over the room—thick and cold, like fog. Only Persis, the cat, seemed unbothered. She rubbed against the base of the clock, purring softly, while the steady ticking carried on.

"Look! Look!" Neda cried, stepping forward. Her hand shook as she pointed at the face of the clock. "The hands—they're moving backwards."

A chill rippled through the room. It felt like time itself was slipping away, refusing to move forward.

Huma's voice cut through the tension. "When the clock hands move backward... time is being bent!"

"Time being bent?" Sam repeated, with a tight voice, "What the hell does that mean?"

Huma replied, "It means time isn't following its usual path. It's not moving in that predictable linear line we're used to. And it's not just time that shifts—everything around us does, too. To move forward, you have to look within."

Without waiting for a response, Huma turned and walked toward the garden door. "I'll be at the cedar tree," she said over her shoulder. "Waiting."

Everyone looked at each other, uncertain. Curiosity tugged at them— but so did hesitation. Would they follow, or stay behind?

Suddenly, Parto felt an overwhelming sense of loneliness. It pressed against her like a cold wind. She took a few steps toward the corridor that led to the garden, then paused in front of the large mirror.

She looked up and, instead of her own reflection, saw something else: a painting she'd once seen in a museum in Europe. Strangely, she wasn't even surprised. It was as though she were simply recalling the image,

It was an 'Annunciation' by an Italian Renaissance artist, a small, modest oil painting on a simple dark background, with no angel, no Gabriel, no dove, no halo, or olive branches. It was a three-quarter-length portrait of the Virgin, dressed in a blue robe and mantle. On the ledge in front of her is an open book. She is raising her right hand slightly. It is as if she just heard that something huge is about to happen—the announcement that she is to give birth to the Son of God. Her eyes are wide open, but she is looking inward.

CROSSING

AS HUMA stepped out to the garden, Bijan motioned to Banoo and Giv to join him in the kitchen. "I've known you since I was a kid," he said, his tone thick with disappointment. "You became my parents... we've shared everything, haven't we? So, what is this, Banoo Jan? Giv, tell me, who are they? What is going on? Tell me!"

Banoo met his gaze, then slowly walked to the far end of the kitchen, pausing by the glass door leading to the garden as though to ensure Huma was still there. She sighed softly and said, "I know, son... I know. Giv and I are often here, coming out of your mind and heart, as well as photos, diaries, and music. But now, it's time for you to step into your journey and make your story. Trust yourself, and Huma will guide you."

Bijan felt like the air had been knocked from his lungs; a sudden emptiness settled deep inside him.

"Won't you come?" he asked, looking at Giv, his eyes wide with the childlike fear of being lost. Banoo glanced back toward the garden and softly said, "No, darling. We're busy in the garden this year. Giv potted so many plants for the spring. And look..." She squinted, then continued, "Your mother needs a hand, especially with those big beehives she's set up by the tree."

Bijan, confused, turned toward the garden but saw nothing.

They paused. Giv nodded and patted Bijan on the back reassuringly. Then Banoo leaned forward, pressing a gentle kiss on his forehead, and whispered, "Go, darling. Go."

Bijan felt the floor beneath him hollow out, as if the ground itself had slipped away, leaving him suspended in a sudden void as he left for the garden to become the first to join Huma.

There was something almost magical in the air, as if the night itself had woken up and was alive with possibility. The twins' mother stood in the doorway, frowning with concern, her gaze darting nervously around the room. It was late. Her fingers twisted the hem of her cardigan, and her voice carried a note of urgency—almost pleading. "We should leave now," she said, her eyes meeting those of her children. "It's getting too late, and... it's unsafe."

Her words were drowned out by the animated chatter that filled the room. The twins, completely oblivious to their mother's growing worry, were absorbed in an intense conversation with Neda and Ayda. Eyes brimmed with excitement and their voices buzzing with anticipation as they spoke of the journey ahead and their shared hope of finding the leader—the mysterious Simorgh.

Across the room, Kamran leaned forward as he spoke in a low, conspiratorial whisper to a group that had gathered around him. Some were certain now that Huma was a spy. The whispers turned into animated gestures—hands pointing, voices rising—as they debated the best course of action. Some were ready to confront Huma immediately; others were hesitant, unsure of the danger they might be walking into. A tense silence fell as the group split into smaller clusters, each deciding to handle the matter in their own way.

Roxy's heart raced. She couldn't take it anymore—she needed to know what Kamran would decide. Grabbing his sleeve, she pulled him into a quieter corner, panic flooding her wide eyes. "What do you want to do, Kami? Tell me, for God's sake! We're not really going..." Her voice broke as the tears welled up.

Kamran gently wiped the tears from her cheeks and wrapped his arms around her. Despite his calm exterior, his mind was also racing with confusion. He wanted to remain strong, to offer solutions, but inside, he was just as lost as she was.

"Ah, darling, don't be silly," he murmured. "We don't have to go. It all smells fishy—either a joke, a spy game, or worse, a trap set by the government, monitored from the outside."

His fingers softly stroked her back, comforting her for a moment.

"I tried to raise the red flags, didn't I? But everyone's too excited, caught up in this game. Let's just wait and see."

He pulled away slightly, a grin spreading across his face—almost playful, as if detached from the confusion around them.

"We'll keep a calm face, pretend we're going, and quietly walk away from the garden."

His eyes locked onto hers as he said, "Deal?"

Roxy nodded, calmer now.

Sam reached out for Ava's hand. She looked at him, confused. "What, Sam?"

He squeezed her cold fingers and mumbled, "I'm glad we came tonight... I mean, to find out there's a way... a path...."

Then he gently placed his other hand on hers and whispered, "I love you, Ava... you know that, don't you?"

Ava quickly pulled her hand away. "The path may offer hope to everyone," she said in a steady, distant tone, "but it has nothing to do with us being together."

Sam shuddered. His disappointed eyes followed her as she moved away.

Atossa called Hooman, and he waved at her casually, walking nonchalantly as if stepping out for a cigarette in the garden rather than heading out on an expedition. It was clear he had made up his mind. As he reached the door, he paused, glanced back, and noticed Parto still inside. Without a word, he continued on his way.

Gitti adjusted Mr. Kayvon's hat, and he buttoned Gitti's coat before they both settled back on the sofa, holding each other tightly. That reminded Parto of a moment in *Titanic*—a brief scene where an elderly couple sits quietly, holding hands in a lounge area just before the ship sank. They seem calm and accepting of their fate, sharing a peaceful moment against the backdrop of the chaos around them.

Just then, Jav passed by, a sarcastic smile on his face, and said to Parto, "You too? Looking for a leader?" He shuffled off to the garden with a mischievous glint in his eyes, as though he were enjoying the game they were caught up in.

At that moment, Parto's gaze landed on Fereydoun, standing with quiet grace at the door like a gatekeeper observing intently. Their eyes met, and he flashed a wide, knowing smile. The intensity in his deep eyes sent a shiver through her, and she felt that something huge and marvellous was about to happen.

DEPARTURE

HUMA STOOD motionless beneath the old cedar tree, staring up at its snow-covered crown, oblivious to the crunching footsteps of others coming into the garden.

Roxy wobbled on her heels, tightening her grip around Kamran's arm and muttering in frustration, "Damn... I should've just worn my Uggs."

"Never mind, darling, we won't stay long," Kamran replied.

When everyone had arrived, Huma finally turned around and looked at the crowd through large crystal eyes that beamed like headlights in the night.

"It is the time!"

Bending down, Huma drew a large circle around the tree. Standing back, he said with a sharp but inviting tone, "Come inside the circle, my fellow travellers!" It wasn't a big ask—certainly nothing to fear and nothing risky, just one simple first step—yet an unsettling tension clung to the moment.

Jav broke the silence with a nervous chuckle and said, "A difficult long journey? It's like walking into kindergarten!" With a deep breath, Jav crossed into the circle. One by one, the others followed.

Before taking her step forward, Parto paused and looked up instinctively. Her eyes followed a lone feather drifting through the air. It floated, suspended in the silence, as though caught in time itself, before gently settling onto her chest. A chill ran down her spine: a feather drifting from nowhere!

As each of them crossed into the circle, a sudden wind whipped through it, spiralling with a fierce velocity no one had expected. It surged around them—wild and unpredictable—tugging at their clothes, ruffling their hair as if the very atmosphere itself were awakening from a long slumber. The wind carried a strange, intoxicating scent—something ancient and unplaceable that seemed to crawl under their skin and lodge somewhere deep.

Ava, who had been rubbing and warming her fingers just moments before, suddenly exclaimed, "Ah... It's boiling in here...I am boiling!" She shook her hands in the air, as if trying to cool them off.

Bijan stood motionless, his eyes narrowing on the old cedar tree. What had once felt familiar now seemed different. Then his heart quickened as he realized it wasn't the tree—it was the air, thick and hot, carrying an unfamiliar scent. In that moment, an overwhelming urge to remember the smell gripped him.

He closed his eyes, and the mantra echoed in his mind: *Trust your memory... trust yourself.* Suddenly, his heart ached with longing—for the garden etched into the fabric of a carpet his father had once shown him. He kept his eyes shut, the warm wind washing over him, its texture almost grain-like. That was it—the scent of their old garden. The trees, the flowers, the familiar paths he had once walked.

It was as if the air had folded time itself, bringing the past into the present. And then, in a heartbeat, he was back—standing in the circle with the others, in the sweltering heat.

Surena found the heat unbearable. He tore off his flannel shirt and flung it outside the circle. Looking at his brother with disbelief and confusion, he shouted, "What the hell is going on?" His voice was hoarse, barely loud enough to pierce the wall of stifling heat.

Neda yanked the band from her hair with a sharp tug and dropped it to the ground. Her curls, damp with sweat, clung to her skin. She swiped at them impatiently, her eyes darting around, scanning the others for some sign of normalcy—anything to anchor her in the chaos.

Dara's heart pounded as he searched for Babak and Shirin, his eyes flicking frantically from one spot to another. Then, suddenly, he froze in terror. His head—he realized—had turned nearly a full circle.

Everyone swayed forward, overtaken by the sudden sensation that they had an inner body moving in a way the outer body couldn't control—no matter how hard they struggled.

Roxy's face twisted with fear as she slammed her hands over her eyes and screamed, "Let's go back, Kami!" Kamran tried to step backward, but his legs wobbled, as if the ground beneath him had turned to liquid. No matter how fiercely he fought to steady himself, he couldn't find his balance—his entire being trembling under the unbearable weight of helplessness.

Atossa reached for the tree, hoping to brace herself against it. But as her fingers brushed its rough bark, a jolt surged through her hand. She gasped, yanking it back as the sensation burned through her skin.

They all stared at Huma, eyes wide with confusion, horrified by what was happening.

"The blessed perplexity!" Huma's voice rang out, bold and vibrant. She laughed excitedly. "You're boarding! This is the pre-departure phase—just like when an aircraft is taxiing before take off. Not a big deal, guys. I assure you; the transformation isn't anything to fear. In fact, you go through a simpler version of it every single night when you sleep. Your outer self retires, and your inner self resurfaces. It's just a swap—like what you do every night."

Poria called out, "The heat... what is this heat for, then?"

"Ah... yes!" Huma continued. "You need a lot of power to take off—you're changing gears, accelerating, preparing to become airborne. So we go through the ignition and burning phase before you can rise!"

"Airborne? Take off?" The words hung in the air, but no one could react or ask any more questions. The heat was unbearable, scorching them from all sides.

Hooman felt something on his skin. He ran his fingers along the back of his neck, a chill crawling up his spine as he touched rough, reptilian flakes—scaled husks shedding from his own flesh.

Everyone sensed something changing inside them, their bones beginning to feel unnaturally light. Shirin winced as the bones in her arms shrank, while those in her hands stretched, elongating as if pulled by invisible forces. Ayda stared at her hands, watching her fingers widen and curve in ways that seemed impossible.

They all watched in horror as their skin began to peel away, falling to the ground like old cocoons. Their feet lost contact with the earth as they started to rise, and they looked down to see their discarded shells ignite in flames, turning to ash and vanishing into the air.

As they ascended higher, the house and garden below shrank from view. They spotted Fereydoun standing by the gate with his two puppies, a serene smile on his face as he waved up at them. But then something else caught their eye. Perched beside him was Persis—but she was no longer a cat. The small creature had transformed into a majestic lion.

THE THREE KEYS

As they began to soar, Huma spoke to them of the three keys: Sun, Symmetry, and Sound.

SUN—"The order of time is merely illusory. What we experience—what we call *reality*—is just a complex network of events onto which we project the past, present, and future. But the most important and real element in defining time is light. We always follow the light—that is our true measure of time.

"Before we departed, I set the grandfather clock to run backward, for the past shone brighter than the present, where all is dark. But as we embark on this journey to find our leader, the great Simorgh, you now hold the power to reshape the present and brighten the future.

"Ahead lie seven arduous paths—bleak, desolate, and unforgiving. I call them *valleys*, for each one descends into a depth where light fades and hope withers in shadow: the Valley of the Quest, the Valley of Tolerance, the Valley of Knowledge, the Valley of Unity, the Valley of Justice, the Valley of Love, and the Valley of Death."

"These valleys are not of the world but are born from within you— manifestations of your own inner void. They take shape according to the trials you must endure to reach the Simorgh. And in each one, you'll find the opportunity to transform darkness, guided by the wisdom of kindred souls on the wing.

"As you invite more light, the sundial will shift, marking Yalda in the outer world—the victory of light over darkness, the triumph of Mithra."

SYMMETRY: "In this journey, you are not alone. But the regions of the unknown you are entering will be different for each individual. For some, it may be a snow-covered expanse, for others, a dense jungle. It could be a desert in an unfamiliar land, or a world lush with lakes and rivers. Each person will face a landscape shaped by the projection of their own mind and unconscious.

"The forces of nature always merge, sharing a common essence unified into one entity. This phenomenon, known as *symmetry*, arises from a single, elegant principle of beauty.

"Symmetry is the expression of equivalence between all things. The fundamental law—the order that governs the universe—resonates deeply within us. This truth is unchanging and profound. Avoid ugliness. Embrace beauty. Trust in symmetry, for it gives wings to your creativity, conducts you to truth, and leads you to grace."

SOUND: "Sound is the barrier between two realms—the intense, concentrated power within, and the earthly ground you have already left behind. It is a celebration marking the dawn of your journey, a ritual that embodies each soul's unique path.

"Listen carefully to the rhythm of life."

"In each valley, hard work is required before you can truly grasp the inner world of these majestic compositions. You will need the flute of your breath and the drumbeat of your heart, as these intricate melodies unfold, take wing, and soar from your ashes."

"It is then that you will hear a simple sequence of tones—whether in a song or the call of a bird—something akin to the magic flute's melody. And in that moment, you will know you have crossed the valley."

Just then, a song began to play.

"By the final note of this melody," Huma said, "you will find yourself dancing through the very essence of your transformation."

And so, they left—with that song.

> ...*voice, voice, only voice.*
> *The water's voice, its wish to flow,*
> *The starlight's voice pouring upon the earth's female form,*
> *The voice of the egg in the womb congealing into sense,*
> *The clotting together of love's minds....*[7]

They could hear everything—the whisper of all *four elements* in perfect harmony.

Together, they rose and flew toward the horizon.

NOTES

1   Sholeh Wolpé, trans., *The Conference of the Birds* (New York: W. W. Norton & Company, 2017), 41.

2   Dasht-e-Murghab is a fertile plain located in Iran's Fars province. Several petroglyph sites have been identified in the region, most of which were carved into the stone walls of Achaemenid era (c. 550–330 BCE) castles within the Pasargadae World Heritage site (*Encyclopaedia Iranica*).

3   Sholeh Wolpé, trans., *The Conference of the Birds* (New York: W. W. Norton & Company, 2017), 44.

4   The Tochal Telecabin (or Telecable) is a gondola lift situated in northern Tehran. It stretches from Velenjak, a neighbourhood at the foot of the Tochal mountain, up to its summit, providing access to ski resorts and hiking trails, and offering panoramic views of the city.

5   Marja' is a title given to the highest level of Shia religious cleric.

6   A Resaleh is a practical, religious handbook that helps Shia Muslims understand and follow the specific religious laws and ethical principles of their Marja'.

7   Sholeh Wolpé, trans., Sin: *Selected Poems of Forugh Farrokhzad, by Forugh Farrokhzad* (Fayetteville: University of Arkansas Press, 2010), 109.

THE SEVEN VALLEYS

Travel is very useful, and it exercises the
imagination. Our own journey is entirely
imaginary. That is its strength.

LOUIS-FERDINAND CÉLINE

THE VALLEY OF THE QUEST

PARTO DREAMT that she wandered through a museum. There was a beautiful painting of the Queen of Sheba reclining beside a stream, a love letter from Solomon resting in her hands, brought to her by the Hoopoe perched at her feet. Parto tried to read the message, but then she noticed that the letter was stamped 'From Iran.'

She still wore a smile when the sound of a bird roused her from sleep.

Quook-koo Quark-koo
Quook-koo Quark-koo

She suddenly remembered that she, too, had become a bird—a Goose. She studied her sleek black-and-grey feathers, neatly arranged in lines, and was amazed by them. But then a sensation made her glance down. She curbed her long neck downward. "Oh no, I'm tagged!" A small metal band around her leg held a solar-powered transmitter, tracking her every move, recording her migratory path. It was not unlike the way the system had tracked her as a human.

The valley around her was enveloped in a thick, damp, foggy cocoon of clouds, with no visibility—but she could still sense him, a familiar presence in the air: a nostalgic reminder that he was near.

A Long-eared Owl glided through the air and slowly sank into the clouds, soaring over her. He called twice: first with a lonely, despairing cry, and then with a more melodic tweet. His rich, mellifluous voice echoed in the silence. *Hooman!*

With a pair of large, glowing eyes, he stared at her, and Parto could see her new bird face reflected in his black irises.

Hooman said, "Hoo," but she thought he was asking, "Who?" Excited, she squeaked, "It's me! Me!"

Parto was worried he'd forgotten her, but she didn't realize he was just hooting. That made him laugh.

"Thanks a lot. Of course, I know you—you're tagged," he said, pointing to her leg.

Trying to sound more formal, Parto masked her confusion. "Oh. So, are we on the same path? Hmm... Do you know where we are? What have we landed in?"

"Cloud," Hooman said. "We're in a cloud. Funny enough, yes—we're sharing the same path. I guess we've landed in the Valley of the Clouds."

He seemed more relaxed and clear-headed in his Owl form than he had been at the party.

"What about the others?" Parto asked. "Is it just us? Where are they? Did everyone come straight from the party? It's still dark... should be midnight, right?"

"Maybe it is midnight—because you were sleeping, and I was awake!"

He was right; he was always up at night and slept during the day. It was annoying, and she didn't like it. They had a lot of differences. Parto still didn't know why she loved him so much, and if she did, what was it that had made her leave him? This thought crossed her mind: *Do we love someone because they are very similar to us, or because they are very different?*

They circled each other, exhaling dust, plummeting downward and plunging upward with playful energy. The feeling of being alone together again was hypnotic—too exciting to begin searching the valley just yet. They reminisced about summers in Bijan's garden, when they lay under the cedar tree, holding hands and watching clouds pass by, searching for meaning in their shapes. It all seemed so distant now, like a lifetime ago.

Suddenly, a strange, sibilant bird call diffused through the clouds, calling: *Quook-koo, Quark-koo,* then faded away quickly.

"Did you hear that?" Parto asked. "I heard it a little while ago too."

"Yes. Is that real? Another bird? I hear it, but I can't see one."

The sound reminded them they had a mission—to escape this thickening cloud and find their way to the Simorgh.

Every now and then, they felt a shudder in the air, the skirmish of wings behind the thick cloud. They tried to follow but always ended up nowhere. It felt as if they were lost in the clouds.

The uncertainty deepened as they were sucked into a vortex of high-pressure air. A sharp black wingtip cut through the icy edge of the cloud, darting in and out. A crow-like feather swept past, but they couldn't distinguish the bird's head from its body—both hidden somewhere on the other side of the cloud.

As the whirlwind passed, a tiny, colourful bird circled and flicked backward through the air at incredible speed. It was Shirin, the Hummingbird.

They rose steeply to meet her, excited and happy to reunite, exchanging greetings and admiring each other's new bodies. Shirin explained that she had been chased by a crow.

"Where the hell are we?"

"Hell, indeed," Shirin replied. "My manoeuvrability helped me escape, but it was dark, heavy, and awful."

After tumbling through the air for a while, the cloud suddenly broke apart. Another little bird jerked into view. It was a Hoopoe, its feathered crest rising like a crown, giving it an air of authority.

"Welcome to the Valley of the Quest, fellow travellers!" The familiar voice of Huma soothed them, filling them with happiness and hope.

Huma continued, "The sky is the canvas of the birds—vast and boundless. Your vision expands with every flick of your wings. But remember: *'The hardest thing of all to see is what is really there.[1]'*"

Then Huma began a tale:

"More than four decades earlier, a hooded crow and a cuckoo stole and hid the winged sun discs, or *farr* and sowed disillusionment among the birds of Iran. Accusing the king and his court of being bird-catchers, the crow convinced the birds that his severe moulting was the kingdom's fault. He urged them to stop flying aimlessly and instead build a grand city in the sky, promising it would grant them power over the kingdom and eternal life after death.

"The birds embraced the idea and agreed to build the city. The crow erased the ancient songs and music the birds had known for thousands of years, replacing them with new lyrics that all the birds of Iran, from every habitat, were required to learn and sing.

"The crow then delivered a speech, declaring himself God-sent. He won over the birds completely and established *The Republic of Cloudcuckooland*—a kingdom built high in the clouds, far from the earth and its truths. The clouds, once mere weather, were thickened and darkened by the crow's design. They became a veil, hiding the sun.

"Beneath this manufactured gloom, he made grand promises—but none were kept. Disobedience was met with punishment: hibernation, exile, a cage, or death. The sky, once open and free, became a prison of fog and forgetting.

"To reach the Simorgh, you must scatter the clouds that shroud the truth. These are not natural clouds—they are spun from lies, from silence, from the fears sown by the crow. Only light and truth can break them. Bring light. Bring truth. Only then can you fly freely beyond the crow's shadow—toward the Simorgh."

"How can we get to the light?" they asked.

"The winged sun. You must bring back the lost winged sun discs. That will scatter the cloud."

The three of them began to make excuses.

"But you said they were stolen by the hooded crow."

"How do we know...?" Shirin asked.

"When you were humans, there were obstacles—both physical and spiritual—in your path. But now that you've become birds, you possess a navigation system, a built-in compass to guide you on your journey: the Earth's magnetic field.

"Don't forget—no one can save you but yourself. No one can, and no one may. *You yourself must take the path.²*"

Huma then vanished into the mist.

QUEST ONE: A CITY, A BOAT, A CHANNEL

Parto followed the pull of the Earth's magnetic field. She rose into the open sky, floating effortlessly, undulating softly. At first, the sensation was thrilling. She was alone, yet free of the fear of getting lost, trusting the force deep within the planet.

No longer a spectator of the sky, she had become part of it, while the land below silently watched her every move. And yes, it was silent. Until now, she hadn't realized how quiet the sky could be. From this height, all the noise below was muted, leaving only the sound of her breath. It was pure liberation.

But then, as she left the familiar landscape behind, an unexpected wave of emotion washed over her. She knew she was leaving home, and with each stroke of her wings, she felt the sharp loss of those recognizable sights as they slowly faded into the distance.

Finally, she found herself above a vast blue sea, spiralling over the white cliffs of the coastline before descending to feed on the water. She submerged herself and, to her surprise, realised she could swim beneath the surface as well—just like when she took her first stroke underwater in a swimming pool.

After a while, she emerged and noticed three Skylarks chasing each other, playing in the sunlight along the shore.

They spotted Parto and fluttered towards her. "My name is Anita," said one of the Larks. "I'm from Sardasht, and I want to be an actress."

Her companions tweeted mischievously. "And these are my brothers, Armin and Artin."

Parto had heard much about Sardasht—a small Kurdish city in western Iran, near the Iraqi border—a harsh place where survival was often the only ambition to pursue.

Parto asked, "This isn't Sardasht, is it, Anita?"

"No, we left Sardasht a while ago," she replied. "First we went to Turkey, then Italy, then... France."

Armin jumped up and exclaimed, "We saw many big ships and boats!" He puffed out his chest and chirped, "We took the boat too... we've *been* on the boat!"

"Wow, so many places you've been... what a long journey!"

Anita smiled. "Yes, like the movies!"

"So, where are we now?"

"This is Dunkirk. Where did you fly from? Didn't you see the Channel?"

"The Channel?"

"Come with us."

Parto followed them, and together they soared high above the sea. The sky grew cold and windy, and rain began to fall. The sea was choppy, but when it finally calmed, Anita pointed and said, "Look!"

There, on the surface of the water, was something shining like a small golden patch.

Parto squinted and said, "That? Looks like it could be a shiny piece of metal. It's not clear from here. Or maybe the wind brought some debris?"

"Wrong!" said Armin.

"What is it then? It's floating?"

"It's not floating. There's something under the water!"

"What?"

"Yes, something's kept under the water... like a treasure!"

Parto trembled. The words reminded her of the conversation at the Yalda party with Mr Kayvon, who had spoken of *farr*—something hidden beneath the water. And, knowing that the winged sun disc symbolised that very concept, her excitement grew.

"We saw it that night during the crossing," Anita said. "We were lost, swallowed by the waves, with nothing but an endless black void around us. The tide pulled us in every direction. And then, we saw it—some kind of light, a flicker, falling into the water."

Armin's voice cut in. "I saw that it was dropped by a crow! I swear!"

Anita nodded. "We were pulled deeper, carried by the current, and I saw it sink with us, further down into the dark. The tide was relentless, kept dragging us deeper. It was suffocating. I tried to reach it, but it was slipping away—too far to grasp. We couldn't reach it, not in time. We didn't stand a chance. It was too late, and we didn't want to stay any longer in that terrible place... so we had no choice but to leave it behind."

Suddenly, it hit Parto—this family was the Kurdish Iranian family from Sardasht, the one that had drowned while attempting the dangerous crossing. Like hundreds of thousands of Iranian-Kurdish refugees each year, they had placed their lives in the hands of smugglers, desperate to reach Europe.[3]

Anita paused, gazing into the distance. "The next day, when we became Larks, we could see the world anew—and everything became clear. That light... it was the light of our homeland, stolen by the crow. Our home had been swallowed by darkness. We ran from it. There are many others in Sardasht who want to leave."

Parto asked, "So what should they do? Stay in darkness?"

Anita's voice was firm. "Leaving doesn't help. Maybe it's better to bring the light back home."

She looked directly at Parto. "Maybe... maybe *you* can reach it. Maybe that light is meant to return with you."

"Me?" Parto exclaimed.

"Yes. Would you go back to Iran? Please? Would you take it with you to Sardasht?"

"But what if I don't want to return? And if I do—how can I carry it? How can I carry light?"

"Don't worry," Anita said. "The light has wings of its own. But the hardest part is breaking the surface and diving deep to retrieve it. After that, it's easy. The light will follow you."

Parto looked at them and took a deep breath, a sense of resolve building within her. She promised to take the light to Sardasht—to fulfil their wish.

Just before she took the plunge, she glanced back. The three Larks were ascending high. Anita's voice called out to her: "We gave it a name. *Mithra.* Remember—that's what you should call it."

Turningher gaze to the shimmering patch below, Parto took one final breath, tucked her wings, and dived into the water.

The shadow on the sundial shifted. The magic flute played.

QUEST TWO: A LAKE, A DAM, A TOMB

Hooman advanced with the wind, circling the sky in confusion. He had followed the Earth's magnetic pulse with instinctive precision and arrived at the place where *Lake Bakhtegan* once shimmered—a sanctuary he remembered well for its serene beauty, Flamingos, and other migrating birds.

Unlike most birds, Owls didn't migrate. Yet now, upon arriving, he felt a pull he couldn't explain. His mission was clear: recover the Winged Sun Disc. But for the first time, the thought of straying from the migratory path tempted him. The darkness in *Cloudcuckooland* had begun to gnaw at his spirit.

He briefly considered seeking help from the Flamingos—if they were still there. But he dismissed the thought almost immediately. A flush of shame rose within him. He exhaled, steadying himself. Fixing his gaze forward, he returned his focus to the mission.

It was cold, but warmer air rose from the ground, brushing his feathers in waves as he descended. Carried on that warmth, however, was a sharp, vinegary stench. The world below felt wrong.

As he sank lower, the landscape began to sharpen into focus. What he had first taken for vibrant fields of lotus or water lilies twisted before his eyes into something disturbing. The terrain was not blooming—it was bleeding. The earth had contorted into an apocalyptic vision. The remains of Flamingos lay scattered across the saltpan, trapped like forgotten sculptures. Some heads were crystallised in saline water, other bodies still warm, half-sunken in sludge. The wind stirred their brittle feathers, fluttering like wilted pink petals. Now and then, a faint gasp cut through the silence—a bird clinging to life, drowning in despair.

Drought had ravaged the lake. What was once a smooth, glistening surface had hardened into a barren, treacherous trap. As the Flamingos descended, their delicate legs gave way, fragile bones snapping beneath them. Hooman shuddered. Had it not been for his slower descent and the sturdier build of an Owl, he too might have suffered the same fate.

A plaintive call pierced the mist—long, low, and aching.

Perched on a weathered stone a little farther off was an old Peregrine, his feathers dulled by time, but his eyes sharp with memory.

He looked as though he'd been there a long time—watching, waiting... calling.

"It's all dried up," the Peregrine said with sorrow. "Beautiful *Lake Bakhtegan*. All that's left is an empty basin, a cradle for broken promises. I still remember the sound of the waves... those innocent birds... all gone. All dried up."

"Who are you?" Hooman asked.

The Peregrine rose heavily from the blend of dust and sludge and settled nearby.

"My name is Eskandar," the Peregrine replied, his orange-teal eyes reflecting a deep, quiet sadness. "I was born just over there," he gestured. "And I'll always carry those memories. We tried to stop it—early conservation efforts, awareness campaigns... but look at it now. A tragedy. Climate change and poor water management have taken everything."

Hooman was captivated by him; his passion for the land was evident. He spoke with fervour about Iran's unique geography, its rich biodiversity, and wetlands of global importance. With quiet pride, he recounted co-founding the Ramsar Convention in 1971—an international treaty to protect these vital ecosystems.

At the end, the Peregrine added, "Here's a little secret for you: if you want to evaluate a country's human rights and freedom, look at how it treats its nature and wildlife. It's the quickest way, even before you dive into any history books. There's always a connection between human rights and environmental protection."

Hooman asked, "So, nothing has been done to protect nature in the last forty years?"

Eskandar sighed. "I wish it were nothing. It's worse than nothing. When they did act, it was either an excuse for corruption or a way to plunder our heritage." He pointed to a nearby dam that had been built despite fierce opposition. It redirected water from *Lake Bakhtegan* and put historic sites like Persepolis and Pasargadae at risk.

"For 2,500 years, Cyrus the Great's tomb stood in Pasargadae untouched," he said. "Now, rising moisture is slowly eating away at it. A legacy crumbling—one bit at a time."

Hooman's anger surged. It felt like an attack on Iran's heritage—like the destruction of the Bamiyan Buddhas by the Taliban in Afghanistan, another erasure of ancient identity. But beneath his rage was helplessness. He sank to the ground, eyes dim, overwhelmed by sorrow. The Winged Sun Disc no longer seemed to matter.

In a brittle whisper, he said, "If they flood it... Persepolis will be gone. This is terrible. I wish we could stop it."

"You could," Eskandar replied. "What's your profession?"

"Me? I was only a writer. Barely a poet."

"Only?"

"Well... what can words do, really?" Hooman's voice was low. "Sure, some people wield them like weapons. But not here. Not now. They don't work." He paused; his eyes gazed into the distance. "Believe me—I had a friend who tried. He spoke with his words, he resisted... and now he's gone. Wilted, like a flower in the wind."

The mention of his old friend Rambod broke something in him. For a moment, silence took over. But then, with that familiar flicker of wit in his eyes, he added, "Unless I write a tragedy about it? Maybe, one day, I'll rewrite *The Persians*—you know, the one by Aeschylus? How about that? That was unique! It was based on real tragedy, not just myth, but history—real loss. The fall of Persia." A weight crept back into his words. "Back then, it was the defeat of the Persians. And now... here we are again."

Eskandar, oblivious to what Hooman had said, asked, "What do you write about?"

"Mostly romance. Sometimes plays. The poem I keep coming back to is *Midnight Angel*."

"Are you in love? Or still searching—like waiting for an angel at midnight to light your way?"

"Yes. Both. I loved my wife. She left me."

"Why?"

"She couldn't stand this country. She was searching for freedom."

"And you? Weren't you?"

"I found mine in words."

"Oh, that's true. Words... writing... language! Absolutely—I won't argue that," Eskandar said, warming to his own thoughts. "Language is a living creature inside us. We shape it, and it shapes us in return. Since becoming a Peregrine, hearing the birds sing—really hearing them—I've started to notice the rhythms of the world. The symmetry in a drumbeat, or the echo of a few simple notes... it's everywhere. A shared rhythm. It's how we connect. How we express joy, sorrow, truth. It is liberating."

He paused, then added, "But we're still animals—driven by instinct, the need for survival. And survival demands action. Take the songbirds: they don't just sing; they serve. They play a vital role in agriculture by feeding themselves and eliminating swarms of insects in the process. Even in cities, sparrows and wrens foraging through fallen leaves or litter help control pests like cockroaches."

Eskandar's tone dropped, quieter but firm. "You said you loved her. So why didn't you go with her? Or try to make her stay? You stayed behind and turned your heartbreak into verses. A poem... where action should've been."

Hooman looked away. The words hit harder than he expected. For a long moment, he said nothing. Then, barely audible, as if confessing to himself, he murmured, "You're right."

Eskandar shook his head and said, "You're not the only one. Too many Iranians speak more than they act. You recite poetry, talk of quests—of seeking the beloved, chasing destiny, reaching some sacred destinations—but when the moment finally comes, you hesitate. You stand still."

He looked Hooman in the eye and said, "We do need poetry. But we need pragmatism too. A wish without action... is just a dream. And you—" his voice softened, but the words struck like flint—"you, my son, you're only a dreamer!"

Hooman started to speak, but Eskandar cut in. "You remember what we said about the destruction of our heritage? That always brings one name to my mind—Sadegh Khalkhali. One of the regime's most ruthless hanging judges. You were probably too young back in '79... but he called Cyrus the Great a liar. A tyrant. Even a queer. And he demanded the demolition of Pasargadae and Persepolis.

"He had Reza Shah's tomb bulldozed. And then he turned on the soul of Iran itself. But Khalkhali was stopped—by the actions of two brave men. Nosratollah Amini, governor of Fars, went on the radio and declared, 'Persepolis will fall only over my dead body.' He rallied the military, the people of Shiraz—they stood up."

He took a breath, the weight of history pressing against his words. "And Professor Shahriar Adl—that legendary archaeologist—he moved fast. He had Persepolis, the Ziggurat, and the Square in Isfahan registered with UNESCO. He didn't just speak. He acted.

"We owe them everything!"

"But even as these legends fought to protect Iran's heritage, we are not safe. The crow is still revered as a god, the cuckoo still stands guard, and the spectre of *Khalkhali* looms over the people of *Cloudcuckooland*. His legacy of destruction is a weapon—a tool for control."

His voice grew more urgent. "This is why action matters. Presence is power. Words mean nothing if you're not there to stand behind them. You must move. Set out on your quest. Your steps are the shape of your words, the body of your wishes."

He paused, as if considering the gravity of his next words. "They fear the light. The *farr*—it haunts them. Wherever it shines, like the winged sun in Persepolis, they tremble."

Eskandar locked eyes with Hooman, the weight of his gaze like a command. "Go to Persepolis. The Winged Sun Disc is still there."

Hooman stood, a flicker of resolve crossing his face. Then, without hesitation, he leapt—soaring into the sky toward Persepolis.

The shadow on the sundial shifted. The magic flute played.

QUEST THREE: A RIVER, A LAKE, A MOUNTAIN

Shirin found herself perched on a pink, plastic, swan-shaped pedal boat. Rows of them were parked in a vast, cracked, dried-up riverbed. She couldn't make sense of it. *Why are the boats here?*

It reminded her of Isfahan, where she and Farhad had spent their honeymoon. They had rented one of these quirky boats back then. At home, she still had a picture of that day—frozen in time—on the fridge door: sitting in the plastic swan boat, their hands raised high, wide open like spreading wings, their heads ducked behind the plastic swan's head.

In her mind, she could still hear their laughter as they paddled down the river. But of course, that had been the beautiful Zayanderud River.

She gasped as she circled back and saw the bridge!

Si-o-se Pol[4], the famous bridge of Isfahan, stood proudly—but where was the Zayanderud? It couldn't be true. The bridge was there, but the river had vanished. An ominous gust of wind swept through the thirty-three arches, now spanning nothing but a dry riverbed. It was a stark sign of the devastating water loss in what, not long ago, had been the largest river on the Iranian Plateau.

She was more angry than anxious. She had lost so much. The river, deeply linked with Farhad, was gone too.

As she hovered above one of the swan-shaped boats, a thought struck her: *Look! Now I'm a bird myself, you pathetic plastic swan!* And she admired her beautiful wings in a fleeting moment of satisfaction.

She left Isfahan and pressed onward with her mission. She flew over one desolate place after another, her heart heavy with despair.

A chill wind rose from the north, carrying crystals of salty air that layered the sky. Her built-in navigation was flawless. The Salt Lake was near. It was the final stop for migratory birds before leaving Iran, and Shirin had a strong hunch that the winged sun disc was there.

Besides, it was Yalda—the start of the migration season—and she hoped the air would be filled with birds that might know something about Farhad.

She flew down, plunging through the warm air rising from the ground, but then the shock hit again. No lake. No water. No birds. The basin stretched out, so white and blinding that it erased all detail. Shirin almost missed the lone Pelican slumped in the distance, like a discarded ghost. She drifted closer.

The bird was massive, hunched on gnarled feet, motionless. Its feathers shimmered, unnaturally white, like salt-crusted pages. Its gaze was fixed on something far off, buried deep in the basin's silent void.

Shirin landed beside the Pelican and stepped forward, salt crunching dry and brittle under her feet. The Pelican jolted, twisting suddenly to face her.

In the stillness, under its weathered, steady gaze, Shirin hesitated. There was something unsettlingly familiar in the bird's presence. She took a small step closer. "I... I'm sorry," she murmured. "Do I know you?"

The bird's beak creaked open slowly, like an old door remembering how to move. "I've been around a long time," she said—and then continued with a voice rusted with age: "My name is Mahlagha Mallah. They used to call me the Mother of Iran's Environment."

"I remember now," Shirin whispered. "I've known you since I was a kid... I couldn't put it together... sorry."

Shirin glanced at the white expanse, then back at the Pelican and asked. "Is this... Lake Urmia?" Shirin asked.

The Pelican didn't answer—just stared, as if the question hadn't quite landed, or as if she were waiting to see for herself. Then came a long pause—too long to be comfortable. Shirin wondered if she had fallen asleep.

"Observation... observation decides the outcome," the Pelican finally murmured, more to the sky than to Shirin.

Shirin hesitated. "Sorry, I'm not sure I follow. Is this the lake? Or where it used to be? I followed the Earth's magnetic navigation, so this must be it, right?"

"It can be both," Mahlagha said.

Shirin tried to stay polite, but frustration crept in. "So... it was a lake, and now it's dried up?"

"No. As I said, it can be both! The cat is both dead and alive—until the box is opened. Unsettling, isn't it? That truth might depend on us."

Shirin hesitated. Was this just the rambling of old age? Maybe. So she didn't argue.

"Well, I guess I missed the cat. Maybe it was here before I arrived."

"No, you haven't," the Pelican said gently. "The cat is still there."

Shirin glanced around—nothing. No cat. But then, a realisation.

Maybe she meant the shape of Iran—so often imagined as a cat on a map.

"Oh! Sorry—I'm tired and slow! You meant the cat of Iran?" she asked.

The Pelican tilted her head. "Hm, that could have been. But I was telling you something else."

She paused, as if measuring the weight of her next words.

It wasn't really about cats at all, Mahlagha explained. She told Shirin about the famous thought experiment she had come across many years ago, when she was studying for her PhD at the Sorbonne and, at the same time, training in librarianship at the National Library of France.

When she finished explaining, there was a brief silence between them before Mahlagha spoke again. "You see... in a way, we're all Schrödinger's cats—our futures suspended, both alive in hope and lost in doubt."

Shirin wasn't entirely convinced. "So, what is the reality, then? What you've said challenges the very nature of reality, doesn't it?"

"Absolutely! There's an explanation for that in quantum mechanics. Particles exist in a 'superposition'—multiple states at once—until... well, until they're observed." Mahlagha paused, letting the idea settle with Shirin before continuing. "Okay, let's peel the science back to normal life.

"The cat is a metaphor for uncertainty and ambiguity. Think about that. Is something only real once it's observed? So the question is: does reality exist independently of observation, or does our act of perceiving bring it into being? And the answer is: our consciousness gives shape to the world. That's why, when you asked about the lake, I said it can be both.

"Yes! This is Lake Urmia. It was once one of the world's largest saltwater lakes, thriving for centuries. It supported livelihoods, nurtured biodiversity, and served as a crucial sanctuary for migratory birds—Flamingos, Pelicans, ducks—along the Central Asian Flyway. More than just a natural wonder, the lake was a bustling hub of trade, with salt mining, tourism, and tradition at its heart. For millennia, people flocked to see its surreal beauty and the shimmering pink of its salt.

"Then the water slowly receded. Resorts were abandoned, turning into ghost towns. The lush ring of life that once hugged the shores withered into dust. What remained was a wound—emotional, ecological, and economic.

It all began with something small: the vineyards uprooted during the 1979 revolution, replaced by thirstier crops—apples, sugar beets. Then came a national unravelling—drought, war, sanctions, a web of politics.

"I told you I've been around a long time," she said softly. "Long enough to see the lake in all its beauty—and as a dried-up mudflat."

She looked out over the white, barren landscape.

"It became politicised, buried beneath speeches, menace, and silence. You see why I tell you this is our consciousness shaping the world. This void of salt is a reflection of people's minds."

Drooping on her withered legs, the Pelican seemed to sag even further—then suddenly jolted upright. Her eyes flickered with renewed strength.

"And people can bring life back to the lake!" she said.

"But how?" Shirin asked. "How could it be possible? Where can the water return from?"

"People's will, people's consciousness—by changing their observations! This is a crisis of our minds more than anything; it depends on how we relate to the lakes or rivers, how we speak to them. The lake is alive—she hears us!"

"Will that bring the water back to the lake?"

"Yes, it will. Your consciousness is capable of anything. The lake is listening... it's responding."

A flicker of hope stirred within Shirin. "You said our consciousness is capable of anything, changing the reality—but this is far from my personal experience!" She then told Mahlagha about Farhad, about the story of his disappearance and her constant quest to find him.

"But I can't find him," Shirin protested. "That wasn't my consciousness."

Mahlagha crouched slightly, her wide eyes locked on Shirin. "Do you know why?" she said gently, "because deep down, you don't believe you can. You've lost hope. You doubt. It's like the cat—either alive or dead. There's no in-between. Either you believe he's out there and you'll see him again... or you don't."

Shirin's voice trembled. "But I want to believe. I try to."

Mahlagha tilted her head. "Trying isn't the same as knowing. Belief doesn't live in effort—it lives in stillness. In trust."

Shirin looked away, her voice barely a whisper. "What if he's gone?"

Mahlagha said softly, "But not in your mind. Don't bury him in doubt before you even open the box."

Shirin blinked. "The box?"

Mahlagha nodded. "The one in your heart. The one holding both the fear and the hope. Open it. See for yourself."

Shirin cried, "You don't know how many places I've searched for him, how many roads I've travelled. You have no idea how dark my life has been. I live in shadows—with no map, no light, no clue. So my box is dark!"

Mahlagha said nothing.

Shirin caught herself, her voice softening. "I'm sorry... I overreacted."

A pause. Then, quietly, Mahlagha added, "In northern Scandinavia, winter stretches on—long, dark, and almost unbearable—for seven, sometimes eight months. The sun barely rises, swallowed by endless night. Yet they endure, sustained by the memory of summer. Summer is short, yes—but it feels like a reward. During those brief months, the sun never sets, and the days never end. That memory becomes their anchor. It gives meaning to the cold and the dark. It shapes how they live. It shapes how they see."

Mahlagha looked at her gently. "You're a Hummingbird. You can fly backwards, can't you? You need to fly back in your mind and find a memory—even a flicker of a moment like a Scandinavian summer—that is short but reviving, that will change your consciousness. Can you do that?"

Shirin nodded, a faint glimmer in her eyes. "Yes. I can."

The air was still, thick with something unspoken. Across the salt-cracked earth, a ripple stirred—like the lake itself had turned in her sleep.

Shirin closed her eyes and flew back in her memory. She felt it—eyes lit up with the warmth of a summer in Bisotun with Farhad. She opened her eyes and saw the colours of her feathers shimmering with a luminous crimson magenta. It was then she had full trust that she could find Farhad—and anything she wanted, including the Winged Sun Disk.

Like an arrow shot from a bow, she darted upwards into the sky. In her mind, she raced back over the dark cloud of all those years—moments of loneliness and uncertainty, seeking, searching, longing for the truth. As if rising from her ashes, she flew towards her love. The whole sky sang for her.

From the land, the Pelican watched her grow small against the horizon —and was happy. She knew that Shirin had shed the weight of her fear and now trusted that the cat was alive.

FARHAD

Farhad the Nightingale perched beneath the smooth expanse of rock on the side of Mount Bisotun. His greyish-brown feathers were mottled with dark streaks. Lost in thought, he stared at the wall until the soft rustle of wings, and the faint vibration of familiar footsteps broke the stillness. As Shirin approached, Farhad's whole body trembled. He wanted to fly forward but held back, calling her name in a brittle, strained cry. Shirin was shaking badly, unable to stand, and gently settled in front of him. Neither of them moved. They just stared at each other for a long time. Shirin leaned forward, but Farhad pulled back with a glaring look.

Shirin, confused, stretched her neck and flicked her head to one side, pleading with him through her gleaming eyes and opening her wings.

"Please," Farhad implored with a shaky voice. He pressed himself closer to the wall of the mountain but lost control and slipped, floundering helplessly onto the rocks below.

Shirin gasped. She could see that one side of his body was burned, blackened from neck to leg.

Farhad lay still on the ground. "Now you've seen it... please leave..." he begged, breaking into sobs.

Shirin stepped closer. She stooped down and gently pressed her head against his side. Her feathers brushed the charred stubble of his skin, and every sense in her stirred to life.

Farhad didn't resist when she leaned in further. Her tears flowed freely as she took in his familiar scent. They stayed curled together, talking through the night until dawn came.

The winter sun was battling to rise over the cold mountain. Shirin rolled herself under Farhad's wings, her mind still turning over his story and all that had happened since the day he vanished.

A car bomb had exploded in Damascus just as Farhad was getting into a taxi to take him to the airport. He felt a searing pain in his side, could smell burning flesh, and then darkness overcame him.

When he awoke, he found himself on a boat crowded with Syrian refugees, drifting along the Tigris River to Iraq. But he was no longer human. He had been transformed into a bird. The only sense he could make of it was that he had died in the explosion and had been reincarnated.

When the boat arrived in Iraq, U.S. troops sent the refugees to the Salman Pak facility[5], which stood beside the ruins of the ancient metropolis of Ctesiphon[6]. Farhad found it difficult to fly because of his injury, so he made Ctesiphon his refuge, roosting beneath the vast arch of Taq-e-Kasra.[7]

The Iraqi birds there, who called the place Al-Mada'in[8], welcomed Farhad as one of their own. Together, they would perch on the arch and watch the American soldiers below darting between the ruins, clad in armour with gleaming weapons and haunted eyes—like ghosts chasing ghosts.

The military base reminded Farhad of the *Epic of Gilgamesh*, the 4,000-year-old tale that serves as a cautionary story about human overreach and its potential for violence. It tells how ambition leads to the destruction of the sacred Cedar Forest and the senseless loss of lives. But even in that ancient tale, amidst the chaos and ruin, there was Shamash—the Sun God, guardian of truth, justice, and law. Shamash observed all things and guided the hero, Gilgamesh, through darkness.

The epic had been written not far from where Farhad had settled—north along the bank of the Tigris, near ancient Nineveh, close to modern Mosul.

Farhad often thought about that story. So much had changed, yet so little. The forests were gone, but the destruction endured. He wondered if Shamash still watched—if some glimmer of light might one day return to this ravaged land, and perhaps, to him too.

Even though Farhad had begun to settle into his new form and found companionship among the other birds, a deeper part of him still longed for something more—for Shirin, for wholeness, for purpose. He lived in a kind of limbo—a space between death and resurrection.

The only thing that grounded him was the scent of honeysuckle that climbed up the back of the arch each spring. It always brought him back to their garden in Tehran—proof that his love for Shirin had been real, not just a dream

Then one day, he saw it—a griffin-like bird perched on the arch, so still he mistook it for part of the ruins. But then it moved. A strange bird, with a crown-like crest—a Hoopoe. "Seen any birds heading toward Iran?" the Hoopoe asked. "I've been counting for decades. They come out, but none seem to go in. It's as if Iran is emptying. The lineage fading. No dynasties, no heirs—just a lost generation."

The Hoopoe looked directly at Farhad. "You must go back. They need you there. If all the birds leave, what will be left to restore?"

"But how?" Farhad asked. "You said there aren't many birds left in Iran. How can I do it alone?"

"You won't be alone. Others are on their own quests. Join them."

Farhad hesitated, then spoke from the ache in his chest. He confessed that he wanted to find Shirin again.

"If love still anchors you to this world, then you must go to Mount Bisotun," the Hoopoe said. "Carve her portrait into the rock. That's how you'll find her."

"Mount Bisotun? Carving?" Farhad hesitated. "With this broken body, I can barely fly. How am I supposed to climb a mountain?"

The Hoopoe tilted its head. "If your mind is strong, the body will follow." He leaned in closer and added, "What stands in the way becomes the way. The obstacle is the opportunity. Adversity is how we grow."

And so, his quest had brought Farhad here—to Bisotun. That was his story.

Shirin thought about it and realised how true it was. Farhad couldn't fly high, nor could he climb with ease—but the struggle to reach Bisotun, despite his broken body, had become the very thing that gave his journey meaning. Without the hardship, there would be no quest, no redemption. It was the obstacle that shaped the story, the resistance that revealed his strength.

Shirin watched him closely, full of quiet admiration. Farhad was waking slowly, twitching his wings as if emerging from a long, heavy dream.

Then, suddenly, he spoke. "We're not dead... are we?"

"Of course not!" she said, rubbing her head gently against his. "I told you, darling, we have a plan. First, we must find the Winged Sun Disc. That will release us from *Cloudcuckooland*. Then we leave the Valley of the Quest and begin our journey toward the Simorgh."

Farhad's heart swelled. He bent his head into hers, softly, gratefully. "You haven't changed at all... I was afraid if you saw me burned and broken, I'd lose you again." His eyes glowed. "I want to show you something. Come!"

He led her to a smooth slab of stone near the mountain's base. With effort, he stood upright, pride in his voice. "I carved it... for you."

The stone shimmered in the light. Shirin's eyes widened as she saw it—her own reflection, a portrait etched in the gleaming surface. Overcome with emotion, she burst into flight, soaring above him, her wings slicing through the air with a mixture of joy and disbelief.

As she glided, she caught a glimpse—far above—of something engraved in the cliffside. "There!" she cried. "Farhad, have you seen that? On the rock face?"

He shook his head. His damaged wing had never let him climb that high.

But together, they began the ascent—slowly, in short flights, pausing often but never giving up. Higher and higher, until the great relief sculpture finally revealed itself: The Bisotun Inscription.[9]

It was all there. The lineage. The *farr*. And the Winged Sun Disc.

Somewhere in the wind, a magic flute played. The shadow on the sundial shifted.

THE VALLEY OF TOLERANCE

KAMRAN'S EYES widened in astonishment as he continued to marvel at his flamboyant chestnut-brown plumage. He lowered his head, letting his beak graze the shimmering bottle-green feathers of his neck. A quiet thrill stirred within him—he couldn't help but feel a secret delight in his new Pheasant form.

It had been a long time since he'd felt anything like this.

As a human, he had become obsessed with plans and outcomes. Anything that drifted outside the margins left him restless, uneasy. But now, in this strange and feathered body, something new had emerged. There was fear, but also exhilaration—like the day his father first tossed him into the water to teach him how to swim. The same wild blend of terror and joy.

Tucked under his wing was Roxy, small and luminous. Her delicate canary head—citron-yellow and downy—peeked out like a golden brooch pinned against the warmth of his copper breast. He drew her closer.

She was quiet now, breathless after a long stretch of sobbing when they first found themselves alone on the slope. Though the tears had dried, her body still trembled with leftover gasps.

Glancing sideways at Kamran, she studied him more closely, and with a shaky voice said, "Sorry, Kami... I didn't mean to make you angry."

Kamran smiled softly and kissed the top of her head. "I'm not angry with you, Rox. I should be the one apologising for shouting. I was just trying to calm you down."

"But your face... your face is all red," she whispered. "Just like when you used to get angry."

"Ha... this is just my pheasant face now. It was dark last night—you probably didn't notice. I'm afraid you'll have to get used to it. At least until we wake up from this very strange hallucination."

"I wish I could be as calm as you," Roxy whispered.

"Best not to take it too seriously," Kamran replied, trying to sound casual. "I'm pretty sure Huma spiked our drink. Psilocybin, maybe. I've tried it before... made me feel like I could fly."

Roxy pulled herself out from under his wing and stood shakily in front of him. "That's supposed to feel good, Kami. Not like this. Unless... unless what's inside our minds made it scary."

They both turned to look down at the valley stretching before them like the open mouth of some ancient beast—jagged red rock rising in stone spires like broken teeth. Mist clung to every surface. Far below, shadowed shapes loomed and twisted, part of a buried world that refused to fully reveal itself. Like a bottomless abyss.

Kamran rose cautiously, his claws curling against the edge of the cliff. His head twitched from side to side as he scanned the hollow. Roxy stepped closer, her breath just above a whisper. "What is that? That bit there... it looks different." She pointed toward a patch of darker wilderness. A few fractured trees pierced the fog like blackened fingers.

Kamran shook his head. "Don't know, Rox."

A sharp screech split the stillness. They spun around.

From the low ridge behind them, two majestic blue peacocks emerged, strutting towards them in perfect synchrony. Their enormous tail fans unfurled like living tapestries, shimmering with turquoise, gold, and green—each feather an iridescent eye of wonder.

Kamran and Roxy stood awestruck.

The peacocks stopped a few feet away. Then, in perfect unison, they shook their brilliant fans in a rustling cascade of colour, performing a slow, dazzling dance. They shimmered like twin walking globes.

And then, as if on cue, they stepped aside.

From between them, emerging with the quiet authority of a legend, came an albino peahen—poised, elegant, and glowing in the mist.

Her feathers were like freshly fallen snow, glistening with silvery light. A delicate crown of pale quills adorned her head, catching every glimmer and throwing it back in diamonds.

Kamran and Roxy stood speechless. They knew—without a word spoken—that she was no ordinary bird.

The albino peahen stepped forward, lifted her head high, and spoke with a voice like soft thunder. "My name is Amytis, Princess of Media and Queen of Babel. Welcome to the Valley of Tolerance."

Kamran and Roxy exchanged a glance, then turned again to the two magnificent peacocks, who stood like statues on either side of their queen.

Amytis noticed their gaze. "Ah yes," she said, "they are my glorious guards. Feminine discernment shaped those spectacular tails—crafted to attract mates. Peahens may not display such extravagance, but we carry something greater: the gift of life.

"In nature, difference is vital. It creates harmony. It ensures continuity."

She narrowed her eyes, and with a soft voice said, "Besides, these dazzling feathers hold, for me, the ancient spirit of the Hanging Gardens of Babylon—alive, shimmering, and never forgotten."

She told them of her origin: a princess of the Median Empire, daughter of Cyaxares, king of Media, married to Nebuchadnezzar II, King of Babylon. To ease her longing for her homeland, her husband built the Hanging Gardens—one of the Seven Wonders of the World.

Trees and flowers from the mountains of Media were brought to the flat earth of Babylon, lifted by tiered terraces, watered by ingenious irrigation. The gardens were her memory, made eternal in stone and vine.

After a moment of awe, Kamran gathered himself and said awkwardly, "That must've been... a very long time ago. I mean, seeing you here, like this—it has to be the hallucinogens, right? I think someone spiked you too."

Amytis turned sharply. "First, I think you're wrong," she said. "Look at the world you live in—hopelessly backward compared to our time. Your era feels like the past to me. A time in desperate need of evolution.

"We meet now because, as birds, you are no longer blind. You see with more than eyes. This is not intoxication."

Kamran tilted his head and let out a small, sceptical laugh. "Did you have electricity back then?"

"No," Amytis replied coolly. "We didn't have electricity. Or petrol. Yet we built wonders—feats of engineering and beauty your people cannot recreate.

"And what have you done with your so-called progress? Burned forests. Poisoned rivers. Dug holes into the Earth for fuel. Choked the sky with smoke—and now run to space, looking for another place to destroy.

"But we... we respected the elements. We kept our pagan heads alert. We listened to the land."

Kamran wanted to reply, but Roxy placed a gentle wing on his chest. Excited to see a woman in charge, she fluttered forward.

"Don't take him seriously," Roxy said brightly, then bowed deeply to Amytis. "You know how men can be! We're on a trip—real or psychedelic—and we have to find our way. We've been told to go to Alborz. Does that name mean anything to you? Could you help us understand where we are... and what exactly this Valley of Tolerance is?"

Amytis stepped gracefully toward the cliff's edge, her white feathers catching the mist. The guards flanked her silently. She stared long into the depths before turning back to them.

"This place is the Middle East," she declared.

Roxy's eyes grew large. "Ah... I mean, I'm not surprised we're in the Middle East. But like... exactly where are we? For example, could you tell us what that dark patch is, way down there?"

Amytis followed her gaze. "That large, scarred patch?"

"Yes," said Roxy quickly. "That one."

"That," Amytis said with calm gravity, "is the man-made wasteland. What you now call Iran."

Kamran's patience snapped. "Wait—earlier you said this was the Valley of Tolerance. Now you're giving us a different address, telling us it's Iran? Or the whole Middle East? We need some clarity here!"

Amytis didn't flinch."I am not lying. This gaping abyss is the Middle East as you've made it—fractured, scarred, and stripped of its ancient tolerance. What once was a cradle of cultures is now a battleground of identities. This valley is what's left. And to reach Alborz, you must go through it. You must descend into the depths and recover the tolerance that has been lost."

Kamran had been listening carefully—until his face twisted with frustration and disbelief. He shouted, "What the hell? Is this some kind of joke? This has nothing to do with us. Our only fault was being born here. This place has always been at fucking war! All the religions started here, didn't they? And that's the problem. It's not us—it's the damn blueprint! There's something in the water, or in the air. Fuelled by rage, hypocrisy, violence, and, yes, a whole lot of bloody oil... It's always been a combustible pit of shit!"

"Kami—language!" Roxy whispered sharply.

Amytis remained still. Then she said, "Every creature must seek its roots to find the way forward. Once, yours was a land of peace, poets, and visionaries. Now? Fanaticism. Division. Racism. A fear of your own reflection. You've forgotten who you were. I am here to help you remember."

She paused, then added, "I have a story to tell."

With regal poise, she turned. But instead of taking flight, she began to walk—slowly, deliberately—as if inviting them deeper into the mystery.

Kamran and Roxy hesitated, then followed. The two shimmering guards fell in silently behind them.

Kamran glanced at Roxy's pale face. "Stay close," he whispered. Together, they descended—into the mist, into memory, into myth—like hikers slipping back through time. Amytis walked ahead, tall and radiant.

And then, she began her tale...

"Long before modern borders were etched onto maps—before the names *Iran* and *Iraq* even existed—the lands they now encompass were the cradle of great civilizations. Sometimes rivals, sometimes allies, they were always forces that shaped history through ambition, ingenuity, and enduring legacy.

"To the east lay ancient Persia and Elam—the ancestral heartlands of what we now call Iran. To the west, between the life-giving rivers of the Tigris and Euphrates, rose the legendary cities of Sumer, Akkad, Babylon, and Assur.

"In 539 BCE, in a clash both epic and inevitable, these two worlds collided—a moment in history that could be considered the first Iran-Iraq war.

"My husband, the great Nebuchadnezzar II, King of Babylon, once marched upon the Land of Judah. He tore down their temples, seized their sacred vessels of gold, and forced their people into exile beneath the towering gates of Babylon. It was a triumph, yes—but one steeped in prophecy and shadowed by consequence.

"By the time war reached our gates, my husband had long returned to dust, and the empire stood under the distracted rule of Nabonidus. But it was his son—my grandson—the proud, impulsive Belshazzar, who held Babylon's fate in unsteady hands.

"The empire's foundations had already begun to crack. The people had grown weary. And as Persian forces closed in, Belshazzar dared to host a feast—a final night of revelry and defiance. He drank from the looted vessels, mocking the gods of his enemies, even as his own downfall crept silently toward him.

"The gates of Babylon opened without a fight. There was no siege. No fire. No prolonged resistance. Only the silent collapse of an empire. A chapter closed for Mesopotamia—the heart of ancient Iraq. And a new one began for ancient Iran. But this was no ordinary conquest. This was a transformation. With the fall of Babylon came a new kind of king—Cyrus, who came not only as a conqueror, but as a liberator.

"Cyrus did not pillage; he proclaimed. He issued decrees of tolerance and restoration. He freed exiles. He rebuilt temples. He etched his vision into clay—what the world would one day hail as the first charter of human rights. Now known as *The Cyrus Cylinder*, it declared that all enslaved and displaced peoples were free to return to their homelands.

"Among them were the Jews, long held in Babylonian captivity. Under Cyrus's decree, they were permitted to return home—to rebuild their temple, their city, and their faith.

"It was more than a political gesture. It was revolutionary."The empire of Iran became the first great world empire—not just the largest, but the first to embrace something far more difficult: diversity."

She lifted her gaze to the horizon, as if seeing it anew.

"It was a state that stretched across the entire Middle East as you now know it—multicultural, multifaith, multilingual. It had to be. To rule such a vast realm, Cyrus wrote not in Persian, but in Babylonian—for the message had to reach Babylonian hearts. He honoured their customs, their gods, their traditions. And that is why the Cylinder matters. It was more than clay. It was a vision."

Amytis turned to Kamran and said, "So, you see? The Middle East wasn't always like it is today. I told you—we were more advanced than you."

A quiet acceptance settled over Kamran and Roxy as they absorbed the weight of the revelation—its beauty, its irony, its truth.

And Amytis added, with a hint of pride and sorrow: "Time erases greatness, but it doesn't make it less true. You are walking on soil that remembers everything—even if you don't."

Kamran bowed his head slightly. "Please," he said. "Carry on."

Amytis nodded. "Very well. Let me show you what was lost—and what still lingers beneath the dust.

"Cyrus, the Great King of Persia, showed the world that a multinational society could thrive—not through fear, but through respect. His empire endured nearly two centuries of peace and stability, until it was finally broken by the sword of Alexander the Great."

"Ah, Alexander…" Roxy murmured.

"One of many Greeks who admired the greatness of Cyrus," Amytis replied. "Alexander conquered the empire, yes—but he could not hold it. Where Cyrus built with wisdom, Alexander blazed with fire. And so, the empire fractured soon after his death.

"But the dream of Cyrus lived on. Xenophon, a student of Socrates and a Greek historian, wrote *The Cyropaedia*, a tribute to Cyrus's leadership. It was no mere biography, but a political vision—a blueprint for ruling a diverse society.

"Centuries later, across an ocean and the vast expanse of time, that book would find its way into the hands of Thomas Jefferson, a founding father of the American Revolution. Jefferson was an avid student of Cyrus. He kept three copies of *The Cyropaedia* in his personal library, returning to it often as he envisioned a new kind of nation—one built on tolerance, liberty, and justice.

"There is," Amytis said, her voice now a whisper, "a link between that clay cylinder... and the birth of the United States."

Kamran looked at her, astonished. "You're saying Cyrus influenced the American Revolu tion?"

"That clay cylinder," Amytis said softly, "planted the seed of an idea. There is a philosophical lineage—a thread of thought that stretches all the way to the birth of the United States."

Amytis lifted her gaze toward the horizon, unfazed. Her thoughts stretched across centuries—the past, after all, was never far behind her. She spoke again, this time of a more recent history—urgent, perhaps even forgotten: "There was a man," she said, "Abdol Hossein Sardari. They called him the Iranian Schindler."[10]

"Sardari, an Iranian diplomat stationed in Nazi-occupied Paris, used courage and cunning to issue Iranian passports to Jews—many of them not Iranian by birth. He leaned on Nazi Germany's own racial delusion: that Iranians were 'pure-blooded Aryans' and therefore exempt from the Nuremberg Laws. And so, through a loophole of cruelty, he saved hundreds of lives."

When Amytis finished her story, she began to pace. Her movements were deliberate, elegant, yet marked by unshakable authority. Then she stopped, turned sharply, and fixed Kamran and Roxy with an intense stare.

"Once, the Middle East was the most tolerant place on Earth. And it can be again. It does not matter who is stronger—Israel or Palestine, Iran or Saudi Arabia, Lebanon or Syria. When there is no peace in the region, everyone is in trouble."

Her crest of silver feathers shimmered as she lifted her head.

"The heritage of Cyrus is not pride or conquest. It is understanding. Human liberty. Courage. Compassion. And above all—tolerance. That is the key to peace. That is what Iran must protect. That is what every individual in the Middle East must guard."

With a flick of her head, the Imperial Peahen scanned the valley around them. "Look around," she said softly. "You have reached the bottom."

And indeed, they had.

Roxy and Kamran looked down. Their feet now stood on the solid bedrock of the valley floor. It wasn't bottomless despair. It had a foundation—one laid over millennia by the quiet strength of diversity.

They looked around with awe. The steep walls of the valley loomed tall and solemn, but they no longer felt trapped. The maze of lotus blossoms that had once seemed tangled and wild now shimmered with a quiet order—an ancient design, built on coexistence.

Wide-eyed, breathless, Roxy and Kamran felt something awakening. A key turned inside them.

Together, they took flight.

Their wings rose on the wind, and with a joyful beat, they soared upward—light, hopeful, free. Across the valley they flew toward the Alborz Mountains. Toward the future.

The magic flute played. The shadow on the sundial shifted.

THE VALLEY OF KNOWLEDGE

THE WHITE STORK

AMONG THE many eggs that had been laid inside the vast cavern, one was ready to hatch. It was Bijan—a Blue Jay. The second followed soon after: a sparrow, Gohar's daughter, Ayda. The third hesitated at first, but then something stirred—the faint, urgent motion of an embryo finding its strength. A sudden crack split the shell, and at last a turkey chick emerged; it was Jav, blinking and confused.

They looked at each other—three freshly hatched beings, still slick with birth. And then, in unspoken unison, they panicked.

Jav looked around the dim cave, bits of shell still clinging to his feathers. "For fuck's sake... what is this?" he thought, utterly bewildered.

Ayda slowly uncurled herself, silent and wide-eyed, staring in disbelief at the strange softness of her own plumage.

"Why didn't we even make it to being full birds?" Bijan muttered, disappointed at the poor, reduced version of what he had imagined birdhood would be.

But beyond the question of status, there was something more urgent to contend with: the cave. It was cold. Dark. Choked with a sulphuric stench. The ceiling hung low, a sparse crust of limestone stretching into a dense, multi-level network—like a maze carved from fossil and time.

Ayda stood shakily on her broken eggshells, her eyes fixed on the dizzying labyrinth above. "So... this is it. We've died." Her voice echoed off the cave walls, growing thinner and more terrifying with each repetition.

Jav shouted back, dryly, "No, it looks like we've just hatched."

She burst into tears, calling out for her mother, flailing helplessly as she searched the dim chamber. The other two watched in silence—perhaps too stunned by their own half-feathered forms to find sympathy, or perhaps just as scared and unable to show it. Eventually, Ayda gave up, collapsing on the cave floor, her tiny wings trembling.

One by one, they eventually began to hop awkwardly along the rocky ground until they reached the mouth of the cave. There, they paused, shivering.

They had emerged at the bottom of a deep valley, its floor buried beneath a thick layer of untouched snow. Not a sound stirred. They scanned the whiteness for a sign—some trace of a path, a hint of direction. But there was nothing. Only snow: endless and untouched.

A little way further on, they came across a patch where the snow was disturbed. Dozens of bird tracks criss-crossed the snow, scattered and overlapping like scrawls on a blank page. Each trail was different: some formed neat, narrow pairs, as if left by the tidy hops of a wren; others resembled arrowheads—sharper, more deliberate—likely made by larger birds. A few were spaced far apart, deep and heavy enough to belong to a Heron or Crane.

It looked almost like a message scribbled in the snow, whispering: "This way."

So, they followed. Before long, the smaller tracks began to vanish, melted away or swallowed by fresh snowfall. But the larger ones remained—deep and clear. Heron? Goose? Swan? It was hard to say. Still, they kept moving.

At first, they could barely manage more than awkward hops. But eventually—with some flapping, some stumbling—they began to flutter forward, climbing inch by inch toward the upper edge of the valley.

After a while, Bijan, who had taken the lead, stopped suddenly. "Look!" he cried.

At the top of the valley, silhouetted against the grey sky, stood the outline of a chimney. A sign of life. Their wings fluttered faster, and they flew toward it as best they could. But when they arrived, their eagerness collapsed into disappointment.

The smoky red bricks of the chimney rose alone from the snow. If there had once been a roof or a home below it, it was long buried under the heavy snowdrift. They gathered around it in silence, their small bodies hunched in despair against the cold. Then there was a sound—a rustle, a shift of weight from somewhere above. They looked up.

Perched on the lip of the chimney pot was a White Stork—tall and spectral, its black-tipped wings folded like a cloak. It stared down at them with one eye, with a face that was motionless and unreadable.

"Who are you?" they shouted.

The stork rose up, stepped forward, graceful on its long legs, and replied in a shrill, rasping voice: "I am a revolutionary. I made a revolution. Like you!"

"We are not!" Bijan stammered. "We didn't start anything... others did... We're here to fix things."

"Aren't you Iranians?"

"So what? I wasn't born then," Jav muttered. "I mean—I was, but I didn't ask for any of this."

"We're looking for the Simorgh," Bijan continued. "A leader. Someone to save us from all this."

"Do you know the way out? Where are we?" Ayda asked with a trembling voice. "Do you know?"

The White Stork looked down at them silently and then turned its eyes to gaze distantly into the snow-covered valley.

"To find the Simorgh," it said slowly, "you must cross this valley. The Valley of Knowledge."

Jav exploded. "Valley of Knowledge? This damn place? That bloody Huma gave us this ridiculous form—turned us into this, an absolute joke!" His wings flailed. "A bloody nightmare," he raged. "Even if this is a dream—I'm telling you—I've had enough of being the fool."

Unfazed by his outburst, Ayda asked, "So, are you our guide? Huma said each valley has a guide."

The stork said, "I am not! But I know this is the Valley of Knowledge!"

"What do we do in the Valley of Knowledge?" Ayda asked. "Learn something, I suppose?"

The stork tilted its head. "Unlearn. And learn. Both. You're here to experience the joy of discovery." It paused, then continued with a note of scorn in its voice. "You Iranians get caught in a cycle of overconfidence—when false knowledge fuels belief. Like when so many of you insisted there was a human face on the moon.

"Yet beneath it all, there's deep insecurity. You forget how extraordinary you are. Most of your people don't even know the basic geography or history of their own country. Or they know just enough to be dismissive. You're simply... uninterested."

Bijan blinked, stunned by the sharpness of the comment. "Wait," he said. "So I gather that you're not from Iran, that's at least clear. You said you were a revolutionary—what revolution were you talking about?"

The stork spread its wings, towering now, and declared in a ringing voice, "The Copernican Revolution. I am the one who placed the sun at the centre of the universe!"

"So, let me get this straight," Ayda said slowly. "Is that when everyone thought Earth was the centre of everything for thousands of years?"

"That's right," the Stork replied. "People once believed the sun and stars all revolved around us. Then, in the 1500s, I came along, did my research, and posed the question: 'What if we've got it all wrong? What if the sun is at the centre?'"

Ayda's eyes flickered. "That must've caused a stir."

"It did. Tremendously. I was an astronomer but a canon in the Church too, so I knew how dangerous that idea was and kept quiet about it for a long time. I only published my book right at the end."

"And then what happened?" asked Ayda impatiently.

"Well, the book was dense—meant for mathematicians, not the average person—but still, it got banned for almost seventy years. Even so, it changed everything. It helped people start asking questions that reshaped how we see the universe."

Ayda was quiet for a moment, her eyes searching the stars. Then, with a hint of hesitation, she said, "I know we're dead, but I didn't think we'd gone that far back in time."

"You're not dead," the stork said gently. "When you look at the stars, you're actually looking into the past. Many of those stars died ages ago— their light is only just reaching you now. So you are alive; what you're witnessing is the echo of what once was, or simply you are looking at history!"

Ayda tilted her head thoughtfully. "So, you're history too?"

The Stork said softly. "Exactly! The universe tells its story mainly through the light from these stars. And now that we're birds, we have an exceptional vision that can penetrate different layers of the atmosphere. We can see the stars much clearer."

Jav made a strange noise, like snorting.

Ayda leaned in eagerly. "So, why are you here? Are we going to learn about the stars?"

The stork smiled thoughtfully. "I'm fascinated by Iran. It's a special case for me. About five hundred years ago, I turned the world upside down—that was during the Renaissance, a time when the world shifted from the Middle Ages to modern times. I thought that change was irreversible, like a bell that can't be un-rung. But the revolution in Iran showed me otherwise."

"Pile of rubbish," Jav moaned, preening his plumage with clear contempt for the conversation. "All this doesn't help us out of this damn freezing cold, does it?"

Bijan bristled slightly. He flicked the air with his wing and dropped down to the ground. "With all due respect, as I mentioned earlier—we didn't. That was just a group of Mullahs. You can't reduce the whole country to that. Besides, the 1979 revolution happened because foreign powers backed the regime change."

The White Stork stretched his neck. "And with due respect, as I mentioned earlier, I am part of history. So I know. The Mullahs owe their victory to the people of Iran—they were the main force that made it happen. And the revolution didn't begin in 1979. It was 1946."

Their eyes widened. Jav's sarcasm sharpened instantly. "Leave it, old bird... You're from Europe, right? Then you must've picked up that rubbish over there—or from your American friends. You're way behind. Time for a top-up, Mr White History."

The White Stork stared at them for several long moments, noisily bulging air in and out of his throat, as if preparing himself to push back.

"May I ask you a simple question?" he said. "Do you know how many explorers Iran has had?"

"What do you mean by 'explorer'?" Jav asked harshly. "Like someone who travels to discover new places?"

"Yes."

"I don't know... do you, Bijan?"

"No, I don't... maybe a couple?" Bijan replied, looking sideways.

Ayda giggled. "Apart from us, obviously!"

The White Stork gave a slight nod, then spoke with calm gravity. "A large part of Iran's history has been written by non-Iranian explorers— foreigners who were curious, who wanted to learn more about you. From Marco Polo to Edward Browne, and many others today. Meanwhile, you're often not even curious about your own land. You don't explore it. Even now, with travel easier than ever, and so many Iranians living abroad, your adventures tend to stop at the shopping malls."

Jav looked away, slightly ruffled. "Maybe we are not as nosy as you! Just that!"

"Sometimes," the Stork continued, "you don't even learn the language of your adopted countries. Libraries go untouched. Books sit on shelves like decorations. Even the Quran—the very book many base their deepest convictions on—is rarely read or understood. Yet you believe in its truth without grasping its meaning. In that sense, I suppose it is a miracle!

"So, please, before jumping to conspiracy theories and blaming foreign powers, maybe it's time to ask harder questions. The image of the hero on horseback in the moon—that wasn't planted by outsiders. That came from within. What you need isn't another revolution imposed from the outside. What you need is a revolution from within."

They fell silent. Then, breaking the stillness with his new turkey-like voice, Jav shrilled, "Okay, suppose you're right—but what's it got to do with you? What the hell are you doing here in our land?"

The White Stork gazed up at the sky. A few feathers on his head lifted with the breeze. "Well, young poult," he said calmly, "as I told you, I'm an astronomer. And this"—he pointed to the tall chimney—"this is my observatory.

"I look deep into the past, searching for dying stars. I hunt for supernovae. Stars die all the time, but I try to catch those rare, spectacular moments when a star goes out with one final, brilliant flare. You can only see them when the sky is truly dark... and I've never found a sky darker than Iran's."

He smiled faintly. "And I was right. A magnificent Iranian supernova died a few decades ago. Its light waves only just reached us today. They were... breathtaking."

His voice softened, tinged with sadness. "You see, when a star dies in a supernova, it doesn't vanish. It leaves behind a remnant—what's left of the explosion. Sometimes it becomes another star, but sometimes the collapse is so intense that it turns into a black hole.

"The heat in the core... the pressure from outside... it all crushed the star's light inward. And so it was with the Iranian Revolution in 1979. It was like a supernova exploding, but what remains now is not light, but absence: a black hole."

"So, I'm done," said the White Stork, with a firm voice. "I'll fly away from here, and I won't dare return to such a dark sky."

He stood tall on his long legs, spreading his wings slightly, preparing to leave.

The birds panicked. Bijan and Ayda rushed beneath him, chirping and fluttering, pleading to be taken along. But Jav hesitated. Despite his fear, he declared, "That's good! Go back to where you came from. We've had enough of explorers—or even worse, *histor-o-nomers!*"

The Stork looked down at them with his cool, distant eyes. "You can only leave the valley if you find something of your own," he said. "A discovery. An outcome. Something real that came from your experience."

He pointed his beak skyward. "Until you find your guide, follow the stars. They guide lost travellers like you."

They looked at each other, unsure, fear flickering in their eyes.

Ayda looked up at the towering chimney. "So... your observatory... can we use it to search for stars?"

The Stork gave a deep sigh. "My observatory? No, I'm sorry—that's a personal space. It means different things to different people. I built it to watch *my* sky. If you want to see *your* sky, you'll need to build one of your own.

"In the Valley of Knowledge, there's no shortcut. You have to evolve from within. Each of you must make your own observations, do your own homework. You can't learn to fly unless you actually fly."

Then he added, with a wry glance, "Besides, I'm a foreigner. If I handed it to you, you'd turn that into another suspicious story. I'd rather stay clear of your conspiracy theories."

Ayda's wings drooped. "But I want to explore... I just don't know how." Her voice cracked, and she began to cry, making a strange, rhythmic sound that echoed gently with each tear.

The Stork paused, glancing down at their frightened faces. His wings lifted slightly, then lowered again. He hesitated. Something in him stirred— perhaps duty, perhaps guilt.

And for the first time, he did not look away.

"Alright," the White Stork said at last. "There's one thing I can do. I can pluck you from where you are and drop you into the Chimney of Rethinking. That'll set you up. But the rest is up to you. From there, you'll need to discover the frozen land beneath your feet. Turn it into a real home. a place you truly know—from the foundation to the roof, the floor to the garden. Every room, every brick—kitchen to bedroom, inside and out. Make it yours."

He snapped his beak open and then shut it with a clattering sound that echoed through the cold air, amplified by the pouch in his throat. Then, with a sharp movement, he flung his head backward until his crown touched his back. Slowly, he arched it forward again—only to repeat the gesture several times in a ritualistic display.

Startled, the three birds crouched closer to each other.

And then, with a powerful stroke of his wings, the Stork launched himself from the chimney, hovered for a moment, and swooped down toward them. His wings spread wide, casting an enormous shadow over the snow.

Jav panicked, squealed, and rolled away, sprinting in fear toward the direction of the cave.

The Stork plunged into the snow with a thud, then rose again with surprising force, lifting Bijan and Ayda in his strong claws. In a single, soaring arc, he carried them up to the top of the chimney—and dropped them, gently but firmly, into it.

Everything went black.

THE MUTE SWAN

Bijan and Ayda shot out of the bottom of the chimney and hit the rocky slope hard, tumbling onto the uneven surface of a sea wall.

The snow was gone. Everything around them had changed.

Behind them, sharp cliffs loomed, rising out of the valley like a barrier. A faint scarlet glow flickered on the horizon, like the last trace of sunlight. The tide had pulled far back, revealing wide stretches of dark, glistening mud. The shoreline had retreated so far that the sea was now just a sliver of water at the edge of sight.

They stood still for a long time, disoriented.

A shriek of wings tore through the air. A black shape crossed the sky, and a large crow slammed down in front of them.

Frightened, they ducked behind a stone. But the crow was already striding toward them, sharp and deliberate. They couldn't escape his cold, merciless gaze.

He fixed his eyes on Ayda and rasped in a hoarse, chilling voice: "Do you know why this water has turned red? It's because they took off their hijabs—those foolish women."

She and Bijan hurled themselves into the air in a panic, wings beating frantically. They darted toward the sea and hovered above the water, hearts pounding in their chests.

The crow hadn't lied. The water below was red, clearly visible, even in the fading light.

They were instantly alarmed and swerved into the southern wind, knowing they couldn't just drift aimlessly; they needed a plan. When they spotted a small island below, they veered towards it, deciding to wait there until nightfall, when the stars might guide them.

They perched quietly on the shoreline. The sea had calmed, but the coast was still tinged red, like blood smeared along the edge of the land. As the last light faded, something caught their eyes, a small white shape floating in the distance. It shimmered faintly in the growing dark.

Bijan said, "What is that? It looks like... a giant letter S?"

"S? To me, it is like a white question mark," Ayda said.

As the tide rose, the object drifted slowly closer. It wasn't an object—it was a Swan: slender, proud, and graceful. It floated buoyantly on the dark water, as if suspended in a timeless space.

For a moment, they felt almost happy. The approaching bird looked harmless.

"Maybe we can ask it where we are and what's going on with the red water?" Ayda said.

The Swan was close now, gliding silently just a few metres away.

"It looks like... a Mute Swan," Bijan said.

The Swan drifted towards them, head tilted upward. At last, it came into view and spoke: "They tried to mute me in 1946," the Swan said, reaching the shore. "But by then, I had already sung my song and left my books behind. Those pages still spoke. My story remained loud—the throbbing beat of my wings during my final flight still echoes in the sky above Iran."

He paused, then added softly, "And yes... I heard you. The water is red."

He looked around and spoke again. "It's getting dark now, but I'll tell you where we are. This is the Strait of Hormuz, in the Persian Gulf. More precisely, about eight kilometres off the coast—on Hormuz Island.

"The soil here holds a high concentration of iron oxide, drawn from sediment rich in ochre. That's what gives the land its deep crimson hue. That's what tinges the water red. The locals call it *golak*—'the little flower.'

"It is a hidden gem, long treasured by travellers. Even Marco Polo is said to have visited in 1290. Yet today, many Iranians don't know it exists. Instead, myths have taken root—superstitions born of fear and ignorance. It is a tool easily used by those who seek control."

Ayda thought it was comforting to finally understand that there was science behind the red water. She hopped playfully on the crimson soil before turning to the Swan and asking, "Who are you?"

Bijan, who had been walking slowly, eyes on the ground as if studying the soil, followed behind. With a cautious but curious voice, he asked, "And what happened in 1946?"

The Swan replied calmly, "My name is Ahmad Kasravi."

Bijan and Ayda exchanged a glance.

Bijan spoke gently, "I'm sorry...the name rings a bell, but I don't really know who you are. It's been a long road. Forgive us."

The Swan looked up. Far above, a star shimmered in the night sky—one with a tail. Like a comet. He watched it for a moment, then said softly: "It all began when I looked at the stars."

And then, he began to tell his story.

"I was born in the suburbs of Tabriz into a deeply religious family. My father was a modest merchant, and from the beginning, it was assumed I would follow tradition and become a mullah. At the age of six, I was sent to the local *maktab*, but the semi-literate teacher there couldn't keep pace with my curiosity. Still, with support from my father and relatives, I completed the traditional studies in just four years.

"When I was eleven, my world changed. My father passed away, and I had to pause my education to help with our family's carpet business. Those were difficult years. But about three years later, at my family's urging, I left the trade behind and returned to theological studies.

"In 1905, the Constitutional Revolution swept across Iran, and Tabriz became a centre of resistance. I was seventeen then, and I was drawn to the ideals of a national assembly and constitutional rule. But it didn't take long for me to see that many of the conservative clerics around me were opposing progress. Some even aligned themselves with foreign powers to block reform. I began to speak out, criticising those who twisted religion to serve their own interests. It was then I began to walk a very different path.

"By the time I was twenty, I had become a mullah—not out of passion, but out of duty to my family. Yet, I could no longer accept the dogma that surrounded me. I distanced myself from the rituals, limited my role to officiating marriages, and began to reflect more deeply on the meaning of faith. During this period, I memorised the Quran and spent long hours contemplating its verses. Doubt began to grow in my heart.

"A turning point came in 1911, with the arrival of Halley's Comet. It appeared during a time of great turmoil, and many around me believed it was a bad omen. But I couldn't accept such superstition. Every night, I climbed up to our rooftop in Tabriz to observe it with my own eyes. Eventually, I found an article in the Egyptian magazine *Al-Muqtataf*, explaining the comet through modern astronomy. That discovery shook me. It revealed the vast gap between scientific truth and the traditional teachings I had grown up with. From that moment, I became a devoted student of modern science.

"In my mid-twenties, I began learning French and English to explore the world beyond our borders. I taught Arabic, wrote textbooks, and even learned languages to translate scientific articles. Eventually, I moved to Tehran and became a judge, committed to reforming Iran's legal system. I fought corruption, resisted clerical interference, and worked to bring reason and justice to a system plagued by stagnation. I gained respect—but also powerful enemies.

"Language fascinated me. I was fluent in several, including Armenian, and I studied Iran's many dialects. I was among the first to argue that dialects like Old Azari were distinct languages rooted in ancient Iranian heritage. This insight became central to my vision of a unified and modern Iran—diverse in culture, yet united in purpose.

"To me, Iran's greatest threat wasn't external; it was our own internal divisions, exploited by outsiders. I believed unity was essential. I once wrote, 'Our younger intellectuals cannot understand the reign of Reza Shah—they were too young to remember the chaos from which he emerged.'

"History, I believed, taught us that even Persia's defeat by Greece in 480 BCE was due to our own fragmentation. I championed reform of the Persian language and cultural identity, publishing my book, *Pure Language*, to promote a clearer, simpler Persian that could unite the nation.

"But my beliefs didn't stop there. I openly criticised Persian mysticism and Sufi poetry. While the nation cherished mystical verse, I saw it as a fog that obscured truth and encouraged passivity. In my book, *Sufigari*, I argued that mysticism weakened our people and made them vulnerable to manipulation.

"I was not just a historian—I was a reformer. I challenged the clergy, particularly after the fall of Reza Shah in 1941, when religious factions regained influence. I warned that their growing power threatened the secular progress Iran had made. I spoke out against their use of media, like radio, to inflame emotion rather than address real social issues.

"In 1942, I published *Khoda Ba Mast* (*God Is With Us*), accusing the clergy of distracting people with empty rituals while neglecting the nation's deeper problems. I was perhaps Iran's most outspoken critic of organised religion. I came to believe that nothing was left of the original Islam, and that what was being promoted in its name was an institution for the benefit of mullahs—one from which the people received nothing but colossal misery. In my book, *Shi'igari* (*Shi'ism*), I questioned the divine status of the Imams and denounced rituals that I believed hindered progress.

"'If this institution survives,' I wrote, 'it will restrain the masses from progress, as it has in the past. While the world witnesses scientific breakthroughs, our religious institutions will continue to bring misery, keeping us forever backward.'

"The clergy branded me a blasphemer. Some accused me of claiming prophethood—a charge I firmly denied. I never sought to be a prophet. I sought only truth, clarity, and justice. Though I could not break the power of the clergy, I know my words planted seeds. I stood alone at times, but I spoke fearlessly. And I hope that, in some small way, I helped shape a future where reason and reform might finally triumph."

It was early dawn when the Swan finished recounting his life story. Bijan and Ayda remained silent, absorbing the complexity of Kasravi's story. He seemed like many men rolled into one—remarkable for countless reasons. Their minds brimmed with curiosity. Above all, one question burned brightest: "What happened to you then?" Ayda finally asked.

"Another long story," the Swan began, "but it's important to understand the historical context. In August 1941, Iran faced the Anglo-Soviet invasion. Though Reza Shah declared neutrality early in World War Two, the Allies launched the invasion to secure their supply routes—what they called the Persian Corridor.

"Supplies from the British and American armies travelled from the Persian Gulf through Iran to the Soviet Union. There were other key reasons too—like securing Iran's oil fields. The Allies feared the Abadan Refinery might fall to the Germans. So the British advanced from the south and central Iran, and the Russians from the north. As you know, Reza Shah was forced to abdicate in favour of his son and went into exile.

"As World War Two came to a close, the British began withdrawing their troops, but the Soviets refused to follow suit. Under Stalin's directive, Soviet influence expanded into Azerbaijan and Iranian Kurdistan, while the communist Tudeh Party—backed by Moscow—emerged as the government's primary rival. Fearing the rise of another large communist state on their doorstep, the British shifted their support to clerics and religious groups, using them as a strategic counterbalance during the early Cold War. Meanwhile, the Tudeh Party remained the main opposition force against the Iranian government. This intense power struggle created an atmosphere of openness—and at times even encouragement—towards religious movements.

"Understanding this is crucial, as it directly connects to the current affairs shaping Iran today."

Ayda listened, disbelief etched across her face. "I never knew any of this—no one ever told us what really happened."

"Listen to the rest," the Swan urged. "In 1941, I founded an independent group called 'The Society of Free Man', dedicated to fighting what I saw as religious superstition and illusions. I also launched a daily newspaper, *Parcham*, to spread these ideas.

"But that alone wasn't enough, given the country's turbulent direction. I had no choice but to engage openly with the people. In 1943, I published my book on Shi'ism—a work many say was the moment I signed my own death warrant. At first, clashes broke out between passionate Muslim crowds and supporters of my philosophy in several cities. I reported and documented everything carefully in my newspaper.

"I can tell you this much—until the spring of 1945, no one had dared to attack me directly. The threats were there, of course, but they remained just words. That changed when a young seminary student—someone I had never heard of—named Navvab Safavi decided to act.

"In April of that year, he and an accomplice came after me in the streets of Tehran. They were armed with knives and a pistol—bought, I later learned, with money donated by the imam of a local mosque. I was badly wounded in the assault and taken to hospital in critical condition.

"And yet—can you believe it? —the attackers were jailed only briefly. Just a few days. Then they were released, thanks to bail paid by a wealthy merchant from the Tehran bazaar."

The Swan's expression darkened as he recounted the saddest part of the story—not the attack itself, but the authorities' response.

"The police report was vague and dishonest," he said. "They accepted Navvab's claim that he acted in self-defence with a knife, even though the medical report clearly showed my back wounds came from a gunshot. I publicly rejected and mocked their findings, publishing my own account in the press. I even sent a detailed open letter to Prime Minister Bayāt titled 'Government Should Respond'. But nothing was done. Navvab was released!"

Ayda asked, "Sorry, but who exactly was this Navvab Safavi? At school, they told us he was a hero!"

"Hero? Maybe to Islamic fundamentalists. But there's no denying his impact. Born in 1924, he was among the first to demand that Islam take political control in Iran—not just spiritually, but as the state's ruling force. He turned religion into a weapon, justifying political violence as a path to religious purity.

"His story began in Tehran, where he completed eight years of school. But after his father—a cleric jailed for slapping Reza Shah's Justice Minister—died, Navvab walked away from formal education. He spent a short time studying in Najaf, but he wasn't after quiet piety. He returned with a mission.

"Safavi founded *Fadā'iyān-e Islam*, 'The Devotees of Islam', a radical Shia group committed to 'cleansing' Iran through targeted assassinations. Secular figures were seen as enemies. The goal? An Islamic utopia. He even took his vision abroad, pitching it in Jordan and Palestine as the beginning of a faith-fuelled revolution.

"His ideas weren't just about violence. He pushed for strict Sharia law, religious taxation as social justice, Fatwa and the purification of the clergy. After the 1979 revolution, much of this agenda would become reality in the Islamic Republic—echoes of Safavi's vision in the policies of a new regime.

"In the early 1950s, as the oil nationalisation movement gained traction,

Ayatollah Kashani, a prominent cleric with widespread popular appeal, allied with Mossadegh, uniting secular nationalists with a religious populist base. Navvab Safavi saw this as a chance to advance his vision of an Islamic state. Kashani's popularity lent credibility to Safavi's radical agenda, and his group viewed the alliance as a strategic opening to push their goals."

"This is unbelievable... connecting all the dots like this," Bijan said, eyes wide. "It just hit me—you said his father slapped the Minister of Justice, got jailed, and died there. What if... what if that slap started it all? His obsession with violence... everything?"

The Swan said nothing.

Ayda, still struggling to piece it all together, spoke softly. "But in your case, you were a judge, part of the judiciary. How could Navvab do this to you?"

The Swan turned to her and said, "Listen, daughter of Iran. I'm afraid the worst was yet to come.

"A few weeks after the failed attempt on my life, Khomeini made his move. He called on young 'martyrs for Islam' to rise up, mocking me as 'this illiterate Tabrizi'. Around the same time, Navvab Safavi—fresh out of prison—released a declaration titled *Blood and Revenge!*, officially launching *Fadā'iyān-e Islam*.

"Then came the legal assault. Under pressure from Prime Minister Mohsen Sadr, a cleric in civilian clothes, the Minister of Education filed charges against me. They claimed my writings violated Sharia law, digging up an obscure 1922 decree to justify their case.

"In the early hours of 11 March 1946, two brothers—members of *Fadā'iyān-e Islam* and operating under direct orders from Navvab Safavi—stealthily entered the courthouse. Armed with knives and pistols, they made their way to the courtroom where I was present during a court procedure, unaware of what was about to unfold. With swift brutality, they attacked—first my long-time assistant, whose scream echoed through the marble halls, and then me. They used knives and guns. I remember the coldness of the knife, the pain of the bullet in my chest, and the smell of gunpowder in the air.

"But what truly killed me was seeing blood stain the steps of the Palace of Justice. I didn't want this for Iran. I feared what lay ahead. And as crimson spread across the marble—justice itself defiled—I knew I had lived long enough to see the signs, the unravelling of a nation I loved. I feared the silence that would follow the gunfire... mourning for my country. I closed my eyes and slipped away."

The Swan paused for a long moment, then looked intently at them and continued: "There was no guard to intervene, no voice to stop them. The Palace of Justice had become a place of slaughter."

He went on to explain how several of the assailants were never even charged. Those who were arrested—including the two brothers—claimed self-defence, accusing him of initiating the confrontation with a gun.

Grand Ayatollah Hosayn Qomi, at the time the second-highest religious authority in Najaf, sent a telegram to the prime minister demanding the attackers' immediate release. He praised their "heroism" and condemned the government's failure to protect the faithful. Under immense pressure from top-ranking clerics, powerful religious figures, and influential merchants, the government released them after a swift and superficial trial.

"My story ended in sorrow far beyond what I imagined," the Swan said. "My murder was not just a tragedy—it was a deeper failure of conscience, born from ignorance and silence. Only a few left-leaning papers spoke out. Most secular thinkers and the press remained silent. Meanwhile, religious groups celebrated. The *Fadā'iyān-e Islam*—the ones who killed me—were hailed as heroes. Ayatollah Qomi claimed their act was as sacred as prayer or fasting.

"My family tried to bury me at Zahir-al-Dawla Cemetery, where poets and writers rest beneath ancient trees. They pleaded with the caretakers, but the Sufi custodians shook their heads. 'He spoke against the Sufis,' they said. So I was turned away from the place of the honoured dead.

"In the quiet that followed, no ceremony marked my passing. No public mourning. Just a small group and a journey north on a dark night into the foothills of the Alborz Mountains. There, in a place few know and fewer speak of, called Abak, they laid me to rest in secret.

"The *Fadā'iyān-e Islam* did not stop. Between 1949 and 1953, they assassinated two prime ministers and a minister of education. They also attempted to kill the Shah, the foreign minister, and another prime minister. In 1965, they claimed responsibility for the assassination of Prime Minister Mansour. Although Navvab Safavi never lived to see his vision of an Islamic state realised, his ideas left a lasting impact. He was among the first to advocate religious rule in Iran, promote political violence, and inspire many of the revolutionaries behind the 1979 Islamic Revolution. In many ways, he planted the seed and laid the groundwork for what was to come."

"I was silenced. But my real grief is for the silence that followed."

With sorrow in her voice, Ayda asked, "This is the saddest story I've ever heard. What's left of us when the truth is silenced? What happens to hope when ignorance rules?" She paused, then let out a strained, nervous sigh. "And now, what are we supposed to do with this rising tide of darkness and dogma?"

Bijan replied quietly, "Not much, I'm afraid. Especially when it's rooted so deeply in our history."

The Swan looked from one to the other with an intense gaze and said, "Be an *Übermensch.*"

"What?" Bijan and Ayda exclaimed in unison.

Kasravi's sharp gaze softened. In German, he said, *"Alle Götter sind tot: nun wollen wir, dass der Übermensch lebe."*

Then he translated: "All gods are dead; now we want the Superhuman to live."

"It comes from *Thus Spoke Zarathustra*—Nietzsche's timeless masterpiece. Now that you've journeyed through my words, perhaps it's time to explore his. More than oil, more than any treasure, what Iran truly longs for is the gift of reading."

He paused, letting the silence speak, then continued with quiet conviction:

"We must remember—the Nazis later twisted and corrupted the term *Übermensch*, bending it to serve their racist ideologies. That's why I chose to translate it as *Superhuman*—to return to what Nietzsche originally intended, not the dark distortion history remembers."

"So... what did he actually intend by *Superhuman* and all that? Was he an atheist?" Ayda asked.

"Maybe he was, maybe he wasn't. But Nietzsche's idea of the 'death of God' wasn't just about disbelief. It wasn't simply that God doesn't exist—it was about truth. About daring to face reality without self-deception, without the comforting illusions of tradition, religion, or dogma.

"The key idea is this: if there are no absolute, pre-given truths, then the courage to seek and live by truth—no matter how uncomfortable—becomes essential."

Bijan asked, "So what really matters, then?"

The Swan replied, "The power of the individual—the ability to shape yourself, master yourself, and discover your own meaning

"In *Thus Spoke Zarathustra*, Nietzsche urges us to 'overcome' ourselves—to rise above our limitations, desires, and the suffering that comes from ignorance. It is a bold call to take responsibility for our lives and create our own purpose in a world that doesn't have one built-in.

"Being a Superhuman isn't about dominating others—it's about becoming a better version of yourself, a deep drive to grow and transcend your own weaknesses. It's an inner strength, a constant striving to evolve."

"As Zarathustra insisted that disciples not follow him but to become seekers themselves : *Now I go alone; you too must go alone. Make your own path and be true inquirers.*"

Kasravi then made a gentle turn and, without a word of farewell, made his way to the middle of the red sea. Spreading his powerful wings, he ran across the water's surface and took flight. The rhythmic beats of his wings echoed as he soared and glided into the distance.

Bijan and Ayda's eyes followed him until he disappeared beyond the horizon.

Many questions that had lingered for years were finally answered. They saw clearly why the violence, dogma, and assassinations that began in 1946 were not isolated acts—but a growing tumour that spread unchecked, eventually erupting in the revolution of 1979.

They exchanged a glance, content in their silence. Understanding had unshackled them.

Ayda murmured the first verse of Ferdowsi's famous couplet from the *Shahnameh*: 'He who has knowledge is powerful.'

They felt weightless—able to fly, far and high, without fear.

Somewhere, a magic flute played. The shadow on the sundial shifted.

THE VALLEY OF UNITY

A MALE NIGHTINGALE hopped from branch to branch in a tree, singing an unending refrain of *"tew, tew, tew…"* He wasn't singing for joy, but out of desperation. Babak was frustrated, not knowing what had happened to the others—or exactly where this valley was that he had stumbled into.

He finally settled on a branch and glanced at his feathers: plain brown plumage, a lightly flecked cream-buff chest, and a reddish-brown tail.

What would Dara say, he wondered, *about his new look?* With a shake of his wings, he rose again into the sky to search for him.

Somewhere in the woods, he heard a strange, rhythmic tapping. He looked down but saw nothing. He swooped lower. The sound repeated in short phrases—almost like the lulling purr of a cat.

A Turtle Dove burst from the shadow of the stones, lifting his head. His striking red-and-black ringed eyes gleamed. His plumage trembled with the rhythm of his breath—in recognition of his beloved.

Babak's heart leapt as he descended.

Standing among the rocks and rubble, Dara and Babak took a moment to observe and complement each other's new looks, laughing lightly. But the laughter quickly faded as restlessness set in. The uncertainty of their situation gnawed at them, and tension escalated when they realised Shirin was missing.

Dara decided to soar high above the valley to get their bearings. Babak had always suffered from vertigo, and even being a bird didn't help much—nightingales may be efficient fliers, but they typically stay close to the ground.

Below, Dara spotted a small wood: a cluster of leafless trees standing starkly at the centre of a brown basin. The valley's gentle slopes were barely marked, dotted with stubble and scattered tussocks. After taking in the view, he descended to report back to Babak.

They perched together on the ground for a while, deep in thought. It was cold but calm beneath the overcast sky.

A sudden whoosh rushed through the air. They glanced at each other, perplexed. The wind shifted, stirring the dust into restless swirls. On the horizon, a vast cloud began to rise, darkening the sky as it surged forward.

The air grew heavy, and the light dimmed. The cloud was coming fast.

"What on earth is that?" Dara asked, his voice tight with fear.

The cloud rose and fell as it crossed the sky. As it drew nearer, their anxiety gave way to wonder. It was neither a storm nor an illusion, but a cluster of dots circling and curving gracefully left and right: a vast, dazzling display of birds swooping and swirling in perfect synchrony. They dipped low, skimming the ground with rippling echoes, then soared upward again, tracing a figure-eight over and over. The air shimmered with motion, filled with the whispering beat of wings. It was mesmerizing, as if the sky itself were breathing—a living cloud rising and falling. The two friends stood stunned, watching thousands of wings rise and dive in perfect, dizzying rhythm.

Among the circling shadows of birds, they spotted a haze of blue—a dazzling figure moving as though the others followed its lead. It twisted and turned in the air, its wings flashing from afar with a sword-like glint of silver. Its feathers shimmered with a striking blend of amber and blue, glowing against the darkening sky.

Dara asked, "Did you see that? What is it?"

Babak answered uncertainly, "Hard to say from here. Might be... some kind of Eagle... or maybe a Falcon... but..."

Suddenly, the bird turned and glided toward them. As it drew closer, Babak shouted, "Good Lord—it's a Royal Eagle! A Shahbaz!"

The bird hovered above them with astonishing power and control. Then he swooped majestically—swift, deft, and deliberate—toward the ground. His strong, dusty-yellow talons clenched the rock in front of them with precision.

He was a magnificent creature: broad, barrel-chested, and strikingly poised. His feathers gleamed a golden buff, and there was a crushing intensity in his eyes—sharp, commanding—impossible to look away from. He was a blue-eyed Eagle.

"That is a murmuration of Starlings—ninety miles per hour," the Eagle said, nodding toward the swirling cloud.

As he took to the air again, he commanded, "Rise up!"

Babak and Dara stood stunned on the ground.

"Follow me!" he called, rising higher.

Babak still hesitated. "But our friend is missing."

Dara added, "And… sorry, but we don't even know where we're supposed to follow you to. And we don't even know who you are."

The blue-eyed Eagle dipped low again and spoke calmly, deliberately: "There is a possibility your friend will join us along the way. Not all travellers take the same path to reach the Simorgh. Each journey is different."

He paused, then dipped his head politely. "You're right—I should have introduced myself. I am no ordinary bird. I'm a crossbreed—descended from the Shahbaz, the Persian Falcon of legend, and the Golden Eagle, both among the fastest fliers of the North.

"My name is Nader. Though among many, I'm better known as Lieutenant General Nader Jahanbani."

He paused, then added with quiet pride:"The last of my kind. Guardian of the sky. I fly not only through the clouds, but through history. And today, I am your guide."

Dara and Babak were stunned. They saw it then—in the fire of his eyes and the power of his flight. He was a hero they had crossed paths with.

The realisation that they stood before such a towering figure—a legend carried on the wind—filled them with awe. They could hardly speak. If this journey had led to *this* moment, then it had already been worth it.

Lieutenant General Nader Jahanbani was no ordinary Eagle. He had once walked the earth in full command of the skies—a decorated Iranian fighter pilot born into a lineage where Persian and Russian gentry met. But more than a soldier, he was a visionary—a builder of wings for a nation still learning to fly. Known as the Father of the Iranian Air Force, he also founded 'The Golden Crown', Iran's first aerobatic team, turning the skies into a theatre of strength and precision.

On the ground, he served as director of the National Sports Organization, guiding the Iranian football team to its first World Cup appearance. But beyond his achievements, he was admired for his manner—the way he stood with his men, whether they wore stars or stripes.

When the 1979 Revolution swept across the country, many begged him to flee. But he refused.

"I am a soldier of this country," he said. "I will never leave my homeland."

Dragged before the dreaded cleric-judge Khalkhali,he faced a litany of accusations: "waging war against God", "corruption on earth", "loyalty to the Shah". There was no trial, no defence; only silence—and his unbroken gaze.

Yet even in chains, he carried himself with the quiet pride of a man with nothing to conceal. A guard would later speak of his calmness, a journalist of the fire in his words: "Write it down that Nader Jahanbani is proud of everything he has done so far."

And so it was written. On the thirteenth day of March 1979, just before dawn, he was taken to Qasr Prison's courtyard. The rifles were raised. He did not flinch. With unshakable dignity, he cried— "LONG LIVE IRAN" —the final words of an Eagle who refused to fall.

Ever the intuitive instructor, he now seemed to read Babak's and Dara's thoughts and spoke before they could ask. "This isn't what you imagine," he said. "It's not a passage from death to life. It's part of the transformation—from human to bird. Humans see in fragments, bound by limits. Avians, by contrast, possess a far more expansive vision. We see the full spectrum.

"I was always here. You just couldn't see me—your lens was too narrow. But now, as your eyes begin to adapt to avian sight, you see beyond the visible, the unseen wavelength, a wider range of lights... and therefore you can see me."

He beat his wings with renewed determination, climbing higher into the thinning air. "I often mentor in the Valley of Courage," he said, "But today, I've come for a greater purpose. This valley now holds strategic importance—for the unity of Iran itself. We are about to perform the 'High Show'—a flight that demands unity, precision, and absolute trust. A test not just of skill, but of spirit.

"We will ascend to an altitude between 9,000 and 12,000 feet from our base. Once there, we'll climb vertically, forming a dense cloud column to signal other flocks to join us. When our echelon is complete, we will dive in unison, flying horizontally at speeds of up to 200 kilometres per hour, before rising again to our original altitude. This manoeuvre demands exact timing and flawless coordination. Every bird plays a part in building the formation."

Babak stared sideways at Dara, his face pale with panic. He could barely follow the flight instructions.

Dara glanced back—his friend's fear echoed in his own chest. He drew a slow breath, steadied himself, and asked, "Is it really necessary to fly that high?"

"Yes, it is!" Jahanbani replied and continued, "Lesson one: Symmetry and unity are inseparable! Symmetry is a visible form of order, while unity is the force or relationship that holds that order together. This is a law of nature—it applies to everything, from something as small as a molecule to something as vast as a country. For example, when a society is no longer beautiful, you can be sure of one thing: it has lost its unity. Without unity, balance cannot exist, and without balance and symmetry, beauty cannot arise."

He paused, looking intently at Babak and Dara in turn.

"Each of us has a role to play," he said. "Only together can we bring about the 'High Show'."

In the distance, another cloud of birds rose and fell with rhythmic grace. The blue-eyed Eagle fixed his gaze on them, measuring their formation with quiet admiration. "Look at their precision," he said. "They were the flyers of the Nojeh coup[11]—rising into the sky on the tenth of July in 1980."

Dara said, "Oh, that's them? I always wonder... what if they had succeeded? Maybe the Islamic Revolution could have ended within a year. I was only one year old. Imagine—my whole life under a different, democratic government. What it could have been... what a shame."

Babak interrupted, turning to the General. "Do you know why it failed?"

"Well, I was watching from the sky," Jahanbani replied. "There were many reasons—intelligence leaks, arrests, even alleged opposition from the U.S. But above all, there were disagreements. No unity.

"And beyond all that... it was destined to fail. The people wanted the Ayatollah. Their vision was too narrow. They had already made peace with the night."

As the array of birds swept past Jahanbani, they tipped their wings in a silent, triumphant salute and fell smoothly into formation.

Leading them was a peculiar-looking bird that prompted Dara to ask, "What kind of bird is that?"

"He's one of their leaders," the General replied. "Dr. Shapour Bakhtiar— we call him the 'Bird of the Storm'. They rose when the skies darkened...but their moment came too soon. The people weren't ready. And so, they fell."

Jahanbani kept his gaze fixed on them, watching in silence as they passed overhead until they disappeared beyond the horizon.

He turned back to Babak and Dara to continue his lesson on flying. "The ever-changing shape of a flock in murmuration comes from each bird mimicking the movement of the six or seven closest to it with astonishing speed. Their reaction time is less than a tenth of a second. In essence, each bird becomes like the next."

Dara looked up at him, squinting against the wind. "Sorry, Lieutenant General... but is there a particular goal you're hoping to achieve with all this?"

"Yes!" he said calmly. "The first goal is safety—there's strength in numbers. A predator can't easily target a single bird in the middle of a thousand. The second is warmth. At night, flying together keeps us alive. And the third is communication. We share information: feeding grounds, danger zones, enemy movements.

"But above all, our ultimate goal is this—to become one giant bird. A single, pulsing organism."

He hovered, his wings outstretched against the sky. "To get there, we must first perform the 'Mirror Display'. Then, when all the birds have gathered, we'll form our most powerful demonstration—the 'One' display. That is our most powerful demonstration, and why I call it the 'High Show'."

Babak glanced at Dara, panic widening his eyes.

Dara gave a calm shake of his head. "Leave it with me," he whispered.

It wasn't long before masses of flocking birds plunged into the valley from every direction, as if the entire land had been lifted into the sky. They circled around them—birds not only of every kind, but in every condition: young and old, weary and spirited, grand and colourful, down to the tiniest fowls panting breathlessly.

The 'Mirror' display began, a prerequisite for the 'High Show'. It wasn't particularly difficult, as each bird simply mirrored the movements of the one beside it. But as they began shifting into position for the 'High Show', tension surfaced. Disagreements broke out.

Some didn't want to be at the edge of the flock, nor among the first to land, dive, or take flight. Hearts pounded and muscles tensed. Some birds grew jittery; others subtly edged their way toward the safety of the centre.

Dara glanced at Babak, who had emptied his bowels more than once and looked visibly ill.

He leaned toward the bird stacked in the middle of the canopy and asked, "Is there any option for birds with vertigo to move to the middle? Can we swap?"

The other bird guffawed. "A bird with vertigo? Are you serious? Never heard of such a thing! You're having a laugh, aren't you? I guess the only option is falling out of the sky!"

Above the noise, Jahanbani's voice rang out, sharp and commanding: "Fear—what is it for? Is it bad or is it good? Bad fear stops us in our tracks. It feeds our excuses, keeps us from taking risks, from living life to the full. But there is good fear, too. The kind that sharpens us, keeps us alert, prepares us for danger. It can save us from predators.

"So why is it so hard to trust our good fears? Unity is the only way we can respond to that kind of fear. By compromising in our differences, we hold together against the predators. That's how we subdue the bad fear— even vertigo—and survive the journey ahead.

"This is the only way to cross the valley. The only way to reach the Simorgh."

The 'High Show' began as swirling clouds of birds filled the sky. Some broke away and escaped, but crashed into cliffs, breaking their necks and falling lifeless to the ground.

Jahanbani cried sharply, "Stay close to the birds in your position. DO NOT CHANGE your position!"

The sky was a whirlwind of feathers, spluttering and crackling all around. The air was thick with the scent of blood. Somewhere within the chaos of beating wings, Babak became hopelessly lost. He had left his position and was slipping downward.

Dara dove after him, but Babak had already vanished from sight.

As Dara cut through the air, memories of his entire life with Babak flooded his mind in an instant—along with the poem they had always loved.

Everyone knows—
You and I have seen the garden
through that cold, grim window,
and have plucked the apple
from that far, flirtatious branch.
Everyone fears.

But you and I—merged into one
before the water,
before the mirror,
before the lamp.
And we were not afraid.
They will carry the news of us
to the town.
Everyone knows.
Everyone knows
We have found our way
to the cold and silent dreams
of the phoenix.
We found the truth in the garden,
and we asked the young eagles—
in that lofty mountain of victory —
What should be done? [12]

Murmuring the poem, Dara felt something shift deep within him. The memory, their bond, their oaths—and above all, their shared goal to find the Simorgh—all steadied him. And suddenly, he turned. He had to finish their quest. Even if Babak was gone.

The Eagle had said, "Do not change your position!"

He soared upward, wings burning with resolve, rising to return to his place. In that moment, he no longer felt alone—he was part of something greater.

Above him, the Eagle circled with silent grace, then pointed with his wing to a far corner of the line below. Babak was there. He was alive, held safely between two tiny Robins who had responded to the Nightingale's call.

As they left the Valley of Unity behind, the sight was breathtaking: all the surviving birds merging into a single living cloud—a single, pulsing organism. A perfect "One".

A golden shaft of sunlight drifted through the shimmering cloud of victory.

The magic flute played. The shadow on the sundial shifted.

THE VALLEY OF JUSTICE

DAWN BROKE gently over the desert, brushing pale light across the cracked earth. Gohar jolted awake, the persistent buzzing in her ears pulling her from restless sleep. Heat pressed against her like a weight, making her eyes flutter open. Her grey wings were coated in dust and crawling with wriggling insects. With a sharp flap, she shook them clean.

At last, she rose—lifting the weight of her wood pigeon body and pulling her wings free from the gritty sand beneath her pink-tinged chest. She stood unsteadily, her dry beak slightly open, gazing out at the desert and up into the blinding sky, trying to get her bearings.

A voice broke the silence.

Atossa tilted her head, exposing her beak. She had become a Woodpecker, her head marked with a red patch and black-and-white plumage. "Seems like we fled from humanity," she said, a spark of enthusiasm in her voice. But her eyes drifted to the barren hills and clumps of cracked earth, as if searching for meaning in the desolation. After a moment, she added more soberly, "But I don't know why we ended up in this desert. There's nothing for miles. No sign of water either." Gohar waddled uncertainly. "Was I sleeping that long? Oh… sorry. Have you seen Ayda, my daughter? Where is she… my beautiful girl… where are we?"

Atossa shook her head gently. "No, I'm sorry… I don't know. But we flew together—don't you remember? All of us, for miles. I think Ayda and Neda were ahead… they were faster."

She nudged Gohar lightly. "Maybe they grouped the younger ones together—and left us old birds to figure things out."

"Oh yes… I remember that," Gohar murmured, "But where has she gone now… my Ayda…?"

"I don't know, Gohar-jan… maybe we've all been scattered," Atossa replied, her voice trailing off in uncertainty. "Look at us. How do we even know who we really are? I know I'm Atossa—but this?" She tucked her head in, flared her wings slightly, and glanced down at her bird body. "Well… maybe I became a Woodpecker because I was always picking at things."

They flew on aimlessly, the searing heat pressing in from all sides. It was everywhere now—thick, oppressive, inescapable. They dipped low in wide circles, desperately trying to avoid the scorching gusts. Atossa grew dizzy from the spiralling descent, a bitter, coppery taste creeping into her mouth.

Suddenly, Gohar shouted, "LOOK!"

On the shimmering horizon, a lone bird appeared, swerving through the waves of heat. "A Seagull?" Gohar said as the Seagull came closer. "In the desert? That must be a trick of the light... a mirage, maybe?"

"Well, I am a mirage," the gull replied calmly. "A mirage of justice in the Islamic Republic—because that never existed."

She hovered in silence for a moment, her small frame steady in the burning air.

"But my pain? That was real. The noose around my neck? That wasn't a mirage.

"My name is Atefeh Rajabi Sahaaleh. I was born in 1987, here in Neka— on the shores of the Caspian Sea." She gestured with a wing toward the cracked, blistered earth below.

Atossa looked down, confused. "Here? This place? But there's no sea... only sand."

Atefeh nodded slowly. "Yes—here. Once, waves lapped over this soil. This was the sea I grew up beside. But after I was arrested... after I was executed by the Revolutionary Guards—hanged in the town square, just over there by the railway station"—she pointed toward the dry, shimmering horizon—"everything changed."

Her voice dropped, quieter now, but heavy with sorrow.

"People watched. My own neighbours. Some stood still. Some shook their heads. Others just kept shopping. Some boarded their trains and travelled where they wanted to go. A few even went swimming in the sea, as if nothing had happened."

She looked down at the desert below, her wings barely moving.

"But the Caspian Sea saw. The Caspian cried for me. It wept for so long—for so many—that it dried up. It became this... this cracked silence."

Her eyes lifted to meet theirs, glowing with a light not entirely of this world.

"What was once sea for me is now desert for you. The Caspian Desert. A lifeless plain where something as vital as justice has withered away. A place stripped of empathy. That is what a true desert is. And now you see it—only because you've finally chosen to."

A heavy silence followed. The air felt unnaturally still—like before a storm.

Gohar looked at the gull, guilt tightening in her chest. She remembered the news, faint now, from so many years ago: a girl, far too young, silenced too soon. Her eyes hadn't just been sad—there had been something deeper. Shame. Gohar too knew what injustice felt like, but only after she had lost her own son. Something had cracked inside her after that.

Atossa spoke softly. "Tell us more. What happened to you? I... I'm not sure I remember."

Atefeh gave the smallest nod but said nothing. Her silence carried a sharpness, as if to ask: *How could you not remember?*

And then, she told them her story.

Atefeh was a 16-year-old schoolgirl who was imprisoned and sentenced to death just a week later, accused of adultery and "crimes against chastity" by the head of the city's clerical court. Atefeh's childhood was marked by relentless loss. Her mother died in a car accident when she was just five. Not long after, her younger brother drowned in a river. With her father spiralling into drug addiction, Atefeh was left to care for her elderly grandparents—barely a child herself yet burdened with the weight of an entire household. She was arrested after being raped by a 51-year-old ex-revolutionary guard turned taxi driver who had picked her up on the street. During torture, Atefeh admitted to having had a relationship for three years, from the age of 13, with that man, who was married with children at the time. In the court, when Atefeh realised she was losing her case, she removed her Hijab, an act seen as severe contempt of the court; she argued the man should be punished, not her, and removed her shoes and hit the Judge with them. The Judge sentenced her to death. While in prison, she was further tortured and raped by the judge himself and prison officers. She told this to her grandmother, who visited her, saying that afterwards she could only walk on all fours because of the pain. Judge Haji Rezai carried out the execution of the teenager himself by placing the noose around Atefeh's neck before she was hoisted on a Crane to her death, telling her, "This will teach you to disobey!" She was publicly hanged from the Crane in Neka on August 15, 2004. She was left hanging for forty-five minutes while the Judge boasted that "she had been taught a lesson for her sharp tongue."

Atefeh saw the shock on Gohar and Atossa's faces and said gently, "It wasn't just me—this has happened over and over again, with the silent permission of our people. Indifference isn't neutral; it's an active decision not to care. And that decision has quietly corroded the soul of our society.

"We stopped seeing one another. We stopped speaking out. And in that silence, injustice found its roots and the regime grew bolder, unchecked. That's how people disappear—not just from the streets, but from memory.

"But injustice doesn't stay in one place. It spreads. It always comes knocking. The question is no longer *if*. It's *who's next?*"

She went on to speak of other children who were executed—voices lost too soon. But she hesitated when she spoke of Nasrin Shojaee. Her voice lowered.

"I used to call her Nightjar," she said softly, "because she was a bird in the longest night of Iran. She was born in 1970, the youngest child of a Bakhtairi tribe from Isfahan; she was executed in Isfahan's prison. The regime's cruelty tore her family apart. Two of her older brothers, Mehran, 15 and Massoud, 21, had been previously executed, so she was the third child to be put to death after enduring prison and torture. She was arrested at the age of 13 and repeatedly ganged-raped by the prison guards and the religious judge who ordered her execution. In her last minutes, as she entered the execution hall, Nasrin stood tall and resolute. The religious judge asked her, 'Are you not willing to confess?' An eyewitness recalled that she looked at him straight, but he wouldn't look back. Her green eyes glowed with resolve yet innocence."

Gohar broke down in tears and said , "Why did they arrest her, she couldn't be a political activist at that age?"

"It was during the 1988 massacre[13], following Khomeini's fatwa that led to the execution of at least 20,000, and possibly 30,000, political prisoners. Nasrin was arrested simply because she came from an anti-government family—labelled a political activist as part of a brutal effort to exterminate the next generation.

"Another horrific fatwa came from Ayatollah Misbah Yazdi, a member of the Supreme Council of the Cultural Revolution and the Assembly of Experts. This fatwa explicitly gave interrogators and jailers the right to rape prisoners before execution, stating: "It is allowed to rape a non-believer, especially virgins." It was even published in the newspapers. And yet, people just turned the page. I don't understand how those who read it could lower their heads and stay silent—then still show up to vote, year after year. There is a saying, 'The opposite of love is not hate—it is indifference.'"

Atossa's stomach churned. "We always blamed foreign powers, conspiracies," she whispered with a shaky voice. "But this... this is something else. It's shameful. Outrageous. I hate calling myself Iranian now. How did I keep living, breathing, eating under this regime? It's too dark—too dark!"

She paused, her eyes burning with a quiet fire. "We must fight back. This silence—it's deafening. We need to find our leader. We need the Simorgh. That's why we're here—to end the darkness and restore light to Iran." The young gull nodded gently. "The moon doesn't stay hidden behind clouds forever. Soon, you'll find the great leader. You're close to Mount Alborz. Neka lies at its foot, near what used to be the seacoast. See that line over there?"

Atossa gazed toward the horizon. "That copper haze there?"

"Yes," the gull nodded. "Well spotted. There's always a sign—a clue, a trace—that shows the way. That's where the Caspian Desert meets the foot of Alborz—where the old sea once whispered."

Atossa's eyes settled on the gull, a flicker of recognition stirring deep within her. She reminded her of a book she'd read long ago, *Jonathan Livingston Seagull*—the story of a young gull who refused to live a life limited by fear. Jonathan believed flying wasn't just about survival, but freedom and meaning. He chased the edges of possibility, then returned—not to prove anything, but to share a truth: every soul holds the power to rise above the boundaries carved by fear, tradition, or silence.

Atefeh's voice was soft. "So... you're our guide, then?"

The Seagull met her gaze with calm certainty. "This journey is yours—a story of self-discovery, breaking free from cages of conformity, and remembering your true path. I'm not here to lead like a master, but to fly beside you... as you remember what you've always known."

Atossa's tone was cautious. "Just one question—for clarity, and I think Gohar would want to know too—have we died, then?"

The young Seagull smiled gently. "No, you haven't died—you're in flight mode." Her expression shifted, turning solemn. "You don't have to die to see the truth."

Gohar let out a weary sigh. "Well... I can only speak for myself, but I wouldn't mind dying after losing my son. I've been dreading this life ever since. If it weren't for Ayda—my daughter…" Her voice cracked, and she broke down in tears. "But where is she now? I need to find her."

The gull leaned forward and said, "You will meet Ayda later in your journey. I promise. But first, we must leave this valley."

She turned and gestured with her wing. "As I said before, you're close to your destination. This is the final stop in the Valley of Justice—just before the steep ascent to Mount Alborz, where you'll join the other travellers. But first… you must find the well."

"The well?" Gohar asked, puzzled.

"In the desert?" Atossa echoed.

The gull nodded. "What makes the desert beautiful," she said, "is that somewhere… it hides a well."

Atossa raised an eyebrow. "Hmm. I think I've heard that somewhere before."

The gull fluttered her wings, slightly bashful. "Well… it's from *The Little Prince*. The only book I read before I became a bird."

Gohar smiled through her tears. "Darling, if you only had time to read one book, that's a lovely choice."

Atossa looked unconvinced. "But why do we need to find this well? If it's just to quench our thirst, I'd rather press on and leave this valley. Surely it's easier to find water on the mountain, isn't it?"

Atefeh shook her head gently. "This isn't about thirst," she said. "You will find water on the mountain, yes. But the well holds something far more important."

She paused, her feathers catching the light like brushed silver.

"Two ancient creatures live in its depths. The Belugas[14]. You must look into the well and see them from above. Only when you see them—and they see you—will you earn the right to leave the valley."

Atossa and Gohar looked surprised, and Atossa, as outspoken as ever, asked, "But what is the point of that? What would we be achieving with it?"

"Everything's connected, thread by thread," Atefeh said. "We're all tied together, not because we chose to be, but because we need each other. There are all these hidden relationships we barely notice, but they matter."

"Beluga sturgeons are ancient—almost prehistoric," Atefeh said. "Some live over a hundred years. There are sturgeon in the Caspian older than the boats that hunt them—older than the borders drawn above their waters.

"They move like shadows from another era—slow, deliberate—carrying the threads of life through these waters. For generations, they shaped entire ecosystems. They returned to rivers to spawn, to keep the balance. But their eggs—caviar, called 'black gold'—came at a cost.

"Greed, ignorance, and indifference choked off their ancient paths. And if they vanish, the balance goes with them.

"The Beluga is more than a fish. It's the heir to an ancient legacy, carrying the wisdom of deep waters. Its silence mirrors the fading tapestry of life below. This isn't just one species disappearing—it's a connection coming undone, and everything starting to fall out of place."

Atossa leaned in. "So... are they extinct?"

"Not yet," Atefeh said. "Almost. They're ghosts now—only two remain."

Gohar flinched. "Only two? I didn't think it was this bad."

Atefeh fell silent, then said softly, "There's still hope."

Atossa frowned. "If the sea's gone, where are they? Russia?"

"No," Atefeh said. "They're here. But so are the hunters—vile, massive things that dive from the clouds and prowl the waters... searching for the Black Gold."

"When you find the well, you'll need to dive deep. As deep as you can go. And when you reach the bottom of the well, don't rush. Wait. Listen. The Belugas are vocal—very vocal. They sing. If you're patient, you'll hear them. But listen closely: you must not leave the well until you've seen them. Hearing them isn't enough. You have to see them. Only then will your path become clear."

Gohar asked, "But... the Belugas, as you said, usually stay deep underwater, don't they? How are we supposed to see them? We're not waterbirds."

"Yes, they usually live deep in the sea," Atefeh said. "But things have changed. The depths are vanishing, eroded by drought and hunger. Everything's growing shallow now. Too shallow. It's become so bad that what once stayed hidden in the deep is becoming revealed. The old secrets... the buried wounds... all of it is surfacing."

They circled upward, steady and slow, catching the wind's thrust. A vast flock of Geese appeared, like a silver cloud unravelling from the horizon.

"Look! They are Geese!" Gohar shouted.

Atefeh's eyes lit up. "Those are the Bahá'ís of Iran."

Their formation was strong and elegant, but each bird flew with grief woven into its wings. They were the ones whose names had been erased from school registers, whose jobs vanished overnight, whose fathers were taken and never came back. Yet they still flew.

Atefeh continued, "Even if they are not recognised by the regime, the sky knows them. The wind knows their names."

For Gohar and Atossa, it was a chilling reminder—all those terrible stories of what happened to the Bahá'ís after the revolution. Homes raided. Cemeteries desecrated. Children barred from education. They were accused of words they never spoke, condemned for beliefs they were never allowed to explain. And yet—they hovered above cities that tried to forget them, refusing to be erased.

"They too were sacrificed as people remained silent," Atefeh said, watching them pass.

"Will they ever be allowed to land?" Atossa asked.

Atefeh smiled—softly, but with fire behind her eyes. "Not yet, but as long as they keep flying, hope stays aloft. And one day, they'll return to their land. They're excellent flyers. Their social bond is strong."

She pointed to the seven Geese at the tip of the V-shaped formation. "They are the Yaran[15]—the trusted ones. The leaders."

As the Geese passed, they honked in unison, signalling to those below. Then one of the Yaran broke from the line.

"We must migrate now. We have to leave Iran. We tried to stay. But the land is burning. Only a few can remain, to be guides for others."

Atefeh spoke no more; the lesson was finished. Atossa and Gohar didn't speak either. Now, it was time for them to find the well.

They flew forward over the endless desert, their eyes searching for any sign of the well: a glimmer of water, a patch of green, anything. Every now and then, Atossa would break from Gohar, heading off alone, only to return, shaking her head. Then, just as the weight of exhaustion threatened to pull them from the sky, something changed. A subtle shift in the air. A coolness.

Atossa tilted her wings, circled lower, and let out a sharp cry. Gohar followed.

There, hidden in the folds of the earth like a secret too sacred to speak aloud, was the well.

They landed gently on the rim, their eyes fixed on the dark opening. Atossa stepped forward and peered into the depths. The water was clear, reflecting a sliver of sky. She let out a soft, reverent call that seemed to rise from deep within her. Gohar trembled with joy, her whole being lit up.

They hovered above the surface, waiting. Hours passed, and nothing stirred. No sound, no movement. From time to time, they dipped into the well, hoping for a glimpse of the Belugas. But the water remained still, silent.

As night spread its dark veil across the desert, they drifted into sleep, wings folded, eyes closed. Then, at some point in the deep of night, the earth trembled. Atossa jolted awake, her claws clenching the stone rim. Gohar was already calling beside her. "What is this... an earthquake?"

A low roar rose from the horizon. A cyclone—or a tornado—was tearing across the desert, as if the earth itself had risen into the sky.

The predators had landed.

The creatures looked like something out of another age—part bird, part beast. Massive, with jagged beaks jutting from hairy faces. Their stubby wings twitched uselessly, and bloated bellies sagged over short legs. It was as if they had escaped evolution entirely, like fossils that somehow kept breathing.

With each lumbering step, they drew closer. Gohar and Atossa stood frozen. The dinosaurs had never truly vanished. They had returned—to kill.

They looked at each other, then at the well. They knew. They must hear and see the Belugas to save them.

Without hesitation, they dived into the well—tumbling through cold darkness, limbs flailing, hearts pounding

Then, a sound began to rise: the song. The Belugas were there. They were singing.

Atossa and Gohar hovered above the water, panting hard. A ripple stirred the surface. Then, a shimmer of light moved beneath, slow and deliberate, like a secret unfolding.

An albino Beluga, heavy with glowing eggs[16], moved in slow spirals, winding gracefully around a larger, black-armoured Beluga sturgeon. The two swam together, opposites in harmony—like yin and yang etched in scale and bone.

They were singing. A lullaby from a time before borders. Before boats.

A predator's call tore through the deep. They were coming to hunt.

As the shadows surged toward the well, Atossa and Gohar froze. They couldn't swim, but without hesitation they plunged into the water to shield the fish.

Through the ripples, the magic flute wove itself into the Belugas' song, its melody trembling like light on water. And far above, the shadow on the sundial shifted.

THE VALLEY OF LO VE

HEART

SAM WAS hunched over, his feathers clinging in awkward clumps. His wings twitched uselessly beneath them—odd forms, hardly wings at all. He shifted with a groan and glanced down at his legs: long, ropey, and twisted in strange ways, like nature had given up half-way through and stopped bothering with the details.

He was in a long, narrow passage. Visibility was low. The air was warm and damp, heavy with a strange movement—like an endless ebb and flow. It felt as if the tunnel had flooded long ago, and somewhere deep inside, it was still trying to drain a slow, stubborn trickle that hadn't yet let go.

He felt confused and anxious, and angry in his old, familiar way. Bending his neck, he pressed his small head into the mud, wishing he could just disappear.

"Man or bird," he muttered, his voice cracked and bitter, "I'm still the same useless thing. A flightless, bloody Ostrich."

It was a familiar feeling—not liking himself. That dull ache of depression, thick as fog.

"Do... I... care? Do I?" he mumbled, suddenly craving a cigarette. That thought stopped him. Birds weren't supposed to want to smoke.

Of all the uncanny things around him, it was that detail—small, stupid—that cracked something open. He could see his bird-body: the feathers, the twisted legs, the useless wings. But in his mind, he was still human. Bitterly human.

Sam pressed his head back into the mud. This had to be a nightmare. He decided to stay still, to wait it out—to vanish into the wet dark until he woke up.

But he couldn't. Stillness made the anxiety worse. The tunnel, the damp breath of the walls, the unfamiliar limbs—it was too much.

Then a thought yanked him upright, like a hook in his chest. His head was stuck in the sludge, but suddenly he jerked it free. The movement sent gooey liquid squelching down his long neck.

Ava!

Mud was everywhere—even in his mouth. It tasted metallic and had a tang faintly like seawater. *This place had to be connected to the sea,* he thought.

He became aware of a low, constant rumble. Maybe it was a distant wave crashing on a shore. The mud shifted beneath him—slick and unstable—swaying gently from side to side as if stirred by a tide.

Was this tunnel inside a cave? By the estuary of a river? Or maybe... the Caspian Sea?

"Might be," he whispered. It made a strange kind of sense.

Then a memory flickered—something half-remembered, a fragment of a plan or maybe a prophecy: they were supposed to go to Alborz. To find the leader—the Simorgh. And the Caspian Sea wasn't far from Alborz.

Sam stumbled through the tunnel like a sleepwalker. His long legs, half-submerged in sludge, felt shaky and weak. His left leg throbbed with sharp, excruciating pain, but he pushed on, dragging himself forward—searching for light, for a way out, or just something familiar.

He called out for Ava, but his voice was swallowed by the heavy, damp air. Fear gnawed at him—fear of being alone, of not knowing where he was going, of drifting aimlessly. It was just like one of his old nightmares: endless tunnels, no exit, nothing but darkness stretching ahead.

A few steps later, his foot slipped. The ground disappeared beneath him, and he dropped into a narrow duct, landing hard. The mud here was thicker, stickier—and something was moving. He could feel it skimming across the surface nearby.

Squinting into the dim light, he slowly lowered his neck—and then he saw it. It was a bird. Its barrel-shaped body was cloaked in feathers, casting a silhouette of immense presence. An Owl—to be precise, an Eagle Owl—stood not far from him, distinctive and statuesque, like the Sphinx.

Sam was flabbergasted.

The bird's large head dipped down, eyes locked on the floor. Sam stepped closer. The Owl seemed preoccupied with something. He followed its gaze and saw a flower on the ground—an orchid. Its petals were withered and collapsed, as if the Owl had been trying to piece them back together.

Finally, the bird noticed him and slowly looked up.

Sam gasped, his heart skipping a beat. He recognised the face instantly. Though he'd only ever seen it in photographs, there was no mistaking it. This was the man who had been the subject of countless conversations among his colleagues—someone they talked about with respect and admiration.

Sam felt a sudden rush of disbelief mixed with awe. Not only had Iran's sugar industry flourished under this man's visionary leadership, but the entire country had experienced rapid modernisation and remarkable economic growth during his time.

He was the longest-serving prime minister in Iran's modern history: Amir Abbas Hoveyda, a towering figure whose name symbolised progress and courage.

"Beauty is missing from our world today... because it's been neglected," the Owl said. "But it does matter. Beauty and truth—they're the same thing, aren't they?"

"Prime Minister?" Sam asked, his voice barely a whisper.

The Owl tilted its head slightly, feathers rustling in the still air.

"You know," Hoveyda replied, "there was a time I believed we never had to justify such things. I thought they were self-evident—values so essential they didn't need defending.

"What we admire, we become. And when we begin to honour ugliness—not just accept it, but praise it—it changes more than the world around us. It changes us."

Sam hesitated, then spoke quietly. "But... if I may, sir—when the Islamic Revolution started, we began to forget what beauty even was." He paused for a long moment, as if gathering the courage to say something important, and then, with rancour in his voice, said: "My parents' generation... they turned their rage on you. After everything you did for Iran—all the progress, the reforms—and despite your humble life and the enormous impact you had... they vilified you, as if you were the face of everything they wanted to erase." His voice wavered, tight with frustration. "I wish you had fled. But you didn't—you stayed. You looked straight into the heart of that darkness. And I still don't understand..."

Sam looked away, ashamed of what he was remembering. "They watched as you were humiliated, imprisoned, executed... and said nothing. I just don't get it. How does a nation choose to be that ugly?"

Turning to the wilted orchid, the Owl gently nudged a crumpled petal and murmured, "We once protected beauty. Now, you've grown used to its absence. Some even celebrate its destruction. No wonder people feel lost."

Sam lowered his eyes. The words echoed something he'd always felt but never dared to say. "Sir," he whispered, "I grew up with two stories.

One was of pride and progress, peace, happiness, music. It sounded like the world my parents once knew. A story full of light.

"The other was what I lived—struggle, death, war, corruption... sadness and silence. We were told beauty was weakness. Questioning was betrayal. And we believed it—or maybe we were just too afraid not to.

"But it doesn't matter now. If I see you, it means I'm dead—and that's good, because I wanted to see no more. To die and close my eyes."

"But you haven't died," the Owl said gently. "You're here to heal—to remember who you are. To find your way out and fly to your sovereign."

Sam's face fell, disappointment washing over him. "So... that story—Huma and the rest—is true, then?" He raised his arms slightly, then let them drop. "But look at me. I don't have wings. I'm flightless. So how do I travel? How am I supposed to fly?"

"You ask how to fly," the Owl replied, "but you're missing the more important question—what must awaken before flight is even possible?"

Sam stayed silent, unsure.

Then, with a soft French accent, the Owl added, "Le cœur."

"The core?" Sam echoed, puzzled.

The Owl nodded gently. "Yes. The heart. Iranians mostly have a heart problem. What's inside your chest—the centre. That's where everything starts. This world, this place—it moves by the heart's rhythm. Without it, no wings will carry you."

He sighed softly and added, "I was born in Tehran in 1919. But since my father was a diplomat, I spent much of my youth abroad. Living and studying outside Iran gave me a broad, cosmopolitan view of the world.

"I attended the Lycée Français in Beirut for high school and later earned a degree in political science in Brussels, in 1941. After that, I joined the Ministry of Foreign Affairs, serving in embassies across Europe and at the United Nations in New York.

"All of this was before I became Prime Minister of Iran—for thirteen years. I had the chance to travel extensively, and along the way, I discovered a quiet truth: the countries that were most successful, happy and beautiful were the ones where people loved, cared and respected one another the most.

"Love and beauty are fundamentally connected. That was the lesson I learned.

"To forsake love is to abandon beauty itself—a quiet, dangerous betrayal of what makes us human. And that, I believe, is what was missing in the Revolution: the love of one soul for another."

He turned his eyes to the wilted orchid, his voice softening.

"You see, Sam," he said, "beauty, love, and happiness are deeply connected. You can't separate them—they feed each other. That's why regimes go after beauty—not just the superficial kind, but the beauty of thought, of feeling, of spirit.

"When people clear their minds, they begin to see. But when they clear their hearts, they begin to choose differently. That's where real change begins." He looked down at his chest, as if remembering something personal.

"I used to wear an orchid in my lapel. A small thing, really. But it reminded me—every day—of nature's quiet defiance. There's a message in beauty that can't be put into words, but it matters. It grounds us. In a world bent on ugliness, even a flower can be an act of resistance.

"When the Islamic regime forced women into cloaks and encouraged a shabby, grim look for men—when even shaving became suspect—it wasn't just about control. It was about erasure. They wanted to break us down, to make people feel small—ashamed of their bodies, suspicious of joy, wary of love, numb to beauty. Because how we see ourselves affects how we feel.

"Strip people of colour, dignity, and self-expression, and you leave them either mentally starved—or obsessively fixated—and in both cases, easier to control. Make everyone look the same, think the same, feel less. That's how you remake a nation."

He leaned forward, and said in an urgent tone: "Now, listen carefully, Sam. This is important. It's a MAYDAY call."

Sam blinked, caught off guard by the intensity.

"A May Day?" he repeated slowly. "But... it's Yalda. Almost winter. Not the first of May."

Hoveyda shook his head. "Not that kind of May Day. A distress signal. We're in danger—and there's a Blue Whale that needs immediate help."

Sam stared at him, bewildered. "A whale? Here?"

"I know how it sounds," Hoveyda said gently. "But I promise—I'll explain everything. Just stay with me. This goes deeper and stranger than you think."

He gestured to the arched tunnels around them. "This is the Valley of

Love and Happiness. And to heal—to learn more about both—we've come to the very core. *Le cœur.* The heart."

He looked directly at Sam. "Can't you see? You're inside the heart. We're here so you can travel through it—to understand how vast it truly is. There's room for everyone. This is a huge heart—the heart of the Blue Whale."

He pointed to the damp wall. "Look! This tunnel? It's the aorta. The main artery."

Sam wanted to speak, but nothing came.

"There's no pulse," Hoveyda said, his voice dropping into a low, sorrowful note. "No rhythm. The streams come and go, but the Whale can't move. Time is running out. If it doesn't stir soon, it will perish. Decay. And so will you. To save yourself... you must heal it."

Sam stood frozen, wide-eyed, staring at the walls and ceiling. He glanced down the massive chamber ahead, then back at the Owl, suspicion creeping into his voice.

"Did you say... the Blue Whale? What even is that? And why am I here?"

"This is supposed to be your home."

"My home?" Sam snapped. "My home is Iran."

"Exactly," the Owl replied, unshaken. "And isn't that what Iran has become? A massive Blue Whale, trapped in stagnant water?"

He let out a sharp screech that echoed through the chambers. *"Bring back the pulse!"*

Something broke inside Sam. He staggered backward, then collapsed, haggard and hollow, onto the warm, living floor of the heart. His body sank slightly into its yielding surface. And there, with no fight left in him, he cried—quietly, brokenly—like someone who had finally run out of excuses.

When he eventually lifted his head, his face was twisted with rage. "What if I want to die with the whale? I don't care...I don't give a damn. I can't conceal it...I'd rather die...I am decaying myself ... my desires are all gone... I just...I just want to see Ava one last time."

"Well...Ava's here too," the Owl snapped. "All of Iran is here! But until you care for one another, you'll stay blind—selfish and jealous. You won't see her. Or anyone. But this is your choice! To stay like this and die!"

He flared his wings, then abruptly turned and began to hop away.

Sam's shout stopped him. "Ava? Where is she? Take me to her. Please—wait!"

The Owl paused. "As I said…you're all here. This place holds you all. But if the heart dies… you all die with it. Ava is in the whale's eyes. They're closing now. And once they're shut—it's over."

He turned again, locking his eyes on Sam. "Fix the core. Bring the pulse back—before it's too late. It's the only way."

"But how?"

"Dance!" the Owl replied.

"Dance? I can't! I've never danced."

The Owl tilted his head, calm and steady as ever. "You can. Think of Ava—the love you hold for her. Let that love move you. The dance will follow."

Sam swallowed hard, feeling the weight of those words settle on him. A tiny spark of hope flickered to life. He held his breath, squeezing his eyes shut. His face tensed until it flushed purple. He pictured Ava—her warmth, her beautiful mind, the way her hair slipped through his fingers, the light in her eyes. In his mind, he kissed her forehead like greeting the sun.

The Owl watched quietly.

Then something stirred inside Sam—like a faint vibration bubbling just beneath the surface of his feathered chest. He shifted his weight, claws scraping the tunnel floor. His beak parted slightly. A sound clawed its way up from his throat. A croak escaped—hesitant, rough, like rusted hinges forced open. Then another followed, wet and awkward, like gurgling water rising through a dry throat.

His broad body trembled with the effort. He wasn't made for this, and yet he pushed on. The purple flush on his featherless neck faded, turning to red before softening to pale pink.

Then… a note, shaky… a high-pitched hum. It was an unclear tune, but alive. The sound rose from his throat, unexpected, and it caught him off guard. He was humming! His eyes widened. A laugh, small and startled, broke free, like a bubble surfacing. He blinked in disbelief, as if unsure the sound had come from him at all.

"Now dance!" the Owl urged.

Sam froze, his feathers rustled. "I can't, I can't…" he whispered.

"Then move! Walk, jump, run! Get your feet moving. Feel it."

Sam started walking, and then, without fully understanding why or how, his steps quickened, shifting from a steady march to a sudden surge.

He was running. He poured everything into it; whether it was his Ostrich body or the spirit within didn't matter. He raced through the chambers, not on wings, but with feet pounding like thunder through the vast heart: Boom... Boom... Boom... Boom.

The rush was electric, like speeding down a highway with the wind whipping past. But this was different. He wasn't standing still while the world moved around him—the world moved with him. He felt the rhythm deep inside, the echo bouncing off the walls. He laughed wildly, breathless.

"Ava! I wish you could see this," Sam cried.

His feet thundered like drums against the cavernous walls, each strike sending ripples through the vast, echoing chambers. He didn't notice how far he'd run until another sound joined the pounding of his feet. He spun around, eyes wide with wonder—but the Owl was gone. It was just him and the heart.

"It's beating!" he gasped. "The heart is beating!"

With every fierce, relentless step, the heartbeat grew louder and steadier; the whole chamber pulsed with life as the whale finally took a deep, powerful breath.

A sudden blast of air whooshed through the tunnel, rattling the walls and scattering cool mist that tasted of salt and sea. Water droplets sparkled in the dim light, swirling with the vapour that poured from the whale's blowhole—a live, breathing pulse of hope filling the cavern.

A weight lifted from Sam's chest. For the first time in what felt like forever, he could breathe.

He wasn't just running. He was part of the pulse.

The magic flute played. The shadow on the sundial shifted.

EYE

Ava unfurled herself as if she were a delicate sheet of paper, creased and hidden in layers—fold upon fold, pressed and tightly tucked. Slowly stretching her wings apart, she snapped her head free from its cocoon. A sharp flick ran down her spine like a shiver, and her body came to life like a figure emerging from a flat page, fragile, but breathing.

She recalled Yalda: the crossing, the metamorphosis, the journey, the quest for the Simorgh. Yet none of it made sense. The space around her was pitch black, a chamber with no visible door or window, except for one tiny hole in the wall. Light flashed through it once, quick and sharp, just enough to catch a glimpse of herself: wings, feathers, her bird form. The sight rattled her. This might be a nightmare. The heavy weight of darkness pressed close. Dizzy and overwhelmed, she had no choice but to wait.

A narrow beam of light eventually pierced through the hole once more. The incoming light spread momentarily through the gloom, casting a sharp, upside-down silhouette of a bird on the chamber's inner wall—the delicate shape of a Crane.

Ava gazed at the silhouette, a wave of sorrow washing over her as it reminded her of the delicate origami cranes she once folded with her students—something meant to fill the emptiness they felt in their art classes.

"No... no... this must be a joke, a trick, or a nightmare," she whispered, her voice trembling.

"It is just a camera obscura," whispered a young voice from the dark.

Ava trembled; a chill racing down her spine. She wasn't alone.

Her head snapped around, and her wide eyes caught a movement—a young, graceful Crane stepping forward from the shadows. Its feathers were pale, almost luminous, catching what little light there was in the room. In the dimness, it was the only shape she could clearly see. The bird bowed its head gently.

"Who are you? Where am I?" Ava asked, her unsteady voice barely louder than a breath.

"I've been sent to help you, Miss, through your valley," the Crane said, calm and soothing.

Now that she was closer, Ava could see her clearly: a red-crowned Crane, strikingly beautiful, with snow-white feathers, jet-black wingtips, and a crimson crest that caught the faint light. Something about her presence stirred a memory—she reminded Ava of the Japan Airlines logo: elegant and precise.

The Crane spoke, her voice calm and measured. She explained that a camera obscura was a dark chamber with a tiny hole pierced in one wall. Light passing through that small aperture projects an image of the outside world onto the surface opposite. Because light travels in straight lines, the image appears upside-down and reversed—a perfect but inverted reflection of reality. The eye worked in a similar fashion: light first enters through the cornea, then passes through the pupil to focus on the retina—a delicate, thin layer at the back of the eye.

She gestured toward the upside-down image shimmering faintly on the wall and continued, describing how the retina converted the light into electrical impulses. These impulses raced along the optic nerve to the brain, where—within a fraction of a second—they were transformed into the images we perceive.

"All of this is fascinating," Ava said, with a hint of frustration, "but you still haven't explained how this will help me escape—this place, this darkness you called the valley. I need to find the others... and reach the Simorgh."

"You're here to learn how to be happy, Miss. That's what you need to complete your journey."

"You've got to be kidding, child! How can I be happy in all this...?"

The Crane's eyes twinkled with a spark of youthful mischief. "You need to see better, Miss."

"What do you mean?" Ava snapped impatiently.

"The final verdict lies with the brain," the Crane said calmly. "All the images that land on the retina—just like in a camera obscura—are upside down. If not for the brain, we'd see everything inverted. There is no fixed reality—only what your mind chooses to see. "

"But how come?" Ava asked, more curious now.

"Because even though the light hitting your retina stays the same, the way you see depends on your brain—on how it processes that information. It's shaped by your memories, your emotions, your expectations. The brain doesn't just flip the image—it builds your entire visual world."

She stepped a little closer and said, "So you must sharpen your mind. Train it to see clearly—to find the beauty woven into everything, even the darkness. Only then will the way forward begin to reveal itself."

"But how can I?" Ava's voice cracked with pain. "When all I see is misery—my husband's betrayal, the deprived children in schools or wandering the streets, endless wars, this dying society. How can I look at the avalanche of ruins we call home and find anything positive? How can I see Iran like this and still think clearly? This is why we decided to look for a saviour. If we truly knew how to fix these issues, we would."

The young Crane's eyes gleamed with excitement, seemingly oblivious to Ava's despair.

"It's not that hard," she said with a bright smile. "Ignore what your eyes tell you! Use your mind—your head—and choose what you want to see. It's a secret I learned myself, and it's pretty good fun! Maybe it's easier for kids to understand. Like that story about the big snake that swallowed an elephant, but grown-ups only saw a hat."

At that, Ava thought of her classroom and the paintings the children made about Yalda. She smiled softly. "I know... and I know that story too."

The young Crane nodded eagerly. "A great scientist once said something I love deeply: 'When you change the way you look at a thing, the thing you look at changes.'"

She then began her story. Her name was Sadako, and she was an innocent victim of World War Two, suffering from leukaemia caused by the atomic bombing of Hiroshima. Knowing she was dying, she set out to fold a thousand origami cranes before her death at the age of twelve—because she wanted to live."

"But you said you died," Ava said. "Does that mean I have died too?"

"No," Sadako replied. "When I first realised how sick I was, I had many fears and questions. I worried about my family and their future, and I asked myself, 'How can I make the world a better place while I'm still alive?' I wanted to leave behind something good. And look—I am one of the few, if not the only child who survived the Hiroshima bombing. My name lives on as a symbol of peace through the thousand paper cranes I folded, and my story still touches many hearts. So I didn't truly die in that hospital—I survived through the better days of Japan. That's why you still hear me; my story never ends, it never dies."

Ava's heart tightened. She recognised Sadako's story, which she had read and been deeply inspired by when she was a child.

Sadako continued. "Back then, Japan was a ruin. People, including my family and friends, struggled with illness, poverty, food shortages, and an uncertain future. But I never lost faith. I trusted in the origami cranes. Despite my pain and the sickness that was taking me, I held a strong vision in my mind—of life, and peace for Japan and the world. And it worked."

Ava hesitated. "So... what should I do? Make a thousand origami cranes?"

Sadako smiled warmly. "Well, everyone has to make their own origami. But if you are a visionary, you can create something from nothing. You can discover the joy of shaping the world with your own hands, starting from a simple piece of white paper—while believing in infinite possibilities."

Ava closed her eyes. In her mind, she took a piece of white paper and thought of all she wished to change. She made her first fold—and saw Iran at peace. No terror, no misery, no homeless children on the streets, no rage or extremists, no oppression. She folded again, wishing freedom for the many political activists, including her best friend who was a children's rights activist on hunger strike in prison. For each name, she made an origami Crane.

She imagined Sam, searching her mind for more white paper to fold, to picture their lives as happy ones. Her paper crumpled under the weight of painful memories. But then she pushed the creases aside and flattened the paper. In her mind, she patched the holes and torn edges with tape, trusting it would hold. She forgave him. She focused on his good qualities. She saw only what she wanted to see.

Suddenly, she yearned for one of Sam's warm embraces—those moments when he ran toward her, eyes wide and fearless, hands steady and strong. Ava felt happiness bloom inside her.

Light flickered like a camera flash, making her eyes snap open. A glowing spot rose from the light, growing larger and closer until it became a bird. It was Sam, emerging from the heart of the whale, moving with deliberate grace as he approached her. They smiled.

Together, they walked slowly, head-to-head, drifting through an ocean of sky toward the white reefs of clouds.

The magic flute played. The shadow on the sundial shifted.

THE VALLEY OF DEATH

NEDA DIDN'T know where she was. Thick, putrid air clung to her skin like a damp cloth. It dragged her from the edge of sleep, and then a sound jolted her, pulling her into full awareness. Instinctively, she reached for her watch—but froze.

Her arm felt wrong. Where her hand should have been, there was a wing. Sleek. Feathered. She blinked. Once. Twice. Her heart fluttered with confusion as she took in the small, streamlined body that was now hers. She felt impossibly light, hollowed out—as if her bones had been replaced with air. But she couldn't see much of herself. Darkness pressed in from all sides.

Then the sound came again—clearer this time. A pause. A heavy stomp. An eerie, rhythmic whistle, like footsteps pacing above her. Nausea churned in her gut. The motion was familiar: a slow, relentless sway. But it wasn't coming from within—it was the floor itself, rocking back and forth.

A ship? she thought. *Am I below the deck?* She held her breath, listening. Beyond the metal walls, the sea rolled and surged—distant but steady.

Yes. Definitely. She was floating on water. Around her, faint rustles and murmurs stirred in the dark. She wasn't alone. The thought sent a tremor through her.

A strong wave rocked the vessel, and a hatch above groaned open—a shaft of dim, indigo light spilled in, scribbling pale shapes across the floor. And that's when she saw them.

Birds. Dozens of them, cramped together in piles, feathers limp, eyes shut in fear or sickness, heaped into what looked like a cargo container. She stared, stunned.

Slowly, she dared to look at herself—tracing the glossy indigo sheen of her back, the cream-white of her belly, and, as far as she could twist, a smudge of red at her throat. A Swallow. Nimble and impossibly real.

Her throat burned in the stifling air. Around her, the other birds fared no better, pressed together, wings overlapping, crawling over one another behind high metal walls. No room to perch or stretch. "Hey!" a whisper. "Hey... Neda!"

She jolted upright. "Who's there?"

"Down here... look beneath the rail."

Neda leaned over the edge. Two small kestrels crouched on the floor side by side, nearly identical—speckled backs of reddish brown, chests pale and flecked. One stepped forward with a flutter. The other—just a little smaller—stayed still.

She knew them instantly. The twins, Surena and Pouria. Relief surged through her. "Oh my God, you're here!" She tried to leap down, but something yanked her back, holding her fast.

"Careful!" Surena called. "That's the crate. You have to free yourself first."

"I'm... trapped?"

"We all were," he said gently.

"What is this? What happened to us? Our bodies! How did you get out?"

Around her, low murmurs rippled from the other birds.

"Quiet!" Surena whispered. "You're waking them."

Neda looked around uneasily.

Surena's voice was steady. "Let's focus. We'll talk after you're free. Try first, okay? If not, we'll help." He sounded like a coach—calm and sure.

"Look for a wider gap... see up there? That latch. Good. Now, stand tall. Move your right foot forward—keep the other parallel. Bend into a lunge. Squeeze your wings together, slightly down. Yes, like that, exactly like... like the warrior pose, from yoga. Hold it." Neda held her breath. "Now jump!"

It took her a few tries, but finally Neda landed beside them, tumbling into a heap of feathers—bruised and breathless.

Surena stepped back to look her over. Then, gently, the twins helped her along the floor to a corner of the space: a narrow tunnel beneath a long row of crates. One by one, the three of them squeezed in.

Surena settled near the edge of the tunnel and gestured toward the metal corridor beyond.

"This leads down to the ship's drive shaft and engine—we checked it. It looks safe there. So glad we found you. Honestly, you could barely be seen in that crowd. Well spotted, Pouria!"

"Thank you, both. I'm so glad too," Neda said. "So—what's going on? This is a dream, I suppose. I mean... we're like this!" She pointed at their birdlike bodies. "Still, somehow, we know who we are! All very odd! Do you know anything?"

Surena glanced at his brother. "Not much. Like you, we just... woke up here. No idea how or why. But we remembered something Huma said—that we'd each end up in different places. So, we assumed... maybe this is our path."

"It's still weird though," Pouria cut in. "We had a quick look around and tried to find our mum. No luck!"

"Yet. We will find her, Pouria," Surena added firmly. He continued, "We're assuming it's a ship—a big one—but we don't know where it's headed."

Neda pointed in the direction of the rows of cages. "What about the others? All these birds—who are they?"

"We don't know, except that they are in an awful condition, either injured or starved," Surena said grimly. "They've been divided into groups. I'll show you."

He led her to a small slit in the middle of the tunnel, pointing to a section near the back. "See those identical rows?"

"Those cages?" Neda squinted. "Oh, yes... they go on forever."

"Yes," Surena said. "That's where they keep the battery hens. Dozens, maybe hundreds. They're loud when they're awake—constantly pecking at their feathers. It's awful."

"Bloody hell..." Neda muttered. "Are they... all going to find the Simorgh too?"

"I doubt it," Surena said. "They seem pretty dumb. Bred to lay."

"Don't say that!" Neda said. "It must be so hard—constantly laying, locked away in the dark. Do they even know what sunlight is? Have they ever seen outside?"

"No, even when the hatch was opened," Surena said, "they just peeked out and then went back in. I guess they're afraid of the unknown or maybe scared of losing what little they have. Or maybe they don't believe there's anything beyond the cage. Whatever. We need to focus on our escape."

They agreed to make their move once the hatch was again opened.

Eventually, the floor trembled, and there was a deep mechanical groan as another cargo load was being winched on board. The hatch opened, and they immediately escaped to the safety of the engine room.

The air was thick with heat and the hum of machinery. Shadows danced across the metal walls. And then, they saw her.

A Peregrine falcon stood majestically on the engine's shaft, her feathers shimmering black and gold like satin catching the evening light. Slowly turning her head, she gazed at them intensely through her amber eyes.

After a long, silent moment, she gave a slight nod and spoke. "We're working down here—plenty of us—on different floors." Her voice had a crisp, melodic quality—rather friendly and unbothered by what was above them. Then she said, "I was expecting you. Huma said you'd be joining this leg of the journey."

They looked at each other in wonder. Surena, impatient and nervous, stepped forward and said, "What is this? A ship—we figured that much. But who are the birds? Where are we heading? We're supposed to be in the Alborz Mountains, not floating out here... There must be a mistake. Did you mention Huma? That's good... Can you tell us anything? Or call Huma for us?"

"This is an old ship," the Peregrine said. "A cursed one. She set out in the early days of 1979, from Guadalupe in the Pacific Ocean. I remember those days very well. Her destination was the Persian Gulf. The cargo was explosives and weapons. She was supposed to deliver them, take on oil, and return west. But something went wrong. Someone miscalculated—badly. The ship got stuck and never made it back.

"Over the years, this ship has had many owners—Americans, Russians, Chinese. No one could fix the problem. Some of the crew left. Some changed. Some died. And some were never allowed to leave.

"Recently, the Iranian government seized the ship over unpaid bills. At first, they wanted to sink her. But she proved stubborn. So now they're loading her with Yellowcake[17]. Once she's full, they'll set her on fire. This ship will sink easily. And no one will take the blame."

The three listened in disbelief. Neda asked, "And the birds? Who are they? Why are they here?"

The Peregrine's gaze darkened. "They're here until their usefulness ends. Each bird serves a purpose. Some feed the crew. Some lay eggs. The ducks—well, their feathers pad pillows. But most of them... are sick with a disease that only affects birds."

She nodded toward the dimly lit cages. "Did you see their pale faces? Some of them—toward the back—carry a terrible stench."

"Yes, I did," Neda said softly. "Poor things. What is it they have?"

The Peregrine replied, "Some have Stockholm Syndrome. Others suffer from something deeper. The sickness has a French name, what the existentialists call *Mauvaise Foi*. I'm afraid there's not much can be done for them here."

"Is it contagious?" Pouria asked, alarmed.

"If you stay up there long enough—yes," the Peregrine replied. "The first few days, you're immune. After that... not so much."

Surena leaned forward. "How about you? Are you immune?"

The Peregrine gave a slow nod. "Yes. But immunity comes at a price. That illness? It only touches the surface. I live deeper—where the roots are stronger. Besides, I'm a doctor."

"A doctor?" Neda blinked. "Wait... seriously?"

"We didn't even get to ask your name," Pouria added. "Who are you? Did you live in Tehran before... well, before you turned into a bird?"

The Peregrine tilted her head slightly. "Yes, I lived in Tehran—a long time ago. Long before either of you were born. I was actually the first woman to hold a cabinet position in Iran."

She spoke with a calm, steady voice. Every word felt intentional, like it was meant to stay with them.

Neda frowned, thinking. "Wait... I'm sorry, I didn't know. What year was that? Were you the Health Minister?"

The Peregrine smiled softly. "Close. I was appointed Minister of Education. It was 1968. I am Farrokhroo Parsa. I was born in 1922 to a mother who was a fearless women's rights activist—and I followed in her footsteps. I became a doctor, not just to heal bodies, but to serve my country.

"While studying medicine, and even after receiving my degree, I taught biology at several high schools in Tehran. I still remember walking into those classrooms for the first time. In one school, there were only 110 girls enrolled when I arrived. By the time I left, 1,850 young women were studying there.

"But it wasn't just about numbers; it was proof that Iranian girls were hungry to learn. I was determined to help them. Those years taught me that real change begins in the classroom, and that education is the most powerful weapon to transform lives. It was from those blackboards and science labs that I stepped into politics, ready to fight for every girl who wanted more.

"After the 1979 revolution, everything changed. I was arrested and falsely accused—not for crimes, but for my beliefs, and for my service. They claimed I spread corruption because I stood for freedom and education. "At my trial, I told them: I am not afraid to die."

She paused and looked them in the eye. "If you're seeking freedom, you have two choices: fight for your values—knowing you may die, or you may succeed. Otherwise... you can stay and join the sick birds."

Neda asked, "What did they do with you then?"

She answered, "Because I had lived true to my values, I did not beg, and I did not regret.From within the prison walls, I wrote my final message to my children: *'I am a doctor, so I have no fear of death. Death is only a moment and no more. I am prepared to receive death with open arms rather than live in shame by being forced to be veiled. I am not going to bow to those who expect me to express regret for 50 years of efforts for equality between men and women. I am not prepared to wear the chador and step back in history.'*

"The Hanging Judge, Khalkhali, sentenced me to death. On May 8, 1980, they executed me. But I do not consider myself defeated. My life was a testament to what women can do—and I hope it still is.

"They did not give me the dignity of a death befitting a doctor, a teacher, a minister—a woman who gave her life to her country. No. They put me in a sack like an animal, wrapped ropes around me, and dragged me to the gallows. But the ropes failed. They tore. I woke again—still alive. I imagine they were furious that I had not yet surrendered to death. So, they tried again. This time, they used wires. And again, my body resisted. Even in death, I refused to go quietly.

"Three wounds were left on my body. Not just wounds from execution, but from defiance, from endurance, from the cruelty of those who feared the power of an educated woman. My death was not quick. It was meant to humiliate. But in truth, it revealed only their fear—and my strength.

"Let the three wounds on my body be three lessons: that silence is not safety, that courage often costs dearly, and that even in the face of inhumanity, a woman can remain unbroken.

"The day after they killed me, they buried my body in Behesht Zahra Cemetery. No ceremony. No dignity. Just a hurried grave for a woman they wanted to erase. But I was not forgotten. My children came, brave and grieving, and placed a gravestone with no name. It bore only one word: *'Mother'*.

"To them, that was enough. That word held my entire life—my love, my strength, my sacrifices. But it was too much for those who feared remembrance. The bulldozers returned. They tore the stone away, and this time they erased even the soil. My resting place was lost.

"They thought that by destroying my grave, they could silence my memory. But a mother's legacy does not lie in stone. It lives in every girl who dares to learn, in every woman who stands tall, in every voice that speaks for freedom. They buried my body—but not my fight. Not my truth."

She paused for a few moments before continuing. "This is the valley of death. But what scares me isn't dying. It's living like those broken, silenced birds, wasting away in quiet misery. That's a real death.

"You've got two choices: join them or stand up and fight for your freedom. There's no in-between."

Surena stepped forward, his voice steady with determination. "We want to be free. No matter what." He looked at the other two, who nodded in agreement.

"What should we do now, on this ship?" Neda asked the Peregrine.

"There's only one way to get rid of the Yellowcake," she said. "You have to plant a seed."

"A seed? Seriously? What kind of seed?" Neda asked.

"A seed from a special cedar tree," the Peregrine said. "It holds an ancient power. It can grow in any condition—even here, on this ship. When its roots take hold, it will start breaking down the Yellowcake. And when the buds appear, you'll know the work is done."

They stared at her in disbelief. "Don't underestimate a seed," she said. "It carries immense biological intelligence."

She stepped closer, as if she were revealing a secret and said, "Our seed comes from a cedar in Chak Chak[18], a village deep in the heart of our land. Have you heard of it?"

They shook their heads. "Never!"

"No surprise," the Peregrine murmured. "Chak Chak is where Nikbanou, daughter of Yazdegerd III—the last Sassanid ruler—was cornered by invading Arab forces in 640 CE. Instead of surrendering, she prayed to Ahura Mazda, and the mountain split open before her eyes and took her in, sealing shut behind her like a fortress.

"Some say she became one with the mountain. Others believe she still waits—deep inside—watching, listening. But the point is: she was never captured. Not by sword, not by men, not by force, not by fear. The mountain took her, and in doing so, it preserved her defiance forever. Her resilience is buried deep in your roots.

"Just beyond, a spring of water still trickles from the rock—blessed by Anahita, goddess of water. It runs in Nikbanou's name. Beside the spring rises the 'Old Green', an ancient cedar born from a single, destined seed. It stands as a quiet testament to the enduring spirit of Persian women: resilient, rooted, and radiant, even in the face of fallen empires and relentless adversity."

Neda's eyes lit up. She leaned forward. "So... how do we get it?"

"Ah," said the Peregrine, a gleam flickering in her amber eyes. "Now we reach the heart of the matter."

She lowered her voice slightly. "The seed is with the Swifts."

"The Swifts?" Neda echoed. "Who are they?"

"A magnificent kind of bird," the Peregrine said. "Unlike any other. Once they take their first flight, they never land again. They feed, sleep—even mate—in the air. In their lifetime, they travel far enough to reach the moon—five times over."

"Unbelievable!" Neda exclaimed.

"So... they must be huge?" Surena asked.

"Quite the opposite," the Peregrine replied. "Small. Tough. Sharper than they look. Their wings curve like scythes, built for sky and silence.

"Twice a day, they ascend to the apex of their flight—to the boundary layer where Earth brushes the edge of sunlight. From there, they see everything: the present, the past, the storms that haven't yet arrived. They see the stars, the twilight, the hues of other planets. They are aligned with the magnetic force of the universe.

"They flock together, but at night, they drift down singly. Then, in the morning, they rise again—together."

"So... what about the seed?" Surena asked.

"One of them carries the seed—a warrior Swift called Navid[19]. He built his strength by pressing against the wind, like a soldier doing push-ups. He was born in a trench, made to endure turbulence—strong, focused, steady even in a cyclone. Before he ascended for the last time, he took the seed. He's carried it ever since."

"So... how do we get it?" Neda asked. "Is he coming here?"

"Yes," the Peregrine replied. "But you must prepare—like soldiers before battle."

Pouria's breath quickened. "What exactly should we do?"

"The seed must land on the Yellowcake," said the Peregrine. "I've worked down there. It's stored at the bow of the ship. There are two access points: one through the upper deck, sealed by the crew; the other through the cargo hold, under the crates. We can use that one. But first, we must move the birds out of the crates and then wait for the right moment—when the gates rise. The Swift will descend and drop the seed."

"Wait! Move all the birds? That's impossible!" Surena said.

The Peregrine smiled, stepping closer. "Just sing to them. All of you. One song. Together."

"Sing?"

"Yes. That's how you'll wake them up. Stir something deeper. One rhythm, one voice. Mingle with them. Be among them."

Neda, Surena, and Pouria exchanged glances.

"But... what song?" asked Neda. "I can't think... nothing comes. It's like my mind's gone blank."

Then Surena began to tweet a faint tune—"Da daaa da da daaa dada?" The others listened.

"Got it?" he asked.

Neda chuckled. "Not the way you're tweeting it."

"That's 'We Shall Overcome' by Joan Baez," Surena said. "I used to play it on my guitar. Remember?"

"Spot on! Yes!" Pouria said. "And the Persian version—remember? We used to sing that too."

Neda blinked. "Oh! There's a Persian version of that song?"

"Yes," Surena said. "Baez recorded it in 2009 in support of the protests. Even sang lines in Persian—*Ma Pirooz Mishim.*"

They closed their eyes—and sang. "Ma Pirooz Mishim."

At first, it was only three of them, humming the song. Shortly after, a faint vibration stirred beneath their voices—like rain brushing the ship's edge. But it wasn't rain. The sick birds were waking.

Chaos erupted in the cages. The crates trembled under the fury of beating wings. A sudden surge of energy flung the birds upward, pushing against the walls and breaking them free from captivity. Still singing, they poured onto the deck.

On the deck, as the mayhem faded, the air shivered, as if something vast was approaching. Then the swifts—thousands, tens of thousands—arrived in a river of silver wings spiralling into the sky.

Surena saw one of them break away—sleek, bright, impossibly fast.

It was Navid.

A seed of light glowed in his beak.

Surena took flight to meet Navid mid-air, snatching the seed, and turning toward Neda and Pouria. They reached for him, passing the seed between them, and planted it onto the deck—right above the Yellowcake.

The wind tore through them—wild and unrelenting. The sky cracked open with a blinding flash. The roaring waves dragged some of the birds into the sea, while others fought desperately to stay aloft. Pouria saw his brother vanish into the depths and lunged after him—but the waves were faster. His wings sliced through the spray; but he couldn't reach him. Salt stung his eyes. The storm drowned his screams. Around him, the surviving birds spiralled upward, clinging to the wind.

Then, silence.

***

Neda didn't know where she was. A fresh sea breeze stirred her half-awake. Then came a twittering—a distant buzzing—pulling her fully into the moment. It was dark, like early dawn. The sky stretched above her, a deep blue canvas dotted with wheeling specks. For a heartbeat, she thought she was underwater, at the ocean's bottom, and that the specks were shoals of fish circling in the gloom.

But the sounds grew louder, and the dots grew bigger. They weren't fish. They were birds—vast flocks of swifts crossing the wide sea.

Neda realized she wasn't beneath the waves, but at the edge where ocean meets sky, floating at the threshold between two worlds.

She tried to remember. The seed. It had been planted.

Closing her eyes, a rush surged through her chest—something new, fierce and pure.

"Hey!" a voice called. "Hey... Neda!"

She jolted. "Who's there?"

"Look up—right above you. Fly up."

From the far side of the sky, a Kestrel glided in: Pouria.

She struggled to lift herself; her body was heavy, unresponsive. Pain shot through one side. She looked down—one of her wings was torn in half.

Still, she fought with every ounce of strength to catch a breeze. She began to fly.

"Where's Surena?" she called.

Pouria's face twisted with grief. Neda cried mournfully. Pouria drew closer to the surface and said, "But he showed us the way—this way—toward Alborz. to the Simorgh"

He pointed to the horizon, where light was breaking.

Neda heard a soft, high melody of a flute drifting through the sky.

She looked up and wished that Surena was watching them from the upper air. Maybe he was there with Navid and all the defiant young Iranians, looking down on them.

Neda and Pouria pressed onward toward the Simorgh.

The shadow on the sundial shifted.

NOTES

1 J.A. Baker, The Peregrine (New York: New York Review Books, 2005).

2 Gautama Buddha, The Dhammapada, trans. Eknath Easwaran (Tomales, CA: Nilgiri Press, 2007), verse 276

3 In October 2020, the Iran-Nejad family—Rasoul (35), Shiva Mohammad Panahi (35), and their children Anita (9) and Armin (6)—drowned when their overcrowded migrant boat capsized in the English Channel while attempting to reach the UK from France. Their youngest child, Artin (15 months), was presumed drowned. The family was Kurdish-Iranian and originated from Sardasht, Iran.

4 The Si-o-se-pol (Bridge of Thirty-Three Arches) is a prominent Safavid-era bridge in Isfahan, Iran, built c. 1599–1602. It spans the Zayandeh River and features an innovative double-tiered structure with thirty-three arches. The bridge served as a vital thoroughfare and a social hub during its time.

5 The Salman Pak facility, also known as al-Salman, is an Iraqi military installation located approximately 15 miles south of Baghdad on a Tigris River peninsula. It was (falsely) assessed by U.S. military intelligence to be a central site for Iraq's biological and chemical weapons programs.

6 Ctesiphon was an ancient city on the eastern bank of the Tigris River, near present-day Baghdad, Iraq. It served as the capital of the Parthian Empire (c. 57 BCE–224 CE) and subsequently the Sasanian Empire (224–651 CE), both significant Persian dynasties, marking it as a major political and cultural hub.

7 Taq Kasra, or the Arch of Ctesiphon, is an iconic ruin of the ancient city, notable for possessing the world's largest single-span brick arch. Dating from approximately the 3rd to 6th century CE, this massive vaulted hall stands as a testament to Sasanian architectural prowess.

8 Al-Mada'in (Arabic for "The Cities") designates a cluster of ancient urban settlements situated along the Tigris River in contemporary Iraq, near Salman Pak. The most notable among these historical sites is Ctesiphon, serving as a key center in the region's ancient history.

9 The Behistun Inscription, located on Mount Behistun in western Iran, is a crucial Achaemenid royal inscription from the reign of Darius the Great (r. 522–486 BC). Its trilingual text (Old Persian, Elamite, and Babylonian) details Darius's autobiography, lineage, and the suppression of rebellions throughout his empire. This inscription proved invaluable for deciphering cuneiform writing, shedding light on ancient Mesopotamian cultures.

10 Abdol Hossein Sardari, an Iranian diplomat, is celebrated as the "Iranian Schindler" for saving thousands of Jews during the Holocaust while serving in Nazi-occupied Paris. His courageous actions, often defying official directives, protected both Iranian and non-Iranian Jews. For more, see Fariborz Mokhtari, "Abdol Hossein Sardari and the Fate of Iranian Jews in Vichy France," Iranian Studies 32, no. 1 (1999): 71-77.

11 The Nojeh Coup was a failed military attempt on July 9–10, 1980, to over-

throw Iran's newly formed Islamic Republic, resulting in widespread arrests and 144 executions. The coup was supported by Dr. Shapour Bakhtiar (1914–1991), the last prime minister under Mohammad Reza Shah Pahlavi (January 4–February 11, 1979), who was later assassinated in Paris by agents of the Islamic Republic on August 6, 1991.

12   Sholeh Wolpé, trans., *Sin: Selected Poems of Forugh Farrokhzad*, by Forugh Farrokhzad (Fayetteville: University of Arkansas Press, 2010), 67–68.

13   The 1988 massacre in Iran, often referred to in connection with Khomeini's fatwa, was a mass execution of thousands of political prisoners in Iran during the summer and fall of 1988. This event is one of the most severe human rights violations in the history of the Islamic Republic.

14   The Beluga Sturgeon belongs to the oldest group of fishes, estimated to be 200 million years old. They can live more than 100 years. They are the largest freshwater fish species in the world

15   The term Yārān (meaning "Friends") refers to a group of seven Iranian Bahā'í leaders who were arrested and imprisoned in 2008 by the Iranian government.

16   Glowing eggs refers to the Almas caviar, meaning "diamond" in Persian. It comes from the rare albino Beluga sturgeon of the Caspian Sea. Only one in 6,000 Belugas is albino, and they can take up to fifty years to mature. This makes Almas one of the rarest and most precious caviars in the world.

17   Yellowcake is the concentrated form of uranium that emerges from the mine and milling process, before it undergoes the complex steps of enrichment.

18   Also known as Pir-e Sabz ("The Green Pir"), Chak Chak is a significant Zoroastrian pilgrimage site in Yazd Province, Iran. The name "Chak Chak" ("drip-drip") refers to a constantly dripping spring within the shrine, which is central to its mythology.

19   Navid Afkari Sangari (22 July 1993 – 12 September 2020) was an Iranian wrestler who was executed by the Iranian authorities. He had been accused and convicted of murdering a security guard during anti-government protests in 2018. Afkari stated his confession was obtained under torture, a claim supported by numerous human rights organizations. His case became a global symbol of state repression in Iran, and his final words reportedly expressed his innocence and his love for his country.

ARRIVING

They saw the face of the Simorgh,
But...

ATTAR, *THE CONFERENCE OF THE BIRDS*

THE SIMORGH

"Ich habe genug."

—Johann Sebastian Bach, Cantata BWV 82

I MPATIENT to arrive, Parto dived into the wet, shuddering wind, beating her wings through the heavy flurries of snow, her eyes burning with fatigue. The storm wouldn't clear for at least another hour—she knew this now, having learned a little about the sky.

She turned back, retreating to the shelter of the trees, where she crouched in silence, her eyes fixed on the horizon in the direction of the Alborz Mountains. Waiting.

She was close now. Just before the snow began, Mount Damavand had appeared in the distance. The highest peak in Iran, it soared above the Persian Plateau, watching over the land like a silent guardian—timeless and resolute.

Parto felt a deep reverence as she gazed at Damavand in the distance. It brought back the view she'd seen from the airplane window when she flew back to Iran—but this was different. It wasn't just a scene behind glass; but something alive. From the ground, it shimmered like a diamond—a precious gift from the earth to the blue sphere above. And yet, she reminded herself, Damavand was also a dormant volcano: a flame of forgotten fire, a symbol of resilience.

Throughout the journey—when her wings trembled in the wind, when fear brushed against her—Parto had clung fiercely to the vision she carried. It kept her going. She followed the mountains, quiet signposts guiding her toward the Simorgh, never far from her thoughts.

Parto reflected: "A mountain's spirit shifts, much like the languages of the world—Feminine in French: *la montagne.* Masculine in German and Arabic: *der Berg, al-Jabal.* But in Persian, it has no gender; it transcends such distinctions. And that duality was so visible in Damavand. From its summit, it watches maternally over its beloved child, Tehran, but from the plains below, it stretches its head to kiss its bride, the sky."

Between longing and exhaustion, Parto slipped into a deep sleep—and dreamed.

She was holding a bowl, clutched tightly in both hands, walking toward a mountain. When she arrived, she placed the bowl at its base as an offering and pleaded: "Let me see the Simorgh. I have crossed my valley." She pointed to the bowl.

The mountain trembled. A rift split it from crown to root, spilling searing light and living flame. It opened—but she could not pass.

The mountain spoke: "The Simorgh does not come in darkness. First, you must find Mithra."

She did not flinch. Meeting the fire with steady eyes, she answered, "I already have."

When she awoke, dawn had come. Broken columns of snow lined the mountain slopes, glittering in the morning light. Cold air rose from the ground—still and sharp.

She found herself staring at her wings—studying them closely as she lifted and lowered them, as if unconsciously mimicking the gestures of human hands. In her dream, she had been human. It had felt so real. She remembered having fingers—warm, separate. She could grasp and let go.

But she also remembered the fearful vulnerability, the stumbling way of being human—the constant reaching without knowing what for, not knowing the beginning or the end. But now, awake, her wings and feathers were still there. She gazed at them and hopped a little. Yes—she could still fly. Easily.

Parto wasn't sure if she had ever truly been human. Maybe that had only been a recurring dream. Or maybe she had once been human—and this life, feathered and sky-bound, was the lingering illusion she could never quite wake from.

The boundary blurred.

And for a moment, the question struck her: which dream was the real one?

Her chest tightened. She wished she could see herself—something to confirm the truth. Wasn't there anything to verify it? A proof. Anything!

Or perhaps she was dead. Yes... yes, maybe that was it. A relief at last.

But no—she wasn't. She checked it. The Earth's magnetic pulse was still there, humming beneath her. She was still alive.

It all unsettled her. She perched in silence, unresolved, suspended in the haze of uncertainty. Perhaps there never was a waking world—only layers of dreaming. Or was waking just another dream, with rules we had agreed to forget? Or was she trapped in a dream that had forgotten how to end? What if she had only ever wandered between shadows of thought?

Yes—thoughts. That was a hint. A thread in the fog. She clung to it, fragile as it was, and took it as a clue. If she could think, she could seek. If she could question, she could answer. She would work to resolve the mystery. Or at least find an edge—something that could hold. To understand the truth and establish herself, she needed a point of reference. Something solid. A place to stand.

She searched her mind, trying to find what remained constant—what had existed in both realms. She recognized two certainties, two enduring calls that transcended all boundaries. Two feelings that had lingered in every shape, every dream, every waking: a quest for something supreme—a purpose, unreachable yet ever-present. And love. A deep, inexplicable love.

Those were two threads that tugged at her—whether bird or human—binding her to something true. And that was what anchored her. She no longer cared which was the dream and which was reality. It didn't matter. That question had lost its hold. She was free.

She soared into the misty sky. A sudden, overwhelming joy filled her. Like a fish breaking the surface of the sea, she swam through the air, drifting into the cold north wind, resuming her pursuit.

Below, the forest stretched frozen across rolling hills—ridge after ridge, each folding into the next, all drawn toward the distant peak. She cast her eyes across the vast landscape, watching the world unfold beneath her.

Birds approached from every direction, their wings stirring the silence of the sky. Among them, Parto spotted familiar figures: a Woodpecker sweeping ahead, followed by a pigeon fluttering weakly—Atossa and Gohar, coming from the direction of the Caspian Sea. A tiny blue flake shimmered in the distance at first, and then grew into a Blue Jay—no one but Bijan. Dara spread his gentle, rounded wings—soft and curved, like all Turtle Doves—with Babak, the Nightingale, drifting close behind. Farhad—her friend who had been missing for years—was there too, in flesh and blood; and beside him, Shirin, radiant as a rainbow. She saw Ava and Sam working it out together, blending their differences into a gift: her wings, his stride. She saw Roxy and Kamran burst from cover, the air stirring with the sudden lift of their wings. She saw the muscular undulations of Pouria's wings, and felt a rush of relief when she spotted Neda—injured, but still weaving her way through the sky. She saw Gohar reunited with her daughter, Ayda. But she did not see Jav.

She heard a melancholic, indescribably forlorn cry. It was the twins' mother, wailing. Pouria had returned alone; his twin, the other Kestrel, was missing. It unnerved Parto. Her wings trembled as a cold knot tightened in her chest and fear crept over her. What if the others she cared about were lost?

Where was Hooman? Had he arrived already?

She dipped lower, traversing the terrain corner to corner, her eyes sweeping the open air for any sign of him. Then she rose higher again, climbing for a clearer view. As she searched and scanned, a memory surfaced—a conversation they'd had years ago.

They had spoken about messenger pigeons, released at the front during the war, forced to fly over battlefields to get home—never looking down. "You must look forward, or you'll never reach your destination." That had become Parto's mantra.

Hooman hadn't liked it then—and now, she found herself agreeing with him. No, she must look downward. Otherwise, she would never truly arrive. And just as she was about to scan the landscape one last time, she spotted something. There—an Owl, perched on a steep slope. Her heart thundered. Could it be him?

With a sudden surge, she drove her wings skyward, then plummeted like an arrow loosed from a bow. It was him, wraith-like and frozen.

She let out a mournful cry as she landed beside him. A sheet of ice masked his eyes and beak, and icicles clung to his eyebrows.

Parto stepped closer, her heart caught between terror and hope. After a long moment, Hooman's eyes flickered faintly. He was still there.

He tried to speak, but only thin needles of ice formed in the air with his breath—fragile threads that vanished as quickly as they came.

"I know... I know, Hooman. We've arrived—we made it," she whispered, blowing warm air onto his face, trying to melt the rim of frost between them.

Alborz stood before them—regal, immense, eternal. Parto pointed to the sky, showing Hooman what gleamed ahead. In the far distance, Damavand's peak shimmered faintly—a silent beacon of hope. The sight filled them with a quiet joy. They soared together, rising to join the others in flight. They were close now—only a few wing-beats remained.

And just as their strength began to falter, there it was: The radiant crown of Damavand. Its white slopes, polished like silver, glistened softly in the light, as if the mountain itself had prepared the way—ready to welcome them home.

It was time to land.

Against the whiteness of Damavand, a speck of colour emerged—gradually growing into a bird. Effortless and majestic, it rode the wind, darting and swooping with graceful precision. It was the Hoopoe—its cinnamon-orange wings catching the light at every turn. The tall crest atop its head quivered gently, fluttering in the breeze.

It rose higher, tracing wide, deliberate loops, as if attuned to an unseen shift in the air. Pausing mid-flight, the Hoopoe turned toward the peak and let out a resonant cry—a sound that echoed through the stillness like a summons—and then darted back to stand on a high rock along Damavand's steep slope, watching the birds descend, waiting patiently for everyone to arrive. By sunset, the survivors of the arduous journey perched along the mountainside. The birds from Bijan's Yalda party scanned through those who had landed, searching for missing companions. Among the flickering wings were unfamiliar faces: birds from distant regions, drawn by the same call. Together, they numbered thirty.

The birds turned their eyes to the Hoopoe, who stood motionless, its shadow cast against the mountain wall—resembling the shimmering silhouette of a winged sun disc.

Damavand roared, casting orange bursts of heat and smoke into the darkening sky. But the birds did not flinch. They stood unmoved, as if hypnotised, stripped of every sense but one: the yearning to stand before the Simorgh—the one they had come to find.

"Fly to the peak," the Hoopoe ordered, "but beware—do not get too close to the crater. It's a bottomless pit of fury and ignorance, boiling dark and deadly below. You only need to reach it. The moment you arrive; it will begin to cool slowly. Over the course of tonight, it will grow still and become dormant. And only then will it allow you to find the truth. Remain there until dawn. When the sun's first rays break the sky, the lightning of glory will appear—and the Simorgh will descend to greet you."

The birds beamed with joy as they followed the instructions. Some climbed on foot, others soared toward the summit. The final stretch was steep, and their bodies ached, but their hearts were light, charged with a restless, impatient hope.

Dusk deepened. Rivers of lava spewed from the summit, bleeding crimson into the darkening sky. The air thickened—blazing hot, laced with the bitter sting of sulphur and the dry sting of ash. It scalded their throats and burned their eyes. Beneath them, the crater churned, its molten pools seething, pulsing with light and heat. Then they heard it: the voice of the mountain. At first, it was a low, guttural groan rising from its depths. But as they neared, it fractured into brittle cracks—like glass shattering under pressure.

The birds hovered above the glowing crater, circling in tense, fevered agitation, their wild flight colliding with the raw fury of the burning earth below. In that moment, their scorched feathers fell away like ash. Wings curled inward, reshaping into arms; talons and claws stretched and lengthened into hands. Their bones thickened, luminous and strong, glowing with an inner light. Skin bloomed over their new forms—fragile, and human. Their souls rose—freed from the bodies they once inhabited. No longer birds, yet not entirely human.

At dawn, golden sunlight stirred their eyes open. They were themselves again, seated in a circle, gazing into the crater. The molten lava had cooled, hardened now into dark stone. Hot steam condensed into shimmering droplets, pooling into a small, still pond at the crater's heart, glistening beneath the blue sky. The wind swept away the ash. A single ripple spread across the water's surface, then another—as if the earth itself were exhaling.

Together, they rose and looked around cautiously, waiting, then stepped forward and peered into the still water's surface.

They looked into the water— and there, a glimpse of the Simorgh appeared.

But as the ripples cleared, they saw only themselves. Like a mirror.

They looked again. And again.

Each time, the same reflection.

In beholding the Simorgh, they dared to understand: the thirty birds were themselves—the thirty seekers who had made the journey, and each of them was the Simorgh.

The Simorgh was not another. The two were one.

From the peak, they looked back. Below them, Tehran gleamed— the whole land shining. The fresh scent of newly fallen rain hung in the air. Yalda—the longest, darkest night—was over.

Light had prevailed.

It was the first day of Day.

WORLD TWO

The world's great age begins anew,
The golden years return,
The earth doth like a snake renew
Her winter weeds outworn:
Heaven smiles, and faiths and empires gleam,
Like wrecks of a dissolving dream...

FROM 'HELLAS' BY PERCY BYSSHE SHELLEY

2584

A SOUND WOKE Parto. Something like a flute—controlled, emotional, haunting. It sounded like the memory of something lost... and almost remembered. Maybe she had heard it before. Maybe not.

She shifted under the blanket, still half-asleep, as the final note rang out—lingering in the air before fading into silence. That was enough to wake her fully. She sat up in bed, confused. *What was that? Who would be playing music at this hour?*

The window blind was down, but through the narrow slats she could see the night beginning to pale, soft light casting faint patterns on the wall. Dawn was coming.

She pushed herself halfway out of bed, thinking she should check who might be playing out in the street. But just as quickly, she stopped and sank back down.

No, the music hadn't come from outside—it had been part of the dream.

She lay back and pulled the blanket over her shoulders, trying to hold onto the details before they slipped away. She closed her eyes and focused, hoping to remember. The flute's melody echoed in her mind, gently tugging a fragment of the dream back into reach—something deep and distant, like standing at the edge of a memory she was never meant to revisit.

Parto reached across the empty side of the bed. Her hand touched the cold pillow. She paused there, fingers resting in the hollow, then glanced at the clock on the bedside table.

4.46 am.

She got up, a small shiver running through her. The bedroom was cold; the soft creak of the floorboards beneath her feet broke the morning stillness as she walked to the bathroom. Reaching for the gown on the hanger, a familiar scent rose. It wasn't hers—it was the bulkier one. His.

She slipped it on and wrapped herself in the thick, chunky fabric. It was comforting. A quiet tug of longing stirred deep within her. She wished he were home.

She filled the basin with warm water, lowered her face to the surface, and submerged—as though the water could open a door, a passage back to whatever her dreams had tried to tell her. On the way back to the bedroom, she paused by the other room to check on her daughter. The little girl was asleep, shifting slightly before settling again. Parto leaned over and kissed her forehead. It was pleasantly warm.

She gently turned the knob to close the door, then stood there for a moment, completely still, her hand resting on the handle. She was still thinking about the dream—letting the images play again in her mind, sliding one after another, as if trying to pin them to the cloud of memory.

For a moment, it became vivid again. Not just a dream anymore, but something she was stepping back into—like re-entering a play. Not as a viewer, but as someone inside it. An actor returning to her role.

"I should write it down," she murmured.

She hurried back to the bedroom, flicked on the light, and sat at her desk. But instead of reaching for a notebook, she opened her laptop and emailed the details of her dream to Hooman—fresh, before they could slip away.

Subject: Strange dream

Hooman-jan,

It's very early, I know—but I couldn't wait until you woke up to call. Don't worry, everything's fine. I just had a strange dream and wanted to share it before it slips away.

I dreamt I was standing under an arch. At first, it looked like the Arch of Ctesiphon—solid, ancient, majestic. But the top was unexpectedly modern. Somehow, I knew I'd seen this arch a thousand times, though I couldn't quite place where.

I looked up. The arch soared above me—tall, proud, triumphant. I stood right beneath its centre. It felt layered, as if each part came from a different era, stacked and woven together over centuries. My eyes followed the curve of the vault, where delicate geometric grids linked the old stone base to a sleek, modern peak.

And then I knew exactly where I was—under the Shahyad Tower[1]. The gateway to Tehran. No wonder it felt so familiar. In that moment, I felt safe. I felt happy. But then I looked down.

Everything had changed. I was still standing at the centre, but to one side it was dark as night. On the other, sunlight poured down from a clear sky. I was caught between two worlds: one cloaked in night, the other bathed in light.

The daylight side was the present. I stood there on the first day of winter—the first of Day—in the year 2584[2], the current year. Everything felt normal. Iran was still a good country—beautiful, thriving, and peaceful, just as it is today. People moved with vibrancy and ease—young and old, women and men alike. There was the same deep respect for difference, and a quiet, genuine love for one another. But when I looked to the other side—the night side—my heart skipped a beat.

It was also the present moment—the first day of winter, the first of Day. But instead of 2584, somehow, I knew the year was 1404. I couldn't understand how that was possible. It was horrifying.

Iran had become dark and broken. Silence weighed heavy in the streets. People looked worn down—poor, hungry, some digging through bins for food. Gallows hung everywhere. Thousands of young lives had been lost to them. Grieving mothers wandered, howling, hollowed by loss.

Books lay torn and scattered. Women were veiled. Clowns with halos chased them through the streets, beating and torturing... it was really disturbing. The air was thick with smoke and darkness.

Lakes had dried. Rivers vanished. Trees stood like skeletons; orchards crumbled to dust. Children ran, begging for water no one could give. Lips were sealed with tape. People—even dogs—were hiding, fleeing, desperate to escape.

I recognised many among the dead—our friends, noble figures, scholars and artists, even sports heroes. It was horrific...

Then came a terrible, dark, menacing laughter from somewhere unseen. Suddenly, fire erupted—flames roaring to life and consuming everything, turning it all to ashes. It was so real, Hooman... painfully real—a pandemonium, as if I'd stepped into a dystopian parallel to the world, we live in. I was looking for you—everywhere. You weren't there. I couldn't find you. I was terrified and began howling.

But then—something rose from the ashes. A golden bird with long, luminous feathers circled above, singing a hauntingly beautiful song.

I couldn't take my eyes off it. It flew out of the darkness, glided over my head, and landed on the bright side. I followed it—crossing into the light.

I woke up still hearing that bird's song—something like a flute. Magical.

I'll call you at breakfast.

Love you. See you soon in Shiraz.

When Parto hit send, a quiet sense of relief settled over her. She knew, however, that it was a bit inconsiderate—he had a long day ahead, with the final rehearsal for his play at the Winter Festival of Art in Shiraz.

THE PERSIANS BY AESCHYLUS

Subject: Re Strange Dream

My love,

I just read your dream. It gave me chills.

I tried calling, but you didn't pick up—maybe still resting or wrapped up in a morning cuddle with our little angel. I miss you both more than words can say. So here I am, taking a few quiet moments to write before the madness kicks in.

You've always had a way of seeing more than others, even in sleep. And once again, you're there—this time standing in the space between what is and what could be.

I can't stop thinking about that moment in your dream—standing beneath the arch, caught between two dimensions, two realms. Such a powerful, striking image, revealing parallel worlds... It reminded me of something you once said— that dreams are places we've already been. Remember?

I just wish I could remember mine more clearly—so you'd be the one trying to interpret them for a change!

But Parto–jan, even though your dream was so unsettling, I feel like it came for a good reason. Maybe it's a reminder that we carry both those worlds inside us—the light and the dark, the joy and the grief. Maybe it's our job not to forget either. Everything feels so fragile, doesn't it? Freedom, democracy, nature, health... Maybe your dream was about that too—about being grateful and staying vigilant.

And that golden bird... I could picture it exactly as you described. I'm not surprised it led you into the light, and you've always known how to follow the good music! But honestly, the one thing I've wished for most is that I'd been there with you.

Sorry I didn't call you last night in the end—you know how Rambod gets, talking for hours after the performance. I was pretty sleepy by then, but if I had let him, he'd have gone on till morning with all that energy! Bless him though, made a brilliant choice. He really knows his stuff. Out of all the international productions, he picked The Magic Flute from the Royal Opera at Covent Garden, performed right here in Eram Garden in Shiraz. And wow—what a choice!

It was such a vibrant, powerful performance—full of thrilling textures, energy, and life. I just know you would've loved it.

But it wasn't just the music—the story really got me. It was this rich, layered fairytale about darkness and light, good and evil. Basically, the whole thing was like a journey—from the darkness of ignorance and superstition (that's the Queen of the Night) to the light of wisdom and reason (Sarastro).

Pretty deep stuff for an opera, but it worked so well. It was really about growing up, in a way—the transformation from raw instinct to something wiser, more human. Like the soul figuring itself out. And somehow, all of that was wrapped up in this light, funny vibe.

Oh, and there was this bird-catcher guy, Papageno, with a set of magic bells. You'd have totally loved him. I think I connected with that character the most.

The final scene really stuck with me—especially the Temple of the Sun part. That moment when Sarastro triumphs over the Queen of the Night felt like this beautiful, glowing celebration of light overcoming darkness. And in the end, he welcomes a new era—one of wisdom and unity. We must go together—I've already booked it for next week when you're here. Honestly, I couldn't think of anything more perfect for our Yalda. It felt like it was made for the occasion.

Today is our final rehearsal.

That's partly why Rambod and I needed a change of scene last night—he says I'm obsessed, that I've been haunted by The Persians. And maybe he's right.

You know how often I think about that tragedy, that defeat—about how Aeschylus portrayed us. Reading your dream and thinking about the darker chapters in Iran's history took me right back there. What really gets me is how Aeschylus treats the Persians with a kind of reverence, even while showing their tragic flaws. It's complicated—and it stays with you.

He paints them as noble people wrapped in luxury and wealth, but also excessively emotional. Their mourning is intense— tearing robes, singing lyrical laments—raw, public grief that probably came across as weakness or a lack of control to the Greeks. In the play, their downfall comes down to hubris: too much arrogance, too much certainty, and not enough unity. And the sheer size and diversity of the Persian Empire, stretching from Asia to Africa, didn't help either, it left them feeling scattered, less rooted.

But you know, though Aeschylus was from the enemy side, his words carried a quiet sympathy for the Persians—a gentle pity rather than harsh scorn or humiliation. It's as if he somehow knew the Persians had the potential to be better but were held back by neglect and indifference.

Also, he didn't glorify war; he made it feel like a sorrowful wound, not a triumph. Okay, yes, his play was a commemoration of the Greek victory—but more than that, it's a deeper reflection on the dangers of arrogance, disunity, and unchecked emotion. Perhaps not just for the Persians, but for anyone who holds power.

It unsettled me when I first wrote about it, and it still does now. What troubles me most is that history didn't end there. The pattern kept repeating... again and again.

After the Greeks came Alexander, then the Islamic invasion, then the Mongol. Over and over, we've been brought to the edge—for reasons that feel eerily familiar.

When you told me about standing between two worlds in your dream, a question surfaced. It hit me like a blow. I didn't have an answer then. I still don't.

Can it happen again?

Can our chapter of peace and glory one day end with the same tragic flaws?

Anyway—I should really stop here. I'm running late now. No idea how tonight's play will go—I'm tired, a little overwhelmed, but excited too. Then again, you know how I get before the final run. Everything usually falls into place after this.

I miss you. I love you. And I can't wait to hold you—and that cheeky little ray of sunshine.

See you both soon, in Shiraz.

H

THE END

NOTES

1   The Shāhyād Tower, renamed Azadi Tower after the 1979 revolution, is one of Tehran's most iconic landmarks. Completed in 1971 to commemorate the 2,500th anniversary of the Persian Empire, the structure blends traditional Iranian architectural elements with modernist design. A prominent feature is its grand arch, which is a modern interpretation of the classical Sassanian arch from the palace at Ctesiphon. Originally called Shāhyād—meaning "King's Memorial"—it was renamed Azadi ("Freedom") following the revolution. It stands at the entrance to the city, symbolizing both a gateway and a complex intersection of Iran's history, identity, and shifting political narratives.

2   Had the Islamic Republic not reverted to the Islamic-based Solar Hijri calendar in 1979, the current year in Iran would be 2584. The Imperial Calendar, introduced under Mohammad Reza Shah Pahlavi, began in 559 BCE—the year Cyrus the Great founded the Achaemenid Empire. Intended to emphasize Iran's pre-Islamic heritage, it was rejected by the religious establishment as a departure from Islamic tradition. Following the 1979 revolution, the Imperial Calendar was abolished and the Solar Hijri calendar reinstated. This system begins with the Prophet Muhammad's migration (Hijrah) to Medina in 622 CE. As of 2025 CE, the official year in Iran is 1404 SH.

ACKNOWLEDGEMENTS

Writing this book has been both a journey and an adventure. Along the way, I have faced my share of valleys, and I could not have made it through alone. My heartfelt thanks go to all who made this book possible—and to three people in particular:

To Maurice Sweeney at Menma Books—thank you for believing in this story and for walking this path with me, step by step. Your extraordinary patience, insight, and wise counsel kept me writing without a flicker of worry. I will always be grateful for your sharp eye, which pruned and polished every line until the heart of the book shone through. At the journey's end, I hold not only a completed book but also a friendship beyond measure. Working with you has been an immense honour.

To Ally Bunbury, whose generosity, quiet encouragement, and faith in my work gave this story wings—my deepest gratitude.

And to Michael Bevan, one of the finest people this world has known, for your unwavering support. Your presence throughout this journey has meant more than I can ever express.

I wish to extend my deepest thanks to the internationally acclaimed illustrator Peter Sís for his phenomenal contribution to the book cover. I am truly humbled by your artistry and generosity and will be forever honoured and grateful for this remarkable gift. Your own book, *The Conference of the Birds*, has been a source of profound inspiration—in spirit and in visual language. I often found myself returning to your artwork before writing, as it helped me stay connected to the very essence of the narrative.

So many people have walked beside me on this journey—offering friendship, love, and encouragement when I needed it most. Though I cannot name them here, each of you is woven into the fabric of this book, and I hold my gratitude close to your kindness.

This work was born from the inspiration and learning I've drawn from many extraordinary writers, poets, historians, and thinkers whose words have shaped my path. My greatest thanks to Helen Macdonald, author of *H Is for Hawk* and *Vesper Flights*, for her meditative reflections on nature and survival; J. A. Baker, author of *The Peregrine*, whose work continues to haunt and inspire; Sholeh Wolpé, poet and editor, whose poetry and magnificent translation of Attar's *Conference of the Birds* and Forugh Farrokhzad's *Sin* bridged cultures with grace; Andrew Scott Cooper, author of *The Fall of Heaven*, for his illuminating historical insight; Serge Michel, author of *Marche Sur Mes Yeux*, for his vivid storytelling and fearless exploration of contemporary events in Iran; Dick Davis, translator of the *Shahnameh*, for bringing the grandeur of Persian epic to life; and the scholars of Zoroastrianism, especially Mary Boyce and Jenny Rose, for their guidance in understanding ancient wisdom.

With deep respect, I acknowledge Michael Axworthy, author of *Revolutionary Iran*, whose lucid, profoundly human account of a nation in transformation remains a guiding light, and Roy Mottahedeh, author of *The Mantle of the Prophet*, who offered a remarkable exploration of Islam and politics in turbulent Iran. I am also grateful to Jason Elliot, author of *Mirrors of the Unseen*, for his evocative portrait of the country; to Anno Birkin, author of *Who Said the Race Is Over?*, whose voice carries the stillness and fire of a spirit that sought infinity in fleeting moments; and to Leonard Lewisohn and Christopher Shackle, authors of *Attar and the Persian Sufi Tradition: The Art of Spiritual Flight*, for their scholarship illuminating the mystic path that inspired this work.

I am indebted to George Lenczowski, editor of *Iran under the Pahlavis*, for his clear and authoritative historical perspective; Hannah Arendt, whose *The Origins of Totalitarianism* reminds us of the moral weight of thought and action; Doris Lessing, author of *The Golden Notebook*, for her fearless exploration of identity and truth; John Berger, author of *Confabulations*, for his profound meditations on art, perception, and the human condition, which deepened my understanding of seeing and meaning; Leon M. Lederman and Christopher T. Hill, authors of *Symmetry and the Beautiful Universe*, for inspiring wonder at the elegance of the cosmos; Colum McCann, author of *Apeirogon*, for demonstrating the power of empathy and narrative to connect distant lives; Houzan Mahmoud, editor of *Kurdish Women's Stories*, for amplifying voices of courage and resilience; and the legendary Joan Baez, whose song *We Shall Overcome*—and its Persian version, *Ma Pirooz Mishim*—embody a timeless spirit of resistance, hope, and compassion that continues to inspire this journey.

To Mark Breckon, my first editor—thank you for your early guidance and encouragement.

To my beloved family—for your endless patience, love, and faith. You have been my constant ground and quiet strength, and this book carries your presence in every line.

And finally, with deepest reverence and gratitude, to Farid ud-Din Attar, whose *Conference of the Birds* continues to illuminate the path for all who seek a leader—reminding us that the journey itself reveals the truth, and that what we search for is often already within.

www.ingramcontent.com/pod-product-compliance
Ingram Content Group UK Ltd.
Pitfield, Milton Keynes, MK11 3LW, UK
UKHW041903140126
466955UK00003B/85